THE UNQUIET DEAD

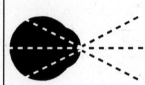 This Large Print Book carries the
Seal of Approval of N.A.V.H.

THE UNQUIET DEAD

AUSMA ZEHANAT KHAN

THORNDIKE PRESS

A part of Gale, Cengage Learning

Farmington Hills, Mich • San Francisco • New York • Waterville, Maine
Meriden, Conn • Mason, Ohio • Chicago

GALE
CENGAGE Learning·

LIBRARY OF CONGRESS CATALOGING-IN-PUBLICATION DATA

Khan, Ausma Zehanat.
 The unquiet dead / by Ausma Zehanat Khan. — Large print edition.
 pages cm. — (Thorndike Press large print reviewers' choice)
 ISBN 978-1-4104-7872-6 (hardcover) — ISBN 1-4104-7872-6 (hardcover)
 1. Murder—Investigation—Fiction. 2. Murder victims—Fiction. 3. Large type books. I. Title.
 PS3611.H335U58 2015b
 813'.6—dc23   2015001859

Published in 2015 by arrangement with St. Martin's Press, LLC

Printed in Mexico
1 2 3 4 5 6 7 19 18 17 16 15

For my parents,
Dr. Zehanat Ali Khan
and
Mrs. Nasima Khan,
whose love and shining example
are everything

Let justice be done lest the world perish.

— HEGEL

1.

I will never worship what you worship.
Nor will you worship what I worship.
To you, your religion — to me, mine.

Esa Khattak turned his head to the right,
offering the universal salaam at the conclusion of the evening prayer. He was seated
with his legs folded beneath him on a prayer
rug woven by his ancestors from Peshawar.
The worn red and gold strands were comforting; his fingers sought them out when
he pressed his forehead to the floor. A moment later, his eyes traced them as his
cupped palms offered the final supplication.

The Maghrib prayer was for Khattak a
time of consolation where along with
prayers for Muhammad, he asked for mercy
upon his wife and forgiveness for the accident that had caused her death. A nightly
ritual of grief relieved by the possibility of
hope, it stretched across that most resonant

9

band of time: twilight. The dying sun muted his thoughts, much as it subdued the colors of the *ja-namaz* beneath him. It was the discipline of the ritual that brought him comfort, the reason he rarely missed it. Unless he was on duty — as he was tonight, when the phone call from Tom Paley disturbed his concentration.

He no longer possessed the hot-blooded certainties of youth that a prayer missed or delayed would bring about a concomitant judgment of sin. Time had taught him to view his faith through the prism of compassion: when ritual was sacrificed in pursuit of the very values it was meant to inspire, there could be no judgment, no sin.

He took the phone call from Tom Paley midway through the prayer and finished up in its aftermath. Tom, the most respected historian at Canada's Department of Justice, would not have disturbed him on an evening when Khattak could just as easily have been off-roster unless the situation was urgent.

CPS, the Community Policing Section that Khattak headed, was still fragile, barely a year into its existence. The ambit was deliberately vague because CPS was a fig leaf for the most problematic community relations issue of all — Islam. A steady shift to the right in Canadian politics, coupled with the spectacular bungling of the Maher Arar terrorism case in 2002, had birthed a generation of activist lawyers who pushed back vigorously against what they called tainted multiculturalism. Maher Arar's saga of extraordinary rendition and torture had mobilized them, making front-page news for months and costing the federal government millions in compensation when Arar had been cleared of all links to terrorism. A hastily concocted Community Policing Section had been the federal government's response, and who better than Esa Khattak to head it? A second-generation Canadian Muslim, his career had seen him transition seamlessly from Toronto's homicide squad to national counterintelligence work at INSET, one of the Integrated National Security Enforcement Teams. CPS called on both skill sets. Khattak was a rising star with an inbuilt understanding of the city of Toronto's shifting demographic landscape. At CPS, he was asked to lend his expertise to sensitive police investigations throughout the country at the request of senior investigating officers from any branch of government.

The job had been offered to Khattak as a promotion, his acceptance of it touted as a public relations victory. Khattak had taken it because of the freedom it represented: the chance to appoint his own team, and as with INSET, the opportunity to work with partners at all levels of government to bring nuance and consideration to increasingly complex cases.

And for other reasons he had never offered up for public scrutiny.

His mandate was couched in generic terms: sensitivity training for police services, community support, and an alternative viewpoint in cases involving minorities, particularly Muslim minorities. Both he and his superiors understood the unspoken rationale behind the choice of a decorated INSET officer to head up CPS. If Khattak performed well, then greater glory to the city, province, and nation. If he ran into barriers from within the community as he pursued his coreligionists, no one could accuse the CPS of bias. Everyone's hands were clean.

It didn't matter to Khattak that this was how he had been lured into the job by his former superintendent, Robert Palmer. He loved police work. It suited an analytical nature tempered by a long-simmering hunger for justice. And if he was being used, as indisputably he was, he was also prepared to enact his own vision for CPS.

What flame-fanning bigots across the border would doubtlessly call community pandering, a fig-leaf jihad. Take anything a Muslim touched, add the word jihad to it, and immediately you produced something ugly and divisive.

But Tom wasn't one of these. Chief historian at the Department of Justice, he was a gifted academic whose fatherly demeanor masked a passion for the truth as sharp and relentless as Khattak's own.

He had called to ask Khattak to investigate the death of a Scarborough man named Christopher Drayton. There was no reason that CPS should have an interest in the man's death. He had fallen from a section of the Scarborough Bluffs known as the Cathedral. His death had been swift and certain with no evidence of outside interference.

Khattak had pointed this out to his friend in measured tones, and Tom had let him. When he'd finished, Tom gave him the real reason for his call and the reason it encroached upon Khattak's jurisdiction.

Khattak heard the worry and fear beneath Tom Paley's words.

And into the remnants of Khattak's prayer intruded a series of recollections from his youth. Of news reports, hurriedly organized meetings and volunteer drives, followed too slowly by action. He saw himself as a young man joining others in a circle around the flame at Parliament Hill. He absorbed the thick, despairing heat of that summer into his skin. His dark hair flattened against his head; he felt in that moment his own impotence.

He listened to Tom's labored explanation, not liking the hitch in his friend's breath. When Tom came to the nature of his request, Khattak agreed. But his words were slow, weighted by the years that had passed since that summer. Still, he would do as asked.

"Don't go alone," Tom said. "You'll need to look objective."

Khattak took no offense at the phrasing. He knew the unspoken truth as well as Tom did.

Because you can't be.

"I'll take Rachel." He had told Tom about his partner, Rachel Getty, before.

"You know her well enough to trust her?"

"She's the best officer I've ever worked with."

"She's young."

"Not so young that she doesn't understand our work. And I find her perspective

14

helps me."

He meant it. But even as he said it he knew that he would work with Rachel as he had done in the past. Withholding a part of the truth, of himself, until he could see the world through the clear, discerning eyes that watched him with such trust.

He knew he could turn to his childhood friend, Nathan Clare, for background on Drayton. Nate lived on the Bluffs and would understand why he'd agreed to Tom's request. Nate would understand as well the toll compliance would take. But Khattak's bond with Nate had long since been severed. It was a mistake to think Nate still knew him at all.

He'd meant the last words of his prayer to be a blessing asked for his family, in a space he tried to keep for himself, exchanging solitude for solace. Lately, he'd come to accept that there was no separate peace. His work, and the harshness of the choices he had made, bled into everything.

He rose from his prayer rug to find that dusk had given way to dark. He thought of the tiny documents library in Ottawa with its overflowing shelves. He'd spent most of that long-ago summer there, collecting evidence.

And he remembered other words, other

blessings to be sought with a premonition of ruin.

They are going to burn us all.

2.

I keep wondering, where have all the good friends gone?

Rachel took her own car to the Bluffs. A couple of times when she and Zach were young, their father had taken them to Bluffer's Park for picnics. She remembered the suppressed pleasure in Don Getty's eyes as his son dragged him to the marina to watch the boats. Even then, the park had been filled with immigrants. Children scrambling unsupervised, shrieking with pleasure. She'd been an afterthought, but her Da had taken time over Zach.

She got out of the car, scuffing her runners against the dirt in the road. She had driven around the crescent slowly so as not to miss the house called Winterglass, an imaginative name for the three-story structure settled at the edge of the Bluffs, as much a part of its surroundings as the trees that framed the park or the wind that had worn down the stone over time.

The first and second stories were separated by a horizontal band of stonework that wrapped around the house. Above the white doors, a pediment supported a recessed arch. On either side of the arch, chimneys flanked an elegant arrangement of windows.

On the east side of the house, a balcony set on white columns floated above a ground-floor terrace. The long, curved drive was edged by maple trees, the small garden before the house embroidered by a gathering of roses. A single ornament rested within its diamond-shaped border: a chipped stone eagle balanced on a plinth.

A weathered house and a thing of beauty, its name subtly inscribed on the plinth.

Khattak hadn't given any reason for meeting at this house. He'd provided a short summary on Christopher Drayton, but unless she missed her guess, Drayton's house was at the opposite end of the circle. She'd already called Declan Byrne, her junior team member, for background on Drayton. As far as Dec could tell her, a man had gone for a stroll at night and fallen to his death. An ordinary man leading an ordinary life.

The only drama she could squeeze out of this was the possibility of suicide. Yet the coroner's report had ruled it an accident.

So why was CPS being asked to dig around Drayton, and why had her boss asked her to meet at Winterglass?

Restless, she kicked at her front tire just as Khattak's BMW pulled up behind her.

"Bit upscale, isn't it, sir?" she said by way of greeting. She meant the house, not the car. Her envious appraisal of his car had been documented on previous excursions.

"Hello, Rachel."

It was too dark out to read his expression. He sounded withdrawn. Fatigued, maybe, though it hadn't dampened his good looks.

And he wasn't gotten up in one of his closely tailored suits. He was wearing black trousers and a dark, fitted shirt. No tie, no cuff links, grappling a string of beads in his right hand. When they stepped under the house's porch light she saw the beads were green agate. He was fingering them in a nervous gesture unusual for him.

"This isn't Drayton's house, sir."

"No. This is Winterglass."

Which sounded like he expected the name to mean something to her.

Biting back the temptation to remind him she could read, she countered, "Never heard of it. Did Drayton use to live here?"

She heard Khattak's quick intake of

breath, saw the string tighten around his fingers. He turned to face her and, as always before his direct attention, she squirmed a little.

"This is the home of Nathan Clare. I haven't been here in some time."

"Nathan Clare? *The* Nathan Clare? The writer?"

She was babbling. Everyone knew the internationally acclaimed author. His last book, *Apologia,* had outsold all his previous works combined. He had made a name for himself intervening in national debates on multiculturalism. Every few years his essays would be collected together and published in a volume, cementing his credentials as a somewhat reclusive public intellectual.

She'd heard him on the radio and had liked his voice and his dry sense of humor. She had meant to purchase the book selection he'd endorsed, but time had gotten away from her. That, and her job. She wasn't on duty tonight, but CPS hours were irregular, and she worked at being someone Khattak could rely on.

She felt a little awed at the thought of meeting Clare. Then she grasped what Khattak had just said.

"You've been here before, sir? You know Mr. Clare?"

He rang the doorbell.

"Yes. Drayton lives nearby. I thought that Nathan might know him."

Now she remembered that the writer was also the son of Loveland Clare, a diplomat in the Stephen Lewis tradition, a fact she correlated to the spike in her nervousness.

When the door opened, they were greeted by a tall man with a slim, straight nose and a delicate face and jaw. His straw-colored hair was worn long in the front, obscuring his gold-rimmed glasses: he was the perfect example of Rachel's idea of an English gentleman. He was even wearing a tweed jacket. Well-fitted, she observed, and though Khattak was tall, this man had an inch or two over him.

"Esa?" He sounded shocked.

Rachel's eyes widened. Khattak hadn't called to set up the visit?

"May we come in?"

The man in the doorway stepped back, his attention occupied by Khattak, who offered no identification, Rachel trailing behind them. They were led through an entrance hall with a sculptured staircase to a double-height room that defied her every expectation of grandeur. Or was it grand? At least fifty feet across, something about the room managed to suggest warmth. Its

floor was a bleached pine, off-setting fur-
nishings in delicate green and the most
elaborate Chinese carpet Rachel had ever
seen. Velvet sofas anchored the carpet across
from a wall of glass that must have given
the house its name. Situated on a curve of
the Bluffs, the wall overlooked white cliffs
and black water extending over a limitless
distance.

She didn't know where to look first. The
blue and white porcelain that shimmered
on the room's tables? The painted white
chandeliers suspended between a set of
peacock chairs? Or the classical architecture
of pilasters and arches that ran the perimeter
of the room to support a gallery on the
second level? Under a set of casement
windows, a grand piano with a raised lid
occupied an antechamber that led outside,
sheet music scattered across its bench. A
silk banner was flung over a nearby chair.

Gawking, she turned back to hear herself
being introduced.

"Sergeant Rachel Getty, my partner at
Community Policing."

Nathan Clare took her hand. She was
surprised at the strength of his grip: there
was something romantic, almost effeminate,
about the elegant bones of his hand. She
took a green-and-white-striped chair at his

invitation, ducking his assessment of her, knowing the picture she presented to the world. Boxy, square-shouldered, round-cheeked, indifferently dressed.

When Nathan smiled at her, she said awkwardly, "You must like music. You don't have any photographs on your piano."

She'd seen plenty of soap operas where a Steinway served mainly as a repository for antique picture frames.

"Nate believes pianos are for playing."

The "Nate" caught Rachel by surprise. Both the nickname and the comment implied familiarity, making her wonder how well her boss knew Nathan Clare and whether that had been a sneer in his cultured voice.

Nathan sat back on the green sofa, watching Khattak string the beads together around his wrist.

"I haven't seen that in a while. Does it help while you're working?"

There was a hint of challenge in his manner.

Sitting next to Khattak, Rachel was able to see the string of beads more clearly. Every now and again, the agate stones were sectioned off by a little marker, dividing the string into segments. It was a rosary or — what was the word Khattak had taught her?

A tasbih, the Muslim equivalent.

She realized that Nathan was watching her. He had swept the hair from his forehead, and now she could see the hazel eyes behind his glasses, intent but also kind.

"We've come about your neighbor, Christopher Drayton. I was hoping you might have known him."

"Everyone in the neighborhood did. He was well regarded here, generous with his time. People were shocked to hear of his fall, myself included, but I suppose no one was quite as distraught as Melanie. Melanie Blessant, his girlfriend."

"You knew him well, then."

"As well as I know all my neighbors, I'd say. He was an educated man, he enjoyed books, art. He'd been here for dinner several times to discuss various projects he was interested in with mutual friends. On some of the same nights you were invited. He was funding a small museum — something that would interest you. I can give you a list of the guests, if you'd like." He rummaged in a small drawer and handed the paper to Rachel.

Khattak brushed it aside.

"Did he often walk by the Bluffs?"

"I believe so, but the people who live here are well versed in the dangers of erosion.

It's easy to lose your footing out there."

"Had you ever seen him from these windows?"

"You know these windows don't face the path, Esa."

There was a note of chiding in Nathan's voice that took Rachel aback. The tenor of the whole conversation seemed strange to her, the room imbued with an inexplicable anxiety. The tasbih was taut around Khattak's hand; Nathan Clare's posture was stiff. That both men knew the source of it was clear: it was Rachel who was in the dark.

Nathan turned to her.

"Do you like the house?"

She couldn't help being caught by the cloudy expanse of lake beyond the windows. Waterfront views were not to be had off the dim streets of Etobicoke, where she lived.

"It's stunning. From the outside, I thought it might be a little pompous, but it isn't."

She bit her lip. Sometimes she was too honest and in this case probably naïve as well. There were thousands of dollars worth of antiques within the room, pieces she could neither name nor identify, yet all possessed of a consonance that pleased the eye. Things to live with rather than admire. The careless sprawl of music suggested as much.

"You can play the piano if you'd like," he

said, following her gaze.

Rachel couldn't play. Though Don Getty had done well for himself in life, the arts weren't a luxury he'd encouraged his children to indulge in. It was her mother's old recordings she had listened to when her father was out of the house, the needle scratching over Chopin's nocturnes, her mother's favorite composer. Part of her mother's life before she'd married Don Getty, as inaccessible to Rachel as her mother's thoughts.

Rachel made her way to the piano, called there by a secret longing. The banner casually placed on the chair beside it looked like a miniature flag, a blue Superman shield imposed upon its green background, the initials *CK* appliquéd at one corner.

The two men followed in her wake like an entourage, Drayton forgotten.

Khattak reached around her and took the banner.

"You still have it," he said.

He deposited the tasbih in his pocket, his hands relaxing.

"It was a pledge, Esa. You know that."

Khattak's gaze switched to the fireplace, taking in the blank space above the lip of white marble.

"The portrait's gone."

"It was more than time."

A rectangular space between the white and blue chinoiserie was less faded than the rest of the wall. Something had been there, and again she was the outsider, in the dark as to why they were here at all when they should have been at Drayton's house, searching for indications of homicide.

"I'm sorry, Mr. Clare. How do you and the inspector know each other?"

Nathan smiled at her and she blinked. The smile transformed her notion of the introverted writer into something much more visceral. A more than ordinarily attractive male, with glints of light turning his straw-colored hair gold.

"Didn't Esa tell you? We were at school together. We're old Seatonians." And when she still looked blank, he clarified, "Upper Canada College."

Openmouthed, the piano forgotten, she turned to Khattak.

"You went *to school* with Nathan Clare, the writer?"

"He wasn't 'Nathan Clare, the writer' then. And we've come about Christopher Drayton, not my unsavory past."

Nathan grinned at him, the first unforced gesture she'd seen from either man.

"It was unsavory, wasn't it? At least, all

the good parts."

Her eyes lit up at the teasing. Here was someone who might deflate the always unruffled, ever-so-proper Inspector Khattak. She wanted to delve deeper into the mystery of this hidden friend, megawatt writer or not, who must be awash in particularly useful inside information. Despite their rocky start when she'd first joined CPS, she'd come to admire Esa Khattak and to value his opinion. She just wasn't sure that she understood him as well as she'd like to. And if Nathan Clare could help her with that, she wouldn't object.

But the mood died in an instant as Khattak answered, "Most of the bad parts as well, I'm afraid. I'm sorry to have bothered you. We should go."

"Sir —"

There were at least a dozen questions she could think of that they hadn't asked Nathan Clare — at least he could clarify the list he'd given them, why he'd had it to hand, and why it even mattered.

"Now, Rachel."

She scurried along behind him, swallowing a grimace. Whatever brief connection she had felt to the author, Khattak was her boss. Her boss who ignored the question Nathan called after him.

"Did you ever read *Apologia*, Esa?"

And that wasn't a question he seemed ready to answer.

3.

He was a modest and reasonable man.

They left their cars where they were. It was a silent ten-minute walk from the far end of the circle to Drayton's address. There was no cordon of police tape around the house, a large home typical of those built on small lots when fifty-year-old bungalows were scraped down to make way for new luxury models. The exterior was stuccoed in white, a color Drayton must have repainted yearly, because the outside bore no traces of wear.

She wasn't sure what they were looking for, wasn't sure why a name like Christopher Drayton would pop up on the CPS radar. On the face of it, it didn't seem like a minority-sensitive situation. All she knew was that her boss was doing a favor for a friend on his own time, and he had asked her along to the party.

"Figure the girlfriend did it, sir?"

"What?"

"Melanie Blessant. The one Clare mentioned. Maybe followed him out after dark, pushed him over the edge."

They were meandering their way through the well-proportioned living spaces, a family room and salon that mirrored each other in dimension, furnished with expensive if generic taste. Everything was in order, well tended, as if death had not visited this house.

Her question was meant as a gentle reminder that nothing about this assignment appeared to fall within their purview.

They had reached the kitchen at the back of the house: dark cabinets, earth-colored stone, stainless-steel appliances, a desk where the mail was tidily sorted. She thumbed through it. Credit card statements, utility bills, a landscaping service, the usual. Adjacent to the kitchen was the study, a glimpse through its French doors disclosing bookcases and a wide desk. She tried the handle. The doors were locked.

Khattak produced the keys.

"Local police were asked to leave this room locked so we could take a look for ourselves. Take some photographs, will you?"

Rachel pondered this. Drayton's body had

been found two days ago. Why had Justice moved so swiftly to secure this particular scene when the body had been found at the base of Cathedral Bluffs?

She had her answer when the doors spread wide to reveal a room twice the size of any other on the main floor. She unearthed her camera and set to work.

The chair from the desk was situated in the center of the room, facing windows that looked out upon the garden. It was an old-fashioned oxblood leather chair without casters, but that wasn't what had captured Rachel's attention. Nor was it the reason Khattak stood still beside her.

On the floor in front of the chair lay a 9-millimeter pistol, pointed away at the windows.

"Uh, sir . . ."

"I see it."

"What's it still doing here? Has it been printed?"

"There are only Drayton's prints on the gun. It isn't loaded. The forensic team was asked to leave the room once it had finished, so we could take a look."

Rachel knelt down for a closer look. She knew it was a 9-millimeter, but the make was unfamiliar. There was a black star inside the circle on the plastic grip. Something else caught her eye on the floor not far from the gun. It was a resinous puddle the size of a quarter plate. She scraped it lightly, her nails raising a white line on the puddle as the flaky residue came off beneath her finger-tips.

"Candle wax," she breathed. She rose to her feet, perplexed. "Sir."

She described a semicircle with her index finger.

"There's several of them."

She counted the puddles under her breath.

"Someone's tried the door as well."

He showed her the scratch marks around the keyhole.

"But they couldn't get in or they would have cleaned this mess up?" Rachel haz-arded. "What does any of it mean? Drayton didn't die here. The gun hasn't been fired, his injuries were consistent with a fall." She looked around.

"There aren't any candles in the study, sir."

"Rachel."

Khattak was at the desk, trying the draw-ers. One was locked.

"Maybe he kept the gun there."

Her guess proved correct. The wide drawer yielded to Khattak's key. Inside, a kerchief was folded to one side, boxes of ammunition were stacked on the other.

"What did Drayton do?" she asked slowly. There was no permit in the drawer. It didn't make sense that a retired man in his sixties would need a small army's worth of firepower.

"He was a businessman."

"What kind of business, drugs?"

Khattak shrugged, not meeting her eyes.

That was Rachel's first clue. Khattak was never evasive with her. When he withheld information, he told her the reason for withholding it. His leadership at CPS had been characterized by a spirit of inclusion. He wore his authority more lightly than any other police officer Rachel had ever worked with. He was certainly nothing like the old bull Don Getty, thirty-five years in the police service, the last fifteen as superintendent, and God help you if you got under his skin or in his way. As Rachel, being his daughter, was prone to do.

Khattak was the polar opposite of Don Getty's bluster. Urbane, soft-spoken, respectful, decisive. The only thing he had in common with her Da was his insight into human behavior. And he'd been candid about his shortcomings as well, something Don Getty could never be. With the great Don Getty, one didn't participate or contribute ideas. One merely bowed and scraped like the rest of his sycophants. *Yes, Chief. No, Chief. Of course you have it right, Chief.*

Khattak allowed her to tell him when he got it wrong. He *asked* her to tell him. Just as he had told her to do during their first case in Waverley, when she'd thrown his affair with Laine Stoicheva in his face, using the well-known sexual harassment claim Laine had brought against him like a machine-gun attack. His composure hadn't altered. He'd taken her aside and in simple, blunt phrases told her the truth about Laine.

There'd been no need to share the truth with Rachel: she was no threat to him. Rachel had fallen as far as she could go before Khattak had brought her into CPS. She'd thought it a consolation prize of sorts, won for her by her father's influence when no one else was prepared to take her on.

But Don Getty had had nothing to do with it. Esa Khattak had asked for her. He had chosen her specially.

We're not just two birds wounded by the same stone, Rachel. Your evaluations were phenomenal.

They had been. It was the claim she had brought against her former boss, Inspector MacInerney, that had seen her fall as swiftly

35

as she had risen. The claim that had died for lack of evidence when his other victims had stayed quiet to salvage their careers.

And just like that, she was a pariah in the service.

You know what it's like to be judged, Rachel. You know in your bones what it's like to shatter the truth against a wall of disbelief.

Khattak had been cleared of all charges brought by his former partner, Laine Stoicheva. He hadn't gone into details, Rachel hadn't asked. It was enough to know they had this in common. His confidence earned her trust. She didn't always agree with him, but she'd learned to respect him. She didn't want to take a step back.

His catlike eyes were watching her. She could tell he knew what she was thinking.

"What's up then, sir? You know more about this than you're telling me."

Blunt as ever. Direct and to the point. It was the thing about her she knew Khattak valued most. And she couldn't change her spots if she tried.

The handsome face that looked back at her in the dimmed light of the study was troubled. And not about the case, she thought, or noncase, as it were. It was something deeper. His fingers were working the beads again.

"Tell me what you see," he said.

She nodded, trying to ignore the stale, slightly smoky scent in the room. This was often how they began.

"No photograph of Drayton yet, but here we are in a house that looks and feels expensive, probably about right for a retired businessman. It's a little large for a man on his own, at least four bedrooms, I'm guessing. It's well kept, somewhat impersonal, suggesting he might have had a touch of OCD and maybe not much personality. There's no art anywhere on this floor, just a map above the desk. He keeps a gun in a locked drawer with plenty of ammo, but on the night of his death the gun is found on the floor in this room, although it hasn't been fired. And there's several puddles of what looks like candle wax on the floor without any sign of candles. Maybe they're in the garbage. Maybe he took them with him on his walk and dumped them over the Bluffs."

She ran over the summary in her mind.

"I haven't seen that make before," she added. "Nine millimeter is my guess. We'll have to look more thoroughly to see if there's a license anywhere. Has it been identified?"

"Not yet."

"I admit it's odd, but there's no sign of a struggle here, nothing in the coroner's report to indicate that he was restrained or dragged or pushed over the cliff with unusual force. But, if he was taken by surprise, I don't know that we'd see any evidence of that. He was probably sitting here looking out at his garden before he went for his walk and lost his way. So I ask you again, sir, what's going on?"

Khattak hesitated, then he picked up a set of picture frames that rested on the desk, handing one to Rachel.

"There's Drayton for you. Possibly with his girlfriend. I don't know who this is."

Primming her lips at the evasion, Rachel studied the first photograph. It had been taken in broad daylight in Drayton's garden. A stocky man with a head of white hair and a square jaw had his arm around a beautiful woman who came to his shoulder. She was petite and curvy. Rachel squinted at it. Maybe not beautiful, with those bloated lips and that hyperinflated chest. She looked like a Barbie doll, her clothes straining over a nipped-in waist and the flare of her hips. Her loosely curled hair was an unlikely shade of platinum blond. It tumbled over her chest in a style suited to a much younger woman. Like Drayton, she wore sunglasses.

The other photo was of two teenage girls in tank tops and shorts. They looked alike with their clever heart-shaped faces, a smattering of freckles, and long, straight, toffee-colored hair. The younger one was smiling at the camera.

"His daughters? An estranged former family?"

Khattak shook his head.

"I haven't answered your question, I know. There's a reason for that. I'd like to see what conclusions you draw without the weight of prior knowledge."

Weight was a peculiar choice of word, Rachel thought. Maybe that was the reason that Khattak looked almost haggard. Or spoke to her so formally.

She gave him back the photographs, marched over to the bookshelves she hadn't inspected yet.

"But eventually you'll tell me. It's not exactly a thrill to work in the dark."

"The light's no better, believe me."

As Khattak worked through the other drawers, she turned her attention to Drayton's library. Nathan Clare had said he was an educated man. The books reflected that. An educated businessman with a more than passing interest in languages. Italian, Russian, Albanian, German. He also had a complete set of the works of Nathan Clare. Several volumes of essays and at least a dozen novels. All except *Apologia.* The rest of the selection was unremarkable, available at any bookstore display. Some new fiction, some books on health, a little political humor, and a set of gardening books. Plus the classics, with new hardbound covers.

On the last shelf she found a curious assortment of teen fiction interspersed with atlases and books on medieval history. A navy wool jacket hung on a peg beside the shelf. Absently, she checked the pockets.

The outer pockets were empty. The inner pockets held a pen and Drayton's wallet. She went through this. Driver's license, check. Credit cards, check. Gym membership, check. The discount cards of various retail chains. The billfold contained a modest amount of cash and a folded piece of paper. She withdrew it, frowning at what she read.

"Sir. Here's something."

She handed the paper to Khattak. Its edges were torn at the top and at the bottom, leaving no more than half a page. Even that was more than enough for the single sentence typed at its center.

Is this waiting more desperate than the

40

shooting?

"Something's been torn away. There must have been more to it. It explains the gun, doesn't it? Maybe an indication of suicidal ideation?"

Khattak didn't answer, so Rachel went on.

"Of course, we could ask why he typed it. There's a computer and printer on his desk but suicide notes are usually handwritten, unless there's some kind of manifesto attached."

"Was there anything else?"

"I haven't been through these cupboards yet." She pointed to the cabinets at the base of the bookshelves. "His taste in reading is pretty bland. What about the desk?"

"Paperwork, mostly. Bills, mortgage information, insurance policies. I'll read those in a moment. There's a folder here on the museum Nate mentioned. I haven't gone through it yet."

She went back to work. Most of the cupboards were empty. Some contained computer gadgets, speakers, printer cables, and the like. There were no photo albums, no congratulatory cards on retirement, no evidence of the business Drayton had run. Midway through, though, she found what she was looking for. The central bookcase was anchored to the wall because its cabinet contained a safe. Not a high-tech safe but the standard kind available at Walmart, weighing in at several hundred pounds with a digital lock. To open it, they'd need to call in a team member or unearth the combination among Drayton's papers.

"This is where he should have kept the gun."

Khattak joined her at the safe, hunching down.

"Perhaps he needed the safe for something more important than the gun."

"Like what? A will? A fortune in black-market diamonds? The guns that go with that ammo?"

"We need that combination if we're to find out."

"It might be in his papers. It's probably not anything as obvious as his birth date."

Khattak was studying the digital display.

"It's five digits."

"I'll keep looking."

There was a filing cabinet beside the printer. It was jammed tight, but most of it was old tax returns on a business Drayton had run. A profitable parking lot he had owned downtown. No evidence of drugs or guns or anything else out of the ordinary. Nothing that would necessitate the deadly black weapon on the floor. She yanked the lower drawer forward. It was caught on a file that had slid in over the others. When she pulled it out, the papers inside spilled through her fingers.

"Sir."

The pages were identical to one she had found in Drayton's wallet. The tops and bottoms torn away, a few chopped-off sentences in the center of each page.

She read through them slowly.

This is a cat-and-mouse game. Now it's your turn to play it.

What was it you told me? You survive or you disappear. Somehow you managed both.

As you took everything from me, you asked if I was afraid.

How could I not be afraid?

Do you hear as we did the starved wolves howling in the night?

Do you feel as if you'd never been alive?

Can you right all the wrongs of the past? Because I tell you that the sky is too high and the ground is too hard.

Something about the words frightened Rachel. Alone each sentence meant nothing. Together they ran like a kind of damaged poetry.

She looked up to find Khattak's face had changed, his weariness shed for animation. The randomness of the words meant something to him.

"This doesn't read like a suicide note, sir. Maybe a confession. And what's missing here? Why are the pages torn?"

He already knew, she could tell.

"He didn't write these himself," she went on. "Someone was sending them to him. That's what's missing from each page. The salutation and the signature. Someone was threatening him."

"I don't think these are threats."

"Then what?"

"Reminders. If someone did send these pages to Drayton, it's because they wanted to remind him of something."

"And you already know what that something is," she concluded, exasperated. "I'm not much help to you like this, sir. Wouldn't it be easier on both of us if you just told me what you know?"

Khattak set the pages down on the desk, sizing her up.

"There's nothing concrete for me to tell you. I'm relying on your clearheadedness. You have a knack for digging things up that most people would leave alone."

Rachel rubbed a hand over her lank, dark hair. How many times did she have to remind herself not to wear a ponytail at night? It did nothing for glamour and it gave her a headache.

"Right now the only knack I have is for some fresh air and my bed. Call it a night, sir?"

He handed her the pages.

"Take these with you. Something might come to you."

"What about you?"

"I'm going to see if I can find the combination to that safe. And if not, we'll call someone in."

He didn't want any of this to be true. He didn't want the words on the pages to have the meaning that Tom Paley's phone call suggested to him.

The sky too high, the ground too hard.

He ran the name Tom had given him over his tongue, hating the way it sounded, hating the rise and fall of its syllables.

Would the past not serve them better left in the past? Its muted face buried, its gravestones a world away? Things he wished he hadn't seen, people who rose like ghosts in his mind. And always that music — its trenchant melody, insistent, unrelenting: there was something here once. *We* were something.

He heard his wife's voice raised in reproach.

We owe the living the truth. It's the only coin of justice left to offer.

Samina had always been braver than he, able to see things as they were, able to shoulder her way forward to difficult truths.

This truth wasn't difficult.

It was devastating.

That was what he hadn't been able to bring himself to tell Rachel Getty, despite the trust in her dark eyes.

He knew, of course, why he had gone to see Nate. Throughout his life, every one of his sins had been confessed to Nate. The only letters he had written, the only stories he had told, had been to Nate. If he'd said to Nate, "I think Christopher Drayton was murdered and here's why," Nate would have understood him instantly. There would have been no need for further explanation.

Esa and Nate. Clare and Khattak. Seaton's diabolical duo.

He'd seen the pleasure in Nate's eyes at the door, the hope. The hope that Esa had finally let go of the anger and judgment that had characterized the last two years of their friendship. The banner should have made it easy, the absence of Laine's portrait even more so.

He told himself he was a compassionate man, not one to judge lest he be judged. As

46

Nate had once judged him, staring across the divide as if he'd never seen him before.

So he'd wanted to tell Nate about Drayton, wanted to seek his help, except that one moment was always with him. Nate turning away when nothing could have hurt Khattak worse than Nate's defection.

His wife's death was still the emptiest part of him. His deep-rooted faith and the seven years that had passed since had made it bearable — but if he was honest with himself, it was the presence of Nate, always beside him, that had enabled him to see the way forward again. It had given him a means of putting his tragedy into perspective: he wasn't alone to suffer. Others had suffered and would suffer far more than he ever had. With hardship would come ease. *Lo, with hardship comes ease.*

Lately, there had only been hardship.

He knew what he sought from Nate, as much as he knew why Rachel had become a friend. A friend he would protect and shield in any situation even as he kept a part of himself from her. But who besides Tom Paley could he discuss Drayton with? Tom, who wanted the knowledge less than Esa did.

That Drayton was a man risen from hell.

4.

Father, take care of my children, look after my children.

"I've learned a little more about the museum," Khattak said.

"How long were you at Drayton's house last night?"

"Enough to discover two important things. One, the will's not at hand, but there are two insurance policies that name Melanie Blessant as the beneficiary. And two, Drayton was preparing to a make a major donation to a local arts project called the Andalusia Museum."

"How major?"

"At least a hundred thousand dollars worth, maybe more."

Today Rachel was in Khattak's car, cautioned to leave her breakfast sandwich in her handbag until she could remove herself from its immaculate environs. Her stomach rumbled but they both ignored it. Khattak had gotten used to her habit of eating on the fly.

"Pickup game this morning?"

It was Rachel's most common excuse for missing breakfast. She was a forward on a women's hockey team and her schedule was erratic.

"We lost four to one. Looks like I'm not getting in enough practice." She smirked at him. "Who's David Newhall and why are we meeting him?"

"One of the neighbors from the list Nate gave us. Someone who might shed some light on Drayton and the museum. He's listed as a director on the project. He works at the university up here. Have you been here before?"

"No, thank God. I was at the downtown campus. I heard they used this place as a stand-in for a nuclear bomb shelter on *War of the Worlds.*"

As they pulled up the long drive to the Scarborough campus, Rachel could see why. The new signage wasn't fooling anybody. It was still just a series of concrete blocks.

"I think they call this brutalism," Khattak offered.

"It's brutal, all right."

They made their way to the administrative

offices where significant reconstruction was under way. From the outside dark and dour, inside it was all glass walls and newly minted light. The corridors were thronged by students lining up to arrange for their photo ID. A pert Asian receptionist waved them through the line to a small inner office.

"Mr. Newhall's expecting you."

So that was one phone call Khattak was prepared to make.

Inside, they were greeted by a man of middle height with a wedge-shaped face, cropped black hair, and close-set eyes behind square frames. His speech was clipped and he spoke with pronounced impatience.

"How may I help you, Inspector?"

Rachel, he ignored. She sat back in the chair he had offered, fascinated by the thick, dark eyebrows that bristled when he spoke, an outlet for the nervous energy he exuded.

"As I mentioned on the phone, we were hoping for some background on Christopher Drayton. I understand he was a friend."

Newhall didn't answer right away. On the desk before him was a plentiful amount of paperwork, cordoned off into separate piles. He ran nail-bitten fingers along the edges of these, his gaze moving between Rachel and Khattak. She was struck by an impression of guardedness.

"I knew him in passing. We live in the same general area but I doubt I knew him better than any other of my neighbors."

"Nathan Clare told us you were working together on a museum project."

Newhall stopped drumming his fingers on his desk. "I'm afraid Nathan is mistaken. Chris Drayton had nothing to do with it."

"He was planning to make a sizable donation. We found a list of museum directors among his papers with your name on it."

Newhall adjusted his glasses. His scowl took in Rachel as well. "I thought Chris fell from the Bluffs. A simple accident."

"As far as we know, that's correct. We're merely following up. As a director, you must have some idea why Chris would be interested in supporting your project."

He laid a slight stress on Drayton's name. Newhall dismissed it.

"He was a latecomer to the museum. He wanted something to stamp his name on. He had a passing interest in Spanish history, he must have decided it would do."

"A hundred thousand dollars suggests more than a passing interest to me. In his papers, the museum is called the Christopher Drayton Andalusia Museum."

For some reason, this information rendered Newhall motionless, his nervous energy concentrated. When he spoke, his tone was thoughtful. "He had a certain grandiosity about him," he admitted, "but nothing about the museum is for sale. Mink would never allow it."

Rachel straightened in her seat with interest, brushing an imaginary crumb from her rust-colored jacket. She'd been out of uniform for a while now but hadn't done much to supplement the track suits that made up most of her wardrobe. The jacket was an exception. She wanted to reflect well on Khattak, who was never at a loss in this department.

"Who's Mink?" she asked.

"I'm sorry, I meant Mink Norman. She's the director of the project, the sole reason it exists. I'm surprised her name wasn't on your list."

Rachel couldn't decide if Newhall was pointing them to someone else because he had something to hide or because he was genuinely attempting to be helpful.

"I'm not sure I understand what the museum has to do with Chris's death," Newhall added.

"At the moment, we're simply getting a

52

sense of the people Drayton knew. Nathan Clare mentioned he'd invited you both to the same dinner."

"Did he also happen to mention that as far as social events go, it was a disaster? The great man pontificating about his largesse to anyone who would listen? He used his wallet to shunt aside people who'd put in two years' work on the house. He even had that ghastly Melanie Blessant work her dubious magic on a few of the directors. We heard him out, but that was as far as it went."

"I'm sorry, what house is this? I thought we were talking about a museum."

Before he could answer Rachel's question, the receptionist knocked at his door. "Your first appointment is here," she mouthed through the glass.

Newhall jumped to his feet like a spring unbound. Khattak and Rachel followed suit, Rachel trying to place his flattened manner of speech.

"One moment, Mr. Newhall. What *about* the house? And what is it you do at the university?"

He patted the files on his desk, a look of quiet pride on his face. "I'm an administrator. I work with the student body on bursaries and scholarship applications. As for the house, if you've been to see Clare you must have seen it — it's on the same circle. The museum *is* the house. Its name is Ringsong, which I might point out is the only name we ever considered for it."

"May we have your home address, sir?" They had it already from Nathan Clare's list, she just wanted to see if he would give it to them.

Newhall raised his eyebrows but didn't demur. He lived on Lyme Regis.

Rachel was familiar with it. It cut across both Scarborough Heights and Cathedral Bluffs. It was also within walking distance of Drayton's house.

"We may stop by sometime," she told him.

Again there was that fractional pause that made Rachel think of a fox warily skirting a trap. She knew death brought out hitherto unsuspected depths in people, but this was something else.

"Come by any time you like. I'm glad to help on any matter related to Chris. I didn't appreciate his attempts to railroad us, but for all that, he was a kind man."

There was no sorrow on his face as he spoke, nor as he ushered them from his office.

"Works with people, does he?" she muttered under her breath.

"We'll talk in the car," Khattak said easily, as if he'd gotten everything he wanted from Newhall. And maybe he had. He had a head full of information as to why they were meandering after Drayton in the first place. They hadn't seen his body. Their search of his home had been cursory. No background information had been pulled beyond the commonplace. And there'd been nothing the least bit interesting about the man except the fact that he'd had money to burn and, apparently, an inexplicable desire to turn patron of the arts in the golden years of his life. And he gardened. If something about this was making Khattak anxious, she'd have loved to know what it was.

She hoped the trust they'd established during their case in Waverley wasn't a chimera. She valued it. She wanted it again, because it had been a long time since anyone had trusted her and she'd felt the same in return. She was looking for the equalizer.

Rachel lowered her window. It was a crisp fall day outside, with a coruscation of wind that arranged the air in rippling phrases. The broken spindles of leaves were assembled in piles along the sidewalks as they drove.

"What now?" she asked Khattak.

He made a show of consulting his wrist-watch, one of the few men she knew who still wore one in the days of the iPhone.

"We should visit Melanie Blessant, if only to rule her out. She seems to have loomed large in Drayton's life. And if possible, I'd like to view this museum."

Rule her out of what? Rachel wondered. A fall from the cliff? But she knew the cherished maxim of "follow the woman, follow the money" as well as Khattak did.

They had an accidental death, they had a woman who benefited from it, and they had a great deal of money in play. Or at least, they would, once a will turned up.

"What about the safe? We could get Paul or Dec on it. Paul, most likely."

Paul Gaffney was the tech expert on their team, a viable choice. Khattak's agenda didn't seem to suggest any hurry to unlock the safe, however.

As if in answer to her thoughts, he said, "Let's give it a day or so before we start using up resources. We may find there's nothing here after all. A man fell to his death, that's it."

From the tone of his voice, that was what he was hoping for. A short, simple solution that was anything except what was rattling around in his thoughts.

His face was paler than usual today, the line of his mouth tightly held, his movements edgy. Something was weighing on him like an anvil. And it was either Drayton or Nathan Clare.

"What did you think of Newhall?"

She waited for him to brake at the crosswalk ahead, which he did at the last minute. An elderly woman in a pair of green flannel pants glared at them over her shoulder as she sped through the crosswalk.

"He seemed cagey, I thought," she went on, without waiting for his answer. "Also a bit intense. A little quick to take offense."

"He didn't like Drayton, but if he's comfortable with us coming by his house, he must have some notion of public duty."

Rachel pondered this. She hadn't found Newhall remotely attractive, yet there was something compelling about his lean-limbed energy.

"He did a fair bit of finger-pointing. Gave us two other names to go for."

Khattak looked at her briefly. "There may be no fingers to point. It could be he thinks there's nothing to hide."

"We didn't ask him much about Drayton himself," she observed.

"I think Ms. Blessant will be able to tell us what we wish to know."

"The grieving widow?"

"She isn't a widow, and for all we know, she may not be grieving."

"The insurance policies speak for themselves. So might the will. A hundred thousand dollars that doesn't go to some froufrou museum might end up lining her pockets instead."

Khattak grinned. "Newhall said they weren't going to take the money."

"I'm thinking given Drayton's Barbie doll taste in women, maybe Newhall's real beef is that Drayton didn't waste much time on him. He may have focused a little more on the lady with the strange name. Mink something. Maybe she had plans for the museum that Newhall didn't know about. Maybe the blessed Blessant wanted to put a stop to that."

Khattak looked at her, his cat-eyes shrewd. "So you're no longer proceeding on the accident theory."

"Murder, murder everywhere," she replied airily. She could smell the freshness of the lake in the air. They had arrived at Ayre Point, a street that was bordered on one side by a park, its shade trees spread wide in stately indifference. Bluffs, park, forest, and lake made it splendor to splendor without the people and their crumbling homes.

Ayre Point consisted of a succession of 1970s-style houses: bricked-up bungalows with low roofs and small front yards, vans and pickup trucks serving as one wing of a crowded assembly. Rachel smoothed down her slacks, tweaked the lapels of her jacket. Remembering last night, she'd abandoned her ponytail, content to brush her sleek hair down her shoulders. Nothing could be done with it, and not for lack of trying. It was like Asian hair minus the silky gloss. She'd secured her side part with one of her mother's gold hair slides, a fact that made her self-conscious when she thought of her no-nonsense hockey team. She shrugged it off. Melanie Blessant wasn't going to bother about her. Not once she got a look at Khattak, who epitomized the female holy grail of tall, dark, and handsome, if you subtracted a certain ascetic quality.

Nobody likes a preacher boy. She chuckled to herself. Whether he was saint or sinner, she didn't know. His private life was difficult to read. What was far more explicit was the reaction of every woman who came within his radius. Although why she was so sensitive to it was a quality she preferred not to examine in herself.

Melanie Blessant's house was at the corner, its green roof steeply sloped over an exterior of dust-colored brick. Cement slabs piled on top of each other provided access to a front door. Telephone wires and a giant fir tree blocked any view afforded by the bay window that fronted the street. Maples covered the rest of the space.

Straddling a pair of lawn chairs on the neatly mown front yard were two teenage girls. They were sipping lemonade, dressed in the teen uniform of blue jeans and jerseys. One was listening to her iPod. The other was reading a book.

Rachel checked her watch. They should have been in school.

Khattak showed his identification, greeted them politely, and asked for the woman he assumed was their mother.

"Mad Mel's not here right now," the older girl informed them, setting aside her book.

Rachel took a closer look at them. These were the girls from the photograph on Drayton's desk, so much alike in appearance that they had to be sisters. They were tawny-haired and bright-eyed, with the clean young limbs of saplings. The younger girl removed her earphones, her face as clear as the cup of a lily rising on its stem.

"Don't call Mum that, Hadley," she scolded without heat. The face she turned to the older girl bore the kind of warmth that Rachel had long since ceased to expect of siblings. The girl tugged her sister up from her lawn chair and extended her hand in a mimicry of adult courtesy. Khattak shook it gravely.

"I'm Cassidy Blessant and this is my sister, Hadley. Our mum won't be home until later this afternoon."

"Would you happen to know where she went?"

"She's in her natural habitat," Hadley drawled. "Getting closer to Chris in death than he'd ever let her in life."

"Hadley!" The younger girl's face fell. Spoonfuls of light that leaked through the trees splashed across her clear complexion.

Hadley shrugged. "It's true. You may not like it, God knows I don't, but that is in fact what our dear, devoted mother is doing. Going through Christopher's things as we speak, hoping to dig up one final, pricey bauble."

"You're referring to Christopher Drayton, the man who fell to his death from the Bluffs?" Khattak asked the question gently.

Cassidy's face clouded in response. "Mum's really upset about it. They were in love. They were going to get married and we were all going to live in Christopher's house."

Her childlike manner of expressing herself coupled with the wistfulness in her voice made Rachel appreciate that she *was* a child. At most, a very young thirteen.

"Bull." Hadley contradicted her without compunction. "Chris didn't want that crazy wedding and I never had any intention of leaving Dad. If Mel had ever shacked up with him, I'd have gone to Dad in a flash."

Cassidy bit her lip. "Chris was really good to us, Hadley. You said you loved your Italian lessons with him. He was nice to us. We had our own rooms whenever we stayed over."

"Did it ever occur to you that he wanted something in return? Like Mel at his beck and call? She wouldn't have been much use to him if she'd had to come home to us every night. And if she abandoned us, as she obviously wanted to, there'd be no reason left for us not to go to Dad."

"I don't want to go to Dad. I loved it with Mum and Chris."

Her lip trembled and Rachel felt a pang of compunction. They had let the dialogue between the sisters play out because it was more revealing than anything they could have asked, but Cassidy was too young to face up to Hadley's brutal truths. If, in fact, any of it was the truth.

"Where is your father?" she asked, curious.

"Our parents are divorced," Hadley said bluntly. "We're the prize they fight over to make each other miserable. Or at least, Mel makes our dad miserable, since he's the one who actually cares about us. Mel only wanted custody for one reason. She keeps us for the money. My dad has a lot of it."

Her attention switched beyond them to a boy on the other side of the street. She shook her head at him. It was a small movement that Rachel caught. She was warning him off. The boy didn't appear to notice. He was dressed with considerable panache in slim-fitting jeans that tapered down to his ankles and a loose shirt with its sleeves rolled up to the elbows. Beneath the long-sleeved shirt was a blue Dr. Who T-shirt that bore the legend, *Time Travel, It's Easier by Blue Box.* The hair that fell forward across his brow had been styled with close attention. He crossed the street toward them, and once he brushed past her, Rachel caught the unmistakable tang of marijuana on his clothes.

"These are cops," Hadley said, her voice fierce. "They're looking for Mel."

The boy ignored her, genially tugging at Cassidy's red-gold hair. "What's up, Goldilocks? You look like someone's stolen your porridge."

She responded at once, her face lighting up. "Hadley's being mean about Mum. Make her stop, Riv."

Rachel liked his aura of emo-chic, but she really hoped that the name he presented to the world wasn't some hippie-go-lucky version of River.

It was a hope dashed. He extended his hand, looking up at her from under his side-swept bangs, through meltingly long eye-lashes. "Marco River," he said. "Most people call me Riv."

He really did belong in a boy band, Rachel thought, suppressing a grin. "That's a great name," she said. His smile in response was good-natured.

"My parents call me Marco, of course. So does Mink — but you know how it goes with the kids." He shrugged one arm over Hadley's shoulders, the other over Cassidy's. Both girls seemed to relax in his presence.

Rachel couldn't decide if she was more disarmed by his candid blue eyes or his casual charm.

"Hadley's my girlfriend but Cassie's my best girl," he went on.

Apparently, smoking pot made one loquacious.

"Mink Norman?" Khattak asked. "Do you know her?"

The sharpness of the question didn't faze him.

"Sure. We all do. Hadley and Cass have summer jobs at the museum, and Mink lets me hang around if I'm useful." He grinned at the girls. "Which as anyone will tell you, I am."

"I imagine so." Even saying it, Rachel felt a hundred years old. This good-looking boy, like all men of varying sizes, ages, and temperaments, had probably dismissed her already, but he was somehow managing to be generous with his charm. His easy smile encompassed her along with the girls.

She waited to see if there was anything else Khattak chose to ask.

"The Andalusia Museum," he said. "The same one Christopher Drayton took such an interest in." He made it a statement, the kind he often used as a fishing line.

"Ringsong," Hadley corrected sharply. "It's named after the great Andalusian poetic tradition, a blending of cultures and faiths, the holy and the vernacular."

"She writes the descriptions for the exhibits," River said drily. "That's why she talks like that."

Rachel couldn't resist. She smiled back at him, liking his sense of humor. It was a cheerful teasing absent of mockery. Hadley poked him in the ribs.

"Is that all you wanted to know?" she asked Khattak. "Do you need to know where Chris's house is?"

"We've been there, thank you. I apologize if we've disturbed you."

"Wait," she said. "Why are you looking for Mel? Why did you want to know about Chris? He was nice to everyone," she added, reluctantly.

Cassidy reached out and squeezed her sister's hand. "He really was nice," she confided. "It's too bad for Mum. He made her so happy."

Hadley might have said otherwise, Rachel thought, but she was not as abrasive a sibling as she'd seemed at first. Or perhaps the boy mellowed her. She opened her mouth, only to shut it without saying anything.

Khattak was careful with his answer. "These are routine inquiries into an accidental death, to make sure we haven't missed anything."

Not careful enough. Riv's fingers tightened on each girl's shoulder.

"Like what?" he asked. "What could you have missed?"

"Depression, financial concerns, health worries. At this stage, we simply don't know."

Hadley and Riv exchanged a quick glance.

"Cass," Hadley said. "Go into the house."

"Why? I want to hear too."

Hadley signaled the boy with a subtle movement of her eyebrows.

"Take her in, Riv. I'll fill you in later."

She wouldn't, Rachel guessed, but Riv obeyed her at once. So he possessed the charm while this possibly no more than fifteen-year-old girl held the actual authority. Hadley waited to hear the door close and then she rounded on them.

"Are you talking about suicide? Do you think Chris killed himself?"

"I'm not sure we should discuss this any further without your mother present."

"Forget my mother. You'll get more sense out of me than you'll ever get from her. The only thing she can concentrate on is whether Chris left her anything and which of her little black dresses she should wear to his funeral. Now, I want to know. Did Chris kill himself?"

"Why would you think that?" Khattak countered.

Hadley tossed her long hair back over her shoulders. "Well, why would you be here if something wasn't wrong? Why would you even care?" Her expression altered, lost its edge. "Look," she said in a rush, "I didn't mean any of that other stuff. It's not Chris's fault that I wanted to live with my dad. He's my dad and I love him. Chris knew that. I'm sure he understood. It's just — he didn't want that big wedding Mel was always on about, so he couldn't have thought that Dad would just allow us to move in. Do you think Chris thought it might still happen?"

She was looking for reassurance, for some kind of expiation. If she had resisted Drayton's parental overtures and Drayton in turn had come to view his future as grimly unmarked by the things he wanted most, there might well have been some connection between Hadley's fears and Drayton's stark reality.

"Did you notice anything different about him these last few weeks?" Rachel asked, neither confirming nor denying Hadley's suspicions.

Hadley stilled. She was standing close enough to them that Rachel could tally the freckles on the bridge of her nose and spy out the gold flecks in her intelligent brown eyes. Unlike Marco River, no whiff of marijuana rose from her clothing.

"He was a bit more serious, maybe," she offered, then added swiftly, "I don't know why. He spent more time in his garden. He was really happy with the landscaping Aldo and Harry had done at the back."

Rachel considered this. A man improving his property, whether for the sake of its value or for his own creature comfort, hardly seemed the kind of man to contemplate a spine-crushing end to his existence.

And what explained the gun and the absence of candles?

"Did the power ever go out at his house?"

Hadley looked blank, as well she might.

Rachel hastened to clarify her question.

"Did he use a lot of candles during the evening?"

Because if he had, that might explain one mystery, although it didn't account for the gun.

Hadley grimaced as an unpalatable thought surfaced. "Maybe he and Mel did? I mean, I think he tried to be discreet around Cass and me," she said, weighing her words. "But he wasn't perfect."

Meaning, Rachel translated, that this more than on-the-ball teenager had quickly deduced that her mother was having sex with her tutor.

Khattak cut across her thoughts.

"Why Italian lessons instead of other languages?"

"Oh, that. He was fluent in Italian because of the businesses he'd owned in Italy. He said we could pick what we wanted to learn. I would have chosen Spanish, but he didn't speak Spanish. I couldn't see the point of German or Russian, and Cass has always wanted to go to Italy. For the fashion," she tacked on, fondly.

Khattak's face tightened with sudden knowledge. Rachel began to feel irritated. She didn't mind that the boss wanted her to look at the scene with fresh eyes and come to her own conclusions. What she minded was that she had no context for filtering the information that was coming through in dribbles from the people who had known Drayton.

Was the business in Italy significant? Did Drayton's fluency in Russian matter? Did the books on Albania suggest a financial interest in trans-European organized crime? What about the unfamiliar 9-millimeter gun? How could she make any of these deductions if she didn't have the faintest idea of what they were investigating? The dark halls of her imagination were pretty

70

unlikely to conjure the truth from smoke.

She sighed.

"Who are Harry and Aldo?" she asked for want of anything more to the point.

Hadley gave her the quintessential teenage shrug, embodying all things from indifference to disgust. She was rubbing her shoes in the spongy grass, which when Rachel did it was a sure sign of boredom.

"Gardeners. They have a local landscaping business that's doing pretty well. They did the gardens at Winterglass and at the museum. They take on plenty of individual jobs like Chris's house as well."

More connections to Drayton. They'd been on Nathan Clare's list, she remembered. Not on the guest list for his dinner parties, but mentioned tangentially. The Osmond brothers, like the singing group. Maybe they were Mormons too.

She wanted to scuff her own shoes.

"I guess we'll head over to Mr. Drayton's house then. Does your mum have a key?"

"Not to everything," her daughter said, with no small measure of satisfaction. "Just the front door. She's been dying to get into his office, but I guess despite their amazing mystical connection, Chris still had his secrets."

The bitter words stabbed at the air like

fingers of lightning. They left her looking after them with her thin arms crossed over her chest, her eyes like bronze metalwork, unblinking and inscrutable.

5.

*I took my mother's head into my hands
and I kissed her.
I never felt anything so cold before . . .*

In the car, he didn't wait for Rachel to ask. "I know nothing of Drayton's past or any businesses he might have run. I've only suspicion, Rachel. I'm not even sure I'd call it that."

"What would you call it, then?"

"Dread."

Rachel accepted this without knowing why. Maybe it was the hunted look in his eyes.

The day was warming up, a languid sleeve of blue draping the air with heat. As she did most days when the outdoor ice rinks were closed due to warmer than average temperatures, Rachel cursed mightily at global warming. She hadn't spent a lifetime recycling to suffer these miniature blows.

"You've known Nathan Clare for years," she said after a while. "Haven't you ever seen this house or museum or whatever you want to call it?"

"Ringsong? I haven't. It must be newly built. We'll go there after this stop."

This stop was Drayton's house, with its burnished aisles of flowers, the autumn grass rising vast and green, a backdrop to roses with gleaming thorns and orange-shouldered lilies that shifted against bright filaments of air.

The Osmond brothers knew what they were doing. And the back of the house, where the windows of Drayton's study broached the glassy expanse of lake, must have been even more peaceful. A place of dreams. A place to lose oneself in a solitude of light. A whimsical thought. One to be expected from a student of literature though not necessarily from a hockey-playing policewoman.

"I'll meet you in a moment," Khattak said. "I'd like to see what the landscapers have done around the house."

More secrets. Or a chance to size up Melanie Blessant on her own. She could take it either way.

She let herself into the house. They were too late to prevent Melanie from tinkering with the lock on the den again, but Rachel doubted she'd gained access. Drayton had fortified his study well. She was right: she found the woman mixing herself a drink in Drayton's kitchen.

"Ms. Blessant?" Rachel held up her ID. "I'm Sergeant Rachel Getty. Hadley told me you were here."

Melanie Blessant snorted, choking on her drink. From the bleary-eyed look of her, it wasn't her first.

"Of course she did, the little rat. Anything to screw me over."

Not the first words Rachel expected from a woman as lushly upholstered as Melanie Blessant. The photograph had given her some indication and Newhall's description of her dubious magic had confirmed it, but in the flesh the woman was something else.

She'd want to be thought of as enchantingly helpless. What else, with those pillowy lips and the white-blond hair that set off china-doll eyes? Not to mention the ridiculously high heels and deep-necked zebra print that hugged her curves. It was an excess of everything. Divine effusion in the form of expensive European scent. Shiny teeth, tiny bejeweled hands, perfectly set hair. Ropes of gold and diamonds blazed between her breasts, dangled from her ears and smothered her delicate wrists. Her makeup was subdued but still eye-catching: blue eyes rimmed with smoky liner, lips emphasized by semi-nude gloss, bronzer defining nature-defying cheekbones. Altogether too much woman, too much perfume, too much everything. Rachel's back ached at the thought of lugging around the other woman's double-barreled weight.

"I've come about the death of Mr. Drayton. I'll have to ask you for your key to his house."

Melanie set her glass down unsteadily on the quartz countertop. Her flawless complexion hardened into a mask.

"I'm not giving you anything until I've seen his will. This was supposed to be *my* house. We were supposed to be married. Then the damn fool had to go and get himself killed."

"Killed?" Rachel echoed.

Melanie waved her glass at the other woman.

"He fell, didn't he? He fell and he didn't even think about what that would do to me." She yanked the bottle on the counter closer to her, possibly a plum brandy, and a potent one from the look of things.

"I'm very sorry for your loss, Ms. Blessant."

"My loss?" Melanie snorted. "Forget my loss. What about that wedding he promised me? What about the money?"

With some effort, Rachel kept her expression impassive. Had Christopher Drayton really wanted to marry this woman? Granted, her breasts were enormous, but was that the only thing that counted with men anymore? How had he missed her mercenary nature? Or maybe he hadn't cared. Maybe a man in his late sixties was looking for nothing more than ready comfort or the sexual indulgence he had long since thought himself past.

Somehow that didn't figure with her notion of the Italian lessons. He hadn't only wanted Melanie. He'd cared for the girls as well.

Khattak tapped at the patio window. Rachel moved to let him in. She nodded at Melanie Blessant, hunched over Drayton's breakfast bar.

"Ms. Blessant, this is Inspector Khattak of Community Policing. He has some questions for you about Mr. Drayton."

The woman ignored her, pouring herself another drink. And then she stopped cold when she saw Khattak's face reflected in the mirror that hung on the far wall of the breakfast nook. Without speaking, she performed a series of subtle motions: arranging the expression on her face, running a quick tongue over her lips, drawing in her breath to boost her décolletage, sucking in her waist. Straightening her back, she turned on her stool and extended a limp hand.

"Ms. Blessant," he offered, as Rachel had, "I'm so sorry for your loss. I understand you and Mr. Drayton were very close."

"Melanie, please," she breathed. Rachel watched, amazed, as Melanie's blue eyes filled with tears. "It's been terrible," she whispered. "I don't know how I'll manage without my sweet Chrissie."

She glanced up at Khattak from beneath a thick fringe of lashes before continuing, "He was everything to me and my girls. My poor, sweet girls. They're absolutely devastated."

Rachel choked back a snort of disgust. Check one for the ingenuous glamour-puss. Check two for the doting mother. Her performance went some distance toward explaining Hadley's naked hostility.

Melanie shifted onto her feet, putting an unsteady hand on Khattak's shoulder. Her fingers tested the flesh beneath his shirt. Even with her heels, she reached no higher than his collarbone, a fact she clearly delighted in.

"How can I help you, Inspector? I'd do anything for Chrissie."

With a swift look at her shoes and a perfectly straight face, Khattak asked, "Shall we walk in the garden? It's a beautiful day for it."

The shoes meant that Melanie would have no choice but to avail herself of the Inspector's strong arm. A sardonic grin on her face that Khattak ignored, Rachel followed them into the garden.

She listened absently as he asked the routine questions about Drayton's state of mind, the unexpectedness of his death. Melanie clung to his arm, her fingers gripping like talons. She was adamant in her denial of any suggestion of suicide. Not her Chrissie. Not when he had so much to live for. The wedding. The girls. The family they would become. He'd already prepared the house for them, both girls had their own rooms. And he'd given her a free hand in redecorating the master, paying the extravagant bills without batting an eyelash or asking her to account for any of it. If his little Mel was happy, Chrissie was happy.

She'd been planning a gala reception at the Royal York. She had a wedding planner on retainer, one of those artsy downtown photographers booked to do the pictures, florists, caterers, wedding announcements — they'd been so busy these past few weeks. Her Vera Wang gown was hanging in Chrissie's closet, along with the accompanying bridesmaids' gowns he'd simply insisted on buying for Hadley and Cassidy. It doesn't have to be Vera for them, she'd assured him. That was spoiling them too much, but Chrissie wouldn't hear of it.

"What's good enough for my Mel is good enough for her girls."

She produced a sob on cue, turning her face into Khattak's shoulder. No tears now, Rachel noted with a wry twist to her mouth.

"Hadley said Mr. Drayton was against an elaborate wedding," Rachel interjected helpfully. Well, pseudohelpfully, anyway.

She caught the look of malice Melanie shot her from the shelter of Khattak's shoulder.

"I was excited, can you blame me? I might have gone a little overboard. Chrissie was the type to prefer something smaller, like in his garden. He'd crown me with lilies, he said. He was romantic like that." This time a genuine sob escaped her throat. She stared at Rachel defiantly, attempting to disown it. "That didn't mean he wasn't going to do what I wanted. Chrissie always did what I wanted. Besides, he knew I wouldn't move in with the girls until the wedding had taken place. I didn't want *Dennis* accusing me of negligence." She spat the name of her ex-husband at them.

A negligence of the heart, perhaps.

Rachel glanced around the garden. Its vivid spires balanced against the scroll of waves that rolled and unrolled to a distant rhythm. It would have been a lovely place for a wedding, intimacy rendered sacred in these groves. In Melanie's place, she would have agreed to it. Except she could never see herself in Melanie's place. When she thought about what the future might hold, she saw only her work. Instead of the promise of love and companionship, there was the constant presence of loss. And work was the one thing that could make her forget, the one place she could do something that mattered, that healed. Even if Melanie didn't seem in need of healing.

Rachel did some quick calculations in her head. Landscaping, the Royal York, Vera Wang — it added up.

"Perhaps Mr. Drayton had some financial troubles. A wedding in his garden would have reduced the expense considerably."

"No," Melanie said petulantly. "He just didn't like fuss. He didn't even want to sit for our wedding photos."

She patted down her dress, admiring herself, inviting them to admire her also, bathed in the glow of autumn light.

She pouted, an action that made Rachel think of an inquisitive puffer fish with its same moist oval of a mouth.

"I guess I don't blame him. Chrissie was nearly thirty years older than me. Maybe he didn't want everyone noticing."

A possibility, Rachel conceded. Perhaps the contrast of so much plush flesh barely bounded by her clothes had made Drayton feel his years. The years that may have hinted at future inadequacies.

"Was Mr. Drayton in a rush to be married?"

Melanie released Khattak's arm and gave Rachel a purely woman-to-woman look. "He wasn't missing out on anything, if that's what you're asking."

It hadn't been, but it was as good a lead as any. "Was it you who was eager to get married, then?"

Everything about the woman suggested haste. With her ex-husband no longer on a leash, maybe it had been a straightforward exchange of sex for security. The woman had a libido; the way she was eyeing Khattak was ample evidence of that.

Melanie swept her arm wide, knocking petals from several of the roses as she did.

"If you think this is about Audrina, let me assure you it isn't. I'm the only woman Chrissie cared about. The only one he wanted to marry, and he was in no danger of changing his mind."

"Who's Audrina?"

Khattak was busy admiring the fruit of the Osmond brothers' labor, so Rachel kept at it. One conversational thread was often as good as another.

Melanie's pouting lips snapped tight, but the massive injections of collagen she had endured meant they couldn't look anything but sultry.

"Some tart he picked up somewhere. I never met her, she was never at the house. Sometimes when Chrissie couldn't sleep, I'd hear him talking about her, but if I asked him in the morning, he'd say it was nothing. Some silly crush from his past. There were no texts from her, no phone calls."

Khattak turned back to them, his fingers absently handling the peach-colored petals of a rose known as Joseph's Coat.

"Your fiancé wasn't sleeping well?"

Melanie renewed her pout, this time attempting a sexier twist on it. "Not for my lack of trying, Inspector. A woman does what she can." She brought a platinum lock of her hair to her lips and twirled it. Rachel smothered a laugh. This was the Scarborough version of Marilyn Monroe's *Niagara.* "I told Chrissie not to worry about it, but I guess he couldn't get those letters off his mind."

"What letters, Ms. Blessant?"

"Melanie, please." She pressed Khattak's outstretched hand, removing the rose from his grasp. "Oh, every now and again Chrissie would find these letters on his doorstep. Typed letters, stupid ones. They never made any sense to me."

As Khattak's interest sharpened, Melanie blossomed before Rachel's eyes.

"Mr. Drayton showed them to you? How were they addressed?"

Her thick-coated eyelashes flickered. "The envelopes weren't addressed and Chrissie didn't exactly show me the letters. I'd find pieces of them in his desk drawer from time to time."

The same things that Rachel and Khattak already knew.

"Once, I found them shoved into an atlas like he was trying to keep them from me. My Chrissie never liked me to worry." Nor would any man, her tone implied. Her raison d'être in life was to be cosseted. "It was total nonsense, anyway. What does it even mean, 'I think it would be better if none of us had survived'? Why would anyone say that?"

She didn't seem to care about the answer.

"Can you tell us anything else about the letters?" There was a stiffness in Khattak's voice that Rachel couldn't place.

"I wish I could, Inspector, but Chrissie agreed with me. He said they were nonsense and he should probably burn them." She tilted her blond head to one side, her china blue eyes widening in sudden awareness. "But he always dreamt about Audrina on those nights when he got one. Maybe the little slut was sending them to him."

Rachel made a note of the name. Could the candles have been for the purpose of burning the letters? If so, why had she found so many remnants in Drayton's file cabinet? The puddles of resin had consisted only of candle wax, not residues of ash.

She signaled Khattak. She was finding Melanie Blessant both vulgar and tedious. She wanted to get to the museum.

"I wonder, Melanie, would you have the combination to your fiancé's safe? Or access to any of his papers?"

Melanie shook her head, her platinum locks bouncing, displeased at this reminder of her limited prerogatives in Drayton's life. "I need to know about his will. Chrissie said he would take care of me. He *promised* he would. I know he wouldn't leave me all alone in the world."

The subtraction of Hadley and Cassidy from her life didn't surprise Rachel at all, but Khattak's response was kind.

"For the time being, we'll have to ask you for your key and that you stay away from this house until we've completed our inquiries. You should know, however, that you are designated as the beneficiary in Mr. Drayton's life insurance policies. Regarding his will, if you know his lawyer's name, you should contact him. He'll be able to guide you further."

Melanie's impossible heels saw her sway into Khattak's chest.

"Thank you, Inspector, thank you! You don't know how worried I've been. Does the policy say — ?"

"One hundred thousand dollars each. There are two of them. But they won't be settled until we've ascertained that Mr. Drayton's death was no more than an accident."

Melanie stared at them shrewdly, her whole mood brightening.

"Chrissie didn't kill himself. He had no

reason to. I'll swear that to anyone who asks."

She had the confidence of a woman who knew that the objections of any rational male could be softened by a comprehensive glance at her cleavage.

She turned in her key without protest, a spring in her step as she let herself out of the garden.

6.

Do you still believe that we die
only the first death
and never receive any requital?

"I want to look for that atlas, Rachel."

"I'd like to get to that museum before it closes, sir. And shouldn't we get something to eat?" The breakfast sandwich being a faded memory at this point, leaving her purse redolent of egg whites, cheese, and sausage.

"After this, I promise."

Rachel screwed up her face in concentration. Only one section of Drayton's bookshelves held any atlases — the same one that contained the teen fiction she now ascribed to Hadley and Cassidy. They were heavy books. She took them out one at a time, shifting them to the surface of Drayton's desk. Khattak shook them out. No letters fell loose, none were concealed between the endpapers or slipped inside their covers.

"No luck, sir," she concluded.

She was in the act of setting the final one back when she saw that Drayton had folded down the corner of a particular page. She opened the atlas to study the borders of the country mapped on its pages. It wasn't Russia or Albania.

In a quick flash of intuition she connected the name of the woman Melanie had called a little slut. Audrina. Shortened, it was a five letter word. A word dark-penciled on the map.

She left the atlas open on the desk to make her way to the safe, adrenaline juicing her veins. The glimmer of an idea was taking root in her mind.

"What is it?"

She pointed Khattak to the atlas.

"I think I might be able to figure out the combination."

If it was as simple as a substitution code. Numbers for a name Drayton hadn't been able to get out of his mind, a name that kept him up at night. A preliminary attempt taught her that a straightforward substitution wouldn't fit the five-digit display. Using paper from Drayton's desk, she tried another tack. If she divided the alphabet in half and assigned the numbers one through thirteen, only one combination would spell the name she had found on the map. She punched in the numbers 45911 and the digital display lit up. As she pulled the small lever forward, she heard a click. The safe opened without resistance.

Drayton hadn't been mumbling the name of another woman in his sleep.

He'd said *Drina,* not Audrina. The name on the map was also the code.

Dozens of letters cascaded from the safe into her lap. She shifted through them, catching odd phrases here and there.

Yellow ants, your days are numbered.

Bend down, drink the water by the kerb like dogs.

Take the town. Comb the streets house by house.

Make them shoot each other. Then kill the rest.

They took my son. They shot him before my eyes.

I'm thirsty, so thirsty.

How sorry I am to die here so thirsty.

A terrible sense of dread pressed against Rachel's heart. Her stomach dropped, her palms went damp. She knew what she was looking at, but she wanted to hear it confirmed. She needed Khattak to admit what he long must have known.

The letters were never meant for Christopher Drayton.

They identified another man altogether.

Her voice raspy in her throat, she skewered Khattak with a look.

"Who the *hell* is Dražen Krstić?"

7.

Under a big pear tree there was a heap of between ten and twelve bodies. It was difficult to count them because they were covered over with earth, but heads and hands were sticking out of the little mound.

There's never any joy.

Khattak's phone rang, a temporary reprieve from questions he could no longer ignore. He didn't believe the truth would set him free. The truth in this case was a trap. One he had willingly entered, on the word of an old friend. Because friendship was more than a source of comfort, or a place of belonging. It was a responsibility. One that Nate had failed. He wouldn't fail Tom in turn.

That's not the only reason, Esa, you know that. You're not detached, pretend as you must. This is about identity. Yours. And his.

The phone call corroborated his fears. He'd told Rachel not to use up resources, not to widen the circle, but he'd sent a picture of the gun to Gaffney. And now Gaff had told him what some still resistant part of himself didn't want to know.

"Bring those with you. You said you were hungry," he said to Rachel.

"Sir —"

It wasn't an evasion. He had never meant to keep her in the dark this long.

"I'll answer your questions while we eat."

And Rachel, ever loyal when she should have been screaming at him, bagged the evidence without a word and followed him to the car.

Evidence? What evidence? A man fell to his death.

If he kept repeating it to himself, it might prove true.

He chose a restaurant near the marina, familiar to him through colleagues at 43 Division. And through Nate. He and Nate had eaten here all the time. The food was good, the views abundant.

His salad arrived swiftly along with Rachel's grilled chicken sandwich.

She tossed the bag of letters beside his plate.

"Talk," she said.

Glad of the excuse not to meet her eyes, he turned his attention to the bag. A disjointed phrase slipped toward his salad.

Not one of our leaders remain. No one returned from Omarska.

Rachel was already putting pieces together.

"Who called you from Justice, sir? Who asked you to find out if Christopher Drayton really fell from the Bluffs?"

His salad tasted dry in his mouth. This was Rachel. This was going to be a nightmare for every branch of government involved, but Rachel he trusted. She had more than proven her loyalty in Waverley, but it wasn't loyalty alone that had shown him her real worth. Rachel had a dogged commitment to the truth that outstripped her pride and ambition alike.

"Tom Paley," he said at last. "He's a friend." There was no point delaying the truth further. "He's also the Chief War Crimes Historian at Justice."

Rachel's mouth fell open, disclosing an impressive amount of chewed-up chicken.

She was bound to know Paley's name. Every now and again, his Nazi-hunting endeavors surfaced in the press.

She swallowed with difficulty, setting down her sandwich so she could count off her fingers. "The map Drayton marked. It was of Yugoslavia. The code to the safe — it was Drina, like the river on the eastern border."

"Like the Drina Corps," Khattak amended. "Like the gun. It's a Tokarev variant, the M70 model. Standard issue for the Yugoslav National Army — or the JNA, as it was known."

"What are you saying, sir? That Drayton owned a Yugoslav army weapon? Where would he have gotten it?"

"Not Drayton." Khattak looked at her steadily. "Dražen Krstić."

She stared back unblinking.

"Lieutenant Colonel Dražen Krstić was the Chief of Security of the Drina Corps of the VRS in 1995. He was General Radislav Krstić's direct subordinate. He was a superior officer to the security organs of the Drina Corps brigades. He also had a unique relationship with the Military Police and the 10th Sabotage Detachment of the Main Staff."

"Hold up," Rachel said. "I'm lost. Main staff of what?"

"The VRS." He folded his hands to cover the letters. "The Bosnian Serb Army."

There was a deadly little pause. It had never bothered Rachel that Khattak was a decade older than she, but she could see now that it had its disadvantages. He spoke of a war he had witnessed, whereas she had been a child during the dissolution of Yugoslavia.

Memories of news coverage began to filter through. The secession of a republic known as Bosnia Herzegovina. A UN force on the ground. Shrill politicians. Hand-wringing. Yes, there had been plenty of hand-wringing.

"Did you say 1995?" she whispered. He nodded, his expression not quite impassive.

"And the Drina Corps's area of responsibility?"

"It was Srebrenica."

Srebrenica.

Now the dread had meaning.

So too the letters.

"And Drayton?"

"Tom thinks Drayton may have been Dražen Krstić."

The notorious war criminal at large. One of the chief perpetrators of the executions at Srebrenica, where eight thousand Muslim boys and men had been murdered near the endpoint of a war that had seen Yugoslavia dissolve into flames. Eight thousand dead in less than a week.

Their hands tied, their bodies smashed,

bulldozed into mass graves in an attempt to obscure the war's greatest slaughter. An act commonly described as Europe's greatest atrocity since the Second World War.

Overlooking the rape, terror, and destruction that had characterized the three long years before the culmination of so much death.

Khattak could never hear the word *Serb* without thinking of its dark twin, Srebrenica.

And he could not think of Srebrenica without remembering his younger self, a self whose ideals and vocation were nearly lost to him now. The younger self that had participated in a student network against genocide, brave or foolish enough to accompany a humanitarian aid shipment to the once exquisite city of Sarajevo.

On Tuesday there will be no bread in Sarajevo.

He heard the cellist's melody again: mournful, insistent, accusing. It had sounded as a requiem in the streets of Sarajevo.

You failed us.

And then you watched us die.

The shipments had been no more than a bandage. Inadequate, deficient, robbed at airports and checkpoints by the same guns that had wiped the history of Bosnia from the map. The theft of United Nations fuel had supplied tanks and convoy lines, enabling the war to continue unto a world without end.

Memory itself erased.

A fig leaf in the end, for stone-faced passivity in the face of mass murder and the camps created for the purpose of torture and rape. The names indelibly stamped in memory: Omarksa, Manjača, Trnopolje, Keraterm.

It wasn't passivity that had defeated the Muslims of Bosnia. He thought now that such merciless slaughter could never have been possible without the international community's intervention. Forestalling air strikes. Appeasing the architects of the war while military units with names like the White Eagles and Drina Wolves pillaged and burned. Equivocating over "warring factions," eager to accept the fiction that a people under threat of extinction had fired mortars upon their own marketplaces to generate international sympathy or to provoke military action.

Action that couldn't be provoked, no matter the horrors on the ground.

Until Srebrenica.

Srebrenica that crystallized a truth acknowledged far too late.

The obliteration of Bosnia had been a slaughter, not a war.

Enabled by an arms embargo that had left its victims helpless in the face of VRS tanks, guns, propaganda, and hate.

The tragedy of Srebrenica will haunt our history forever.

Just as it haunted Khattak. Too many dead, too little done for the innocent. He still believed in a community, an *ummah;* in his best moments, he saw himself as a guardian. If he failed to discover the truth about Drayton, would he still be able to think of himself that way?

It had never been a question of ethics because nothing his work required of him had been in conflict with the truth. His counter-terrorism work had been a requirement of faith, not an abjuration.

During its three-year siege, Srebrenica had known terror enough for eight thousand lifetimes.

He read the letter he had covered with his hand.

Lt. Colonel Dražen Krstić,

It took some persuasion to convince my Serb neighbor with whom I had lived my whole life that I was suddenly his enemy

99

and that I was to be killed. And yet you managed it.

"Unless someone identifies him as Krstić, how can we really know?"

"Is that why you left me in the dark? You hoped it wasn't going to be Krstić?"

"There's a fairly significant Bosnian community on both sides of the border. How do you think it will play that a war criminal managed to acquire Canadian citizenship?"

"Does that matter?" Rachel pushed back. "If Drayton was Krstić, isn't it far more important we confirm that he's dead?"

"It will matter like hell to the Bosnians. They've a mosque not far from where you live, Rachel. And it's largely a refugee community."

Rachel pulled the bag of letters back toward herself, smoothing the plastic with her fingers.

"Sir," she said, carefully. "Did Tom Paley ask you to look into this for the purpose of covering it up? Because the biggest storm this will unleash will be at CIC."

Canadian Immigration and Citizenship. If they had granted Drayton his papers.

"Justice will take its share of opprobrium too. No, Rachel, that's not it. If they wanted it left alone, Tom could have left it alone. He didn't need to call me. He wouldn't want this on his conscience, and no one at CIC would have wanted Drayton in the country. He might have come across the border with forged papers, we'll find out eventually. What matters is that someone knew who Drayton was. Someone was sending him these letters. And then Drayton died."

"A fall," Rachel countered, playing devil's advocate.

"A fall," he echoed, a tightness in his chest. "Was it a fall? If this was Dražen Krstić, there are thousands of people who'd want to see him dead."

"Wouldn't they rather have justice? See him exposed and paraded in front of the press before he's locked up for good? That's what I would want."

Muslims, you yellow ants, your days are numbered.

Khattak couldn't be quite as confident.

A flush rose in his face, the moment of confession upon him. "They tried, Rachel. That's why Tom called me. For nearly two years, he's been receiving letters about Drayton. Anonymous letters. Someone's been asking him to investigate. Persistently. Tom meant to do it, he always meant to. Time got away from him."

"And now Drayton is dead."

101

"It's not all on Tom. In seventeen years, very few of these men have been apprehended, even fewer convicted. In the towns and cities of Bosnia, victims see the men who abused them walking free every day. Profiting from their crimes while the crimes they perpetrated can never be undone. Rapists. Sadists. Torturers. Thugs. And the missing —"

He ran out of words.

Rachel tried to understand. She'd read enough of history to appreciate the destruction of Yugoslavia for what it was. A bloodbath. Overseen by an intractable, perhaps even complicit, United Nations. As a police officer, she didn't have an ounce of Gandhian blood in her. She scorned those who genuflected at the temple of nonviolence, their voices ringing with praise of the defenseless victims of butchery while they sat on their hands when the gods of carnage came calling.

And she'd followed a bit of the general's war crimes trial.

General Ratko Mladić, commander of the Bosnian Serb Army, in the dock at the Hague's International Criminal Tribunal for the former Yugoslavia.

Charged with crimes so monumental they

had required the formation of a separate court to hear them.

Genocide. Complicity in genocide. Crimes against humanity. Violation of the laws of war. Deportation. Murder. Extermination.

Seventeen years the survivors of Srebrenica had waited to see Ratko Mladić account for his actions.

On the day he had faced them in court, Mladić had drawn his finger across his throat.

In a recorded statement of guilt, VRS officer Momir Nikolić had confessed little more than: "I am aware that I cannot bring back the dead."

Whatever hatred these men had spewed had consumed them, unable to recognize the civilization they had destroyed.

There was never a place called Bosnia.

We deny the existence of a camp called Omarska.

We deplore this time of war and hatred.

We are working for peace, peace is what we want.

All were sentences glimpsed from the letters.

"What was the letter writer doing, sir? What does it all mean? Was Drayton being threatened?"

Neither one of them had finished their

lunch. Rachel had been starving. Now her stomach was unsettled, protesting any thought of food.

Khattak raised his hands, as she had sometimes seen him do in prayer, and brushed them over his face.

"God knows." He said it seriously. "Perhaps reminding him of his crimes. Perhaps documenting them." He turned the bag over, sifting through more of the letters. "It's not as if these are threats." Through the plastic, his fingers measured first one line, then the next. "It's testimony, Rachel. These letters are testimony."

"From what? War crimes trials? You said yourself, there haven't been many."

"Not just the trials. These read like statements of witness. To the war itself. Perhaps reminding Drayton of what he and his confederates so pitilessly wished to obliterate."

A place of belonging for all of its people.

"Muslims weren't the only victims of that war," Rachel said, a trace of worry in her voice. She'd come to believe in Khattak's utter impartiality.

"No," he agreed. "But they were the only victims of Srebrenica. The only people of Bosnia under threat of extermination."

He pushed one of the letters at her.

104

The mosque in Foča burned for days. They danced the kolo *over its embers.*

"Foča?" she asked.

There was an expression on Khattak's face that she'd never thought to see. Haggard, haunted, almost without hope.

"A town in southeastern Bosnia. After the war, it was renamed Srbinje. The destruction of the Aladza was the least of its tragedies." He hesitated. "You could find out more from the witness testimony at the trial of Dragan Zelenović. There are a few others who have been tried for crimes at Foča as well. It's not — easy reading."

Rachel swallowed.

"So this is not just about what Krstić did at Srebrenica."

"There's been a tendency for history to cling to Srebrenica like a touchstone while ignoring the crimes that transpired before." He shook his head, his dark hair disarranging itself across his brow. "Srebrenica wasn't the beginning. It was the end."

He seemed to be taking a largely forgotten conflict much too personally, which worried Rachel.

"You're not Bosnian, sir." Her attempt at subtlety. "You seem rather — invested."

Khattak smiled. He always smiled when she expected him to take offense, something that continually caught her off guard. Not to mention the smile itself. Disconcerting at the best of times.

"You're not a Muslim girl. And yet, you were rather invested yourself in the death of Miraj Siddiqui."

Their last case and the first time she and Khattak had worked together to solve a murder. Miraj Siddiqui had been a young woman from a small Ontario township. They had caught the case because her death had been flagged as an honor killing.

It was a fair point. How to respond?

"I'm just saying — look, your background is South Asian."

"Pakistani," he added helpfully. "Don't beat around the bush."

She glared at him. "That didn't require security clearance, did it, sir? It's just — you seem to know an awful lot about this. You seem to *care* an awful lot about this."

"Empathy," he said easily. "The reason we work so well together. You have it in spades."

"I was a kid when Yugoslavia fell apart. I had no reason to know or care anything about it."

At once he became serious. "If it had fallen apart, I don't know that I would have cared much either. But it was severed, Rachel. By gangsters on the ground and cowards at the Security Council."

"That's exactly what I'm talking about. Who carries that kind of conviction around in their heads?"

"I wasn't a child then." He ate the last few bites of his salad. "Let's talk about this more later. We should be getting to the museum."

Prevarication.

She was the queen of prevarication, so she had no trouble recognizing it.

If Christopher Drayton was really Dražen Krstić — a man who had butchered Muslims in their thousands — that might be a reason to call upon the head of Community Policing, especially if that head was also an old friend.

Her gut told her there was more to it — more about Khattak that she didn't know, which was no surprise. She hadn't known about Laine Stoicheva until he'd taken the time to tell her. She definitely hadn't known about Nathan Clare or she would have read all of his books by now. Especially the one he'd mentioned to her boss — *Apologia.* She made a mental note to hunt it down. She was pretty sure there was something more here — something about the war that was more personal to him.

Khattak rarely shied from the truth. In

her working experience with him, what he asked for was time to ascertain the nature of the truth. He was cautious, thorough, and eventually, the truth came to light.

Her own skills in this department were of no little assistance. She made connections quickly, leaps of intuition that were somehow in her blood. She liked to pound ahead wherever they took her, and Khattak usually let her.

This time he asked for patience.

She wanted to see the museum as well. Spanish history wasn't her strong suit, but she'd always wanted to visit Barcelona. Each fresh winter that rolled by, she cursed herself for not having purchased a ticket. Maybe this year.

She'd rather think of Spain than of Krstić, but her bloodhound instincts were up.

What would a man like Dražen Krstić have wanted with a museum on the history of Moorish Spain?

8.

All my life I will have thoughts of that and feel the pain that I felt then and still feel. That will never go away.

It was Tuesday night. It had taken them all day in the blistering heat to walk the four kilometers to Cinkara. It was no uglier than any of the other buildings. It had the same pockmarked face and shattered windows of all the concrete blocks. They had made munitions here once. Maybe, maybe there would be weapons of some kind, a gun she could hold. Maybe there would be food or clean water. One thing she knew was that there would be people. The road was full of them, everyone hungry, everyone frightened, everyone hot.

One of the girls in her class had fainted at the roadside. She wanted to stop and comfort Edina, but her sister wouldn't let her. Her sister kept her slippery hand locked tight within her own, bruising it with her hold, and marched her forward, talking to no one, listening to no one. It was only the two of them now. They had already seen their brothers to the woods. Four boys, ranging in age from thirteen to twenty-one.

"We will meet you in Tuzla," Nesib said. "Look for us in Tuzla. And when you get to the base, look for our neighbors, they will help you. Look for Mrs. Obranovic. She will make sure you are safe."

None of this had been said to her. Nesib, the handsomest and oldest of her brothers, had given his instructions to her older sister.

"And listen," he'd said. "Stay in the middle of the crowd. Keep your faces turned away. Don't go near any of the soldiers. Do you hear me? Always look away from them."

Her sister had nodded. Then Nesib tried to push the last of their food into her sister's hands. She pushed it back, spreading her hands wide, refusing to take it. Her stomach was crying but she knew it was right what her sister had done. Their laughing, joking, beloved Nesib was losing his teeth. He was the skinniest of them all because he gave his share to whichever of them cried the most or complained the loudest. Only her sister was good enough not to take Nesib's food, though she was hungry too.

Her sister was right. It was a very long march to Tuzla.

Her brothers would need the food in the woods.

She thought that maybe Nesib was so worried that he might not even remember to say good-bye to her. But he had kissed her and kissed her, squeezing her tight, before saying to her sister, "Don't let go of her hand."

Her sister had nodded, solemn as an oath-taker.

"All the way to Potočari, don't let go of her hand. If the soldiers come, you run into the woods."

And then he had pulled at her sister's braid and kissed them both again.

"Allah keep you, my little sisters. Allah is wise and protects us all."

He read the Fatiha over their heads, then he took their brothers and left. None of them looked back.

Her sister had obeyed Nesib as if it was the most important thing in the world, the most important lesson she could learn. She had kept them marching despite her complaints. She had cried, begged, even thrown a tantrum, but her sister wouldn't stop.

She held her hand in a death grip.

If they died on their way to Potočari, she would still feel that grip.

Cinkara was even hotter and more crowded than the road had been.

She hated it. She hated that Nesib had left them and that everyone was crying and angry and frightened. They made her frightened too.

Her sister kept pushing and pushing, dragging her by the hand, through the crush of bodies until they got to the center.

And every now and again, her sister, whose head kept turning from side to side, would call out, "Mrs. Obranovic? Mrs. Obranovic, are you here?"

They found a concrete wall to lean against. There had been so much heat this July that even the concrete was warm against her bare arms.

She was so hot and thirsty she thought she might fall to the ground like Edina.

And then, her sister let go of her hand and darted into the crowd.

Stunned, she sat back, too frightened and thirsty to move. She couldn't even call after her. Everyone had left her. Their parents had died two months ago in the shelling. Now Nesib and her sister were gone. She was alone. She wasn't going to make it.

She began to cry, but it had been so long since she'd had any water to drink that the tears wouldn't come. For some reason this made her angry.

She cursed Nesib, she cursed her parents, and loudest of all, she cursed her sister.

And then she remembered that smiling, hungry, skinny Nesib didn't like it when she cursed. She recited his prayer instead.

"Allah will keep us, Allah will protect us. Allah will keep us, Allah will protect us. Allah will keep us, Allah will protect us. Allah keep Nesib, keep Nermin, keep Jusuf, keep Adem, keep my sister."

"She is a good one, this little girl. Look how she says her prayers."

It was Mrs. Obranovic!

Her face broke into a smile of unrestrained joy as she found her sister behind the bulk of their neighbor. Her sister hadn't left her alone in the world. She hadn't broken her promise to Nesib by letting go of her hand. She'd seen Mrs. Obranovic and dashed into the crowd!

And now they were both with her.

Mrs. Obranovic studied their hungry faces and reached into the basket she carried on her shoulder. She had a plastic carton of water. She twisted off the lid, giving each of them a little to drink. Then she reached back into the bag and produced a half loaf of bread. She gave all this to them with a little bit of yoghurt.

"It's gone bad, I think, in this heat, but take it anyway. You girls need it."

She couldn't help herself. She kissed Mrs. Obranovic's hands.

Such a wonderful woman. So blessedly, blessedly kind!

The noise and heat and crush around them faded. She relaxed against the concrete wall, happier than she'd been in weeks. As if in harmony with her moment of contentment, the people around her quieted from their terror. Everyone went thankfully still.

Dutch soldiers in their UNPROFOR gear and blue helmets were approaching through the crowd.

Her stomach full, her thirst a little quenched, she smiled at them and waved her hand.

9.

*I addressed one of the wingborn singers,
who was sad at heart and aquiver.*

*"For what do you lament so plaintively" I
asked,
And it answered, "For an age that is gone,
forever."*

Now that she was standing before it, Rachel couldn't believe they had missed this house upon their former visit to Nathan Clare. It was four doors from Winterglass and roughly double the size, albeit entirely different in style. A style unseen in the climate of southern Ontario, let alone at the edge of an eroding series of cliffs.

The Andalusia Museum wasn't just a museum: it was a house drawn from the rural architecture of southern Spain, where internal spaces expanded outward in a marriage of gardens and stone. In Scarborough, it was impractical at best, foolish at worst.

From the street the house fronted, Rachel could see the lake through a row of French doors and recessed windows. The loveliest part of it was the shining coil of light that illuminated the courtyard within.

She marveled at it. The grace of modeled plaster played against slurried brickwork and roofs of red clay. A portico and forecourt beckoned beneath the rusticated arch that crowned a flight of terra-cotta stairs. Under the sconces on the cast-stone surround, the name Ringsong was outlined in tiny bronze and blue mosaic tiles.

Ringsong.

Something to do with Andalusian love poetry, she recalled.

It didn't belong on this street, yet she had difficulty imagining it anywhere else. It was too rich, too alluring, too beautifully imagined. It made her think of constellations in a southern sky unfolding against the velvet of night or the sweet taste of nectar in a miniature golden cup.

All it required in addition was an encampment of glossy-necked peacocks. There was plenty of space for them to wander in the tiered garden that surrounded the house, plantings she was fairly certain wouldn't survive the winter.

116

The house was filling her head with fantastical thoughts.

To dispel the magic, she pressed the doorbell, Khattak silent at her side.

For someone who'd been agitating about their visit to the museum, he had little to say. She shot him a glance. His face was meditative, absorbed. She could tell he was impressed.

A woman close to Rachel's age, in her late twenties or early thirties, answered the door. She wasn't the coal-eyed, caramel-skinned beauty Rachel's imagination had conjured up to go with the house, a woman of Spanish warmth and languid bones, another stereotype dashed.

If anything, the woman's grave young face made her think of the soft-spoken Jane Austen scholar whose course she had taken as an undergraduate. Dreamy-eyed, a little withdrawn, but there the comparison faltered. The woman who answered the door had a guarded, subtle face with eyes the pale blue of Waterford china. Her sheaf of hair was the color of wheat, neatly captured at the base of her neck. She was narrow-shouldered with wristbones that hinted at a painful fragility. Dressed in a white silk blouse and tailored gray trousers, she was mildly attractive, though too self-possessed

117

for true beauty.

Pale-hearted, Rachel thought in another flight of fancy.

Before they could introduce themselves, Marco River appeared at her shoulder.

"Well met," he said. "These are those cops, Mink. The ones I was telling you about."

So much for the element of surprise. And what kind of kid said "Well met"?

Khattak made polite introductions with more than a touch of warmth in his voice. As Mink led them inward through the forecourt, Rachel wondered if it was the woman or the house that attracted him. They passed under an arch inlaid with a narrow river of Moorish tiles and then through a space Candice Olson would have described as a flex room. It was a space between spaces, inviting them deeper into the house, yet Rachel could have lingered in it for hours. The antique Moroccan carpet that warmed the floor, the assembly of indoor palms potted in sand-colored stoneware, books and pamphlets on Andalusian history — all of these demanded time and care.

She changed her mind in the forecourt, where curtains of wind brushed against her face, carrying the scent of grape myrtle, jacaranda, and chorisia from the courtyard through a wood-planked door. Small pedestals with glass cases were arranged in a circle in the forecourt, each with a manuscript page on display and an accompanying beautifully lettered description of the exhibit.

Was this Hadley's work?

Three sides of the house opened onto a courtyard planted with flowers, olive trees, citrus, and palms. A massive hearth dominated one end, fortifying a large alfresco seating area. Cassidy Blessant was curled up in one of the armchairs, her long legs tucked beneath her as she paged through a magazine.

Rachel expected it to be *Seventeen* or some teen gossip rag; she was surprised to discover a calendar with photographs of Arabian thoroughbreds.

"This is a resting place," Mink informed them. "To give people time to reflect on what they've learned in a space that's purely Andalusian."

"Outwardly impassive, preserving the artistry of its craftsmen for the interior."

Mink nodded at Khattak, pleased. "Like the Alhambra," she agreed, "with its Court of Lions." They exchanged the glance of intimates who spoke an exclusive language.

Mink led them through the courtyard to

the great room, the first room that con-
formed to Rachel's notion of what a museum should be. Exhibits were arranged on
white marble pedestals and in bowfront
cabinets, each with the same hand-lettered
descriptions. Carved beams and a progres-
sion of clerestory windows subdued the im-
mense space; tall glass lanterns were hung
at regular intervals between the beams. The
room was a spectacular contrast of dark
timber against pale stonework. Three pairs
of French doors opened to the courtyard,
dressing the room in a canopy of light. The
entire effect was effortless.

Rachel loved it. From his arrested expression, she could tell Khattak felt the same.

"I hope you don't mind if we keep working while we talk. We're due to open in
October and we're a bit behind."

The "we" included Marco River, who was
now ensconced with Hadley at a huge wood
table in the center of the room. They were
seated on high-backed stools, bent over a
table piled high with any number of dispar-
ate objects, manuscripts, and books. Hadley
was using the fine nib of a calligrapher's
pen on cream notecards that matched the
milky tones of the room. Riv leafed through
a dictionary, presumably assisting with
vocabulary. His knee was touching Hadley's,

who ignored it.

"Why Andalusia, Ms. Norman?" Rachel asked.

"Won't you call me Mink?" She invited them to the table to inspect her collection, sliding onto a stool across from Hadley and Riv.

"That's an unusual name."

"My sister is Sable," Mink said drily. "Our mother had two passions in life: fashion and theater. She respected the animal rights movement but deplored the need to give up her precious furs. So she took her revenge with typical drama — by naming us after them."

Rachel smirked. "No siblings named Otter and Ermine?"

There was the briefest hesitation before Mink laughed. "None. Now, how may I help you?"

Khattak was quick to step in. Rachel had the uneasy feeling that he was more than a little interested in their hostess.

Great. He'd been the one man she'd met who she thought could resist blondes.

"I would love to know more about the museum."

"It's a passion project," she said simply. "I'm a librarian. I've studied languages and history. There's no place that speaks to me

121

more than the civilization of Andalusia. Cordoba, Granada, Seville, Toledo — it was a sparkling moment in our collective history." She was dismantling an ornate picture frame as she spoke, intricate gold decoration incised on black steel.

"Moments that come rarely and are soon extinguished," said Khattak, something indefinable in his voice.

She paused in her work. "I don't know that I would call seven hundred years of Moorish influence on Spain 'soon.' All history is eventually extinguished, but its monuments may well endure. Like the Alhambra. Or this one."

She placed the photograph intended for the steel frame before him on the table. Forgotten, Rachel peered over his shoulder.

It was an exquisite Spanish building with a cascade of horseshoe arches in white.

"A mosque," Rachel said.

"A synagogue," Mink corrected. "Actually, this is Sinagoga de Santa Maria la Blanca, or Saint Mary the White, a structure that seems extraordinary to us now, though it was perfectly appropriate to its time." Her fingers brushed Khattak's at the edge of the photograph. "It was built by Mudejar architects for the Jewish community of Toledo, at their request." She placed a special emphasis on the last words. The smile that edged her lips was wistful. "Muslims," she elaborated for Rachel's benefit. "Moorish architects designing a Jewish place of worship on Christian soil. Can you imagine such a sharing of religious space today?"

Khattak had once prayed at the Dome of the Rock next to a Syriac Christian, a fact he was willing to discuss, if not advertise.

"I think they did it on *Little Mosque on the Prairie.*" Not Rachel's most brilliant offering, but true as far as it went.

"Saskatchewan — the new Andalusia."

Mink said it gently enough, but Rachel caught the undertone of mockery. Khattak was slow to remove his hand, she noted.

"Where do the exhibits come from?" he asked Mink.

"I've been collecting little bits of history ever since I can remember. Nothing very valuable — most of it is just a translation of poetry and religious manuscripts, which, thanks to Hadley, we've prettified. The forecourt exhibits are a series of ring songs, a tradition that began with the Andalusian Arabs who had a genius for assimilating cultures and ideas. Arabic was the lingua franca of Andalusia — admired, almost venerated for its great poetry and expressiveness, not feared and despised as it is today. The ring song rejuvenated Europe's indigenous tongues, gave voice to feelings and ideas that Latin couldn't begin to grapple with. The ring songs from our exhibit are from Arabic, Hebrew, and Romance. It's a remarkable synthesis. Andalusia was a remarkable synthesis."

She would have made a great teacher. Her passion for her subject, her ability to slice through centuries of history to the shimmering idea at the heart of it, would inspire the museum's visitors: it was more captivating than her remarkable endeavor.

But it was a humble project as far as museums went. Scattered objects. More description than representation. For the life of her, Rachel couldn't see why Christopher Drayton would have been prepared to make such a major donation. Just to put his name on a wall or a plaque? If David Newhall's thinking was illustrative of the museum's directors' position, they hadn't wanted his money. Yet a hundred thousand dollars might have purchased more than a few trinkets or seen to the upkeep of this fabulous house.

Where had the funding for the museum come from? Surely not from a librarian's salary. And did she live here? Had she been prepared to turn down Drayton's offer? Rachel's list of questions was growing longer.

"So what happened to Andalusia?"

"Fanaticism, fundamentalism of all kinds. Petty-minded rivalries from within, ignorance and fear from without. The Inquisition. The Reconquista. Before you knew it, Iberia's Jews and Muslims had vanished into history. We think of it commonly as a case of Christians expelling or forcibly converting the peoples of the peninsula. In fact, there were all kinds of alliances between the communities and they changed frequently. It wasn't Christians who burned the Great Library of Cordoba." Mink looked pained at the mention of it, as if it were a loss that had occurred only yesterday. "It was Berbers riding an orthodox tide that swept the Muslim world."

Book-burnings. Those inveterate moments in history when knowledge and the transmission of it was the most dangerous currency of all.

"What they were striking at — as did the Inquisition centuries later — was a culture of enlightenment. Knowledge shared, refined, debated, and ultimately transformed. Ideas, books, histories could come from any source, and the Umayyad rulers of Spain had instantaneous access to everything created and translated in the staggering knowledge-production factories of Baghdad. Knowledge was priceless, whether religious or secular, indigenous or foreign. The prince of Cordoba housed countless scribes, editors, and bookbinders in his palace." Her smile was reminiscent, her blue eyes alight. "They say in Cordoba books were prized more greatly than beautiful women or jewels. In Andalusia, the mark of a city's greatness rested on the caliber of its libraries and the quality of its scholars. That's what we're trying to re-create here, in some small part. That wonderful spirit of inclusion and mutual learning. The Library of Cordoba held over four hundred thousand volumes, with a catalogue librarians only dream of."

Which was an interesting history lesson, and Rachel could see that the librarian was moved by it, but it still didn't explain Christopher Drayton's interest.

Or maybe it did. Khattak, who as far as Rachel knew had no particular attachment to Moorish Spain, was listening to Mink with the fervent attention of the masses in Saint Peter's Square on Easter Sunday. Maybe this idea of a vivid, elastic pluralism gave spark to magic. The kind of magic that opened wallets and turned serious men into dreamers. Or maybe it wasn't Andalusia at all, but the woman herself.

"What was Christopher Drayton's interest in the museum? We've learned that he was to make a significant financial contribution to it."

Mink took a moment to slip the photograph of the synagogue into the steel frame she had prepared. When she looked up at Rachel, her face was composed.

"Chris was a neighbor and a friend." She lowered her voice. "I think he was a little lonely and the idea of the museum was something that intrigued him. People who know nothing of Spain beyond Madrid and Barcelona are often captivated by their first venture into its Moorish past. By what the wonderful writer Maria Menochal has called palaces of memory."

Rachel scowled. Was this a second dig the quiet librarian had aimed at her? Or was Rachel just being sensitive because she'd imagined herself on a sunny Mediterranean beach?

Her answer was overloud. "How could he be lonely with a bosom companion like Melanie Blessant?" She was quite pleased with the emphasis she'd laid on the word *bosom*. Until she saw Hadley and Riv's heads come up.

Mink shrugged, her face tight, searching

for other work at the table to occupy her hands. They fell upon a small book of poetry, its author Arab, its title *The Neck-Ring of the Dove.* Fascinated by it, Khattak took it from her.

Her voice lowered further, she said directly to Khattak, "There are other needs men have beyond what Melanie offered. Understanding. Communication. A certain sympathy of thought."

Khattak held her gaze without comment.

Rachel scratched at her neck. Her boss was being decidedly unhelpful during this interview, neither asking his own questions nor following up hers. Mink Norman was clever, but she was also ordinary to a fault: where was the distraction?

"Are you saying you possessed this sympathy with Mr. Drayton? Was that why he planned to make such a large donation?" Rachel asked.

"We never intended to be too ambitious with Ringsong. We hadn't expected the kind of budget that would permit us to purchase manuscripts and so on. I'm not a curator of objets d'art. I'm a librarian. I wanted to tell the story of a civilization of the word. A civilization in love with language and learning."

"Would Mr. Drayton's money help with

that or not? One of your directors, David Newhall, said that it came with a steep price tag. You'd have to rename the entire project after Drayton."

Mink stiffened, bracing her hands on the table. Hadley and Riv looked up again, sensing that the mood had changed.

"We hadn't decided about the donation. As far as I knew, there were no strings attached. We'd already named the house, and the house is a public trust. We built it with a great deal of grant assistance."

"We?"

"The Andalusia Society. We've over two thousand members."

"Do you live here?"

"The house has a set of private rooms. That's part of my arrangement as librarian. Should I leave the job, naturally I'd leave the house."

There was a thrust and counterthrust to her conversation with Rachel, a suppressed antagonism, as if she recognized in Rachel a cunning, obstructive enemy. There was something wary about Mink Norman, some powerful emotion tamped down beneath a calm exterior.

"If, as you say, there were no strings attached, why the hesitation? Surely the money would come in handy."

"I have no fund-raising agenda," she replied with dignity. "There's a process by which new members are vetted. The same is true of donations. Christopher did wish to help us, but we had to weigh this against his request to come on board as a director."

"So there *were* strings attached."

It was the obvious conclusion. Drayton wanted more than the indulgence of a passing interest in a history entirely unrelated to himself. He wanted a role in directing the museum itself.

Rachel looked through the windows to the courtyard. Maybe it wasn't the museum he'd had an interest in. He'd chosen to live in an unprepossessing home on a pretty street with magnificent views. Maybe what he wanted was the house.

If Mink were no longer librarian, maybe a man of his independent means could talk his way into some form of guardianship.

House, kids, adulation, and Melanie.

The perfect life.

She changed tack.

"Did you see Mr. Drayton on the Bluffs on the night of his death?"

"No." She answered exactly as Nathan Clare had. "You can't see the path to the Bluffs from these windows."

But was it true? Rachel would have to get

out there and walk it to discover just what could be seen of the museum and Winter-glass from the Bluffs.

If everyone had liked Chris Drayton and no one had seen him on the night of his death, what did his death really signify? And yet, she couldn't shake the feeling that Mink was holding something back. Perhaps an affair with Drayton. Was she the reason he'd dragged his feet about Melanie's plans for an over-the-top wedding? Hadley and Riv were whispering to each other across the long table, the boy's hand caressing the girl's neck, another gesture Hadley ignored. She was watching the three of them with canny, glittering eyes.

The conversation was at a dead end. Unless Khattak had something to offer, Rachel couldn't think of anything else to add that seemed remotely connected to Drayton's death. Unless she simply came out and stated: *"Do you have any reason to suspect that Christopher Drayton was a Bosnian Serb war criminal?"*

She was tempted, but she didn't want to tip her hand too soon. It was hardly something Drayton would have advertised if he were Dražen Krstić. And that was another thing — what rational reason could a man accused of exterminating Muslims and

131

eradicating Bosnian history have for his attraction to the Andalusia museum? Weren't the two ideas fundamentally opposed? One a civilization of pluralism and tolerance, the other a culture of hate?

If she'd understood Mink's little lecture properly, the Andalusians had created something beautiful out of their divergent identities. In the hands of the Bosnian Serb Army, difference — whether Muslim, Catholic, or Jew — had meant destruction and death.

There were no personal items in the museum area of the house that could offer further insight into the character of Mink Norman and her association with Christopher Drayton. Rachel tried anyway.

"You mentioned your sister, Ms. Norman. Where is Sable now?"

Mink smiled with genuine warmth at the mention of her sister.

"The music you see everywhere? It's Sable's. She studies piano at the Mozarteum University of Salzburg. She'll be home again for Christmas break."

One sister a librarian, one sister a musician. An educated family. Rachel envied their opportunities.

"Your parents?"

"It's just the two of us, I'm afraid."

Another field of inquiry dried up. The only sensible thing to do was to begin a comprehensive investigation into Drayton's real identity. Without that information, there was little point to harassing those Drayton had known passingly or well.

The music reminded her of Winterglass and Nathan Clare. She mentioned him to Mink, watching her guarded face.

"Come on," Riv said from his side of the table, his dictionary abandoned, one hand on Hadley's knee. "Everyone from here to Timbuktu knows Nathan. He's amazing. And he gives the best parties."

"That's all right, Marco. And yes, it's true. Nathan loves the piano. He's quite proficient. He often loans us music."

On the other side of the courtyard was a colonnade of arches through which Rachel glimpsed fountains that seemed to drop through the air to the lake. She very much wanted to explore further but could think of no reason to stay.

"Shall we go then, sir?"

Khattak caught her glance, moved away from the table. "I'd like to take a closer look at the exhibits. You've been up early, call it a night."

Rachel cleared her throat. Had the museum and its proprietor so bewitched him that he'd forgotten? "You're my ride, sir. I'll need a lift to the subway at least."

He straightened quickly. "Of course. Then I'll return later, if I may."

The words were said somewhere in the vicinity of Mink's burnished hair. Her blue eyes encompassed Khattak, acknowledged a private communication.

In the car, Rachel said, "A blonde, sir? Really?" And left it at that.

10.

Easily predictable events have been proceeding inexorably in the cruelest, most atrocious fashion.

For more than a week now, Rachel had been asked to do nothing further on the Drayton investigation. She'd resumed her regular workload with Dec and Gaffney, saying little about the previous week's excursions, wondering when Khattak would show up at their downtown office again. She had a few ideas about what they should do next and found Khattak's silence troubling. Had he ruled out the idea that Drayton was Dražen Krstić? If so, based on what evidence? Or had he found something that cemented his certainties? Was he even now reporting to his friend at Justice? He'd told her to keep the letters, and she'd spent her evenings digging into the history of the Bosnian war, trying to find out more about Krstić.

Initially, she'd thought that the letters spoke from the perspective of a survivor of the war with a very specific axe to grind, but Khattak had been right. The letters weren't just about the massacre at Srebrenica. They were far more wide-ranging, as if the letter writer was making a darker point, outlined in blood.

Sarajevo, did you hear my warning?
The sun on your face looks like blood on the morning.

She hadn't been able to trace either the letters or the source of those words. The only prints on the letters had been Drayton's. The words she had just read were conceivably from a translated poem or song. And Sarajevo wasn't the only name she had found in the letters. There were others, all of them, apart from Srebrenica, unfamiliar to her. Gorazde, Bihac, Tuzla, Zepa.

She'd looked them up. All six cities had been UN-designated "safe areas," under United Nations protection. All six had come under siege, repeated bombardment, the destruction of religious and cultural monuments, and the recurrent targeting of water, electricity, and food supplies.

The letter writer encompassed it all.

Today a funeral procession was shelled.
Charred bodies lie along the street.

The whole city is without water.

Srebrenica, like Sarajevo, had suffered a three-year siege. In Srebrenica, civilians kept alive by a trickle of UN aid ultimately became victims of genocide. In less than twenty-four hours, safe area Srebrenica had been depopulated of its Muslim inhabitants: women and small children forcibly evacuated under the eyes of the Dutch battalion stationed there, men and boys murdered in their thousands.

Nearby Zepa escaped the massacres but suffered the same depopulation.

All at the hands of the logistically efficient killing machine known as the VRS or Bosnian Serb Army, supplied materially and in all the other ways that mattered by the reconstituted Yugoslav National Army.

We will not reward the aggressor with the carve-up of Bosnia, redrawn along ethnically purified lines.

And yet they had.

Many of the post-1995 online commentators on Bosnia used the satiric term *unsafe area Srebrenica.* Rachel couldn't fault them. It was a compelling history lesson: how quickly the violent ideals of ultra-nationalism led to hate, how quickly hate to blood. If Drayton had been Dražen Krstić, his hands were bloodier than most.

137

The letter writer wanted to remind him of this. More than anything, he or she intended to disrupt the idyllic latter stage of life Drayton had constructed for himself: peaceful home, lovely garden, voluptuous fiancée, made-to-order family.

Had there been a ring on Melanie Blessant's finger? Rachel couldn't remember.

Another line of inquiry to follow up. There was the will to consider, the insurance policies — if Drayton hadn't yet made a bequest to Ringsong, it was possible that his will left everything to Melanie. If Melanie had known as much and if the wedding was slow to proceed — if Mink Norman was somehow seducing Drayton's wealth to fund what she had called a passion project — Drayton's death might have nothing to do with the identity of Dražen Krstić at all.

The letters may have been intended merely as torment, the need of a clever and isolated individual to maintain control over Drayton.

She made a list of things to check out: the disposition of the will, whether the wedding had been confirmed, Drayton's relationship with Mink Norman, the identity of the letter writer.

She was ready to chase down all possible

leads as to Drayton's true identity, including a visit to view the body: she was waiting for Khattak's call.

She glanced up from her desk to the glass doors of his office. Still empty. She could see his bookshelves on the wall, nearly all police business except for a few personal selections, one of which was *Apologia*. Would he notice if she borrowed it?

She slipped into his office and helped herself to the book. Its black and white cover held an undertone of midnight blue. It featured a wrought-iron bench shaded by a tree in a desolate garden. Singularly uninformative.

She flipped through the first few pages until she found the dedication.

To EK, whose friendship I valued too little, too late.

Her intuition had been right. There were deep waters to traverse between Esa Khattak and Nathan Clare. She slipped the book into her bag, closed the lights, and made for home.

11.

All my joys and my happiness up to then have been replaced by pain and sorrow for my son . . .

She walked up the porch steps to their dark two-story in Etobicoke. She noticed, as she always did, that the stairs needed sweeping and that the paint on the porch was peeling badly. Her Da was retired from the service, but he spent most of his time in front of the television, often cursing at it. In the evenings, he went to the local pub where he traded the same war stories that had been doing the rounds for the last thirty years. He was a heavy drinker. His drinking had defined her whole childhood: it had made a victim of her mother and driven her brother, Zachary, to the streets while still a teenager.

Zach had been fifteen the last time Rachel had seen him.

Ray and Zach, they'd been to each other

during those good days. Ray-Ray, she'd been when Zach was little. A seven-year age difference had separated them, but Zach had been the light of her world, the baby she'd done her best to raise. Her father's rages and her mother's efforts at making herself disappear had been successful. There'd only been Rachel for Zach. And that less and less, as Rachel put herself through school.

She and Zach had shared the same dream. She'd get an education and a job, and she'd make a home for herself and Zach. A home away from the paralytic rages of Don Getty and the helpless murmurings of Lillian, his wife. No matter how much she longed for closeness with her mother.

But as Zach had shot up and filled out, it had been harder and harder for him to wait. He'd fought back against their Da, usurping Rachel's role as his protector. Her Da had been prepared to use his hands on his boy. Rachel, he'd never touched. She'd been the one to calm him down, usually with a dose of sharp-tongued humor.

When Rachel was the protector, Zach had gone untouched.

When Zach stood up for himself, everything had changed.

She'd called the cops round a couple of

times, but the men who'd come by had been friends of Don Getty, friends who knew his wife, and when asked by them if everything was all right, Lillian had flapped her hands at her sides and apologized for calling them out. No one had mentioned Rachel.

As a child, she had judged her mother for it and held her accountable. As a police officer with years of training behind her, she knew no one was more to blame for the turmoil in their home than Don Getty.

"You better watch it, Da," Rachel had said. "You'd better not touch Zach again."

"He's just a boy," her mother had felt brave enough to add.

"He's got a man's fists. If he uses them, he'll get what a man's got coming."

In some twisted way, had Zach been proud of that? His father finally acknowledging him? Rachel didn't know. All she knew was that the decision had hardened inside herself. All over the city there were families like hers, kids like her and Zach who needed help and were scared to end up at Child Protective Services. The cops were supposed to help kids like her and Zach. They weren't supposed to look the other way when one of their own used his fists on his kid.

She wasn't going to be that kind of cop. She was going to be the kind that stood in the way of the fists, the kind who took on a guy twice her size, soaked in alcoholic rage, the kind who beat him down, cuffed him, and offloaded him into her car. The kind who talked to vulnerable women who couldn't protect themselves and kept the promises they made to help them.

She'd told all this to Zach, but he hadn't understood.

"You want to be like Da?" he'd raged at her, already a foot taller than she was, betrayal in his copper-brown eyes.

"I want to be the exact opposite. I want to do good things with my life, Zach. I want to help kids, if I can. Kids like you and me."

Two days later, Zach was gone.

She'd seen the blame in her mother's eyes every day after that. What they'd had wasn't perfect, but it had been a family. The best kind of family her mother could manage under the pressure of her husband's outbursts. That's what Rachel's actions had destroyed. She and her brother living together under their parents' roof. A roof that provided little in the way of shelter for her mother or her brother, but she'd promised she'd never leave as long as Zach lived there. Rachel pitied Lillian, but she hadn't been able to understand the chains that bound her parents together. It was no kind of life for them. It had been no kind of life for Zach. And when Zach had left, Lillian Getty hadn't shared Rachel's introspection or her inner struggle. She'd blamed her daughter for the absence of her son.

I didn't make him leave, Mum. It was Da's belt and your silence that chased our precious boy away.

Zach hadn't lived in this house in seven years, which raised the question as to why Rachel was still there, living under the same roof, drinking the same poison night after night.

She hadn't stopped searching for her baby brother and she never would.

One day Zach would turn up.

And she'd be here when he did. Waiting for him to forgive her. Waiting for him to love her again, the one person in the world who did.

She bypassed her parents in the living room. Her Da was in for the night, his glazed eyes watching *World's Worst Police Chases.* Her mother sat quietly in a corner, carefully folding down magazine pages to avoid any telltale rustle. Neither greeted her.

She took the narrow wood stairs to her bedroom, set down her bag, hooked her jacket over the back of a chair. There was no game tonight, and she was too tired to play if there had been. With dragging movements, she turned her computer on.

She'd given the Drayton case less than half her attention, pushed Khattak much less than she normally would have, for a single, pressing reason. She'd turned up a lead on Zach.

After all this time, she'd been looking in the wrong place. Halfway houses, homeless shelters, rehab centers, addiction programs. All the things she'd imagined could happen to a boy fending for himself on the streets. She had a friend in every division in the city and she'd called in a lot of favors. Zach's image was on posters and flyers she'd circulated year after year.

She'd tried bus stations, train stations, other metropolitan areas. Zach's friends, his school, everyone who'd ever met him. Even the cops who'd come to the house.

There'd been nothing. Just seven years of silence.

And a folder of e-mails to a long-defunct address that he'd stopped accessing seven years ago.

How would a kid on the streets get e-mail, after all?

And now this hit, from a friend in North

145

York who had a daughter in the arts program up there. A student exhibit at a gallery inside the university.

Her friend had sent her the list of five exhibitors, five students in the Bachelor of Fine Arts program.

Four of them meant nothing to her.

The fifth was Zachary Getty.

It was maybe her brother, maybe not. She'd chased down leads like this before, only to end up with nothing, coming home to her mother's silent, reproachful eyes.

Because Lillian knew.

She knew why Rachel had joined the service. She knew why Rachel's temper had quickly derailed her career — she knew where that temper came from, and what fostered Rachel's constant need to prove herself.

She hadn't said, *"Sweetheart, it's all right. What happened with Zach wasn't your fault. We miss him too. We're searching too."*

They hadn't searched.

Zach dead or Zach alive was all the same to them.

All they needed was each other and their mutual dysfunction.

Lillian Getty had certainly never said to her, *"Forgive yourself, Rachel."*

Was it because her mother couldn't forgive her? Was that why she withheld her grace and her guidance? Was it the reason for her silence? The conversations that tapered off, the half starts, the eyes haunted by secret knowledge?

What had happened to Lillian Getty?

Had Don Getty happened?

Had there never been any more to her mother than martyred sighs and silent compliance? Had it become Lillian's choice in the end?

Rachel remembered another woman altogether. A woman with a bright spark in her eyes when Rachel had rescued a broken-winged bird on their porch, or played her mother's records. A woman whose loving hands had stroked Rachel's hair when she had cried herself to sleep at night, after her father had turned on Zach again. A woman, who despite Don Getty's strictures, had packed little treats in their lunch, along with notes that reminded them of her love.

She wished she had kept even one of those notes from her childhood, as a means of holding on to the woman she had once fiercely loved — instead of the enemy she had made with her decision to follow in Don Getty's footsteps.

It didn't matter. None of it mattered. Zach

dead or alive, hurt or harmed, lost and confused — none of it seemed to matter to Rachel's parents.

It mattered only to her.

She had a name and a place and a time. And it was three nights to the exhibition.

She wasn't about to share any of that with Don or Lillian Getty.

12.

Whoever was on the list to be killed would be killed.

Friday morning Khattak called her. He gave her directions to the Bosnian community's mosque, which wasn't far from her home at the corner of Birmingham and Sixth. It was too early for the Friday prayer, so she found a spot in the parking lot close to the main entrance, a freshly painted white door. The word *Dzamija* was inscribed above the door, the Bosnian spelling of the Arabic word for congregation or community, a fact Rachel had learned during her training at CPS.

The gray building indicated its character with a modest spire of minaret and a phalanx of long, narrow windows topped off by tiny arches. Sunlight warmed the stone; on its grounds the maples were a soft, crushed gold.

Rachel found the women's entrance and

left her shoes in a caddy near the door. She proceeded inward by intervals: through a narrow aisle, a tidy library and the outer chamber of the women's prayer space. At the threshold to the main hall, she met Khattak.

The week had not worn well on him. His dark hair was disheveled, the crow's feet at the corners of his eyes were more pronounced, there was even a hint of shadow about his jaw. Instead of his usual sleek splendor, he was dressed in a loose-fitting white kurta and tapered cotton trousers. His green tasbih was wound about his wrist.

"What are we doing here, sir?" was her greeting. "I thought Drayton was a dead end by now."

Khattak shook his head.

"I've been asked to tread carefully so I've done a little digging, called in some help. And I have a couple of visits lined up for us today. You've had the letters printed. Did you find anything?"

"Someone was careful. Only Drayton's prints are on them."

"Did you learn anything else?"

"Very little." She'd elaborate later if he wished, though she imagined there were only so many ways she could tell Khattak he was right. He must be tired of hearing it.

"If this is as sensitive as you're suggesting, this might not be the best place for us to be." She cocked her head at the members of the Bosnian community milling about.

"We've a meeting with Imam Muharrem. I was hoping he might know something about Krstić." He lowered his voice as he said the name. "I've brought a photograph of Drayton."

Rachel didn't ask where he'd obtained it. She'd gotten used to the element of mystery peculiar to her boss. She knew he'd tell her everything she needed to know eventually.

They found the imam at the *mihrab* in the main hall. He was dusting the prayer niche in the wall behind him, a selection of Qur'ans reposing on the lectern before the *minbar,* where he would stand to give the afternoon sermon.

He set down his duster and embraced Khattak, kissing him on each cheek, then holding on to his hands in a prolonged handclasp as he studied him.

"Inspector Esa," he proclaimed. "I am very glad to have the chance to meet you, Asaf has told me so much about you. And this is your colleague, Sergeant Rachel." His bright blue eyes beamed at Rachel. "It's a pleasure to welcome you here."

Asaf, she'd gleaned from Khattak earlier,

was the regular imam who gave the services at this location. Imam Muharrem was a visitor from Banja Luka in Bosnia, whose presence allowed his overburdened host to take some time off with his family.

Rachel liked the look of him. He was excessively tall, clad in long, white robes that she thought of as Turkish, with a clean-shaven face and a warmth of manner that enhanced his natural authority. His English was lightly accented, his movements calm and deliberate.

Nothing about multiculturalism antagonized Rachel. She liked all kinds of food, clothing, cultural customs, and music. The one thing that held her aloof was a fear of offending through ignorance.

She apologized for her uncovered hair, but the imam waved the apology aside.

"You were good enough to remove your shoes. It is an honor for us when any guest chooses to visit the *Dzamija.*"

"I didn't realize the imam was responsible for maintenance here." She nodded at the duster, one eyebrow aloft.

His answering smile was immediate.

"There is no work of God's too minimal for His caretaker. But let me take you into my office and give you some tea."

He swept them along the hall to an office

at one end of an adjacent corridor. It was a well-proportioned space made smaller by rookeries of books gathered up in piles. On top of these, letters in several different languages were stacked at random. Dictionaries, travel guides, and Arabic-language Qur'ans filled up a bookcase behind the imam's desk, a tidy space anointed with a desk lamp, clock, and laptop computer. The impression of mild chaos was balanced by the neatly organized bulletin boards that ran the length of one wall.

He poured them small cups of lightly scented tea from a samovar arranged precariously close to his printer. Glass-green light filtered through the open windows, framed by the yellow branches of maples. They could hear birdsong from the trees.

It was an environment of great charm, and Rachel relaxed into her seat.

"Now, tell me why you have come and what it is I may help you with."

Enjoying the tea that tasted of green apples, Rachel let Khattak present his information.

A close-up photo of Drayton was passed across the desk. "Do you recognize this man, Imam Muharrem?"

In one of his deliberate gestures, the imam steepled his fingers under his chin and bent close to study the photograph. "He isn't a member of our congregation, not that I recognize — but I am still a newcomer here."

"What part of Bosnia and Herzegovina are you from?"

"As so many of us are, I am a refugee and a wanderer." The answer wasn't a circumvention, for he went on to add, "Most recently, I have been conducting historical research in Banja Luka."

A shadow crossed Khattak's face. The sun settled at the window's edge.

"Could I ask you to be more specific? What type of research?"

"You know Banja Luka?"

A slight nod from Khattak.

"We are trying to document what remains of our heritage — the heritage of the Muslims of our sorrowful country. A study was done on the mosques of Banja Luka." He smiled at Rachel, his teeth white and even. "I was a scholar at Ferhadija, the Ferhad Pasha mosque complex. A jewel of our Ottoman past, modest perhaps in scale, but certainly our finest example of sixteenth-century architecture." He brooded over the photograph. "Of course, all the mosques of Banja Luka were destroyed, not just Ferhadija. Let me show you."

He set down his glass of tea and turned to the bookshelf behind his desk. There he searched for a few moments before finding the one he wanted and opening it to a centerfold that displayed two photographs side by side. One was a photograph taken in 1941 of the Ferhadija complex. The second was a flattened area of grass where what remained was the merest outline of the mosque's foundation.

"Razed to the ground in 1993." He fingered the photograph. "That was the last time I stood under the doomed shadow of its minaret. Even then Banja Luka was not safe."

"You were a refugee in Banja Luka?"

"I am from Brčko," he said simply. "I ended up in Manjača."

Names that meant something to Khattak, if not to Rachel. The imam was quick to seize on it. "You *know* Bosnia," he said. "I should have known the name Esa signified a connection."

Not from her CPS training but from Khattak himself, Rachel had learned that Muslim names could transcend sects, ethnicities, communities, and nations. The name Esa could be found in the Arab world, the Indian subcontinent, the villages of Turkey and Persia, or further east in Malaysia and China. It simply meant Jesus.

"I've been to Sarajevo," Khattak answered. "During the war." He took the imam's book and leafed through its pages, one at a time.

"You were *mujahid*?" The imam's question was reverent, a tone Rachel had never formerly associated with the word.

Now Khattak smiled, his hands open on the book that documented the ravaged history of a people. "I was a student," he corrected. "A humanitarian aid worker alongside other students concerned about the siege of Sarajevo."

Imam Muharrem shifted in his seat. Rachel had the impression that Khattak's words were not entirely welcome.

Rachel thought of his words: *I am from Brčko. I ended up in Manjača.*

Hesitating, she said, "I don't know the names of those cities you mentioned, sir."

"Brčko is my home town. It has the misfortune to lie on the Serbian border to the north. Manjača was a camp the Serbs ran on the mountain. First, it was where they held Bosnian Croats. Later, it was mainly us they detained."

"Prisoners of war?"

A curious expression crossed the imam's face: part memory, part judgment.

"It was where they sent many of the

people of Banja Luka. All the educated people. The community leaders they hadn't killed outright. The teachers, the doctors, the businessmen, religious leaders — myself. It was a place of unrelenting misery." Under his breath, he recited a prolonged prayer. She caught the word *rahem* — mercy. "I should not speak of it, because then I would speak not only of Banja Luka and Brčko but also of Prijedor and Foča. Of the terrible places where the Serbs ran their rape camps." He took the book back from Khattak and closed it with a snap. "I have counseled too many of our sisters. I do not wish to relive their suffering."

Rachel swallowed. She was a police officer with seven years in the service, but there were entire areas of war crimes testimony she had deliberately avoided in her research.

She was unfamiliar with the names Imam Muharrem had recited. Since Khattak remained silent, she offered, "I thought the great tragedy of the Bosnian war was Srebrenica."

The imam flinched as if she had knifed him in the ribs. "Each of us is the citizen of a fallen city. The killing in Brčko took place three years before the Serbs overran safe area Srebrenica."

Three years. He said it with exactly the

same note of bitterness that permeated Rachel's research. She wanted to know more, yet felt she had no right to ask. After all these years, did anyone have the right to send survivors of the war plunging into the pitiless void of memory?

"We've no right to encroach on your privacy, Imam. I've wanted to understand a little better, that's all."

Imam Muharrem held her gaze across the desk. Something in her face must have reassured him.

"If we do not speak of it, it does not mean we do not dream. Survivors are quiet because they are haunted, because they still cannot entirely accept what happened. Yes, there was a method to the madness of their killing, but what was the reason for it? In Brčko, they loaded refrigerated trucks with bodies and dumped them off at the *kafilerija* to be burned in the furnace. In two months, they killed three thousand people. They slit their throats, drained their bodies, and dumped them into the river. Or they killed people with three bullets, the Chetnik salute, and then robbed the dead. They mutilated the bodies and raped the women in front of their husbands, parents, and children." He went quiet for several moments before adding, "Luka-Brčko also had a torture room. I will not tell you what happened there."

He turned his head to the side, light settling softly on his shoulders. "I was in Banja Luka when they took my family. I thought I would carry the guilt of that forever. Until the day I was sent to Manjača, where my friends were murdered before my eyes. I was the only imam to survive. They asked me to care for their families, and I have tried to do the best that I can."

He spread his hands wide as if what he had done was no more than his duty, when he had just conjured up an unfathomable horror. Her face, like Khattak's, was abnormally pale.

"I don't think you came here to hear this," he said, when neither of them said anything further. Condolences were out of the question. She hoped Khattak would know how to proceed.

"I've troubled you with painful memories of the war, Imam Muharrem," Khattak said at last, sharing Rachel's struggle for words.

The imam's hands were steady as he decanted more tea for them. They took a minute to sip it, its soothing fragrance a balm on the air.

Imam Muharrem's lids lowered over his eyes.

"It wasn't a war, my dear Inspector Esa. What happened in my country was simply a slaughter."

He managed a smile. Rachel admired his ability to do it.

"Didn't our president say, after all, 'Sleep peacefully. There will be no war'?"

"A terrible naïveté," Khattak countered.

"It was the Bosnian spirit. We'd lived together so long, intermarried so deeply, spoke the same language. We imagined ourselves a people of the most enlightened pluralism. The Orthodox and Catholic churches, the synagogues — they were part of us. And thirty thousand Serbs resisted the siege of Sarajevo by our sides. Across all these boundaries the fascists insisted upon between us, we kept our belief in the spirit of our nation." He set down his glass again. "And we paid for it."

"And if I told you that one of the men responsible for these crimes was at large here in this city, what would you say?"

The imam's eyes shot to his. He straightened in his seat. "Is that why you have come? Such a man should be denounced. He must be brought to justice at once."

"He's met his justice. He fell — or was helped — to his death."

"That is not justice. We need these people

160

to answer for their crimes. Whom do you speak of, Inspector Esa? What is this about?"

Khattak showed him the photograph of Drayton again. "Are you certain you do not recognize this man?"

Now the imam tried harder, studying the photo with greater care. From his desk drawer, he removed a magnifying glass and scrutinized it further.

"Could this be Krstić? A commander of the Drina Corps? The international forces said they were never able to capture him. How do you know this is him?"

"That's why we came to you. We don't know. We know this man as Christopher Drayton. Ten days ago, Drayton fell to his death."

The imam's fingers tensed around his glass. "I wasn't in Srebrenica, so I wouldn't have seen Krstić personally. But some of our congregants are refugees from the enclave. Shall I ask them? The Drina Corps commanders mixed with the people at Potočari. Someone will have seen him. Someone will know."

Khattak contemplated this option. Rachel knew he would rule it out.

"Will you give me a little time, Imam Muharrem? I have a few other leads that may confirm Drayton's identity. I would prefer to be certain before this news becomes public to the Bosnian community. And I have something else to show you, something you may be able to help us with."

"You would not plan to keep the truth from us?" The imam's gaze was searching.

"We would not have come to you were we not committed to finding the truth."

Imam Muharrem pressed a hand against Khattak's cheek then let it fall.

"Then show me."

On cue, Rachel removed the letters from her bag. She removed their covering and passed them to the imam.

"These are letters that were hand-delivered to Drayton, as far as we can tell. Can you tell us anything about them — maybe help us to understand them?"

"These are typed," he said in surprise. "In English. It is not my best language. Let me find my glasses."

He produced them from the same desk drawer that held the magnifying glass. One at a time, he shuffled the letters between his fingers. He read several phrases aloud, phrases Rachel had been unable to trace.

I have just been informed that the besieged city of Jajce has fallen to the aggressor.

Massive air attacks continue in Bosnia today. We cannot defend ourselves yet no one is coming to our aid.

For having uttered a wrong word, people are taken away or killed.

The camps remain open.

The enemy ring around the city is being strengthened with fresh troops.

For the past three days, Serb forces have been conducting a fierce offensive against the town of Bihac.

Today Serb forces shelled the city of Tuzla. While writing this letter, the city centre is under heavy mortar attack.

The famous National Library has been set on fire and is still burning.

He came to a halt, his breathing heavy and removed his glasses. He looked at them both curiously. His long, well-shaped hand rested on a letter that contained a single sentence.

On Tuesday, there will be no bread in Sarajevo.

"You do not know what this is?" Their silence answered him. He studied the letters again. "These are statements made by our government before the United Nations Security Council. Our country was burning while they insisted on negotiating their imaginary peace, deaf and blind to the scope of the evil confronting them."

Khattak jerked in his chair.

"Ah. You do not like that I use this word,

Inspector Esa? Yet in your work as in mine, you must see its face, you must know that evil exists in the world."

He showed them another letter as he laid the Qur'an by his glasses.

Defend us or let us defend ourselves. You have no right to deprive us of both.

"That was our president, doing his best to rescue us. Somehow, it reminds me of the Divine teaching."

He held up a translated verse of the Qur'an.

If Allah helps you, none can ever overcome you; but if He should forsake you, who is there after Him that can help you? In Allah, then, let the believers put their trust.

"To hold on to our trust in the aftermath of such evil has been the hardest test of faith one can face."

Uncomfortable with the turn the conversation had taken, Rachel cleared her throat. "What about the rest of the letters, sir? Are they government statements? Some of them don't appear as if they are."

"I cannot be certain. They sound to me like fragments of testimony from those who survived. If these letters were sent to the man from the photograph, does this not prove he was Dražen Krstić?"

"It's a strong indication," Khattak said,

"but it isn't conclusive. We need more."

At his signal, Rachel gathered up the letters and returned them to her bag.

"There is one thing," said the imam. "A sister who is part of the mosque community relayed a story from her mother. She saw Krstić at the gates of Potočari. She said he was more fanatical than most."

"Meaning?"

"If this man you've come about is Dražen Krstić, there will be a tattoo on his hand. It was common among the paramilitaries, but Krstić had it also."

He sketched it for them on a piece of paper tucked into his Qur'an.

Four letters that resembled the Cyrillic *s* written as a *c* filled in the spaces above and below a Serbian cross. Beneath it, the imam had transliterated a phrase.

Samo sloga Srbina spasava.

"Only solidarity saves the Serbs," Khattak translated.

"You know of it."

"As you said, Imam, it was common to the paramilitaries."

"A man named Christopher Drayton would never mark himself this way. If you find it on his hand, he will be Dražen Krstić."

13.

*No one knows what will come tomorrow
and no one knows in what land he will die.*

Rachel pulled in at the morgue and flashed her ID. She was expected. This was the second meeting Khattak had promised for the afternoon, a viewing of Drayton's body. He'd stayed behind at the mosque to attend the Friday prayer. He'd more than fulfilled his CPS mandate if the imam who regularly presided over services was a friend.

The first time Rachel had seen Khattak pray, she'd been embarrassed for them both. Religion figured very little in her life, though she supposed she was a lapsed Catholic. But Khattak was comfortable in his faith, pragmatic: he made so little of it that her feeling of discomfiture vanished. He didn't preach and she didn't listen, a good enough partnership.

She understood the imam's feelings. God

had never helped her with her search for Zach, and she wasn't willing to falter her way back to trust. But then again, perhaps God would surprise her.

Witness the body she was studying on the table. A better-looking man than she'd expected, with a face more youthful than his years indicated. There was bruising about his forehead, yet nothing about his expression indicated terror or pain, nor even the mild surprise she had come across with other bodies that she tried not to think of as corpses.

Lash was the Urdu word Khattak had taught her for corpse.

It seemed right: each dead face she studied was like a whiplash across her consciousness.

She reached for Drayton's right hand and turned it over.

The thumb and forefinger were heavily callused.

From a gun grip? she wondered. What had these hands done? Were they responsible for deeds so dark that Drayton had chosen his fall from the cliff?

And then her questions were put to rest. She found the tattoo, the cross divided by Cyrillic letters.

Only solidarity saves the Serbs.

She waited for the Friday prayer to end, and then she called Khattak to tell him what she'd found.

"I need something else from you," he said.

Startled, Rachel wrote down what it was.

14.

Somewhere life withers, somewhere it begins.

The blue rain sank against the mullioned windows of the pub. The temperature had dropped. It was a good night to be indoors, drinking warm ale that nourished the throat as it spread its warmth to his toes.

"You're nervous," his sister said.

"I am," Nathan admitted. "I didn't expect Esa to say yes. I'm not sure I know what to say to him."

"I still can't believe I missed him at the house."

They turned together to wait for the pub's door to open, each of them cherishing different hopes for this reunion. Nate, an end to the two-year severance of a friendship that had meant everything to him. Audrey, the return of the security she hadn't known since the death of her parents. Nate was to

169

blame for where the three of them had ended up, yet Audrey couldn't hold it against him, couldn't hold anything against the brother who had raised her in the absence of their parents and kept her safe.

There was a fire in the grate, a warm bubble of conversation from patrons divesting themselves of steaming raincoats, and a faint light that anchored it all. The door inched open, bringing Nate to his feet. He'd brought Audrey with him as a buffer in the hopes that the sight of her would melt Esa's reserve. Esa had never been able to withstand her.

Instead, the door disclosed a rain-soaked Rachel Getty, her dark hair plastered to her head, her mascara describing inky configurations about her wind-reddened cheeks. He held back a smile; she looked so lost and disconsolate. Esa needed his own buffer, it would seem, but at least he'd agreed to come.

He went forward, grasped Rachel's hand, and dragged her back to meet Audrey. He was unprepared for the strength and smoothness of her grip. His hand tingled as he let hers go, watching as she and Audrey sized each other up. Was there something between Rachel and Esa? Would she view Audrey as a potential rival? He didn't think so, not for all the diligently recorded "sirs" that peppered her conversation. But there was a warmth there, a trust. Observing others was the habit of a lifetime, and Esa he knew as well as he knew himself.

Esa liked Rachel Getty. Very much. So he was prepared to do the same.

The door opened again, and this time it was his friend.

Khattak's eyes searched the pub for Rachel. When he found her, he visibly relaxed. It made it easier for him to come forward and grasp Nathan's hand. Not what he would have done in the past, but maybe Nate was getting too old for that thunderous back clap anyway. He would take what he could get — a friend who tentatively ventured the customs of friendship again.

And then Esa saw Audrey, who flung herself at his neck.

When he saw the broad smile that chased the last trace of diffidence from his friend's face, Nathan found himself smiling as well.

Rachel's eyes widened at the sight of the small, gold whirlwind that launched itself without ceremony at her boss.

Who was she? Nathan Clare's sister, fair enough, but what was she to Khattak that she could wrap herself so confidently about him and he — instead of starching up and shaking her off — draped one arm over her slender shoulders?

She was everything that a strong, square-built, hockey-playing female police officer most definitely was not. Pretty, petite, girlishly feminine without being cloying. Chic, expensively dressed even for a night at the pub, her russet scarf and body-hugging dress a perfect complement to her figure and coloring. Instead of the babyish tones her squeal of delight had seemed to indicate were at hand, her voice was low-pitched and sweet.

Rachel hated her on sight.

She was wet and disheveled and afraid that she stank of the morgue. Between her lumbering awkwardness and the other woman's easy grace, no greater contrast was possible.

"There's absolutely nothing you can say to make up for your total and utter neglect," Audrey scolded Khattak. "Two years? Two years without a word and everything I've learned has had to come through Ruksh? Is this because of that hijab thing?" Her quick sputter of laughter was as appealing as everything else about her. "Because I thought we were past that."

Rachel studied the trio, bemused. Nathan

and his sister, the masculine and feminine poles of all that was privileged and charming, with the same fine-boned faces and golden grace; Khattak, leanly exotic and entirely at home in the company of his friends.

What was she bringing to the party? Why had he insisted on her presence with that note of entreaty in his voice? She'd said yes because she owed him, and if she was honest with herself, because she didn't want to spend another night of turmoil speculating about the possibility that she might have found her brother. She didn't take her honesty far enough to admit that she drew comfort just from Khattak's presence.

She sipped at her lukewarm Molson Canadian, letting the warmth of the others' conversation wash over her. She was tired. The search for Zach had been long and filled with disappointments, the imam's stories not easily set aside. The day's revelations chipped away at her. Even on a dead hand, the Serb tattoo menaced her.

In death, Drayton's face was unrevealing. Could this have been the man to send so many innocents to their deaths?

There *was* no art to the mind's construction in the face. She couldn't tell. There was no way to know what kind of mind or soul had breathed beneath that invariably brittle arrangement of bones.

Khattak's interaction with Nathan Clare was stilted, but Audrey's presence seemed specially designed to dilute the uneasiness. Maybe she'd been invited for the same reason as Audrey: to preserve a barrier between the two men.

"We're ignoring Rachel," Audrey said, laughing. "That's really rather odious of you two. First you drag her out here after a long day's work and then you don't even ask if her drink needs topping up."

"I'm fine," Rachel said quickly. "I'm driving home in the rain, so this is my limit."

"And where is home?" Audrey persisted. "Surely you can't mean to drive across town at this hour. There's traffic closures everywhere, it will be a nightmare." Her voice was genuinely friendly, genuinely interested — genuinely everything that was affable and good-natured if Rachel had had the patience for it.

"All part of the job." Her eyes met Khattak's. "I should be going now, sir."

"Sir?" Audrey hooted. "How long have you two worked together, did you say? Ruksh says Esa always calls you Rachel."

Rachel didn't know who Ruksh was. She fought down the swift bubble of pleasure that her name was ever mentioned in any context outside of work.

Suddenly abashed, Audrey must have realized how she sounded. "I'm sorry, Rachel, I didn't mean to presume. I know what police work can be like."

How? Rachel wondered.

"First, let me tell you some of the things that *Inspector* Khattak may be too tight-lipped to divulge. Esa has a sister my age — we grew up together. Her name is Rukshanda. Naturally, as the much younger sisters of two devastating men, we developed a *tendresse* for each other's brothers. We grew out of it, of course."

Her face was aglow with laughter in the soft light of the fire.

"Though not before I attempted a religious conversion and started to wear a headscarf. Unfortunately, my lack of flowing tresses made me no more attractive to what I then determined was quite a dimwitted federal investigator." She made a moue of distress, inviting the others to laugh. "Ruksh was equally foolish about Nate, which was the only thing that prevented me from retreating to the attic to die of mortification. I'm sure Esa kept all my love poems, though. Unless Samina disposed of them?"

A swift glance at Rachel's confusion and

she added, "Samina, Esa's wife. I hope you don't mind me telling Rachel, Esa. She's your partner, after all."

Khattak held up his hand. "Yes, Rachel's *my* partner, sprite." He turned to her, his face grave. "I should have mentioned her before. We were married very young, and then some years later, my wife was killed in an accident."

"I'm very sorry, sir." She didn't know what else to say, taken aback by the information. There was more than pain in his face. There was guilt. Was it the reason he'd never shared this with her before? Or was it simply that he was more unguarded around his friends?

"She was the loveliest person, Rachel," Nathan said. "You would have liked her very much."

Despite herself, she felt touched. This was a gathering of old friends — she was the outsider. Yet everyone was taking so much trouble over her. She knew it could only have been because of the way Khattak had spoken of her. She felt valued, respected, a feeling she rarely experienced at home. The only thing Don Getty had taught her was how to be tough. Kindness she had learned from Zach, and in rare stolen moments from her mother.

When she overlooked her outsider status, she realized the story Audrey had confided was actually quite funny.

"Er . . . how old were you during this headscarf incident?"

Audrey seized her hand in delighted response.

"You won't blackmail me with that, will you, Rachel? It really was too dreadful — here I was convinced that anointing myself with new religious credentials would make me irresistible to my very first deathly crush —" She took a moment to squeeze Khattak's hand. "And instead he looked at me as if I'd grown another head. Too, too devastating. If it wasn't for Ruksh, I'm convinced I'd have thrown myself into the lake, painfully itchy headscarf and all."

Rachel's sudden smile was unguarded. She looked up to find Nathan's attention upon her. "Wearing the scarf is an art, I'm told."

He responded in kind. "The art Audrey favors most is drama. It's there in everything she does, even her choice of profession."

"You're an actor?" Rachel asked.

There was another delighted spurt of laughter.

"Nate loves to tease. No, I run a small NGO working with women. I went to university and then I didn't know what to do with myself. I couldn't possibly live up to Nathan's prestige but I thought, here's something I can do. I embroil him in it constantly but I secretly think he uses it as material for his books."

"Then he's overdue," Rachel said, feeling her way. "It's been some time since *Apologia* was published. Have you been working on something new?"

It was an innocuous question. There was no reason why it should have sent the conversation crashing to the ground. She looked from one face to another, puzzled. Khattak's gaze found the window. Audrey bit her lip. Nathan cleared his throat, searching for words.

"I've — not been writing much lately. It seems I can't find anything else to say."

It was clear that he addressed these words to Khattak. They were met with silence.

"Writer's block?" Rachel ventured, though common sense told her to drop the subject. "It's sort of an occupational hazard, isn't it?"

"Like drunken domestics for police officers," he agreed.

Rachel stiffened. His guileless eyes — lovely eyes, really, flecked with bits of bronze and green — indicated it was a

178

random hit.

"All in a day's work," she repeated.

"I hear you're investigating Chris Drayton's fall." It was meant by Audrey as a change of subject. Khattak took it as such.

"There are some leads we're following up," he said to Nate. "Some unresolved questions as to background and finances. I've been wondering about that dinner you mentioned — the one you arranged for Drayton to speak about the museum."

"I've seen your car at Mink's house a few times this week. So it's the museum that interests you."

This was news to Rachel. Khattak hadn't mentioned it to her, and she wondered why. He was often reticent at the beginning of an investigation but seldom secretive.

"She's an interesting woman," he said without emphasis.

Nate stared across the table at him, a sudden glint of discovery in his eyes.

"Fascinating is how I would put it. If she's with a potential donor for less than half an hour, she doesn't leave empty-handed."

"You set up the dinner specifically for the museum, then."

"Not exactly. It was Chris who asked me to arrange it. He was adamant about getting on the board of the museum. He

179

thought of it as a prestige project, something that a man at his stage of life should attach himself to. He was willing to pay his way in. Mink was somewhat resistant to the idea, so Chris thought a dinner might soften her up."

"I'd have thought she'd welcome an influx of moncy," said Rachel. "The upkeep on that place can't be cheap."

"It's not. The house is worth upwards of a million dollars. Most of the exhibits were already in Mink's possession, but if she wanted to expand, Drayton's investment certainly wouldn't have hurt. And from his perspective, gaining a reputation as patron of the arts was essential to his sense of himself."

"How long has Ringsong been here? Inspector Khattak said he hadn't seen it before. In the past, I mean. Whenever you saw each other last."

She stumbled over the words, aware that she'd inadvertently trespassed.

Nate rescued her. "It's been about two years. A year to build and a year for Mink to get the museum on its feet. It's due to open very soon, so I know this phase of things is critical."

"Do you expect it to open on time?" Rachel asked. Probably Khattak had asked

Mink the same questions. She still wanted to hear. "Would there be any reason for Drayton's death to delay it?"

"I can't think of any. Mink is very capable. I've never known her to run overbudget or behind schedule."

"And did you make a contribution, sir?"

"Please. At least call me Nathan. Or Nate if you like, all my friends do. It was Andalusia," he said with a fond glance at Khattak. "The golden age. How could I not?"

"You sound as though you and Ms. Norman are quite close."

It was a question pertinent to the investigation. Somehow it came out sounding as if Rachel were jealous. She found herself blushing. Khattak, too, appeared oddly interested in the answer.

Nathan's glance traveled between them, a suspicion of mirth in it.

"I wouldn't say I've spent as much time at Ringsong in one week as Esa has but yes, we're friends. I find the project mesmerizing: Mink's passion for it is contagious. And it's been good for the girls too — Hadley and Cass. It's saved them from being used as ammunition between their parents and it's given them a sense of purpose. Mink knows how to make people feel valued. It's certainly given Marco more free-

181

dom to hang about."

"Riv," Audrey corrected.

"I refuse to call a seventeen-year-old boy Riv when he has a perfectly acceptable first name."

Audrey punched him good-naturedly in the arm. She opened her mouth to respond when the door to the pub gave way, divulging a new group of patrons. Her face froze in an expression of dismay. In a swift gesture under the table, she pressed her brother's hand.

Rachel swiveled in her seat. The new arrivals were a group of cops, mostly in uniform. They laughed and talked easily, stopping at the bar to give their order. In their midst was an extraordinarily beautiful woman whose dazzling features and wickedly curved body drew the eye of every man in the room. She was dramatically dark-eyed and dark-lashed, raindrops clinging to her hair and gliding down the silky skin of her cheek. She wore a skin-tight dress made of some metallic material that gathered the light inward and clung to every curve. With a sexy pout, she bent before the fire to warm her hands.

It was like a bomb had gone off, sucking all the air from the room.

Conversations were suddenly louder, her

companions jostled each other to get close to her. Her smile beguiled: her movements were sinfully lithe as she touched one man's cheek, ruffled another's hair, squeezed the elbow of a third.

Was Rachel imagining it or were there sparks of electricity in the waves of her jet-black hair?

The woman looked over and caught them watching her. She checked mid-movement, disentangled herself from her companions, and made her way to their table, where she dismissed Rachel and Audrey without a second glance.

"Look who's here!" Of course her voice would be low and throaty. She leaned over the table, enveloping them in the musk of her perfume. Her smile glittered between the heavy wings of her hair.

"Nathan, darling! More devastating than ever!"

She turned the other way, saw Khattak, widened her black eyes fractionally and sailed on. "The old gang, together again. How perfectly wonderful! You've brought along a plaything, I see." Her sleek white hand pointed at Rachel, the dark eyes sweeping over her and away. "Not up to your usual standard, Esa." She dragged the name out, catching her tongue between her teeth. "I hope you boys aren't fighting over her the way you fought over me."

Her laugh was a sexy growl in her throat. She accompanied it with a pivot of her hip, thrusting her décolletage at Nate. "Have you missed me? You never have me anymore." She brought her hand to her lush mouth, miming dismay. "I meant, you never have me over anymore. Surely my portrait doesn't warm your bed?"

Rachel choked on the heady scent that clung to the woman, just able to discern the contempt on Audrey's face through the cloud of fragrance around her.

"You're drunk, Laine," Nathan said with disgust. "Go back to your friends."

"I thought I was among friends," she purred in return. "Don't you remember how to be friendly, darling? Don't you remember lying on your back and begging me not to stop? Or was that you?" Whiplash quick, she turned to Esa. "Men! So easily interchangeable, so easy to forget." Before Esa could object, she leaned down and kissed him full on the lips. "There! I *thought* I remembered you. As decadent as ever."

Khattak got to his feet, politely shouldered Rachel aside.

"If this performance is for my benefit, I'll put an end to it by leaving. Rachel, I'll call you tomorrow. Thank you for coming out."

"Rachel?" Laine crowed. "As gloriously humdrum as the rest of you! Audrey darling, don't tell me you've become so petty that you haven't thought to give Little Miss Dreary the makeover she's gasping for. She'll need it to stoke that libido, am I right?" She stood chest-to-chest with Khattak.

"Shut up, Laine," he said brutally. He signaled one of the men behind her shoulder, offloading Laine into his arms. "Your friend is drunk. Kindly take her with you."

"I'm not drunk, sexy," she called over her shoulder, as she was guided to the fire. "I miss you, Esa, I miss your bed."

Khattak muttered an imprecation under his breath and an apology aloud to Rachel.

"Why did you ask her here?" he said to Nathan. "You've learned nothing, have you?"

Nate scrambled to his feet. "Esa, wait — I didn't call her. This was an accident, you have to believe me."

"Like you believed me?" He didn't wait for an answer.

Defeated, Nate sank back into his seat. "Goddamn her."

"Who *was* that?" Rachel breathed. The

woman had descended on them like a tornado, leaving just as much destruction in her wake.

"That was Laine Stoicheva, total and utter bitch," Audrey said. "Pay no attention to anything she says. She lives for trouble. Eats and drinks it too, I think."

Laine Stoicheva. The last partner Khattak had worked with before Rachel herself. She'd heard the stories. Heard the truth from Khattak himself, yet the woman in person was like an undefused bomb. She oozed sex. And as Rachel could see from the lapdog expression of every man around them, she wasn't accustomed to rejection.

Khattak's account of Laine Stoicheva's demotion had included no mention of Nathan Clare. Laine had divided her attention between both men.

"I should get home," Rachel said to the others. "It's a long drive."

"I didn't know she'd be here," Nate said to his sister. "How could I have known?"

"He'll calm down. He'll realize that's the case."

"He won't," Nate said bitterly. "That's only the second time in two years that he's spoken to me."

Rachel looked from brother to sister, feeling decidedly *de trop.* She murmured a good night and slipped away to her car, caught by an icy blast of rain.

It was a relief to breathe the rain-drenched air, to feel its spiraling wetness against her cheeks. She slid into the driver's side and started the engine.

It choked.

She tried again, her eyes searching for Khattak's BMW.

It was gone. Why did the man have to appear and disappear so quickly? She'd have sworn he was a magician. She let loose a fluent string of curses. Now, she'd have to call in a tow truck for a boost, and she'd still be sitting here when Laine Stoicheva and the Clares eventually found their way to the lot. They'd see her because she'd been stupid enough to park near the door with plenty of lighting. Rain had been her only worry then. Balanced against potential humiliation, it seemed a small price to pay.

She scrabbled in her purse for her phone. Maybe her Da would come.

She choked back a laugh. Not tonight or any night. Her Da wasn't in the business of rescuing damsels in distress. Just like with Zach. Dead or alive, it was the same thing. Why worry about Rachel driving home at midnight? She was a police officer, not a teenage girl. Except that when she'd been a

187

teenage girl, no one had worried either.

Keep the boat afloat. Keep everything the same. Nobody speak. Everyone survives.

There was sharp knock at her window.

She rolled it down: Nathan Clare stood there, dripping with rain. Like her, he hadn't had the sense to bring an umbrella. "Let me give you a lift."

"I can't leave my car here overnight."

"You can. I'll settle it so that it's ready for you in the morning. Now, where can I drop you?"

"What about Audrey?" she asked him, not seeing his sister.

"She's met a friend who will drop her. Get your things while I call."

Common sense told her to refuse. Her personal sense of awkwardness insisted on it.

But there was Nathan Clare, soaking wet and miserable, not budging from her window as he made his calls.

"You'll catch cold," she said ungraciously. "Let me get my bag from the trunk."

The thought of someone else driving through the city to Etobicoke in the rain imbued her with bliss. Not having to worry about her car or fix the problem herself — well, this was the first time someone had stepped in for her. The first time anyone had seemed anxious about her feelings.

The scene in the pub had been insulting and confusing, but Rachel was used to both. What she wasn't used to was the generous offer of help and comfort. She found herself stretching out her legs in the luxurious interior of an Aston Martin, watching traffic lights swing past rain-darkened streets in long green streaks.

Nate glanced over at her, his hands tight on the steering wheel. "I think I owe you an explanation."

"Honestly, you don't. Inspector Khattak told me about the charges Laine manufactured against him, I'd just never met her. I can see why she was a problem."

"That's all he told you?"

"That's all that mattered to our job. He doesn't owe me anything else."

Nate brushed his gold hair to one side. His fingers came away damp. "I wonder why you think that, Rachel. Esa speaks very highly of you to Ruksh. It sounds to me as though he considers you a friend."

Rachel flushed with embarrassment at the thought of herself as the subject of such personal discussion. The suggestion that Khattak might share the quiet regard she felt for him was unsettling. She cleared her throat. "He's also my boss. And I want to do well with him."

"I think you have done. Audrey tells me as much. He has a strong sense of what's right."

And though she hadn't wanted to be drawn into this conversation, Rachel asked, "Then why haven't you spoken in two years?"

Nate kept his attention firmly on the road. "It doesn't mean he's not stubborn. He's stubborn and judgmental as hell. If he thinks his trust has been betrayed, there's no convincing him otherwise. When he brought you to Winterglass, I thought he might be thawing. He wouldn't have brought you, I thought, if he didn't want me to meet you. To let him know what I thought of this woman who figures so largely in his life."

Rachel flushed red. "I'm not — we're not — we work together. We came here because of Christopher Drayton."

"I think that was an excuse for Esa to reach out. You must have seen that he's asked me hardly anything about Drayton. Or Mink, for that matter. When Esa is interested in a woman, he tends to go quiet."

Rachel wanted to ask if there had been many — there had to be something behind the reputation he sustained at work, even if she hadn't seen it herself — but it didn't seem appropriate. And she wondered if Nate was right. Had Khattak wanted to reach out to a friend he had somehow lost along the way? Had he needed her presence as a shield? All the things they should have been doing to confirm Drayton's identity had been delayed. He hadn't called her for a week, and then only to visit an imam unconnected with the case.

"Were you both in love with her?"

Drayton, she cursed herself. *You should be asking about Drayton.*

"No." His sudden awkwardness appealed to Rachel, if only because she identified with it so thoroughly. "Audrey said she would tell you, but she tends to dramatize things. The truth is theatrical enough."

"Two friends fighting over a woman who plays them off against each other?"

A faint color rose in Nathan's face, softening its incipient lines. "I — these are good guesses but they're off the mark. Esa was never interested in Laine. She was his colleague at INSET. She may not seem like it, but she has an excellent brain and a knack for intelligence work. It was a good partnership, but she wanted more, which was something I didn't know. He should have told me about the trouble she was causing him, but he's somewhat conservative in these matters. I suppose he thought he was being gentlemanly. I'd come by several times to meet Esa after work, and I noticed Laine." He shrugged helplessly. "Who wouldn't? What stunned me was that a woman like that noticed *me*. She was interested in me. She didn't have to try all that hard. One look at her and I was besotted." He smiled at the old-fashioned word. "I planned to marry her, and then she brought her claim against Esa."

"That must have been the end of things," Rachel said, in as neutral a tone as she could manage.

"You would think so. You would think I'd know Esa better than anyone — or that I'd learned to trust him in thirty years." He glanced over at her. "Laine was an obsession with me. I couldn't think or sleep for wanting her. I would have done anything she asked. In the end, I did."

"I don't understand." From the wretched expression on his face, she had the feeling that she didn't really want to know.

"Laine asked me to testify on her behalf at a closed hearing. Against Esa. And I did. That's why he hasn't seen me in two years. That's why I wrote *Apologia*."

Rachel clasped her hands together. Her

fingers felt numb.

"He was cleared," she said weakly. "And you never married Laine. He must have forgiven you."

"When he brought you to meet me, I hoped as much. He tried to warn me once, but when I wouldn't hear it, he didn't say another word against her. In your case, there's no reticence. When he brought you to Winterglass, I knew something had changed. And then Laine tonight — let's just say, she destroys everything she touches."

Rachel considered this in silence. She barely knew Nathan Clare, really only knew him through the veneer of his public persona as writer and commentator, yet she felt that she owed him whatever she could bring to bear. Perhaps that was kindness. "It can't be as bad as you're imagining. He came tonight. By the morning, he'll know that Laine's being there wasn't your fault. He just needs time to think."

"That's the most dangerous time, when he's thinking." His smile was brief. "Read *Apologia*. Then you'll know what I did."

On the day of the hearing, Nate had been the last to leave the room. He had shaken Laine's touch from his body but why, *why*

193

had Esa not told him? He had the answer a moment later, agonizing in all it revealed of himself: he shouldn't have had to.

They had known each other since they were seven years old. They had weathered every storm, shared every confidence, loved each other's families, loved each other.

Known each other.

And Laine Stoicheva had detonated a grenade within the stronghold of their friendship.

Esa had left without a word, without a glance. That had been two years ago, and even *Apologia* had made no difference.

On the night he'd driven to Esa's house to stumble through whatever apology he could try to make to rescue the only friendship that mattered in his life, Esa had said simply, "I thought if there was anyone in the world who would know what I'm capable of, it would be you. It can never be the same now."

"Rahem," Nate had dredged out of nowhere. The plea to recognize the Islamic concept of life-giving mercy. He knew there were a lot of things Esa could have said in response — don't you dare drag faith into this now when you've betrayed it so utterly — but what he said with a look of regret was, "I could never wish you ill, Nate."

194

And the door had closed.

On thirty years of friendship, it had closed.

It hadn't opened again, even when he'd written his dedication: *To EK, whose friendship I valued too little, too late.*

15.

While the Serb soldier was dragging my son away, I heard his voice for the last time. And he turned around and then he told me, "Mummy please, can you get that bag for me? Could you please get it for me?"

With no word from Khattak and no clear direction on what to pursue next, Rachel's instincts told her to revisit Melanie Blessant. She had called Khattak and been unable to reach him. She had tried the Blessant house with the same result. And the days until Zach's exhibit were passing, not in suspended animation, but with a concentrated intensity, every hope and whisper magnified until her head began to ache from the pressure of her thoughts.

It was a relief to knock on Melanie Blessant's door, despite her awareness that as poorly tended as the house was, it was still more presentable than her own. A wan light seeped through the canopy of maples that bordered the walk, a reflection of the diminishing day, a reminder that as swiftly as time passed, it offered no reprieve from her restlessness. She didn't know if that long-anticipated moment of reunion with her brother was a source of creeping dread or solace.

No one answered the doorbell or her more insistent knock. Whatever she had tried to make of it, this was a dead end, a lost afternoon. There were no games on the schedule, no extra time she wanted to spend at home with her parents, no diligent partner to be found pursuing his own leads. She returned to her car and rolled the windows down, drumming her fingers on the steering wheel. It was one of those rare afternoons free of the rain that had made the fall so miserable, and yet her expectations made her wretched.

The sound of a car pulling up interrupted her thoughts. A luxury vehicle slowed in front of her Neon to park in Melanie's driveway, flattening the weeds that sprang from cracks in the stone. Rachel recognized the passengers as Hadley and Cassidy Blessant. The man who stepped out to open Cassidy's door resembled them so closely, he could only be their father.

"I'm sorry girls. I think it's better if I don't come in."

There were signs of tension in his otherwise pleasant face as he squeezed his daughter's hand.

"Daddy, you promised!"

From where she was parked, Rachel could hear the longing in Cassidy's voice, could hear them all, an unforeseen opportunity.

"Don't be a baby, Cass." Hadley unbuckled her seat belt, her manner brisk. "You know what'll happen if Mel has to deal with him."

She grabbed her bag and took a moment to glare at her sister in the backseat. "Come on, get out." The smile she turned on her father was unexpected. So expressive of warmth and trust and utterly unlike the front she had presented to Rachel and Khattak earlier.

"You know we love you, Dad. Don't believe anything the Grand Narcissist tries to tell you."

One of her nicknames for her mother, Rachel guessed, more in keeping with what she'd perceived as the girl's sardonic nature. Her father tried to hold back a smile and failed.

"I wish I didn't have to leave you here. I

thought this would all be over once your mother married Drayton."

"What would be over, Dad?"

Hadley answered her sister, her voice tart and impatient. "The child support. The spousal support. The never-ending demands. The custody battle, Cass. Mel didn't want us once she had Chris. We could have gone back to Dad once and for all."

"Chris wanted us," Cassidy protested. "He made room for us. He said it was our home."

"I want you more, honey. Your home will always be with me."

Dennis Blessant sighed and Rachel could well imagine his thoughts. He was a handsome, well-dressed man whose careless appeal had suffered more than the usual depredations of middle age. His sandy hair was graying, and there was an air of general fatigue about him that she attributed to the divorce, along with the custody battle — although she marveled at the thought of a man for whom responsibility and family meant everything. A man who chose the company of his daughters. To Dennis Blessant, fatherhood was a source of ceaseless fulfillment — not an affliction, which was all Rachel knew of the matter.

If Drayton had indeed been planning to

marry Dennis Blessant's ex-wife, Dennis's freedom had been close at hand. Any financial strain caused by Melanie's tactics also would have ended. Rachel puzzled over the custody decision: How had Melanie done it? Had her plea for her children been sincere and well-reasoned? Or had her exaggerated femininity done more to sway the family court judge than any show of saccharine devotion? Leaving Dennis Blessant and his daughters shattered and undone.

They seemed in no hurry to leave their father, leaning against his car, warming their legs against the hood.

"Is that boy still hanging around you, Had?"

Hadley grinned. "Marco, Dad. And yes, he is. I'll bring him with us next time, if that's cool."

"Bring him," Dennis said, his hands relaxed in his pockets. "Just make sure he knows I carry a gun."

Both girls laughed, and again Rachel wondered at Dennis Blessant. He looked at his girls as if they were the only things that mattered in the universe; moon, sun, and stars combined in one celestial profusion.

And then Melanie Blessant descended on them from a considerably less elevated plane, the screen door slamming shut behind her.

"Your time is up, Dennis," she said, weaving her way toward them. "You're not allowed to overstay, so I want you gone right now."

Whatever the very real loathing on Dennis Blessant's face gave away, he responded mildly enough. "All right, girls. I'll see you next weekend, then."

"*Not* next weekend, Dennis," Melanie contradicted sharply. "It's every other weekend, as you very well know. Don't try to mess with the custody arrangement or I'll have you back in court by the morning. *And* I'll be making a motion for the adjustment of child support."

"Still torn up over Drayton, I see."

He would have been wiser to resist, thought Rachel. Those were words to light the tinderbox of Melanie's temper.

"Mel," Hadley interrupted before her mother could go off. "Cass and I are at a museum dinner next weekend. Dad's taking us there and picking us up. We'll be back on Sunday, we talked about this."

Melanie fiddled with the string of her midriff-baring tank top. The temperature was starting to cool off, a fact that didn't appear to have registered on her decision to reveal nearly as much flesh as her outfit concealed. Sugary pink lip gloss and a skin-tight pair of cutoffs completed her ensemble.

How grateful their father must be that his daughters had chosen not to emulate their mother's style of dress.

"I'm sick to death of that museum," Melanie said. "That used-up librarian wanted Chrissie's money and she invented that museum to get it. I knew what she was from the moment I met her."

Hadley made no effort to hide her contempt. "I'm sure she knows what you are too."

"Don't you dare take that tone with me, Hadley! I knew why she was sniffing after Chrissie, but her pathetic little plan failed. He didn't leave her a dime. Everything comes to me." Her face beamed with gratification. "I'm the only beneficiary of Chris's life insurance policies."

"I'm very glad to hear that," Dennis answered. "It should make all the difference to your spousal support."

"You bastard," she hissed at him. Then she rounded on the girls. "You're not going to any party and if he tries to take you, I'll call the police, don't you think I won't!"

Hadley shoved her sister toward the house. "Get inside, Cass. You don't need to hear this." She turned on her mother. "I'd have thought you'd prefer us to go with Dad than Riv. Your choice, either way."

"I knew this was about that boy!"

"Yes," Hadley drawled. "That same boy you slobber over every time he comes by. Could your top be any lower, Mel? Or your shorts any tighter?"

"You're just jealous of what I have. And really, who could blame you?"

Dennis's "Don't you talk to my daughter that way" overlapped Hadley's "Isn't that a case of the pot calling the kettle black, Mel dear?"

And then Melanie slapped her.

Dennis grabbed her wrist.

The entire family was oblivious to Rachel across the street in her car. She knew she should intervene, just as she knew that intervention would cut short the family's revelations. She hesitated, her hand on the door handle.

"Don't, Dad. Once the will is read and those policies are paid out, she'll clear out of our lives for good. And if she takes you to court, ask the judge what happened to the money you gave her for our laptops."

He was torn, Rachel realized. He didn't want his daughter to talk about her mother this way. Especially when everything she said was true.

Spittle gathered in the corners of Melanie's mouth. "It was never about the money with me and Chrissie," she spat at them. "I loved him! I loved him and she can't stand that because no one will ever love her the way that Chrissie loved me."

"I hope not," Hadlcy said, her face deadly serious. "I wouldn't want a man who called me a whore every time he climaxed."

Melanie gaped at her, thunderstruck.

"What? You didn't think we heard you those nights you made us stay over? And obviously you liked it or why else would you put up with it? I have a hell of a lot more self-respect than that."

Melanie's nails bit into Hadley's arm.

"I want you out of my house right now!"

Hadley stood her ground, picking off her mother's fingers one by one. "Can't," she said without humor. "Custody arrangement, remember? How else will you get your money?" She stepped between her parents, urging her father back into his car. "You'd better go, Dad. Cass and I have a shift at Ringsong anyway. We'll see you again on Friday."

She turned to her mother, her tone derisive. "And I don't think you're going to be a problem, are you, Mel? Otherwise, I might have to tell Dad the real reason Chris wanted us to move in with him. In case you thought I didn't know."

She kissed her father calmly and walked to the door to talk to her sister.

Only Rachel noticed that her hands were shaking at her sides.

16.

The National Library of Sarajevo is burning.

A radio broadcast instructed Muslims to put white ribbons around their arms, go outside, form columns and head towards the main square.

He was in love, he decided, with the house. It wasn't a museum to him. It was a place of restful beauty, a space that his layered identities could lay claim to as home. He waited for Mink in the second courtyard reached through a colonnade of Andalusian arches, its tiled fountain at play beneath a stately turret. The white stripe of the Bluffs broke off from the darkness, the lake a gleaming shadow beneath them. Stars and sky stretched above, a timeless motif on an illimitable canvas.

The green coins of Andalusia extolled the

courtyard's virtues.

He sat still and calm between the palms and orange trees, waiting for the woman whose presence breathed life into all.

When she came, it was as if she detached herself from shadow, bringing with her a pale and rarefied light. After a moment of fancy, he realized she held a candle between her hands. She placed it on the table beside him, sliding easily onto his lounger, tucking her delicate feet beneath her. It had been like this between them from the start: a hushed and glowing intimacy, where if he wished, he could reach out and unclasp the golden knot of her hair or lay his hand upon hers, upheaval in so simple a gesture.

"Esa," she said. "You've been enchanted by Andalusia."

"Or by the woman who breathed it into being."

She brushed his words aside. "Look what I've brought you." She placed a dish of fresh dates in his hand.

He knew he should rise, find another seat, place some distance between them, but Mink was as sweetly scented as her garden. It was its own magic, that and the soft words that painted for him a distant civilization, a time of grace and elegance, a grand achievement.

The Library of Cordoba.

Of course a librarian would cherish such a memory.

"Paper was the beginning of it all. From Baghdad it was shipped to all the capitals of Islam. It was a competition of knowledge — who could build the grandest library, fill it with the most books — who would read and translate and comment. They were experts at classification. Such a catalogue they had — the thought of it makes me envious."

"Those words transformed the world."

"Think how little we know of such marvels. How little we appreciate those moments of history where differences were glories yet to be discovered, synthesizing a greater creation. This tribalism we worship now is an ugly thing."

"Tribalism?" he questioned.

"Patriotism, nationalism," she said impatiently. "Call it what you wish. Mine the only flag, mine the only way. All else is inferior, trample it underfoot. Despise it, detest it."

"We've come some distance since then," he suggested. He wasn't sure that he wanted to talk. He was here because of Christopher Drayton, but he thought that what he wanted was for Mink to sit at her table, quietly intent, turning the pages of her manuscripts in her hands. And he would do no more than absorb the luxuries of Andalusia and watch.

"Have we?" she asked him. Her hands did what he had longed to do, unraveling the gold coil of hair, letting it slip down to caress her shoulders as gently as a folio of wind. "You're an adherent of Islam, yes, Esa? Your name," she said, with the curve of a smile. "It declares it for you. So, what of the Ground Zero mosque?"

"A volatile situation."

"Indeed. And what of Murfreesboro, Tennessee? And all the other places where your people are unwelcome. Welcome to live, just. But not to worship or declare their way of faith."

"There's fear and ignorance everywhere. It's not exclusively practiced against Muslims. Look at Rwanda. Or Nazi Germany. Or the barriers Hispanic immigrants face."

"Or the Inquisition," she finished. "The culture of power versus the power of culture. One side consistently loses."

"We've a kind of Andalusia in this country," he teased, hoping to lighten her mood.

"Yes," she said seriously. "That's very true, but less true I think across the border. Inquisitions, pogroms, genocides — those are endpoints. Demonizing, fear, the pass-

209

ing of laws of exclusion, the burning of libraries — these are beginnings. Historians are vigilant as to beginnings. Too often we fail."

"I wouldn't have thought that was their calling," he said. "I imagine them lost in ancient worlds like the palace of the Alhambra or Madinat az-Zahra."

"It's dangerous to be so comfortable — to live in the past alone."

"Isn't that what museums are? Halls of the past?"

"Reminders," she said, reaching for a date from his hand. "Of things that could be, if we dared to dream a little differently. If we opened ourselves up."

"You've made this very personal." He gestured at the great room beyond the colonnade.

"I suppose I like to imagine this time of Muslim princes whose Jewish viziers conducted dialogues with Christian monarchs, reliant upon one another, influenced by one another, respecting one another. The Convivencia. In love with language, learning — what shouldn't I admire?"

He laid his hand on hers.

"Shall we talk about Drayton?" he said gently. "I would like to understand his attraction to the museum."

"You've just praised it yourself. Why wouldn't Christopher have felt the same? He was an educated man."

Khattak hesitated. He'd been coming to the museum for more than a week, finding excuses to stop by and linger beneath the palms, attracted by something he couldn't name. His heritage was neither Arab nor Hispanic, yet he laid claim to the intertwined identities of the civilization of Islam.

He should have asked much more about Drayton. And yet somehow, in her presence, all other thoughts eluded him. There was the material of who she was and the hope of what he still wished to discover. A feeling he hadn't known since the loss of his wife.

Her pale blue gaze challenged him. He cleared his throat and spoke. "Is it possible that Christopher Drayton wasn't who you thought he was?"

"What do you mean? Not a friend or advocate?"

"That." He lowered his voice so that Hadley and Cassidy, at work in the great room, wouldn't overhear. "But more than that. Did you ever have reason to suspect that Drayton might have another identity?"

Her hand smoothed over a palm leaf. "Is that why you're investigating his death?"

She thought a moment. "Was he a biga-mist?"

"Nothing like that. You've no reason to doubt he was who he said he was? A man who'd made money from businesses he owned in Italy and was prepared to spend it on the museum?"

"I didn't know about Italy," she said slowly. "I thought he was a man with a somewhat forceful personality who was searching for a way to put his mark on the world."

"Wouldn't such a man have had his own ideas?"

Mink pleated her hands against the bark of the palm.

"That's very common," she said. "There are dreamers and there are donors. Once they've given their money, they tend to reshape the dream in their own image. In Christopher's case, it was certainly about ego. Does that help?"

It was interesting, he thought, yet not quite the answer he expected.

"There's something you're not telling me," she said. "Is it a question of trust?"

"No, absolutely not." The connection between them was a tenuous one. He had no wish to risk it. "Does the name Dražen Krstić mean anything to you?"

"I feel that it should." She moved away from the seating area to stand by the turquoise tiles of the fountain. The sound of falling water murmured at them. "I can't quite place it."

"Did Drayton have an accent of any kind?"

"No," she said, startled. "His voice was rough, perhaps a little gravelly. I thought it was another sign of a man wishing to impress others with his consequence. Are you saying his real name was Dražen Krstić? That he was putting on some kind of act? Why would he do that?"

"Often when people take on new identities, they try and retain some trace of the old. The names Christopher Drayton and Dražen Krstić resemble each other."

She smiled. "Insomuch as Hebrew ring songs resemble Arabic ones. Who was Dražen Krstić? Does it really matter if Christopher wanted to leave something in his past behind?"

He didn't answer this. "Did you notice anything unusual about him? Any markings? Did he speak any other languages?"

Each time he asked Mink a question, she undertook some small action before she answered it. Now, she dipped her fingers into the upper tier of the fountain, interrupting its minor cascades. In another witness, he would have seen it as subterfuge.

"He spoke many languages. He was teaching Hadley and Cassidy Italian. As to the others, perhaps French, German? He did have a mark on one hand, a cross I believe. But then many people are attached to symbols of their religion."

She glanced pointedly at the tasbih on Khattak's wrist, a gesture that struck at him, collapsing his fluid identities inward like a lightning strike: one a symbol of thousands of the unquiet dead, the other the mark of their murderers.

"I'm sorry, Esa," she said quickly. "What have I said? I don't understand."

"It's nothing." He tried a smile and held out his tasbih. "In its proper context, it embodies grace. I know without the logo, the cross does as well."

He should tell her. There was nothing he should keep from this woman who cherished the complexities of Muslim Spain.

"Logo?"

"Entwined with the cross on his hand. The four *s* symbol: literally, it's translated as 'Only concord saves a Serb.' "

"But that's a twelfth-century motto, attributed to the Orthodox church."

"It has a much more contemporary significance."

She straightened from the fountain
abruptly. "Krstić?" she repeated. "I do know
that name."

"He was a commander of the Drina Corps
in 1995. You're much too young to remember. As Chief of Security, Dražen Krstić was
one of the men who orchestrated the Srebrenica massacre."

She froze. "Are you saying that *Christopher Drayton* was that man?"

"The tattoo is suggestive. And he was
receiving letters addressed to Dražen
Krstić."

He studied her closely.

The soft curve of her lower lip trembled.
She touched a hand to the back of her neck.
"What possible interest could a man like
Krstić have had in Ringsong? It doesn't
make sense."

Khattak had thought about this long and
hard. "If Drayton was Krstić, there may be
two possibilities. First, he had built a new
life for himself in a nation where we're so
intermixed that difference ceases to matter
or points of contestation are immensely
civil. Perhaps he saw his contribution to the
Andalusia project as a means of atonement." He watched the play of emotions

215

across Mink's face. "You don't think so. There is a second possibility, though I find it difficult to contemplate."

"Tell me," she whispered.

"He wanted you to change the name of Ringsong to the Christopher Drayton Andalusia Museum. He wanted a seat on your board of directors. And you've told me that donors often wish for greater say in how their money is spent — in fact, they 'reshape the dream.' So I've asked myself, what is the history of Moorish Spain most known for today? Its palaces? Its libraries?" He shook his head. Nothing about the preservation of memory fit with his knowledge of the ideology of Dražen Krstić.

But Mink, alert and lovely, was with him. "The Reconquista," she said simply. "The Moor's last sigh."

"Seven hundred years of the Moorish occupation of Spain brought to an end by the Spanish Reconquest. Expulsions. Forcible conversions. The implosion of a people's blended history of centuries of coexistence. And always the burning of books. Even memory erased."

Shaken, she said, "He often talked about the Reconquest. He did seem preoccupied more with the end of the period than its achievements."

216

"The culture of power versus the power of culture," he quoted. "One side always loses."

"I may have viewed the past as a loss, but Christopher saw the expulsion that accompanied the Reconquest as a triumph. And yet, I still can't believe that explains his interest."

"Then why were you so reluctant to take his money?"

Somehow, some part of Mink must have known that this was not a man to support a multiethnic, multilingual ideal. Her lips flattened in recognition of it.

"I must ask you not to speak of this to anyone," Khattak said. "If Drayton *was* Krstić, we have a problem of some magnitude on our hands."

Mink looked at him sharply. "Are you here about his identity or are you here because of his death?"

He couldn't stop himself from saying it. "At this moment, I'm here because of you."

It was a risk, a venture, spoken to a woman neither of his faith or culture, a line he had not been able to envision himself crossing. In time, he had thought, there would be a woman as dear and familiar to him as his beloved Samina.

He had noticed Laine Stoicheva. No man could be blind to that formidable sex appeal or powerful charisma. But she had touched no part of him the way his wife had. She was electricity without accord, a magnetism that was all outward. Her thoughts, her heart, were brittle, broken. She had wrung Nate dry. Such a woman could not attract him.

Here in this silent, prayerful space, he'd found something that had been missing in all the long years without the wife he'd adored. He'd found Mink and he wanted her. It was that simple.

When he'd solved the riddle of Dražen Krstić, he would leave behind the killing fields of Bosnia for the contradictions and glories of this Andalusian idyll.

"I need to think this over," she said. "Please leave now, Esa."

His face fell. He shouldn't rush her. They had known each other a week, no more. "I'm sorry. If you think of anything else, please call me."

He'd been dismissed. He should go.

"Esa." Her low voice halted him. "You know you can come back any time you'd like. This —" She gestured at the catalogue that awaited her in the great room. "All of it needs time."

He accepted that, releasing himself from the perfume of Andalusia. At the door he looked back at her, small and sheltered beneath the palms, her thoughts preoccupied by his revelation. He raised a hand in farewell and she smiled.

He moved quietly through the forecourt, so quietly that he had come upon Hadley and Riv in one of its shadowy corners without giving away his presence. Riv was holding her by the forearms, his expression pleading.

"You have to tell him," he said urgently.

"Why?" Hadley's voice was clipped and cold.

"Look, if you're worried about Mel —"

"I'm not. She's the last person I worry about. Ever."

"Then if she's not holding you back, what gives, Had? Why won't you tell?"

The girl's stiff posture unexpectedly crumpled and Riv folded her into his arms. The teenagers clutched at each other as Khattak moved closer, still hidden in the shadows.

"It's too hard," Hadley whispered. "Everything we've done these past six months has been too hard. Keeping Cass safe. Keeping him away. But it's done now."

Riv's hands clamped down on her shoulders.

"You should tell your dad, Hadley. He'd understand. He wouldn't want you to cover for him. And he might have seen something — after the fight."

Hadley swallowed and stepped back. "What fight? I don't know what you're talking about."

"What? Of course you do. The night Chris fell."

"No. No, I don't."

She had seen him, Khattak realized. Her hands were digging into Riv's forearms, warning him off.

Khattak stepped forward.

"Did you want to talk to me?" he asked gravely.

Riv's skin turned white under the pressure of Hadley's fingers.

"No," she managed on a gasp. "I'm — no. We're fine, aren't we, Riv?"

"Fine," he agreed, but Khattak read shame in the body angled away from his.

He studied their guarded faces. "If you know anything about the night Christopher Drayton fell, I hope you understand how important it is that you tell us. We're here to listen and to help. Please believe that."

But he could see the doubt in Hadley's eyes, the underlying panic. Whatever she had debated telling him was locked away again, sealed off by an undeclared darkness. It wasn't something he could demand from her. He would have to wait. And while he was waiting, he would puzzle through Drayton's connection to Ringsong.

"Thanks," she whispered.

"Peace be with you," he said, and meant it.

17.

I don't have a photograph of my child when he was small . . . I want to apologize for crying because you cannot compare this with what has happened but this is also something that is important to many people.

The art gallery was housed inside a university building so ugly it seemed like a contradiction in terms. She and Zach would have laughed over it in better times.

"Ray," he would have said. "Where did they find this architect? In the big-box department at Walmart's?"

After Ringsong and Winterglass, it seemed like a monstrosity: a long, narrow concrete block with ridges of additional concrete arranged at the entrance like a façade. It, too, could have served as a bomb shelter.

The building sat between two other much more decorous arrangements of steel and glass, and the gallery was really a passageway for students in transit between them. There was a fast-food stand in its midst, so she guessed this was an example of art designed as part of a living space. She wasn't impressed. Near the potato chips was a panel of red paintings, delineated by a series of screaming white faces superimposed on each other.

Further down the hall, a second artist had created sculpture from leftover scraps in the recycling bins. The word *recycled* screamed across the bellies of his tortured iron figures. Someone else had bravely attempted a representational field of lilies. Two slender individuals in their twenties dismissed it as derivative.

Discouraged, she muscled her way through the winding coil of students to the exhibit at the end. She had dressed to blend in, wearing jeans and a T-shirt, and when she saw the artist, she was glad that she had. He wore a black shirt and black jeans. Otherwise, he was her twin. Square-shouldered, lanky and tall, with shaggy dark hair worn long over his collar and with deep-set eyes, the color of Rachel's own.

It was Zach.

For a moment she couldn't absorb it. The boy had grown into a man, but it was Zach.

Her baby brother, Zach.

He was dwarfed on both sides by vertical cityscapes painted in shades of gray, blue, and black. Rachel could see at once that these paintings were different. The buildings crowded together, meeting each other at their pinnacles, suffocating the street dwellers below. They spoke of exclusion and hunger and want, loneliness and isolation.

It was Zachary's work, improved a thousandfold, bespeaking the maturity of a boy who had been on his own for the past seven years.

She waited until a group of admiring young girls had walked away, then touched his sleeve. The smile of welcome on his rugged features died on his lips as he recognized her. The things she had planned to say choked in her throat. She waited for him to speak.

"What are you doing here, Ray? Why have you come?"

The words were clipped, his manner frozen.

"What I am doing here?" She faltered. "What are *you* doing here? Do you have any idea how long I've been searching for you?"

"Not very good at police work then, are you? Or maybe you weren't really trying."

She stepped back as if she'd been slapped.

"Zach!" she cried. "How can you say that? Do you know how hard I've tried to find you? Do you know what you've put me through, put us all through?"

Her brother's eyes stared through her. "It's always about you, isn't it, Ray? Well, maybe you didn't give me enough credit. Maybe you were looking in rehab clinics when you should have been trying the local schools."

"I'm sorry." She fixed her gaze on the cityscape behind him to prevent herself from crying. "I tried everything I could think of. You made it so hard. There was never the slightest trace of you."

He shouldered past her to an easel where brochures of his work were arranged. He sorted through them, but she knew it was a delaying tactic, so she reached for his hand.

He wheeled around to face her. "This is one part of my life that no one named Getty has touched or ruined. I'd like to keep it that way."

"I'm not here to ruin it, Zach. Jesus, you're my brother. I care about what happens to you. I needed to know if you were dead or alive. I needed answers."

"And you thought I'd be strung out on drugs, didn't you? You'd made something of yourself, but there was no chance that I would."

"Jesus, Zach! You were fifteen. You may not know what happens to kids on the street but I'm under no illusions."

"That's right." He scowled at her. "You're out of uniform, I see. Does that mean you quit? Because I never could understand why the sister I looked up to more than anyone would want to follow in the footsteps of the man who beat me bloody."

"Zach, please." She took his hand again. "Look, can you take a break? Can we just sit somewhere and have a drink?"

"You look like you need it, Ray." He shrugged but he didn't resist. "Whatever."

They found a spot at the cafeteria where Zach could oversee his display from a distance. She bought them both Cherry Cokes.

She tried to think calmly, act calmly. "You've done really well for yourself. Is this exhibit part of a program here?"

"What you really mean is am I a registered student? Surprise, surprise. I'm a fine arts major. It's amazing what you can do with a student loan."

Something he had chosen, despite Don Getty's attempts to beat it out of him.

"That's wonderful, Zach, so wonderful.

I'm proud of you. Your work is really good."

His eyes softened at this but his tone remained confrontational. "What would you know about it?"

Rachel jerked a hand at the series in red. "I know those are garbage. So are those." She waved at the sculptures. "But your stuff is good. You get something from it."

He shrugged again, sinking lower into his seat, the gesture instantly reminding her of a teenage Zach bent over his homework at the kitchen table.

"I would have helped you, Zach. At any time, if you'd come to me."

He slurped at his Coke. "How could you have? You'd left for your training."

"I thought it would help me find you. Honestly."

She patted her brother on the arm, hardly able to believe that this was Zach Getty, alive and well, sitting across from her, noisily drinking a Coke.

"Why are you still at the house, Ray?"

She wanted to cry. Didn't he know? Didn't he know the only reason in the world she would continue to share a roof with Don and Lillian Getty? "It was the only place I knew you might come back to."

"But I never did." There was a suspicion of moisture about his eyes.

"No, you never did."

A silence built between them as she tried to think what to say next.

"So tell me a little about yourself, what your plans are."

His shoulders relaxed. Instead of meeting her gaze, he kept his attention on the visitors at his exhibit, assessing their level of interest.

"I can't stay here long, Ray."

"Please, Zach."

He folded his straw in two, inserted it through the tab on his can, spraying himself a little in the process. "I live on campus. I'm a year from graduating. Then I head to Vienna for the summer to study the Viennese painters."

She thought of Mink Norman's sister. "Have you ever heard of the Mozarteum?"

Zach looked at her. "Sure. It's in Salzburg. Different city. Why?"

"It came up during an investigation I'm on."

"So you're still in the police. No uniform though."

"I got promoted. I work at Community Policing now."

"That minorities crap?"

"At least Da hates it. That's a plus."

Zach grinned at her and she caught her

breath. It *was* Zach, it wasn't a mirage or her own hopes materialized into delusion. A cautious little ball of hope began to unspool itself in her heart. "Would it be all right if I asked how you got here? How you managed?"

He didn't flare up. If anything, his expression was pensive. "It wasn't easy. I stayed with my friends, at first. Then I moved around a lot. I fast-tracked through school because I knew I could get loans for university and move out on my own."

Rachel's heart seized up at the thought of it: so much danger, so much risk. Anything could have happened to him. "Weren't you scared?"

His level gaze said a lot about the man he was growing into. "I was a lot more scared at home. And I was sick of feeling that way."

Which made Rachel think of their mother. "Seven years is a long time to go without any contact, Zach. I don't — I wouldn't have expected you to want to have anything to do with Da, but what about Mum? You can't let her keep suffering, wondering what happened to you. I mean, I'll tell her, but at least you should make a phone call."

Zach looked at her so oddly that her heart constricted. He would bark at her, telling her she had no right to dictate his decisions when she'd done nothing to help him in the past seven years.

"You've lived at home this whole time?" he said.

She nodded. "I told you. I wasn't going to leave if there was a chance you might come back."

"You were punishing yourself," he concluded. "And now you're lost in that house. You never found your way out. I don't understand why she did that to you."

Rachel's stomach lurched. She had a sick feeling that something bad was coming.

"I wasn't punishing myself." But she had been. She knew it. She just didn't know how Zach had seen it so quickly, so clearly. Maybe it was because he knew her better than anyone. "I hoped one day you might remember what it was like. Not with you and Da or even with Mum. I mean with you and me."

Zach's eyes were wet. He stood up and brushed off his jeans with brisk movements. "Someone's screwing with you, Ray. When I figured out what I wanted to do with my life, I called Mum. She's been giving me cash since I started my program. She knows where I am because I call her once a week. On a cell phone that she bought me. I've gotta go."

There was no bombshell he could have delivered that would have shattered Rachel more.

It simply wasn't possible.

In the desperate years of her search — years of turmoil and misery that nothing could set in balance — Lillian Getty could not possibly have known where her son was. Don Getty managed all her money. She didn't have a dime of her own to give to Zach. Silent, timid Lillian didn't have the wherewithal to find or arrange a cell phone for Zach.

She'd stayed quiet and grieving in the corner of her living room without a word of consolation or hope for Rachel.

Because she hadn't known where Zach was.

No. It wasn't possible.

Rachel trudged after Zach, elbowing her way through students and teachers alike.

"Zach," she called. "That can't be true."

He stopped cold. She cowered inwardly, expecting his rage. But when he saw her ashen face, her pained incomprehension, he did something astonishing. He gathered her in his arms, shoving his face down into her shoulder.

She didn't know if he was crying or she was.

"I'm sorry, Ray. I shouldn't have told you

231

like that. She told me that she told you. She said you didn't want to see me again. I could hear you in the background sometimes. She said you refused to take the phone from her."

And it was clear that her brother still didn't know what to believe.

No, no, no, no, no!

Pain sliced through her heart, exploded in her brain.

What kind of woman would do such a thing to her children? Divide them from each other and kill the memory of the only love and security they had known?

Lillian Getty — pale and timorous on her chair, reading her magazines.

Knowing that Rachel wouldn't leave as long as she held out any hope for Zach. Knowing that her dread for Zach had leached the happiness out of any small moment of personal achievement. Knowing that all Rachel cared about in the world was her baby brother Zach.

Why had she done this?

Don Getty used his fists and only his fists.

Lillian had ripped out her heart.

She gasped out her pain into Zach's ear, her fingers clutching his neck like those of a drowning swimmer.

All this time Zach had been safe and Lillian had known, while Rachel shouldered her burden of terror and guilt.

"Ray-Ray." He murmured her childhood nickname. "Come back another time. We can't talk about this now." He drew away from her, hastily wiping his eyes.

"What if I lose you again?"

"You won't. Here." He drew a napkin from his pocket and scrawled his number and address on it in blue ink that smeared as he wrote. She took it with shaking fingers.

"Take this," she said, fumbling her business card from her bag. "You can find me at this number anytime."

She touched her brother's face, his hair, her fingers trying to memorize the man she saw before her now. She reached around him for one of his brochures and tucked it into her bag.

"I have money now, Zach. I'm working. I could help you. We could find a place together, make some changes —"

He cut her off. "I can't think about any of that now, Ray. I have my own life here. I'm being graded on my exhibit, I have to focus."

She nodded helplessly. "But you'll call me?"

"I'll call you."

"If you need anything —"

"I'm okay, Ray. Try to believe that."

She smoothed her trembling hands over her face, tried to get her thoughts in order. "Don't say anything to Mum, Zach. Don't tell her that we saw each other."

Because if she could make Zach disappear once —

"No," he agreed. "You either."

She nodded again, knowing he wanted her gone but loath to leave.

"Could I have one, Zach? One of your paintings to keep at work?"

He studied her card. "I'll send it to you. Now, please go."

She hugged him once more, aware that even though he was sending her away, insisting that she leave, he was bruising her shoulders with the fierceness of his grip.

They looked at each other uncertainly, their faces mirroring the same pain.

And then she forced herself to turn away and leave her brother behind.

There would be a reckoning of all she had learned. And when it was done, she would walk away without looking back.

18.

Simply, they left no witnesses behind.

The next morning, she called Nate. She'd stayed at the office overnight reading *Apologia*. She wasn't ready to face her mother. Instead, she'd gotten her skates out of her locker, found an indoor rink, and raced around its perimeter for an hour. Spent, she'd ordered pizza and hurtled through Nathan's last book. She'd been bleary-eyed and exhausted, taking her mind off her troubles by focusing on Nate's. She understood what the book was now, the meaning of the dedication. It was Nate nakedly displaying his longing for forgiveness.

He was just as screwed up as she was.

That was why she had called him. That, and for a tour of the Bluffs.

He was waiting for her at the trailhead. She greeted him with a wave.

"Have you ever noticed," she said as an

opening, "that everything about you matches your hair?"

Nate blinked at her. He was wearing a tweed jacket the color of autumn leaves and narrow slacks in the same shade of amber as his eyes. On his feet were the sensible shoes Rachel had proposed for a walk along the Bluffs.

She grinned, getting out of the car. "It's like a palette — the country gentleman's catalogue for fall. Do you have a valet?"

"I have Audrey," he said drily. "She hasn't gotten out of the habit of thinking of me as her personal dress-up doll."

"She has an eye for things," Rachel said. She felt safe in her compliment because it was directed at his sister. From the corner of her eye, she could feel the intensity of his regard.

"Shall we walk?"

He was guiding her down the path Drayton would have walked the night he fell to his death. The lake unfolded before them like a bolt of blue silk, a tangy breeze fresh against their faces. Rachel was glad she had opted for her ponytail and running shoes. The ground was uneven beneath her feet, covered with a sparse, thready grass that gave way in places. She could hear the rumpled murmur of water against the shore.

The Bluffs rose in an illumination of chalk-white cliffs before them, the path winding its way above the headland.

Rachel found the spot marked with yellow police cones without much difficulty, Nate trudging along behind her. Sixty-five feet below them, the detritus of the lake had scrubbed the shoreline clean.

She looked around.

It had rained often during the past ten nights. There were no tracks on the ground, no broken tree limbs, no indication of any kind of a struggle. She looked inland. The walk had taken them fifteen minutes. She could make out the barest outline of Nate's house. Ringsong receded even further into the distance.

If anyone had seen a figure walking on the Bluffs that night, there would have been no way of identifying the man as Christopher Drayton. If he'd been pushed to his death, someone would have had to have been following him closely. And why would he have stood there so obediently, making it easy for the person who wished him harm? Unless the relationship between Drayton and his pursuer had been one of trust — if it had been Melanie Blessant, for example.

If it had been anyone at all, she reminded herself. As Khattak was fond of saying: *a man fell to his death.*

She stood beside Nathan companionably, their hands shoved in their pockets, their faces reddened by the walk. She could taste the lake on her lips.

"Rachel," Nate said after a time. "Why would anyone push Chris to his death? Or why would he commit suicide? There must be something more to the matter here, and it's obvious you think it has something to do with the museum."

She would tell him, she decided. This mucking about in the dark was pointless. It was getting them nowhere. "The chief got a call from a friend at Justice, from the War Crimes division. There's some suspicion that Christopher Drayton was actually an alias. We think his real name was Dražen Krstić."

Nate stared at her, perplexed. "Dražen Krstić?"

"An indicted Serb war criminal. One of the logisticians of the massacre at Srebrenica."

"*That's* why they asked Esa to dig around?" He lost a little of his color. "They think that Chris was Krstić? That's simply not possible."

"Why not?"

She was curious as to how Drayton had

238

submerged his true identity so thoroughly.

"His English was perfect, for one thing."

"He spoke several languages fluently. Why not English?"

"No. He was a patient man, immensely kind and vigorous. He had an appetite for life. He loved teaching kids. He loved beautiful things. He threw himself into the museum — my God, the museum!"

Rachel waited. She was finding this most instructive.

"A man like Dražen Krstić would have had absolutely no interest in the Andalusia project. It would be antithetical to his sense of himself — to the ideology that fueled the Bosnian war."

"You know something about it, then." She filed away the troubling contradiction of the museum for later consideration.

"Of course I do. When Esa went to Sarajevo with his student group, I was the one he wrote to about the siege."

"You didn't go with him?"

"I couldn't. My father was a diplomat. It would have embarrassed him. I did what I could to help Esa from this end."

Rachel tried to remember her student years. She'd been hungry to learn, but her risk-taking had taken another form.

The cops turned their backs on us, Ray.

How could you want to be one of them?

I don't, Zach. I won't be anything like them, you can trust me.

She hadn't begun to come to terms with the knowledge that she no longer needed to carry the burden of guilt and dread that had defined her life for the past seven years. She didn't know if she felt lighter or merely empty. She wondered what Drayton had thought, venturing too close to the traitorous edge of the Bluffs. Had he jumped? Had the ghosts of Srebrenica haunted his peace too fully? Was his support for Ringsong meant to be an absolution? Had he accepted the things the letter writer had said about him?

I would like to appeal to you Mr. Krstić, whether there is any hope for at least that little child that they snatched away from me, because I keep dreaming about him. I dream of him bringing flowers and saying, "Mother, I've come." I hug him and say, "Where have you been, my son?" And he says, "I've been in Vlasenica all this time." So I beg you, if Mr. Krstić knows anything about it, about him surviving somewhere . . .

Were there tears in her eyes, or was it mist from the lake that spread below them?

If she had received such a letter — a mother begging for the whereabouts of her

240

missing son, one body among the thousands in Srebrenica's mass graves — she knew she would have found herself standing at the edge of a precipice, praying for the ghosts to leave her in peace.

But the man whose hands and brain had overseen so much death — how would such a man be moved by a letter? By a mother's agonized plea?

"Drayton was receiving letters addressed to Dražen Krstić. Letters that knew what he had done."

"Blackmail?" Nate asked, threading his fingers through the swoop of his straw-gold hair.

"Reminders, the boss said. I think they're accusations. We took them to an imam at the Bosnian mosque and had him look at them. There was an arms embargo, it appears."

"Yes," Nate said. "It made my father furious, I remember. The matériel of the Yugoslav army remained in the possession of Greater Serbia while the Bosnian territorial units were disarmed in preparation for the war. The international arms embargo prevented any hope of self-defense. My father observed that it was the first time the United Nations had actually supervised a genocide."

"Too harsh a condemnation, surely."

" *'The tragedy of Srebrenica will haunt our history forever,'* " he quoted, his voice soft.

"Where's that from?"

"The UN report published after the war. My father used to wonder if the war could have continued quite as long or reached such a violent conclusion without the role that the UN played. Do the letters speak of it?"

Defend us or let us defend ourselves. You have no right to deprive us of both.

She supposed they did.

"I just can't believe it of Chris. It would have been too great a charade. The thing he loved best was time in his garden. You could find him there in the evenings, chatting with his lilies. People who create such beauty can't possibly possess such ugliness within them."

Of course they could. People were full of contradictions, bewildering even unto themselves.

She'd seen her Da at the marina with Zach, his face alive with joy. And she'd seen her Da take his belt off and beat Zach bloody with it. And when she'd worked the Miraj Siddiqui case with Khattak, she'd seen sides of the human mind she hoped never to see again. Death and loss and betrayal, wound up in each other.

There was a fragile thread of connection between herself and Nathan Clare. He'd opened himself to her within days of knowing her. He'd directed her to *Apologia.* She wondered if she could say anything to him.

"Isn't that what you thought of Laine Stoicheva?"

His head whipped round toward her, his gold eyes like flinty coins. And then he smiled. "Yes, you're quite right. I should know better as a writer. I'm either observing contradictions or inventing them. It's just that Chris was — too normal, too human. And then, why the museum?"

Rain began to spatter lightly over their heads. They turned back.

"Maybe it was a form of atonement."

Nate neither agreed nor disagreed. He struggled to twist his thoughts around this idea of a dual identity. He fell into step with Rachel, conscious of the solidness of her beside him, the fixed, dependable nature of her movements. She moved quietly, without fuss, her ponytail bouncing behind her.

"You'll need to keep this information to yourself, though I wondered: do you think any of the people that you know, perhaps someone you invited as a guest to one of your parties — could one of them have been the letter writer?"

Nate considered this, his steps careful and sure on the precarious surface of the Bluffs.

"I honestly can't imagine so. Perhaps if I went back over my guest lists, something might stand out. Have you studied photographs of Dražen Krstić?"

Rachel glanced at him sideways. "Yes. I've looked at everything I could find. We're a bit restricted as to resources because the boss is keeping things quiet for now. The pictures I've seen are some fifteen years old. If it's the same man, he's greatly changed. Heavier. Older. We found a gun at his house. A JNA army pistol."

"A gun? Chris didn't own a gun. He abhorred them."

"Krstić didn't. They were second nature to him."

Her phone rang. The call was from Khattak. She listened, then turned to Nate. "I've got to go. There's been a break-in at Drayton's. If you could just try to remember if there's anything at all about Drayton that seemed strange or would suggest he had something to hide, that would be helpful."

"I could come with you."

"It's more important that we establish a break in Drayton's cover. He must have slipped up somewhere if he was Dražen

Krstić. Think about it and let me know."

That wasn't the reason she had asked him to show her the path through the Bluffs. And she didn't think it was the reason he wanted to accompany her now. In fact, she knew why.

With his writer's instinct, or whatever it was, he'd recognized a fellow screw-up.

19.

How is it possible that a human being could do something like this, could destroy everything, could kill so many people? Just imagine this youngest boy I had, those little hands of his, how could they be dead? I imagine those hands picking strawberries, reading books, going to school, going on excursions. Every morning I cover my eyes not to look at other children going to school and husbands going to work, holding hands.

Allah knew why this was happening. Only Allah knew. Only Allah could say why He had reached down His divine hand and touched them with the mark of the believers — the mark that cursed them. They had lost everyone else. His father, the brave ammunition courier, killed on the road to Tuzla. His grandfathers deceased from starvation. His uncles, cousins, brothers, and friends — some had stayed in the woods. Some had been executed inside the white house in Srebrenica. Some had been shot point-blank not far from the base at Potočari. Some had been beaten by axes and truncheons, or had their throats slit in the night, during the long wait for deliverance. Some were on trucks and buses that had materialized swiftly from nowhere and just as swiftly disappeared to unknown destinations. He had seen them take the boys from the line that separated the men and women. He knew they would take him, a skinny fourteen, just as they would take Hakija, at ten years old, the baby of their family. They would not say, "These are children, leave them." They would say, "These are prisoners. We will exchange them."

But there would be no exchange.

If they could take the baby that was crying from want in the unmerciful heat and shoot him in the head, why would they leave Hakija and himself? They would not. They would call them out as Turks, as *balija*. They would say, "Fuck your Muslim mothers." They would make them sing Chetnik songs.

Then they would tie their hands behind their backs, drive them away to a school or warehouse as they had done to others at Vuk Karadžić, and murder them all. They would lie there dead, forgotten, the last men of their family. Their mother would never find their bones. In time, she would forget the shape of their faces.

The Chetniks were coming.

There were rumors of more than just the Drina Wolves.

Someone had seen Arkan and his Tigers.

He kissed his mother, three times, four, and on the last kiss, he jerked Hakija's hand away from hers and whispered fiercely, "They are going to kill us. I will take him to the woods. I will find you again at Tuzla."

His mother had wept, pleaded, begged to take Hakija with her on the bus to Tuzla until she had seen just ahead of her in the line, Mestafa wrenched from his mother's struggling grasp.

"We need to question him," the Chetnik said. "He must be screened for war crimes."

Mestafa, Hakija's classmate, was eleven.

She let them go. Pressed her last bit of bread into their hands.

"Take this, my Avdi, my prince, the last hope of our family. Come back to me in Tuzla, Allah keep you safe, Allah bless and protect your road."

They melted away from the line, dodging the Chetniks, dodging the Dutch who were helping them. He saw that not every boy or man had been lucky enough to kiss his mother or wife or daughter farewell. Already, they looked like skeletons to him. He didn't want to be one of them. He would find his cousins in the woods, find a way to reach the column that had broken out for Tuzla. If he was crafty and careful — and how else had he stayed alive all this time — he and his brother would cross the divide into the free territory where they would be welcomed like heroes. There was food and water in Tuzla. His father's men were in Tuzla. His mother, Allah keep and protect her from the animals, would be there waiting. And this nightmare would be over.

He tucked Hakija's hand into his own, placed his other finger on his little brother's lips.

"No matter what they promise us, we don't talk now," he warned him.

Haki had always trusted him. He kissed his mother sweetly and left the line without protest.

Not knowing then that they would be hunted like animals with just as little chance of survival.

Before, there had been other words. A possibility of hope, of survival. He had heard it on the radio. They would send the airplanes. They would all be saved. The former meaning of all good things would be restored. Green fields no longer a killing ground where men he had known all his life collected their ammunition for this purpose. Animals peacefully at pasture, food fresh and plentiful, water sweet as nectar. And all of it a lie.

They were milling around in circles in the heat.

No one knew the way.

No one had a weapon.

They were trapped on all sides.

"Come down from the hills," the Chetniks said. "We will give you a ride. We will give you water. Why do you suffer for no reason?"

There was nothing to do, no one to ask. They hadn't found any member of their family. They didn't see any of their neighbors. It was just this writhing, dislocated circle of men. Boys, too. Others like himself and Hakija, their eyes desperately searching the faces of their elders. Should they go down? Should they surrender? A man had tried to run and been shot. Lazily. Easily. By a soldier adjusting his rifle on his shoulder.

What should he do?

What was the safest thing to do with Hakija?

"This one is just a boy," a soldier said. "Bring him down from the hill. Give him some water."

In that moment, he decided. Hakija needed water. He needed water. For now, they would come down off the hill near Konjević Polje with all the others. There would be another chance for escape and he would seize it. Later.

A soldier gave Hakija water from his canteen while he clung to his brother's hand.

He looked the Chetnik in the eye, polite and determined.

"Don't separate us," he said. "He is only ten."

"No," the Chetnik said. "I won't separate you."

When Hakija was finished, he received his share from the canteen. He sipped quickly, mightily, knowing that next time he might not be so lucky. In that moment, he saw a halo around the Chetnik's head. He saw that his eyes were kind, his hands gentle. He thanked him for his goodness.

"Stay on the bus with your brother," the soldier told him. "Keep hold of his hand."

They were shepherded to the bus like lost sheep. His hands were clammy from the heat; so were Hakija's. Still, they held on. The bus was as hot and crowded as the trek had been. But it was a mercy to be able to sit. He thanked Allah, he praised His glorious names. There was nothing else to do but sit and wonder and be afraid. Without showing he was afraid to his brother.

The drive was short and Hakija slept until they arrived at Kravica where the bus pulled up in front of a warehouse. In the field outside the warehouse, there were hundreds — or was it thousands? — of men. They were sitting on the ground with their hands behind their heads. Resting, their faces were just like his. Stoic. Bewildered. Terrified. They knew what was coming but they didn't absolutely know. They hoped, just a little, that the sun would rise without blood. They begged for water. He wished now he had not been so selfish with the canteen. He should have asked his brothers. He should have asked the thin, petrified men all around him, "Uncle, will you take a sip?"

He had thought only of himself and Hakija.

The engine died. The door opened and the Chetniks began to argue.

The driver wanted the men to get off.

The soldiers who guarded the warehouse refused. "We already have too many here. Take them somewhere else."

From the warehouse he could hear screams. Cries of desperation.

Not the warehouse, then. It would be hard to escape with Haki from the warehouse.

Allah show us a way, he whispered. Allah deliver us from evil.

There was noise all around them. More buses, some trucks. More people. More prisoners. There were too many. It was a convoy now. An officer came with orders. Their bus driver shrugged. He started up the engine again.

For so long, there had been no fuel in Srebrenica. Here, in moments, so many trucks, so many buses. The convoy began to travel again. He pushed Hakija's head down and craned his neck out the window. They were leaving Kravica behind, but where would they be taken next? Where would the road end? Would there be food or water when they got off the bus?

He didn't think so.

Those quiet men in the field told him otherwise. Their pleas for water had been ignored. In the woods, some of the men had drunk their own urine. If necessary, if they got to that point, he and Haki would do the same. He would have to wait and see.

The fields rolled by, the green fields of his country. He felt as if his stomach was being wrenched from him, but it wasn't a physical feeling. It was in his mind. The mind that schemed and planned and thought of survival. The mind that had seen the bodies of the men hunted down in the woods.

Where was the bus going? When would it stop?

He read the signs for Bratunac.

He knew what was in Bratunac. He didn't

want the bus to stop in Bratunac.

It stopped at the school: Vuk Karadžić. The site of the massacre three years ago.

He would not tell Hakija.

Even Hakija knew about Vuk Karadžić and the killing.

He didn't need to know that his brother had made the deadliest decision of their lives, to come down from the hills in the hopes of getting water.

He put his hands over Hakija's ears. Haki knew the sound of screaming and gunfire as well as he did. In the school there was death.

Please, he prayed. Let it be like the warehouse. Let it be full. Let them say there is no room for us.

Abruptly, the convoy came to a halt. A Chetnik rapped on the door.

Don't open it. Almighty Allah, Lord of all that is good, please don't open it.

The driver slid the doors wide, admitting his friend.

"Don't let them off the bus," the Chetnik said. "There's no room. We're not finished in there."

Praise Allah, praise Allah.

He wouldn't think about what the words meant, what it meant to be finished. He would only think about opportunities. Opportunities to escape with Hakija at his side.

The driver shut the door but still he could

hear the screams from the school. Wasn't it wrong to kill people inside a children's school? They had done it three years ago, they were doing it now. What about the day when the children came back and needed a place for their classes? What would they do then? Unless they already knew that no one was coming back.

It was true, but he didn't want to admit it. Everywhere they had stopped, he had seen the faces of dead men.

The convoy came to its final stop.

And he understood that they would spend this night at the execution site, but with the infinite mercy of Allah's grace and favor, he prayed they would not be taken off the bus.

Hakija would sleep but he would stay awake, alert to the sound of Chetnik boots, Chetnik guns. He would watch and see what he could learn. He would think of his mother, waiting for them in Tuzla.

And as he listened to the sounds of his people dying all around him, he would try with all his might not to break down and cry.

20.

All wounds will be healed but not this one.

Rachel took over from the local police with minimal fuss. The person who'd broken into Drayton's house was Melanie Blessant. The local landscapers, the Osmond brothers, were the ones who had called the police. They waited in the garden while Melanie arranged herself in a confrontational posture on the hood of Rachel's car.

"We asked you not to return to the house, Ms. Blessant," she said. There was a hint of exasperation in her voice. "What were you looking for?"

"It's my home, too. I lived there with Chris. You can't keep me out of it."

"As of this moment, we don't know what your legal standing is. Mr. Drayton may have had heirs. He may have debts with regard to the house: a mortgage, liens. These are things we need to clear up before we

256

can ascertain the extent of your rights. And of course, a will would greatly help."

Melanie batted her baffled blue eyes at Rachel. She was dressed in leopard-skin leggings so tight they were in danger of splitting across her rear as she twisted from side to side on Rachel's car. With that and the ample cleavage spilling from a leopard-print bra showcased inside a white hoodie, the entire effect dazzled.

"Wasn't it in the safe?"

"Have you ever seen it there, Ms. Blessant? Did Mr. Drayton tell you that he kept it in the safe?"

"Not exactly, but where else would it be? I didn't see it anywhere else in the house."

Her tone was martyred. Evidently, the police were to blame for her misfortune.

"If he had a will, Mr. Drayton most likely kept it at his lawyer's office. We'll have that information very soon, I'm sure. And in the meantime, do you have the combination of Mr. Drayton's safe? Have you ever removed anything from it?"

Melanie Blessant slid off the car with the practiced movement of a pole dancer at a strip club. She dusted one hand over her derriere, her gaze taking in the Osmonds. She produced a sexy little smirk. As she raised her hand to brush a lock of hair from her face, Rachel caught sight of the ring on her finger — bold, bright, and blinding.

"Chrissie liked his privacy. I didn't mess about in his stuff. He wouldn't have liked it."

Before his death, Rachel thought. Afterward, she wouldn't have been as fussy.

"Did you ever see any of the papers he kept in his safe? Apart from the letters we've already discussed?"

Melanie pretended to think, slipping one foot out of its sandal and rubbing it luxuriously against the back of her calf. Aldo and Harry Osmond watched her, fascinated. She was like a human Barbie doll, but it didn't mean she was any less intriguing. Surely that wasn't glitter she had dusted between her breasts? It matched the dangly earrings she wore. Nate should have inserted Melanie into one of his books.

"I don't think there was anything else. I mean, I wouldn't know." She patted her hair complacently.

He lost his temper with you, Rachel translated.

"You told us before that you'd read some of the letters. What did you make of them?"

"You expect me to remember that nonsense?" She turned on Rachel like a shrew. "Why would I, if Chrissie warned me off?"

258

"Just on the off chance."

Rachel waited her out, knowing an audience would be irresistible to a woman like Melanie.

"Things about maps and rivers, not my cup of tea, I can tell you. Directions, I think?" She made it a question. "And a whole lotta names, too strange for normal people to understand." A look of comprehension dawned over her face like a long-delayed sunrise. "I mean, the strangest thing is that the letters weren't for Chrissie at all. Some idiot just kept leaving them for him. Telling him to take the death road."

Now this was something.

"The death road?"

"That's what I said." Melanie tapped her nails against the side mirror on Rachel's car. "That's exactly what I said. It doesn't make sense. What kind of map talks about a death road or death march?" Her eyes became fatuous and wide. "Unless? Was it Las Vegas, do you think? Maybe Death Valley?"

Rachel sighed. There would be no elucidation here. Still. There was something about the safe. Something not entirely forthright.

Watching Melanie Blessant flounce her way across the street to her dark sedan, the headache that had subsided over her morning walk with Nathan returned to Rachel in full force. She squinted against a watery sun, thinking. Her gaze came to rest on the Osmonds. Why had they been here to call the police? She introduced herself, advancing into the garden.

They were two brothers in their early thirties with square faces that tapered down to narrow chins and eyes the color of steel bolts, sometimes blue, sometimes green, depending on the light. Scrawny, with the thick-skinned hands of gardeners. They wore dirt-stained T-shirts under their coveralls, and Harry, the younger of the two, shaded his face with a wide-brimmed hat. Aldo, the elder brother, fielded Rachel's questions, his eyes wary.

"You've heard about Mr. Drayton's death?"

Aldo nodded. He placed one hand on his brother's shoulder and held it there, his knuckles white against his sunburnt skin.

"Yet, you're still coming round."

"We owe Mr. Drayton two more treatments." His voice had a sliding pitch Rachel found unusual. "We worked well together on his garden. We wouldn't want to neglect it now."

"How long had your arrangement with Mr. Drayton been in place?"

"Two years? A little more? He liked our work very much."

She switched her attention to Harry.

"What did the work involve?"

Aldo reached over to adjust the brim of Harry's hat, pulling it low over his face. Rachel noticed the creeping system of lines about his eyes and mouth as he did so. For a young man, he had a gaunt, watchful quality.

"My brother doesn't talk much." He placed a hand to his head in a speaking gesture. "He has some difficulties."

As discreetly as she could, Rachel peered under the hat. In the first instance, she had missed the childlike nature of Harry Osmond's expression, the obvious befuddlement. Now she saw that his blue-green eyes were uncomprehending, the hand that clutched at his brother anxious and unsure.

"I'm sorry," she said. "Did you plant these flowers?" She indicated the border of sprawling lilies. "They're very pretty."

Harry's grip on his brother's wrist eased slightly. "Lilies," he said with careful accuracy. "My favorites. My favorites, Al, right?"

"Yes, Harry. Harry likes all the flowers. He likes their colors and their scent."

"No," Harry contradicted, his mouth set

261

in a stubborn line. "Lilies. Lilies are my favorite."

Aldo rubbed his hand over Harry's shoulder, a patient, familiar gesture. "Yes, Harry. Lilies are your favorite. There are some at Winterglass too," he told Rachel. "But not at Ringsong." A trace of amusement colored his expression. "Miss Norman had very specific ideas about the garden and the courtyards. I told her the plants wouldn't survive the winter, so she's planning to transfer them to a greenhouse."

"It should be a warm winter," Rachel said. "Getting warmer every year."

"Not warm enough. Not for orange trees. They need special precautions. Now, miss, if you don't mind, we weren't quite finished when we saw the broken window."

With a typical lack of nuance, Melanie Blessant had broken the small oblong window beside the front door to let herself into Drayton's house.

"You're going along to the back?" she asked them. "I'd like to see the back."

In grudging silence, the Osmonds led her to the back of the house. Here, Rachel stopped to take stock. The garden exploded in a profusion of herbaceous borders, roses and lilies — hundreds of plants and flowers that she hadn't a hope of recognizing.

Peonies? Chrysanthemums? Ranks of color, blooms piled high as snowbanks, scent and texture and astonishing variety. The garden gave the house its character, its charm. Drayton had placed comfortable loungers at intervals beneath the shade trees. She leaned against one, watching the brothers at work.

Harry's job was to spray fertilizer on the grass, a simple enough task. Aldo crouched onto his haunches to prune deadheads and trim back the hedges, supplying the appropriate tools from the pockets of his coverall. They were silent as they worked, ignoring Rachel.

She moved closer.

"When was the last time you and your brother saw Mr. Drayton?"

Aldo rose from his knees in a smooth motion, balanced against the handle of his garden shears. He looked from Harry to Rachel, a vigilance in the act that puzzled Rachel.

"Three days, maybe four, before we heard about his fall. He'd asked us to come and consult on new plantings."

"Both of you?"

Again that wary glance across the yard at Harry.

"Yes."

Her instincts told her to separate the two. "Perhaps Harry would like to show me the new plantings." She strolled over to the far end of the garden, her pace easy, her manner relaxed. Aldo followed at once.

"We didn't put anything in. We just discussed his ideas. Look, miss." He gripped her wrist with surprising strength. "Harry can be unpredictable. I can answer anything you want to ask."

Rachel detached Aldo's grip without difficulty.

"Is that so, Harry?" She smiled at him, her voice gentle. "Did you like Mr. Drayton? Chris?"

"He was nice to me," Harry said. Then he frowned. "He wasn't always nice, was he, Al?"

"He doesn't know what he's saying. He was nice, Harry, remember? He let you plant the lilies."

"He was nice," Harry agreed, pushing up the brim of his hat. "He let me plant the lilies. Orange lilies. Yellow."

"When wasn't he nice, Harry? Can you tell me?" And then as Aldo moved to intervene, "Mr. Osmond, would you wait beside the loungers?"

"You have no right to question my brother." His voice became rough, irregular.

"He doesn't understand you."

Rachel placed both hands on her hips and faced Aldo Osmond squarely.

"Do you have something to hide, Mr. Osmond? Does Harry? Do I need to take you both in?"

"We have nothing to hide. I just don't want my brother to become upset."

"You have nothing to worry about, sir. I have a lot of experience in these matters."

Aldo didn't back away. "He's my brother. It's my job to watch out for him."

"You can listen to everything I have to say. Just wait over there, please."

"I'll stand here. I won't interrupt."

"See that you don't. Harry, will you show me where you planted the lilies?"

Harry turned off his sprayer. He motioned Rachel to the very edge of the garden, where the lilies rose and fell in orange rows. Harry's hand caressed their delicate heads.

"These are the pretty ones."

He led her further down the path. With every step, she was conscious of the livid rage Aldo aimed at her back.

"Do you like these lilies?" Harry asked her.

"I do. Very much. Did Chris like them too?"

"He liked the orange ones. He didn't like

the others. He yelled at me. He said I did wrong. The wrong ones."

"Show me."

"It's nothing," Aldo denied. "It was nothing."

"Mr. Osmond, you said you wouldn't interrupt. I'd like to see them, Harry. Will you show me?"

Harry took her to the far side of the garden. Planted in a bed that circled a maple tree was a covey of yellow flowers, their buttery heads bowed on their stalks.

"He didn't like these? But they're so pretty."

Harry shifted from one foot to the other.

"He yelled at me, right, Al? He said it was my fault. But I didn't plant these. I didn't, did I, Al?" He jumped from foot to foot, his voice rising.

Aldo joined them, his shoulders slumped in defeat.

"You've upset him now." He reached for his brother's hand and stroked his own callused palm over it. "It wasn't your fault, Harry. You didn't plant these." The lines in his face hardened as he scowled at Rachel. "I don't know why Mr. Drayton didn't like them. It's not a good place to plant, in the shade of a large tree, but we wouldn't have made such a mistake. He asked us about it and I showed him the landscaping plan we had sketched together. No plantings under his maple. Harry doesn't know how to read people. He thought Mr. Drayton was angry at him."

"Did he yell at him?"

"He wasn't the kind of man to yell at anyone. Especially not Harry. He seemed more disturbed than angry but he didn't explain why."

"Did he ask you to uproot them?"

"No." Aldo sounded puzzled. "He asked us to leave them. He said he needed to think about them. Maybe he didn't like yellow."

"He didn't like yellow," Harry echoed.

Rachel nodded at them.

"I appreciate your help, Mr. Osmond. And I apologize if I upset Harry. It was nice to meet you, Harry. Thank you for showing me your work."

As she made her way back to her car, she heard Harry protest.

"I didn't plant them. That wasn't my work."

Rachel met Khattak at his office and waited for him to finish his phone call. He was speaking to a contact at Immigration, but from his scowl he wasn't getting the answers he wanted. She cast a furtive glance at his bookcase. Would he notice that his pristine copy of *Apologia* was missing? She turned her attention back to him as he ended his call.

"What did you find out?"

Rachel straightened her spine.

"It was Melanie Blessant who broke in. She said she was looking for Drayton's will. Apparently, she's not content to wait to hear from his lawyer. Is there a will, sir?" She hadn't overlooked Khattak's absence from the investigation. Nor did she know what leads he was working on his own.

"There is." He slipped his phone inside his pocket. "The lawyer's name is Charles Brining. We have an appointment with him in the morning. He wasn't prepared to speak on the phone about the terms of the will. You sound as if you didn't find Ms. Blessant all that convincing."

"I'm not entirely sure it's the will she's looking for. She's just *so* stupid," she added, thoughtfully. "I can't quite believe it's real. She saw other papers in the safe, though she'll tell you that she didn't snoop around in 'Chrissie's' things. The amazing part is that she didn't get why Chrissie received so many letters that weren't even addressed to him. Maps and rivers and such."

"The Drina," Khattak confirmed at once. "And the Drina Corps."

"There was more. Something we didn't find in the papers we took from his study. She talked about a death road." She resisted the temptation to roll her eyes. "She thought it meant a trip to Las Vegas."

"The road of death," he echoed.

"You know what it is."

"It's what survivors call the escape route to Tuzla. The men who managed to break out of Srebrenica. Many were killed or captured along the road, to be executed later. Some reported chemical weapon use."

"I didn't know that."

Khattak checked his watch but it was a deflection, not a sign of impatience.

"It came out in a Human Rights Watch report a few years after the fall of Srebrenica. They couldn't definitively substantiate the witness testimony, so they called for a wider investigation. The Yugoslav Army was known to have developed delivery systems for a chemical agent called BZ."

"Christ." Rachel no longer bothered to curse under her breath. "Are you telling me those weapons were used?"

"I suspect as much, but I can't say with certainty. Survivors said the mortars caused a strange smoke to spread out around them.

Some of the men exposed to it experienced hallucinations. They turned on their friends or killed themselves. The physical evidence of chemical weapons use remains elusive, however. Does Ms. Blessant know something about this? Should I talk to her?"

"She'd like nothing better, I'm sure. I can't be certain what Melanie knew. What I do think is that if she did know something — if there was something in that safe that penetrated through what passes for her brain — she simply didn't care about it. Whatever she knew, it didn't change her plans. She wanted to marry Drayton desperately. And she wanted to give him a ready-made family."

"We should be asking ourselves what the girls' father thought of that. It's a fairly steep price tag, giving up your girls to a fugitive accused of war crimes."

"If he knew."

"Someone knew. I wonder if it was Melanie Blessant."

"She's not going to tell us, sir."

"There may be a more roundabout way. Her daughter Hadley strikes me as being quite observant." He recounted what he had learned at the museum, but Rachel was shaking her head.

"She's a minor. We can't question her

without a parent present."

"Then let's ask Ms. Blessant. Let's see how far her motherly concern extends. Perhaps she'll be satisfied if Mink Norman is present." His voice caressed the name and Rachel scowled.

"Do you think that's wise, sir? We can't have interested third parties contaminating a line of inquiry."

"There's no reason to think of Ms. Norman as an interested party."

Rachel's eyes searched his face. "Isn't there, sir? Surely, we can't know who the interested parties are yet. At least until we've discovered the identity of the letter writer. Can you say with certainty it wasn't Mink Norman?"

He didn't concede her point, but he didn't sidestep it either. "I know there's more to these letters than we've understood. We need to go back to the Bosnian community. It's time we started asking questions there."

"I thought we were supposed to keep this quiet. Surely we're not going to treat Bosnians as suspects when we haven't had the nerve to come clean about Drayton."

"I'm saying we should pursue both avenues, Rachel. You've had a good instinct about Melanie Blessant that I'd like to follow up. We need to talk to the parents and, failing that, to their daughters."

"And while you're managing our community policing mandate, what will I be doing?"

Khattak didn't hesitate. "Read the letters more closely. Something may strike you."

"You're seeing Melanie on your own?"

"I think it's the likeliest chance of success."

He was right, of course. Melanie would be eloquent under the spell of his attraction. And if this bothered Rachel, she told herself it was for professional reasons.

To Khattak she said, "And if it isn't?"

"Then I'm willing to bet that she doesn't much care if we interview her daughters."

"And what if the girls aren't there?"

"Then they're likely at Ringsong."

They'd come to an impasse. Rachel thought about objecting again but left it. "Be careful, sir. We're working in the dark here. We don't know anything about anyone."

"I think you'll find once you've gotten to know her that there's nothing to fear from Ms. Norman."

"Is that what you call her?" Rachel asked, curious.

"You don't trust easily, do you Rachel?"

"I wouldn't have thought that was a useful quality in a police officer." She hesitated. "I'm just wary of provocative women, sir."

Khattak's gaze made a slow inventory of the shelves in his office before coming to rest on Rachel's face. "Is that a comment on my personal behavior?"

Nervous sweat soaked Rachel in an instant. "Of course not." She had never, ever wanted to traverse this ground with Khattak. He knew the entire history of her sordid entanglement with MacInerney and hadn't once ventured a personal remark. Her voice stayed trapped in her throat.

"We don't share much about our personal lives, do we?"

There was a rueful note in his voice. She swallowed on a ball of fear.

"That's all right though, isn't it?"

She did not want to talk about Don Getty. Not with Khattak. Not with anyone. If this was an overture of friendship, she'd do her best to deflect it at once.

"But something's been worrying you, hasn't it?" he went on. "Outside of this case."

Oh God. How to answer him?

"The specter of a war criminal walking our streets is more than enough to worry me, sir. I hope I've given this case my full attention."

She studied her fingernails. She'd find time for a manicure if she could just walk out of this office now. When he didn't speak, she forced herself to look at him.

He seemed more than a little uncomfortable himself. "Rachel. This is supposed to be a position of leadership. If you ever wish to speak with me about anything, I can assure you it won't leave this office."

Oh God, she thought again. Did he know about Zach? Had he noticed her lack of focus, her mind constantly wandering to her brother? Was that what this was about?

Tears flooded her eyes and she began fumbling needlessly through her bag. "I'd best get on these letters, sir. Thank you, though."

Without meeting his eyes, she made her way out of his office to her desk.

Only later would it occur to her that his unexpected compassion had skillfully diverted her from the subject of Mink Norman. And that she'd forgotten to mention the lilies.

21.

I apologize to the victims and to their shadows. I will be happy if this contributes to reconciliation in Bosnia, if neighbors can again shake hands, if our children can again play games together, and if they have the right to a chance.

Despite his desire to return to Ringsong, Khattak returned to the Blessant house, where he found Melanie and her daughters at home. He had debated pushing Hadley harder the other night, but now he realized the conversation would be better served away from the museum and Mink's subtle influence. He might have been reluctant to acknowledge Rachel's warning, but he couldn't discount it altogether.

Rain pelted his cheeks as Melanie let him in on her way out. She'd granted his request for an interview with the girls without hesitation. If she knew anything more about

Drayton's will or his papers, she refused to discuss it, her mind preoccupied.

"Talk to them all you want," she said. "Just don't let that boy in, because I'm not running a whorehouse here."

He winced at her manner of indicating concern and watched her go, hips swinging, heels slapping against wet concrete, an umbrella sheltering her crown of blond curls.

"She's headed to the pub," Hadley said, coming to meet him at the door. Her skin was paler than usual, but otherwise she seemed composed. "We're in here."

He followed Hadley to the dining table where Cassidy was seated in front of a polished paper cutter. She was absorbed in the task of measuring cardstock. As he entered the small room, she spared him a shy smile.

He could see why the girls preferred to work in the great room at the museum. The interior of their home was small, cramped, and shabbily kept, old furniture crowded together, yellow wallpaper peeling from the walls in long, damp folds. Whatever money their father had given his ex-wife, it hadn't been spent on this house. The girls were identically dressed in faded jeans and blouses that had seen better days. He caught

Hadley's eyes on him, knew she had understood the judgment in his face, and hastened
to cover it.

"You're not at Ringsong today."

"Mink's busy tonight. What can I help you
with?"

Hadley came to stand in front of Cassidy's
chair, blocking his view of her sister, a
gesture that made him feel inexplicably sad.
Why did it seem to him that this fierce
young girl faced the world alone, bearing
the weight of intolerable burdens? Or was
she alone? Marco River melted into the
room like quicksilver, toweling off his dark
hair. It was obvious he hadn't used the front
door.

"Sorry I'm late. I had to wait for the tiger
to leave."

A kinder way of referring to Melanie than
Hadley's "Mad Mel." For Cassidy's sake,
he thought. It couldn't go on. Whatever
secrets they shared between them, he would
have to find a way to them move forward.

"Your mother gave me permission to ask
you a few questions."

"That's because she's an idiot," Hadley
said without blinking.

"You and your mother aren't close?"

She made a quick, precise movement with
her hands, directing him away from the

table to the adjoining living room. They took seats at the far end in front of the bay window.

"I want to hear," Cassidy protested.

"No you don't. Sit with her, Riv."

The boy obeyed, his eyes gentle on Cassidy's upturned face.

In the living room Hadley turned her full attention on Khattak. "I can't stand her, and the feeling is mutual."

"I'm sorry to hear that."

"Why? I've got one good parent which is better than a lot of kids." She flicked a hand at Riv. "Riv's parents are potheads who got him hooked." She narrowed her eyes at Khattak. "I'll deny that if you try to make anything of it."

Khattak nodded gravely, careful not to look over at Marco. "That doesn't interest me at present. I was wondering how well your father knew Christopher Drayton."

He had been expecting panic, but there was anger in the set of her face, anger and something more. Bleakness.

"Mad Mel was planning to marry him, so Dad had to get to know him a little."

"What were his feelings about the marriage?"

"He was ecstatic." Hadley's voice was dry. "Mel's had him on a very tight leash since the divorce. Chris marrying Mel meant freedom for all of us."

"How so?"

"Dad wouldn't have to pay out the monstrous spousal support that keeps Mel afloat. She's never had to work for anything. And even if she did, minimum wage wouldn't pay for her surgeries." She pinned Khattak with a steely gaze. "Do you think she's beautiful?"

"I'm sure many men would think so."

"They'd be idiots. There's nothing real about Mad Mel — either inside or outside."

Her contempt was undercut by the pain beneath her words.

"Do you think that's what men like?" she went on. "All that plastic tarting-up? So you can't tell what's real or not, just that there's a lot of it?"

She gave her own slender frame an unsparing glance. She was still young enough to need approval, to wonder if she suffered from the comparison to her lavishly endowed mother.

Khattak answered with care. "Without taking anything away from your mother, I think it's safe to say that most men have a more discerning palate. Less can be more." He thought of Mink's elegant hands sliding over her manuscripts.

"You really think so?"

"I think Marco would agree with me. He hasn't taken his eyes off you since he entered the room."

The boy flashed him a grin from the dining table.

"He's probably worried that you're grilling me."

Khattak smiled the smile of a man who'd once stood in an adolescent's besotted shoes. "That's not worry I see in his face."

She heard the humor in his voice and blushed. His words must have been some comfort, because she pushed her shoulders back and raised her head to meet his gaze. "Dad was actually very grateful to Chris. He was taking a huge problem off Dad's hands, and we would have been free to move in with our father after that, so no more extortionate child support either."

She placed a heavy emphasis on the word *extortionate.* It must have been her father's word. It made Khattak think of the letters. He'd get to those in a moment.

"I understood that you were to live with Christopher Drayton after the wedding took place. You have rooms at his house, your mother said."

"No." Hadley's voice flattened. "We were never going to live there. Not in this lifetime or any other. The wedding was the end of the road for us."

"Didn't you like Mr. Drayton?"

"We have a perfectly good father of our own, so why would we settle for a substitute? Why would I want to be around Mel a minute longer than I need to? She makes no secret of the fact that we'd just be in the way."

And yet, she couldn't entirely hide the note of longing in her voice. No matter how harshly she spoke of her mother, there were better memories buried beneath her pain.

"She mentioned that Christopher Drayton wanted a family."

"Did she?" Hadley said without inflection. "What he wanted and what I want are two very different things."

"What about Cassidy?"

He caught the flare of panic on Hadley's face.

"No," she said, a grim anger in her voice. "Cass goes where I go."

"Unless she decides otherwise."

He said it to get to the root of her alarm.

"Cass feels the same way about things as I do," Hadley muttered.

But did she? What did this forthright, clever girl fear so much that she balked at telling him the truth? Because something in her manner spoke eloquently of deception.

"Tell me about the fight."

Instantly, she went still and quiet. She shook her head, freckles standing out against her pallor.

"I can't. I don't —"

"Hadley." He leaned forward, his tone confiding. "This is not your burden to carry. You don't need to protect Christopher Drayton or anyone else."

He'd said the wrong thing. He'd only reminded her of what she thought she had to lose by speaking.

"There's nothing. I don't know anything."

He tried another tack.

"Did you ever see any unusual letters in Drayton's possession? Did your mother ever talk about them?"

The change of subject afforded her no relief. If she held herself any more closely, her bones would snap.

"Letters? No, not letters."

"Something else then? A will perhaps? Papers to do with the museum?"

"No, nothing." She was lying. And the more she elaborated, the more evident it became. "We only went there to study Italian. I wouldn't say we were friends."

Khattak cast about. "Was he a good teacher?"

"He was all right." She bit her lip. "The only reason Mel wanted us to have those lessons was so that she could work on Chris. Flirt with him, get him interested. I guess it worked."

She should have said, "Obviously, it worked." That's what the bitterness in her voice conveyed, a bitterness he couldn't place. Her phrasing told him that there was something else going on entirely.

He raised his voice slightly. "Did you go to these lessons, Marco? With a name like yours, you must have been interested in Italian yourself."

"Sometimes. If Hadley couldn't go and Cass had a lesson, I'd go."

"Why was that?"

A frozen silence stretched between Hadley and Riv. It was broken by Hadley's sharp intake of breath. "Cass likes company. She's younger than she seems. That's why she's not prepared to let go of Mad Mel just yet."

Every piece of information directed him back to Melanie Blessant and away from Christopher Drayton. At some cost to Hadley, he realized.

"I thought you said Cassidy was ready to move with you to your father's."

She faltered for a moment but hit back hard with, "I said *after* Chris and Mel got

283

married. What sense does it make to live in a stranger's house when we have a beautiful home of our own? Cass and I weren't about to be split up for the sake of Mel's libido."

It was a bold performance, but the hint of uncertainty that underscored the last word rendered it false. There was something dark under Hadley Blessant's collected surface, something else beneath the stony front she tried to project.

She was a girl in trouble.

And with a man like Dražen Krstić, he feared what that trouble might be.

He turned his attention to Cassidy, whose head was diligently bent over her work.

Hadley came to her feet with startling force. "I don't think I want to answer any more of your questions, Inspector. And if you want to talk to Cassidy, you'll have to ask my dad."

"I have your mother's permission." He made the observation only to test her response.

"You need to ask the parent who actually cares about our welfare, and that would be my father. Now, please — leave us alone. We have work to do if we're going to meet the deadline for the opening." Her shrill voice rang through the room, causing Cassidy to turn their way, bewildered.

"I appreciate your honesty," he said, his tone mild. "I didn't mean for my questions to upset you. I just want you to know —" He came to his feet as well. "If you ever need help, you can talk to me or Rachel at any time."

He hoped she would believe him.

"Why are you so interested in Chris's death? It's not because you think he fell, is it?"

And just like that, his moment was before him. A moment when he could open his investigation up a little, trading truth for truth, offering honesty in exchange for a reluctantly given confidence, proving himself worthy of a teenage girl's trust.

Yet the cataclysmic secret of Drayton's identity could not be released at will: not without consulting Tom Paley, not without mapping out the implications for the Department of Justice, Immigration, and most of all, for the Bosnian community.

The ugliness of Dražen Krstić's life darkened the space between them. Hadley caught his hesitation, but he went on regardless.

"We don't think Drayton was who he claimed to be. We fear there was another side to him altogether. It's possible that whatever secrets he kept may have led to his death. But I think you already know this."

"The Bluffs are treacherous. People often think they're safe when they're not." She whispered the words through lips so dry they were stretched taut against her gums.

"We've considered that possibility as well."

"Good — I mean, good."

She didn't say anything else, although Khattak gave her time. It wasn't working. Nothing he'd said had convinced her to trust him. She was much too frightened. Not of someone but for someone.

"What did your father and Drayton argue about?" he asked at last.

Hadley raised one arm in front of her body as if to ward off his question. Tears spattered her freckled skin. Throat working, she opened her mouth to speak. And then fainted dead away.

22.

Mr. Stakić is here. He's a physician just like I am, and he made decisions concerning the camps. He knew that we were there. He knew that his colleague Jusuf Pasic, who was facing retirement, had been taken to Omarska and killed there. He knew about dozens of doctors, physicians being taken to Omarska and killed. Why? These people were the Muslim intelligentsia and they meant something. Is there an answer to all of this?

Charles Brining's office was located in one of the gleaming glass towers that stood opposite the Scarborough Town Center. As they traveled through the air-conditioned chill of its lobby and elevator, Rachel cast a surreptitious glance at her boss.

Was it her imagination or was Khattak's smooth front unraveling a little? The knot on his tie lacked its usual exactness. The pen inside his shirt pocket had leaked ink, leaving a small blue teardrop at its corner. His manner was abstracted, his forehead creased as if he was fighting off a headache. Which only made sense, after his disastrous interview with Hadley Blessant. He'd given her the barest of details, admitting candidly to his failure. And his sense of shame.

She hoped their time with Drayton's lawyer would be more profitable. To that end, she'd made more of an effort than usual with her dress code. On the whole, she detested lawyers, although every now and again, she came across one who made her forget their unmitigated unhelpfulness when she'd tried to emancipate herself and Zachary from Don Getty's control. Charles Brining wasn't one of them. He was a twig-thin, nervous man in his sixties with the bespectacled face of an absentminded owl and the irritating habit of clearing his throat before each utterance.

He met them in his firm's conference room, a space that aimed at the glamour of the high-powered conglomerates on Bay Street. The seedy, well-thumbed magazines gave the lie to a shining mahogany conference table and the floor-to-ceiling windows that looked out upon ramps to the 401.

His discreet assessment of the duo from

CPS took in Rachel's crumpled Banana Republic suit in an unflattering shade of taupe and the ink stain on Khattak's otherwise pristine shirt.

"I've considered the will, as you've asked," he said as an opener. He had the querulous voice of an elderly woman unable to follow the bidding at her bridge game. "It's quite straightforward. With the exception of a single bequest, he leaves his fortune in its entirety to a Mrs. Melanie Blessant. The house and the chattel are left to the same — ah — lady."

Rachel pounced. "You've met her, then."

Brining blinked at her through his spectacles. "Yes, ah — yes. Mr. Drayton brought her with him once."

"Did he discuss the disposition of the will with her?"

"I advised him not to do so."

Rachel and Khattak exchanged a glance.

"Why was that?"

"General prudence." Brining cleared his throat, his pronounced Adam's apple bobbing up and down as he spoke. "The lady has a somewhat — grasping demeanor."

Rachel grinned. "Did she ask you about the will?"

"She spent her time in our lounge, refurbishing her nail polish. She did — ah, drop in to ask a question or two, but naturally, I was not at liberty to speak of Mr. Drayton's confidential matters."

"Naturally," Rachel agreed. "You mentioned another bequest."

Brining worried the tip of his tongue against his lips, a motion that caused the tuft of white hair on his head to shiver slightly. "Yes. Of a charitable nature in that it was a bequest to a registered nonprofit. Informally, I believe it's known as Ringsong. The name on record is the Andalusia Museum Project. The fund was to be administered by the museum's board of directors."

"When you say 'fund,' how much money are we talking?"

Brining looked abashed, as if the mention of actual hard numbers was an indecency. "My dear Sergeant Getty, the man had done quite well out of his business. Even with all that's owed in taxes and death duties, he was quite comfortably able to bequeath the museum a quarter of a million dollars."

"What?" Rachel hissed. "You've got to be kidding."

"I assure you I am not."

"But why would he want to give so much money to such a small project?"

"It was quite a passion project of his. He wanted to leave a legacy, and the Reconquest of Spain from the Moors was a legacy he respected very much. It seemed somehow personal to him. Is that helpful to you?"

"It confirms certain theories," Khattak said, echoing the lawyer's noncommittal manner.

"Then perhaps I should add that the amount available to Mrs. Blessant is substantially more."

"How much more?"

"Something in the nature of two million."

Rachel's shock was evident.

"Just what type of business was he in?"

"He operated a parking lot in the city that was remarkably lucrative. And of course, he brought savings with him from his businesses in Italy."

Rachel's knees knocked together. The thought of Melanie Blessant in possession of so much ill-gained fortune made her feel nauseated.

"Do you know the nature of those businesses?"

"Import-export, I believe. Christopher didn't discuss the specifics with me."

"You were on a first-name basis?"

Brining bristled. "It's atypical, I assure you. We were of a similar age, with similar interests. He was a hospitable man: we socialized occasionally."

Rachel rushed to soothe him. "Of course. You say you had similar interests. Might I ask what those were?"

Brining's smile was unexpected. It disclosed a series of irregular, closely corralled teeth with a gap at the center.

"I'm quite fond of vacationing in Italy. The food is divine. And we both enjoy a tinker in our gardens. Peaceable hobbies."

"Indeed." Khattak cut in. "What would happen to Mr. Drayton's bequests, if it became public knowledge that Christopher Drayton was not in fact his true identity?"

The unexpectedly charming smile disappeared. "I'm afraid I don't quite follow."

"If Christopher Drayton was an assumed identity rather than a real one."

A shrewd flash of intuition lit up Brining's eyes. "Is that the nature of your interest in this matter?"

"Yes."

"I suppose it would depend. If the identity was a legal identity, as per a perfectly justifiable legal name change, it would have no impact at all. If he'd never formally registered a change of name, there would be issues, certainly, but none that might not be overcome with careful and thorough paperwork."

Careful and thorough paperwork were

Charles Brining's holy grail, Rachel deduced at once.

"That's not the issue, is it, Inspector?" Brining's rheumy gaze darted between the two detectives. "If Mr. Drayton were some type of fugitive or if the funds themselves were to be of suspect provenance — illegally gotten gains," he elucidated for Rachel's benefit, "then naturally, the bequests would be held up until Christopher's legal right to the funds could be determined. If any of his assets were found to be the gains of criminal enterprise, they would be seized by the jurisdiction most concerned with the crime." He lowered his voice. "Does this pertain to organized crime?"

"We don't have that information yet, although we are in the process of acquiring it. Would you be able to do something for us, sir?"

"That — ah — depends." Ever cautious, the lawyer waited for clarification.

"Would you notify the beneficiaries of their bequests but also warn them that the actual dispensation of funds will be held up until our investigation is concluded?"

"That was within my ambit, regardless. I shall do so immediately."

"And if they press you for additional information —"

"Naturally, I shall say nothing, as I know nothing," he responded with a twinkle in his eye.

"You're very good."

Brining dismissed this. "I must say, however, Inspector —"

"Yes?"

"I cannot imagine Christopher Drayton to have been anyone other than who he claimed to be. A generous man whose greatest pleasure was his garden, with perhaps a weakness for improbable women."

Rachel grinned at the word. It was a brief yet perfectly calculated description of Melanie Blessant's pneumatically enhanced attractions.

"You say improbable, sir. Why so?"

"She presented herself as — what's the common vernacular? Ah yes. No more than a trophy for Christopher's arm. A somewhat artificial woman with a voracious eye for Christopher's credit cards. He didn't seem to mind that." Brining's white tuft trembled as he nodded at Rachel. "Yet I had the distinct impression she knew everything there was to know about Christopher, down to his last cent." His manner became grave. "If Christopher Drayton was indeed an assumed identity, I have very little doubt that Mrs. Blessant knew the truth of it."

"Let me make a call, Rachel."

Rachel cooled her heels by the car, noting anew the sprawling ugliness of the shopping mall across from them. In the last two decades, its big-box stores had multiplied exponentially, robbing the façade of any appeal.

Khattak made no effort to screen his call from her hearing. He made a polite but firm request to be put through to Tom Paley at Justice. Some moments passed before the call was connected.

"Tom? It's Esa here. I think I have confirmation."

Rachel listened without pretense as Khattak described the letters and the gun in Drayton's study, his own suspicions, and lastly, Drayton's tattoo.

"You'll need to trace the money. It's the fastest route to the truth." He listened for a moment. "I can't confirm it through DNA unless you or the ICTY have a sample on file. Do you have that?" Another pause. "I didn't think so. Listen, Tom, we should talk in person. I'll come to Ottawa tomorrow. We need to discuss exposure."

Rachel scowled. Just what in hell did he

mean by that?

As if he'd heard her thoughts — or just read the anger on her face — he went on, "It's time you notified Immigration, more than time. And I've a duty here with regard to the Bosnian community. You can't possibly expect this to remain quiet much longer."

Another long silence, and this time it was Khattak who looked angry. "Who told you about Imam Muharrem? I see. Then let me say this, the Bosnian mosque was our first, best lead in terms of confirming identity. The imam has offered to put us in touch with survivors who were at Potočari when Krstić was there. Survivors who won't have forgotten what he looks like or who he is. I'm well aware of that, Tom. And yes, I'll be discreet."

He snapped his phone shut. "They'll trace the money. It's what they should have done from the first."

"What about Immigration?"

"Yes, that's the question, isn't it?" He stared up at the glass tower to Brining's office. "There was no legal name change, that's one thing I can tell you. However Krstić got here, it was as Christopher Drayton."

"You've been widening the net," Rachel

said. "Why didn't you tell me?"

"If this blows up, as I've every reason to believe it will, I don't want you caught in the crossfire. They'll come after me. I need to make sure you stay above it so we can salvage any justice that's possible from this mess."

"That sounds personal, sir."

"If you'd been through a single day that Sarajevo was under siege, you might find it personal as well. It won't compromise my judgment."

Wouldn't it? He hadn't mentioned the bequest to Mink.

"Sir, what about the museum?"

"What about it?"

"A quarter of a million dollars. That's quite a motive. Money left as a bequest is entirely different from a donor's gift. It comes without strings attached."

"If Drayton is Dražen Krstić, I've every confidence that Ms. Norman will refuse the gift."

"Have you?" Rachel bit her lip. "If the money's dirty, there's no gift to leave. But Mink Norman wouldn't have known that."

Comprehension flared in Khattak's eyes. "Suppose Melanie Blessant did know. Suppose she understood the letters she snooped through all too well. Maybe she did have the combination to the safe and she got rid of anything that definitively pointed to Krstić. Knowing that it might be an obstacle to his fortune."

Rachel wondered if he could hear himself — the thin and paltry hope.

"There's a number of problems with that, sir." She chose her words carefully. "If she married Drayton, she was getting everything anyway. And from all accounts, not to mention the blinding piece of statuary on her finger, they *were* to be married."

"She might have preferred the money without the man. There was a considerable age difference. And Drayton wanted her daughters to move in as well, whereas Hadley's given me to understand that the last thing her mother wanted was to allow the girls anywhere near her love nest."

"All right. Then if she had the combination to the safe, why would she leave the letters behind? If she wanted to obscure Drayton's true identity, surely she wouldn't leave behind dozens of letters that address him as Dražen Krstić and accuse him of heinous crimes."

"That part might have been true. She might not have understood the letters." He met Rachel's gaze and caught himself. "No, you're right. It doesn't add up. She's a calculating woman, not a clever one. She may have seen the letters and the will — Brining said that Drayton retained his own copy, by the way. She may have known what Drayton was and simply not cared about anything except her own security. She wouldn't necessarily have understood that the letters posed a threat to her inheritance under the will, but Rachel — all this presupposes that Dražen Krstić was more likely to have been helped to his death by a mercenary woman than by the person who sent him the letters."

Rachel mulled this over, chewing at the end of her ponytail.

"You're saying that the likeliest answer —"

"Is that he was killed by a survivor of the massacre he perpetrated."

"A man fell to his death from the Bluffs," she mused.

"It can't be a coincidence. I just don't see it."

"Nor I," she agreed. "And Melanie's the type to prefer to have a man around, doting on her every whim. Maybe she didn't know about the will, despite what Charles Brining said. Maybe Drayton alive was her only guarantee of security."

"How long had Drayton been receiving the letters?"

Rachel spit out her hair. "Why? What does that matter?"

"We have to ask ourselves: why now? If the letters had been arriving for some time — months, even years, what precipitated Drayton's fall at this time? Was there a precipitating event? That's what we need to know."

"He's only lived on the Bluffs for two years, we know that much."

"Assuming that he'd been receiving the letters for the whole of that time, what does that tell us?"

"I'm not sure." An idea began to form in her mind as the significance of the dates stamped itself into her awareness

"Sir, there were two precipitating events, if you think about it." She knew he would only accept the first. She offered them both anyway. "One, the wedding was on the horizon. Drayton was about to marry Melanie Blessant, transferring himself and his money into her hands."

"Go on."

"Two, the museum's about to open. He wanted in. The board may have wanted his money, but they had no intention of renaming the project in his honor. Or of allowing him a greater say in directing the museum."

"Melanie marries Drayton, she gets the

money. Drayton dies, Melanie gets the money. In one scenario, Dennis Blessant is off the hook but has to wrangle over his girls. In the other, Melanie no longer wants the girls."

"You're thinking the *father* is a likelier suspect?" Why wasn't he looking at the museum?

"I'm not saying that." His tone was patient. "I'm simply running through all possibilities. I've no doubt at all that Drayton was Dražen Krstić. There are multiple scenarios here, but we can't ignore the letters. Whoever wrote them had a motive strong enough to have seen to Drayton's death." Rachel hesitated before she said softly, "I'm glad you see that, sir, because there's something else."

When he raised his eyebrows at her, she told him about the lilies.

23.

Verily God will not change the condition of a people until they change what is in themselves.

This driving around in the middle of the day was tiring, but at least the city traffic wasn't terrible. They were back at Drayton's garden. Khattak stood under the maple tree. The heads of the yellow lilies sagged toward him on their stalks. He brushed them lightly with his fingertips.

"I know what these are. Do you have your camera?"

She produced a small digital camera from her blazer pocket. He snapped several photos.

"If Drayton was as upset as the Osmonds claim, there's an excellent reason for it."

"He didn't like yellow?"

"This is the Bosnian lily, a native plant. It was a symbol on Bosnia's flag at the time of its independence from Yugoslavia. The coat of arms that bore the original fleur-de-lis is a much older symbol. It represents the arms of the Kotromanić family, who ruled Bosnia during the fourteenth and fifteenth centuries."

"So someone planted these to upset Drayton. To remind him of the war."

"And his role in it. Did the Osmonds say when the flowers first appeared?"

"No. Drayton thought Harry had planted them, but Aldo showed him the sketch for the landscape design. He said they'd never plant lilies in such deep shade."

"Drayton believed them?"

"That's what they said. Plus, they consulted with Drayton over every plant in the garden. They'd hardly throw in something as a surprise."

"You said the younger brother suffers from mental illness. Violent?"

"I don't know. Aldo Osmond was definitely not receptive to the idea of me questioning him. Harry's easily upset, but he seemed harmless to me."

"So what do we have? The letters, the lilies, the tattoo, the gun."

"He's Krstić," Rachel said. "I don't doubt it either."

"We need to pay another visit to the

Dzamija."

"You're planning to tell the imam?"

"I'm hoping there's something more he can tell us."

"You don't expect him to stay quiet, do you."

It wasn't a question. It was an observation that troubled Khattak at a personal level.

"I don't know that I could in his shoes. After what he's been through. Dražen Krstić, here? Living a peaceful, successful life? I don't know that I could stomach it."

"He's a spiritual man."

"He watched his friends and mentors murdered in Manjača. I don't know how spiritual anyone feels after such a thing."

"I don't know what faith has to say in answer to that," she said, after a moment.

"I've struggled with it, but I don't either."

She decided to forego any mention of lunch, caught by Khattak's somber mood. They drove to the mosque in silence, through back roads that bypassed the traffic building on the highways. She palmed a Mars bar from her bag and made quick work of it.

"I've another if you want," she mumbled around a mouthful of chocolate.

"I need to feed you better. Or at least let

you take a lunch break once in a while."

"That place at the marina was good."

"This is your neighborhood. What's here?"

"Popeye's Chicken? Spadina Garden? What are you in the mood for?"

"Those are a little out of the way. I have to drive to Ottawa tonight."

An awkward silence fell. Rachel wasn't slow to understand the reason for it. "If I lived on my own, I'd invite you over and whip something up for us." It wasn't that she couldn't cook. She just didn't like to.

"I'd like to meet your father one day."

That was Khattak. Clear and direct to a fault. He'd seen her discomfort, pinpointed its source, and spoken to its root. She cleared her throat, her skin suddenly clammy.

"It might not be the experience you're hoping for, sir."

"I don't think it will be as bad as you fear, Rachel. I've worked with some obdurate individuals at INSET."

She choked on her last bite of chocolate. "You know a little about my da, then."

He slid the car into an empty spot in the mosque's parking lot and gave her a friendly glance.

"Don Getty's reputation precedes him everywhere. He's enormously popular."

Except in his own home, she thought. Aloud she said, "That's good to know. Maybe another time, then. We're here now."

But there would never be another time. She would make sure of it.

This time they were directed to the slightly shaggy lawn behind the mosque where Imam Muharrem strolled back and forth beneath an avenue of mulberries. He was dressed more casually today, a thin white sweater adding warmth to his robes.

A group of children scampered over the lawn in search of a soccer ball, their ages ranging from five to fifteen. Their playful laughter filled the air, as a particularly determined little girl kicked at the older boys' knees. Rachel smiled. Any girl who fought the odds, convinced that she could win, reminded her of herself.

Although the imam's welcome was warm, a wariness darkened his eyes. "You are back, my friends. With news I hope."

Khattak ran through the information they had gathered so far, giving the imam time to absorb it. His gaze brooded over the children at play, following the progress of the soccer ball.

"He has the tattoo?"

"He has it, but I caution you that it was a

common symbol among the paramilitaries."

"Krstić was not a paramilitary. He was Chief of Security of the Drina Corps. He was General Radislav Krstić's direct subordinate. You know what they say about Lieutenant Colonel Krstić, don't you?"

"I'm afraid I don't," Khattak said.

"I've spoken with some of the survivors since your last visit. I've asked about this man. They told me the same thing: Krstić was everywhere during the murders. He arranged the logistics, he oversaw the executions."

Khattak waited. "Yes, I'm sorry. I did know that."

"Then perhaps you will tell me what you are waiting for. There should be an announcement to the community, to the country. There must be an accounting of what Krstić was doing in this country. How he arrived here."

"I promise you that all those things will be arranged once Krstić's identity is confirmed. We cannot confirm it through physical evidence — we simply don't have any. We're following his paper trail, his money. I can assure you of one thing, though: he did not come into this country as Dražen Krstić. He was already Christopher Drayton when he arrived here."

The imam came to a halt near the shaded entrance to the back of the mosque. A few of the older children had opted out of their game to watch him. He waved them off with a faded smile.

"He fooled your government, this means."

"I think he fooled a lot of people, sir." Rachel tugged on the lapels of her blazer. "I doubt that anyone who knew him then would recognize him now."

"Should we not test this? We can arrange for people who saw him in Srebrenica to identify him. Not just from our neighborhood but from many cities in America: St. Louis, Chicago, Des Moines. We can set this matter to rest."

Khattak hesitated, his movements ill at ease. "I'm afraid that wouldn't settle it, sir. Given the amount of time that's elapsed. They would say that memory alone cannot be trusted."

The imam's lips tightened. "And when memory is all we have? They took everything else. Our papers, our homes, our cities, our loved ones. They even robbed the dead of their teeth."

His words made Rachel think of a line she had read in the letters.

They stripped us of everything. There was no kindness, no decency.

She wondered what Khattak could possibly say to alleviate the other man's anger.

"You insult us, Inspector. The truth is terrible enough. We have no reason to manufacture lies about the horrors my people suffered."

"I know that, believe me I do. I'm not saying that identification wouldn't help. I'm saying we must follow every possible lead until we are certain of Krstić's identity beyond a doubt. Wouldn't you prefer it that way?"

The little girl kicked the ball straight at the imam. He caught it with a deft movement and tossed it back to her, his face grave.

"It would give many people peace to know that Krstić is dead."

"For that peace to be real, they would need to know that Drayton really was Krstić. All I'm asking you for is a little more time. I'm heading to the Department of Justice this afternoon. I should be able to tell you much more once I've had that meeting."

Imam Muharrem studied him.

"So you will be the truth-bearer, Inspector Esa. You will tell your masters what they do not wish to hear, insist to them on the truth of what you've learned. And they will

309

say to you, Inspector, 'How can you trust the memory of these Bosnians? A people too weak to save themselves. We owe them nothing. Let us preserve our silence.' "

"Imam Muharrem —"

"Can you deny it? Was Srebrenica not the worst hour of so many Western governments?"

"The Canadian battalion wasn't in Srebrenica in 1995, sir. And while they were there, they lived on combat rations as an act of solidarity with your people." Rachel had done her research but she didn't know what made her say this; perhaps a flicker of deep-seated shame.

The imam took her up on it. "The Canadian battalion was evacuated at the insistence of your government. Unlike my people, who could not be evacuated and were left behind to be murdered. I'm afraid a ration of two beers a day is not my definition of solidarity, Sergeant. We experienced the same pressures as your commander in Srebrenica, but we did not share his relief from it." He shook his head. "Canbat or Dutchbat, it would have made no difference. The outcome would have been the same. What does it matter to the mothers of Srebrenica if entire governments resign? Will that bring back the dead?"

"Sir —"

"You do what you must, Inspector. I will do the same." He saw their expressions and added, "I do not mean that as a threat. I will wait to see what your government does. I think this will make you unpopular, Inspector Esa. If you expose your government, you may not reach the heights you were otherwise destined for. Your Community Policing may fail before it has a chance to begin."

Khattak slid his hands into his trouser pockets, the gesture unforced. "Please let me worry about that, Imam Muharrem. We cannot possibly fail you twice."

It was a kind thing to say, Rachel supposed, words that reassured the imam but did nothing to dispel her own anxiety. She couldn't quash the feeling that Khattak was far more invested in the outcome of this case than he was prepared to concede. If he'd been brave enough to join a student humanitarian mission, his conscience should be clear. Why did he bear the burdens of Bosnia so personally?

She admitted she didn't know what a person who subscribed to the same faith might feel. The bonds of religious solidarity? A call to action? A sense of failure?

Guilt? Shame? How far did the bonds of this dimension of identity extend? What did faith demand in this instance? Maybe Khattak's recollections of a city under siege were what drove him repeatedly to the golden idyll of Andalusia, to Mink Norman and her museum.

Her steps heavy, she trudged behind Khattak through the narrow passageway that led to the mosque's front door. Both sides of the hall were lined with group photographs that depicted community activities. Cookouts, picnics, basketball tournaments, children's races. A few were the solemnly arranged groups of board members and clerical advisory committees, identified by name but not by date. One of these dominated the others in a massive black frame cropped by a velvet mat. Six men in poses of varying seriousness were gathered before the mosque's *mihrab.* One was a man she recognized.

She tugged at Khattak's jacket.

"Sir," she said. "Isn't that David Newhall?"

24.

We heard it on the radio. They will send the airplanes now. They will save us now.

They were pushing and pounding him from every direction, asking questions he couldn't answer. He didn't have time to take stock of their desperation when the same feeling was oozing from his pores.

It was hot. God of the heavens and earth, it was hot. His neck and hands were slippery with sweat, the shirt he hadn't changed in three days was soaked through. He reeked like a wild animal and he was hungry. There wasn't a scrap of food within three square miles, not a drop of water to spare.

The sky had shriveled, hanging over them like a judgment, corrosive and dull.

The whole place was a rathole.

He didn't care about any of that. All he cared about in a rapidly shrinking world was four irrefutable realities. His mother, father, brother, and brother.

Was it twenty thousand people or thirty?

It felt like every person he had ever met in his life was here, every grandmother who had touched his hair, every girl he had flirted with in high school, every officer who had rotated in and out of this open jail. Yet each face had changed, condensed into a pair of terrified eyes and desiccated lips.

Everyone was carrying something, everyone was searching for someone.

He couldn't help.

Even if he found someone he could use his translation skills on, there was nothing to say.

Today he had only one message to communicate, and he would sound it out over and over again, even if he had to wend his way through every last corridor of this concrete maze, breaking every window the mortars hadn't exploded. Even if he had to crawl over every single body jammed behind the gates that obliterated the name of the battalion stationed there.

He would find the major, take his gun and kill him if he had to.

Today, there was only one truth, one order that mattered. One thought that hammered him through the stench, the cries, the incremental terror.

His family was not leaving this base.

■ ■ ■ ■

He heard a stranger's moan. "I'm not going to any safe place. The Serbs are going to take me."

From every direction he heard similar cries.

Noise. Chaos. Terror. Misery. Four words that now made up his world.

They had closed the gate. They had sealed the hole in the fence. What did the Dutch know that he didn't? There were some five or six thousand people inside the base, but how many more had been left outside? Fifteen thousand? Twenty? Where would those people go? What would they do when the enemy came?

He knew what the gate was. It was a dividing line between those who would live and those who would die. Inside the base was life. Outside, death.

He shoved his family forward. His mother complained and he pushed her harder. They had to get away from the gate. They had to push their way inside as far as the soldiers would let them. If he had to step on other people, if he had to crawl over their bodies he would. You didn't manage three and a half years without running water, electricity, or a steady supply of food just to give it all up at the end. He was valuable. He wasn't going anywhere. And neither was his family.

He expected bad things to happen. He had always expected them: the first shot fired in the war, the first mortar launched at Sarajevo, the first village burned and looted in the east, corpses piled high beside the rubble of the mosque.

Bad things had happened. Worse things were coming. The base was the only safety there was.

The Dutch were the only protection they had, the thin blue-helmeted line between survival and mass murder. He didn't care about the graffiti that marked their compound, adding insult to injury. He didn't care about the lies they had told him up to this very moment. He didn't care about anything except what their blue and white flag represented.

Safety. Survival. The chance to weather the siege for just another day.

He wouldn't think about the faces on the other side of the gate. He wouldn't think about the panic or the hopelessness in their eyes.

Noise. Chaos. Terror. Misery.

That was all there was. That's what he wouldn't think about.

He realized they'd reached the endpoint, his small desk just outside the major's office. He gave the chair to his mother and placed his youngest brother on the desk. Ahmo was a small, wiry thirteen. Malnourished and terrified but trying to hide it.

They were getting to the place where no one could hide anything anymore.

His father and his other brother, Mesha, paced nervously at the door. He knew they wanted cigarettes. He wanted one himself, the way he wanted other things. Water from the tap. A phone call to his girlfriend. An acre full of livestock.

Bread and circuses.

Nothing mattered except survival.

Mother, father, Ahmo and Mesha.

That was it.

The major came. He looked harried and angry. Preoccupied with his orders. Whatever he'd been expecting, it hadn't been this onslaught of refugees. Thirty thousand people at Potočari. Thousands and thousands outside the gate.

He could feel the sweat on his skin, taste the panic on his tongue.

"We waited all night," he said. "Where are the planes? The safe area is under attack. Srebrenica will fall."

The major ignored him, as he'd known he would. He was searching his office for something that didn't take him long to find. A

317

megaphone. He handed it to Damir, his eyes skirting over his family.

"What's this for? What do you expect me to do?"

"We pay you to translate. So translate."

"We waited all night. Where are the planes?"

The major was sweating too, he saw.

"Tell the people they must leave the base. Tell them now, Damir. This is UN property."

"UN property?" He spat out the words. "Do you think we care if this is UN property? Do you understand what's waiting on the other side of the gate?"

"Tell them. They must leave in groups of five. They must leave now. We can't have the Serbs see them as provocation."

"Provocation? They see us as fodder. They see bodies, dead bodies. Fields and fields full of them. Are you crazy?" he demanded. "This base is the only thing keeping these people alive."

His voice ratcheted out of control. He could hear himself raving like a madman, spittle flying from his lips. The major backed away in distaste.

"Don't make me call my men, Damir. Tell the people to leave the base at once. Five at a time. Everyone must go."

"Now you want to call them? Now? Why don't you tell your men to guard the gate?

Why don't you tell them to help the people come in? Why did you seal the fence?"

"Procedure."

Damir threw away the megaphone. "Your procedure will see us dead and buried in the ground. No, not in the ground. They'll shoot us where we stand and leave our bodies to rot. Have you seen what's happening at the gate? Have you?"

The major avoided his eyes. "If you won't translate, you have no purpose here."

"I work for you!" Damir screamed. "I've worked for you through this whole bloody mess, translating your lies, making your lives easier. You expect me to tell my people to march out the gate to their deaths? They're separating the men and women at the gate. They've taken the men. Do you know what that means?"

"They are screening for war crimes, that's all. There will be a prisoner exchange."

"Are you mad? Demented? Didn't you hear Mladić? He said we would have blood up to our knees. What do you think they're doing with the men? And not just the men but the boys? What do you think, Major? How many lies will you tell us?"

The major grabbed the megaphone and forced it back into his hand. "If you won't translate my instructions, someone else will.

But you'll have to leave. You're all going." He pointed at Damir's father. "He can stay. Your father is a negotiator. He can stay with you on the base. Everyone else must go."

He now knew that terror had a color. A red as bright and immersive as blood. "What about my mother? What about my brothers? If they go to the gate, they're as good as dead."

"Everyone must go. No one has permission to stay on the base."

"They're not going. I won't let you take them."

There was no door that protected his small workspace. If there had been, he would have barricaded his family inside.

His father could see what was happening. And Mesha. He was nineteen. He didn't speak English but he could see what was coming, plain as day.

"Tell your family what I've told you." The major's voice was implacable.

All these months of indecision, and now at last the major had found his resolve.

"What is it? What's happening?"

He started to cry. There was nowhere else for his panic to go but tears. And when he started, Ahmo did as well. Huge, gulping sobs.

"You can stay, Father," he managed. "He says you can stay but no one else."

Mesha swore at him.

His father and mother stared at him without answer.

"They are making everyone leave the base. All of us. Except for the negotiators." He gestured at his father. "And those who work here."

"Negotiators — what a joke. We never had any power to negotiate. What are we negotiating? The manner of our death?"

At his brother's words, his mother began to cry.

His father pointed behind him. "I won't stay without Ahmo and Mesha. I won't let the Chetniks take them."

He turned to find that from among the crowded corridors of the base, the major had summoned three of his soldiers and three of the military observers, weapons at the ready.

"What in hell are you doing?"

"Your family will show the others. Tell them to leave."

Mesha rolled forward on his feet. Damir blocked him with an arm across his chest.

"Listen to me, Major, please! Don't make them go out there. Let them stay with me on the base! They won't take up any room. They don't need any rations. I won't tell anyone. Just let them stay. Let them stay, I beg you."

His tears rained thick and fast, blurring his glasses.

"I've said your father can stay."

"He won't stay without my brothers," he shouted. "Can't you see what you're doing?"

"That's his choice. He doesn't have to stay if he doesn't want to. But General Mladić knows who he is."

"I know that! Do you think I don't know that? Please, Major!" His voice tore in his throat. He saw the decision in their faces, the inexorable reality. There was no weakening of the major's voice.

"Please, Major, just my brothers. Just Ahmo and Mesha. Don't send them to the gate. You know what's waiting on the other side of the gate."

The major turned away, nodding at his men. Damir latched on to his arm with desperate strength.

"Stop begging these bastards for me! I don't need you to beg for my life," Mesha said.

He swore at his brother over his shoulder. "Please, Major. This is all the family I have. I beg you, let them stay."

"Take them out."

The soldiers began to shepherd his family through the crowd.

He followed along, desperate, hysterical.

"Please. Just Ahmo then, just Ahmo. He's

only a boy. He's only thirteen."

"Don't worry," one of the observers said to him. "They're not separating children."

"They are. Please. I know they are. Please. Leave Ahmo. Let Ahmo stay. I beg you. I'll give you anything. I'll do anything. I'll tell all these people to go. Just leave Ahmo."

They marched ahead without answering. His family trailed between them, a tiny rivulet dwarfed by mountains.

His father stopped for a moment, turned back.

"Please, Father, stay," he whispered. "Stay with me."

"I cannot leave your brothers. I must protect them from our enemies. You stay, Damir. You stay and look for us when you can. Look for us in Tuzla."

He saw death in his father's eyes. There would be no Tuzla.

For the thousands of men on the other side of the gate, there would be no Tuzla.

He knew at last what he must do.

"Wait!" He hurried along beside them, elbowing the same people he had treated so shamefully in his rush to reach safety. "If they won't let you stay, I'm coming with you. We'll go together."

His father's eyes were kind, so kind.

"You stay here, Damir. You'll be safe and I will know you are safe. Stay."

"I'm coming."

He'd known this day would come.

Cities falling, villages burning. Rape. Torture. Madness. Death.

This last day in Srebrenica had been inevitable from the beginning.

His right hand grasped Ahmo's. His arm brushed Mesha's.

Whatever happened, he would be with them. The last faces he saw would be theirs.

Three years in frantic pursuit of survival would end here.

Mesha took his arm.

"You are not coming."

"I am not staying."

"You are staying on the base," his brother screamed into his face. "You are staying because you *can* stay, that's the end to it!"

"I won't!" he screamed back.

"You will. You are."

He shoved Mesha aside. Mesha grabbed him by the neck and punched him in the face.

He fell back, stunned.

"Mesha!"

"You stay," his brother sobbed. "I will take care of Ahmo and our parents. You stay because you *can* stay." Mesha pulled him close, wrapped his arms about his neck, kissed his cheeks. He felt the hot wet slide of his brother's tears. "You live," he told Damir. "You live and you remember."

The soldiers pressed them forward.

He watched their silhouettes recede into the crush.

He looked down to find the megaphone in his hand.

25.

30 Dutch = 30,000 Muslims.

Khattak met Tom Paley at Café Morala on Bank Street. He'd wanted to meet at Justice, but Tom had sidestepped him. Instead, he'd suggested a place away from his colleagues at War Crimes, this café with its bohemian vibe and sinful Mayan hot chocolate. The proprietor's homemade black bean panini was legendary.

Khattak wasn't in the mood to eat. He ordered a strong cup of coffee and waited for Tom in the café's sunny interior. His friend, when he came, looked as disquieted as Khattak felt. He ordered the panini from the menu and a small bag of alfajor Argentino cookies to go with his hot chocolate.

"Everything here's homemade. You should try the cookies. They're out of this world."

Khattak studied his friend's face. He'd always thought of Tom as a comfortable man, energetic but running to fat, with a shiny pink skull and an absentminded manner that fooled no one. His knowledge of his field was encyclopedic, his reputation international.

"We've a mess here, Tom. I hope you've found something."

"Immigration status." Tom bit deeply into his panini, its melted cheese scouring his chin. He dabbed at it with his napkin. "He came as an investor with the requisite funds tied up for a five-year period. He landed as an Italian citizen with documents to suggest he was the son of ex-pat Americans who made their home there."

"What do we know about the documents?"

"We've requested them. Immigration does its own check, as you know. Police clearances, provenance of funds. He ran textile factories in Italy to substantial profit. Based on his records, they thought the money was clean. We'll need to dig deeper now. The fact that they didn't means the passport forgery must have been first rate."

"He's had seventeen years to learn a new trade," Khattak said bitterly. "Easy enough to erase traces of a past life. What brought him here, I wonder?"

"Too many old associates in Italy, most

likely. Too many people apt to recognize him or come calling for a share of the company's profits."

"Krstić wasn't the kind of man most people would dare to blackmail."

"The Drina Corps and the paramilitaries aren't what you'd call most people. Blackmail would be nothing to them. Krstić worked hard. He was a success. Most people don't and aren't, but they're happy to hitch a ride on someone else's coattails."

"This is all speculation on your part."

"True."

"He may have had personal reasons for moving to Canada."

"He hasn't been here long. Three years. Two at the present address, buried away at the edge of Scarborough. We haven't been able to trace any personal connections."

"Scarborough's not that remote. He's been keeping company with Nathan Clare. Although —" Khattak paused as he sifted through the facts he'd learned about Drayton's plans to marry Melanie Blessant. "His fiancée did point out that he was loath to sit for a well-known photographer. He may consciously have been attempting to shelter his new identity. Where was he for the first year?"

"Manitoba. What about this museum

you've told me of? Wouldn't that raise his profile?"

Khattak sampled one of the cookies. It melted into his coffee, changing its flavor.

"It would have. If people were to associate a much older, much heavier man by the name of Christopher Drayton with a fugitive named Dražen Krstić. His contacts at the museum would have been limited to the intelligentsia."

"Then why not the wedding photos?"

"Maybe he was more afraid of local publicity. Krstić must have known there's a fairly significant Bosnian community in the city. He may have viewed a portrait in the wedding section of the paper as a danger to himself. Tom, I have to ask this. Why did you ignore the letters you were sent about Krstić?"

Tom finished his sandwich and turned his attention to the trio of teenage girls that spilled through the café's door into its warm interior. They jostled each other for seats, draping their handbags over wooden chairs before lining up in front of the chalkboard menu. They were pretty and lively; for a moment, everyone in the café stopped to watch them make their selections.

Tom sighed. "You know how this kind of work is, Esa. You've been in intelligence.

329

You collect so much information, it takes time to sort through it all. We're understaffed, underbudgeted — I can't keep up with my correspondence. This didn't ring any bells. Typed letters in the mail. No prints, no DNA. No reason to think it was anything more than someone trying to work through their personal pain by casting about for answers. The letters were accusations, nothing more. There were no photographs, no proof. In time, I would have asked someone to do a little digging. The last letter made it a bit more urgent. It said that Krstić was dead."

"So you called me."

"I called you." Tom lingered over his chocolate-soaked cookies. "Because I could call you. Because your unit exists, and I couldn't think of anyone more closely connected who would know what to do with the information. And because that last letter worried me."

"Why?"

"It said: 'Krstić is dead. Everything is finished. I don't need you anymore.' And then the letters stopped. In my experience, when someone has a pathology, that doesn't happen. It made me wonder."

"You must have wondered before that."

Again, Tom sighed. "What do you want

330

me to say? Sometimes we miss things. Can you say with certainty that Drayton is Krstić?"

"Come on, Tom. The tattoo and the gun make it certain. And you'll have used facial recognition on the photograph I had the morgue send you."

"Esa, this will be a terrible embarrassment for the government. For me, more than anyone." His evasion answered Khattak more effectively than an open admission would have. "Immigration at least did their due diligence. They only have so many resources."

"And the investment of half a million dollars may have dampened their enthusiasm for a more rigorous examination of Drayton's credentials."

"I don't think so, Esa. They've sent me everything they have. They didn't miss a single step. Drayton went to a lot of trouble to cover up his tracks."

Khattak wished he could feel more for his friend. He had other worries, other priorities. The teenage girls had taken the table beside them and chatted to each other noisily. He lowered his voice.

"Make the same arguments that Immigration will. Your resources were limited. The letter writer offered no proof, not even a photograph. If your letters are anything like ours, it was difficult to pinpoint the source of the writer's information. You can't be held accountable for that, Tom. What will matter is how swiftly you resolved things upon learning of Drayton's death. You called me right away. Based upon my findings, you've made major strides investigating Drayton's background. You've matched the photo. You know Drayton is Krstić."

Tom looked over at the table of girls wistfully.

"Yes. It is Krstić. And we'll have to announce it, and there could be hearings. Someone's job on the line. Maybe mine."

"Never yours, Tom. Not with your reputation. And frankly, shouldn't we be more concerned about the Bosnian community?"

Tom studied him as if seeing Khattak for the first time. "That is your remit," he agreed.

"My God, Tom! There's a limit to objectivity. Krstić was ubiquitous at the execution sites. He's knee-deep in blood."

"I'm not denying that, Esa. And I'm not asking you to do anything you shouldn't. All I need is a heads-up. If you're worried about the Bosnians, isn't it best that we coordinate our response? Or is something else bothering you?"

Khattak looked over at the table beside them in time to see the girl with long, blond braids widen her eyes at him.

"The letter writer worries me," Khattak said. "*Krstić is dead. I don't need you anymore.* Why? Because the letter writer killed him when the government wouldn't act?"

"Christ, are you laying that at my door?"

"Of course not. If he was killed by one of his victims, we have a much bigger problem on our hands. A trial, a scandal, the evacuation of Canbat revisited. All of that and more."

"There's something you're not telling me."

"Drayton wanted to get on the board of the museum, Ringsong. His presence was strongly objected to by one of the directors, a neighbor of Drayton's. I interviewed him during the course of the investigation. His name is David Newhall."

"So?"

"I was at the Bosnian mosque in Etobicoke yesterday. My sergeant found David Newhall's photo hanging there."

"What? Why?"

"Because his real name is Damir Hasanović."

The girls beside them forgotten, Tom stared at him, aghast. *"Damir Hasanović?"* he whispered.

"Exactly," Khattak said. "The translator at the UN base in Potočari. Dutchbat gave him refuge on the base. That's why he survived the Srebrenica massacre."

"It can't be."

"If you check with your friends at Immigration, I think you'll find he came here as a refugee."

The blond girl brushed her leg against his. She apologized brightly. He ignored it.

"That's not all. I think Newhall is the man who sent the letters to you and to Drayton."

"And Drayton is dead."

"Which means Dražen Krstić is dead."

"Damn," Tom muttered. "Goddamn it all."

"I think that sums it up."

"You need to interview him again."

"I plan to. Rachel's looking into his background. With CPS resources."

The two men weighed each other.

"But you'll let me know whatever you find."

"I won't forget that you asked me to investigate, Tom. Of course, I owe you that. I've a long drive back tonight. I'll call you with any news."

"It was good of you to do this for me."

Khattak's answering smile was brief. "I think you know I did it for myself."

26.

*It was a crime committed against every
single one of us.*

Rachel was surprised to find her parents sitting together in the family room, a program
on the television that her mother particularly favored. Her father wasn't napping,
nor was there a beer on the coffee table in
front of him.

"Hey, Da," she said, tossing her keys on
the console in the tiny dark foyer. Winterglass, this was not.

"Where've you been then, girl?" he said in
response.

She debated telling him. Sometimes hearing about Khattak made her father ballistic:
he still thought of her boss as a politically
correct, affirmative-action appointee to a
unit whose purpose he'd once described as
barefaced boot-licking. Once or twice,
they'd been able to discuss the finer points

of an investigation without it ending in tears or slammed doors or a shattered beer mug or two.

She brushed off her weariness and came to sit beside Don Getty. One part of her mind observed her mother's leery glance.

"Mostly up in Scarborough. Trying to figure out if some guy fell from the Bluffs or was pushed."

"The Bluffs, eh. You go by the marina?"

"I did, Da."

Her father was still a handsome man with bullet-gray eyes and a head full of thick white hair that stood on end when brushed. His jowls and neck were thicker because of the drinking, but his bearing was otherwise compact and upright. She had noticed more and more of late that his eyes were more likely to be alert than blurred by booze.

"Rachel," her mother intervened softly. "You shouldn't talk about the marina. You know how your Da is."

She hadn't mentioned the marina. Her father had. She wondered what had made her mother say it with that gently martyred air of hers.

The years had not worn well on Lillian Getty. Her wardrobe rotated through a series of faded-print dresses with full skirts and fitted tops. Occasionally, her lips would be smeared with a coral shade of lipstick that emphasized their thinness. Her dark eyes and lifeless hair were the same as Rachel's own. In Lillian's case, a permanent treatment had transformed it into a gauzy cloud about her head.

"Da likes the marina," she said to her mother. "He always has. He used to take me and Zach all the time."

She rarely mentioned her brother. She still hadn't told either of her parents that she'd found him. Over the past few days, she'd brought up his name in one innocuous context or another to test their reaction. For the most part, her father had ignored her. Her mother, however, had darted anxious glances at her, opening her mouth to speak before changing her mind.

"I did, girl, you remember that?"

Rachel patted her father's hand, another rare gesture.

" 'Course. You taught Zach everything there was to know about boats. Sorry the water wasn't my natural element."

"Seasick. That's what you were. But you were a fine swimmer, Rach. Built like one of those East German girls."

She didn't bother to correct him. In his day, there had been an East Germany, and Don Getty hated to acknowledge change.

338

"Thanks, Da. It's helped me with hockey too."

"Strong shoulders. Nothing wrong with that. Don't let any man tell you otherwise."

"You know our Rachel doesn't date, Don."

It was another subtle put-down. A contradiction for its own sake, intended to annoy her father with little thought to Rachel's feelings. She'd never noticed this about her mother before. But then she'd been blind to her mother's seven-year secret.

"I would if the right guy asked me, Mum. I've met someone, actually."

Her father grinned at her. He wasn't used to her defiance of her mother. He was taking his own small pleasure in it. Christ, but her parents were messed up.

"Good-looker? Cop? Got some heft on him?"

"Be realistic, dear. Rachel has to take what she can get."

She'd been making it up, some hazy thought of Nate in her mind, but now she felt furious. What kind of mother said something like that to her daughter? In that moment, the meek and mild Lillian Getty reminded her of Melanie Blessant.

"I don't, actually, Mum. He's great-looking. And tough, Da. And smart as hell."

"You sure he's real?" Her father slapped

her knee with a laugh. It was the big, blustery laugh she remembered from scarce moments during her childhood. It made her smile.

"I've pinched myself, I can tell you." She eased out of her blazer, folded it across her knees. "It's not serious. We've only just met. I'll let you know how it goes."

"How about some dinner then for our girl?" He narrowed his eyes at his wife. "You've been sitting there for hours doing nothing but turning pages."

Lillian coughed. "I did try to be quiet, dear. For Rachel? I don't think . . . I didn't make enough. She's usually not home."

Rachel was used to this. She lived under her parents' roof but was otherwise completely self-reliant. She took most of her meals on her way to or from a pickup game. She could see her father was getting angry. Best to defuse the situation at once.

"It's good, Da. I've got a game to get ready for and then I'll grab a bite. You know you can't load up on carbs right before a game."

"I know you would if you had a choice." He glared at his wife who held up her hands in dismay. Helpless, useless Lillian Getty. Or had that always been Rachel's own delusion? Had she missed the steely core that had allowed her mother to shield the only relationship whose loss she still grieved?

"Honestly, I'm okay. Thank you, though."

"You don't need to thank your father for watching out for you," Lillian snapped.

Rachel raised her eyebrows. What was this little game of her mother's? She had seen Lillian through the lens of helpless anger for so long that she'd assumed her mother possessed no agency of her own. She was Don Getty's passive foil, her moods conditioned by her husband's rage.

This wasn't the same woman, with her careful jabs and her sly taunts at Rachel.

This was a woman fully equipped to keep a devastating secret, playing some twisted game of revenge against her husband with no regard for the fact of Rachel's loneliness and guilt.

Was she nothing to either of them? Had Zach been everything?

Her mouth turned down. It was enough to know she had caused her mother's pain. It was too much to accept that her mother might wish to hurt her in turn.

Maybe the only way forward was to talk about Zach — to bring her brother out in the open.

"There's something I've been meaning to tell you, Da, about Zach."

"Rachel!" Her mother's voice shook the small room. "I've told you again and again not to upset your father."

It was true. It was the constant refrain of their childhood.

Children, hush. You're disturbing your father.

She must have had reasons that Rachel hadn't known, and still didn't know to this day.

Don Getty scowled at his wife but he stayed in his seat. "Let the girl talk. She's got something on her mind. You've been looking for the boy, I know. I've seen the posters."

Rachel swallowed. It was a day of sea changes, she thought. Before this moment, her father hadn't mentioned Zach in seven years.

"You've found him then."

Tears pricked at her eyes, muffled her throat.

"I didn't know you knew. That I'd been looking, I mean."

"Ah, girl. I'm not much use as a father but I know when my girl's upset. I know why, too."

It was the drink, she realized. Without the veil of alcohol between them, she could see her father as clearly and acutely as he was seeing her.

"Tell me then, Rach."

"She has nothing to tell. It's nothing but foolishness."

The television blared commercials in the background. She heard the anxiety ring clear as a bell in her mother's voice. And made the decision to continue.

"I've been looking and I found him. He's a student at university. A friend of mine recognized his name."

"University."

"Yes." Rachel gave him a tremulous smile. "He's a year from graduating, Da. He's studying art. He'll be going to Europe soon." She held her breath for the last part, afraid of his reaction.

Her mother stood up, her hands shaking. "You're lying," she breathed.

Rachel turned on her.

"You know I'm not, Mum. You *know* I'm not."

Her father disregarded this. His breath came out of his strongly built body in a collapsing whoosh of air. His shoulders sagged. He reached for the remote to shut off the sound from the television.

"He's well, then? My boy's well? He's happy?"

It was the last reaction she'd expected from him.

"Yeah," she said. "He's doing really well. He's not in any trouble or anything. He's really smart. He's standing on his own feet."

Her father turned his face away from her. She could see that his throat was working, choking on words.

"I'd tell you more if I could, I've only just seen him. I don't know very much. Shall I tell you if I see him again?"

Without speaking, he nodded his head.

She stood up, not knowing what else to say, and met her mother's gaze. All the fuzziness and weakness of will she'd associated with her mother evaporated under that gaze. What she saw was a woman, wretched and determined. For a moment, she couldn't speak.

Nothing made sense.

No one made sense.

She grasped at her game like a lifeline. "I'd better go up and change."

Her father brushed a hand over his eyes. He straightened his shoulders and turned the television back on. "You get ready, girl. I'll take you. It's been a while since I've seen you play. Left wing, aren't you?"

"That's right, Da. Are you sure?"

"Sure as sure."

As she turned to the stairs, she caught sight of her mother's reflection in the mirror above the console.

She mouthed six words at Rachel, each as clear as daylight.

You don't know what you've done.

Shocked, Rachel flew up the stairs to her room.

27.

When I close my eyes, I don't see the men.

In fourteen days, Srebrenica will be gone.

Rachel parked in the driveway of the blue and white house at the corner of Sloley Road and Lyme Regis. It was a plain two-story with a double garage, its shutters painted periwinkle blue, its white siding crisp and fresh. The maple that bordered the sidewalk was still aglow with autumn loveliness. The lawn was covered with un-raked leaves.

A wreath hung above the letter slot on a plain blue door.

She paced the sidewalk waiting for Khat-tak. Dec and Gaffney had compiled a first run of background information on David Newhall for her; the house on Lyme Regis belonged to him.

She considered its geography off Cathedral Bluffs. Here was another neighbor of Drayton's. A neighbor of Winterglass and Ringsong. The house was a little further back from the escarpment. A neighborhood or two away from Melanie Blessant. A small stage for the actors of this drama. Significant? She couldn't tell.

David Newhall was a legal name change, unlike Christopher Drayton's alias.

She understood now that Newhall's clipped manner of speaking had been an attempt to mask his accent. He'd come to Canada just after the fall of Srebrenica, legally, as a Convention refugee. He'd changed his name two years ago. Around the same time he'd moved into this neighborhood. Before that, he'd lived alone in a small apartment not far from the mosque.

If their last visit with Imam Muharrem hadn't ended on such bad terms, she would have sat him down for a lengthy discussion on the true identity of David Newhall.

Masks, she thought. First Drayton, then Newhall.

It struck her that in the short time since she'd met Nathan Clare, whom she viewed as a touchstone, she'd been the audience to a pantomime. Players moving together and apart in a complex orchestration.

That was one thing she'd learned from

studying Damir Hasanović's file.

Newhall was the one who'd sent the letters.

She gave a slight wave as Khattak pulled up on the driveway beside her. They'd talked on the phone in the morning. She'd given her report on Newhall, he'd told her what Justice had found. Justice had a statement prepared. They were holding off on the announcement until Khattak's investigation turned up a result.

Time was definitely not on their side.

If Drayton had been pushed, she hardly expected Newhall to own up to it.

If he *had* assisted Drayton to his death, sent the letters, planted the lilies, she couldn't say she blamed him. Newhall's account of survival was harrowing, his losses inestimable.

When the Serbs took Srebrenica, they wiped from the earth three generations of men.

She envisioned grandfathers, grandchildren. Rows upon rows of exiguous green coffins, wept over by the wretched. The resting place of the men of Srebrenica.

The unquiet dead and those who mourned them.

How had she become one of them?

Her Da had always said of her that her

problem wasn't that she thought too much. Her problem was that she felt too much.

As well as she could, she understood Newhall's anger, his terse dismissal. He'd not only had something to hide — he'd had to suppress his tragedy in its entirety.

The young boys were crying out for their parents, the fathers for their sons. But there was no help.

She understood the letters with perfect clarity now, the chronicle of the fate of Newhall's family. Zach had been resurrected after seven pitiless years. Newhall held no such hope.

"This doesn't feel right, sir."

"I know, Rachel, but we need to see this through."

He moved to the door and rang the bell, his elongated shadow falling across the lawn. Rachel's steps crunched over the leaves.

When Newhall opened the door, she had the same impression of jittery energy as before. He ushered them into a parlor with the jumpy movements of a cat, nervy and quick-jawed. The room was simply furnished with a white chesterfield and a pair of suede armchairs placed beneath two windows. Late-afternoon light threw shadows upon a worn Turkish rug with a geometric pattern. Newhall took a seat in the corner that left him in darkness. He didn't offer refreshments.

He focused on Rachel.

"Have you learned anything?"

This time she caught it. The hint of a foreign pattern of speech: she would have guessed it as Russian.

"We've learned a great deal, sir. We know who you are, for example."

He straightened in his seat. Beyond his shoulder, she glimpsed a dining table piled high with stacks of file folders.

"What do you mean? I've told you who I am."

"Your name is Damir Hasanović, isn't it?"

"If you look at my driver's license, you will see my name is David Newhall."

"You're denying it, then?"

"There is nothing to deny. It was a perfectly legal name change." He leaned forward and placed his hands on his knees, composed and at ease.

He'd been waiting for this moment, she realized. Anticipating the confrontation.

Khattak spoke. "Mr. Hasanović, you changed your name to Newhall two years ago. Why?"

"It was a fad. It seemed to be going around."

Rachel sucked in a breath. "Then you knew about Drayton."

"Christopher Drayton, Dražen Krstić. I knew the moment I first laid eyes on him. So?"

"When was that, sir?"

"At Clare's house. Two years ago. Before I moved here."

"And why did you move here?"

He shrugged. "I like the Bluffs. I like to walk along the escarpment." He threw down the words like a challenge.

"Did you ever confront Mr. Drayton with your knowledge?"

"I did not. Next question."

"Why not?"

"I thought there were other avenues. As a Canadian, I imagined I might have some recourse to justice." He stressed the last word.

"You sent the letters to War Crimes," Rachel concluded.

"Yes. Nothing came of it."

"Yet you never accused Drayton directly."

"I did not wish to precipitate his flight."

"He might have fled if he'd known who you were."

He flashed them a wolf's smile, his teeth small and dangerous. "It was one of the wonders of Potočari. Thousands of people desperate for security. How could Krstić notice them all the way we noticed him? He had no reason to know me. We'd never met."

"But you knew him."

"Wouldn't you like to ask me how?"

Rachel cleared her throat. "Will you confirm that he was in fact Dražen Krstić?"

Newhall laughed. "Does my confirmation matter? Have you not seen the tattoo on his hand? Are you asking me if Krstić was there? In Srebrenica, at Potočari? Is that what you want to know?"

She looked at Khattak. He motioned her on.

"Was he?"

"Ah. You are asking me how I recognized him. Was it from his Chetnik tattoo? His military haircut? His thick, squat neck? Was he there when they ordered my mother and father from the base at Potočari? Did he give the order to shoot my brother Mesha? Was he there when they took Ahmo away for questioning? Was it he who guaranteed our safety if our weapons were surrendered? Was it Krstić who promised a prisoner exchange?" He stared into the distance. "They gave us no prisoners, just bones. But not Ahmo's bones. Not Ahmo. No one can tell me where his bones lie."

"Mr. Newhall —"

352

"Call me Damir, dear Sergeant. It must be confusing for you. Christopher, Krstić. David, Damir. I think on the whole I prefer my Bosnian name. They've erased everything else. But you haven't come about that, have you? You want to know how I recognized this man who lived here so safely, so sweetly undetected. Was he there at the base, is that right? Do I recognize him from the gate? Or is it from the execution sites that I remember him? Was he at the famous white house for the torture and beatings? Or was he with the bulldozers they brought in to cart away the corpses? Or at the factory during the night, smoking and laughing when they took away the girls for the evening rapes? Did I recognize him? Yes, I knew his face. I will never forget his face. What does any of it matter now? Didn't he fall from the cliffs? After his successful retirement in this safest of havens?"

How could we know that the little towns would fall and we would run out of these sacred havens?

Without a doubt, Newhall was the letter writer. She couldn't think what to say, so she left it to Khattak to ask, "Did he, Damir? Did Dražen Krstić fall to his death? Or did you help him?"

"I would not help him to anything." His

353

contempt was obvious. He'd said his piece. The energy drained out of him. He leaned back in his chair, his hands limp upon his lap. Rachel noticed a photograph on the table beside the lamp.

She gestured at it. "May I?" Newhall flicked the switch. He handed her the photograph.

An elderly couple sat on a sofa surrounded by their painfully thin sons. The father wore the kind of cap she'd seen Khattak wear at prayer. A kerchief was knotted over the woman's faded hair. The boys were watchful, hollow-eyed.

"My brothers. The last photograph. The last I have of anything. The bones of my parents were identified in 2010. I went home for the fifteenth anniversary of the massacre to organize their funeral prayers. You could see the green coffins for miles, it seemed. The earth was thick with them."

He said it without blinking. His eyes were dry.

"Of Mesha and Ahmo, I have only this photograph. Their bones are cold. Where were they murdered? How were they killed? Where do they lie? This photograph cannot answer me. Beside my father and mother, their graves are waiting. Do you think Krstić knew? Do you think he could have told me?"

Is there any hope for at least that little child they snatched away from me, because I keep dreaming about him?

Why was she crying when Damir Hasanović wasn't?

"Did you ask him?"

He seemed surprised at her tears.

"He wouldn't have known. He gave orders, he supervised execution sites. He wouldn't have known a single one of our faces. *Balija* were all the same to him."

She palmed her face with her hand, deeply embarrassed. "You wrote him letters," she said. "In your letters, did you ask him?"

All the men of our family were killed. I can read you the list of their names.

I realized then that nothing good was in store for us in Potočari.

"What letters?"

"You sent letters to Dražen Krstić. Dozens of them. And you planted the Bosnian lily in his garden to remind him."

"Ah. His garden. His small, safe haven." When Newhall smiled his knife-blade smile, she felt her blood run cold. "Do you think a man with his finger on a trigger that killed thousands of Bosnians needed a reminder? Did he feel haunted? I doubt it, Sergeant."

"You've admitted you sent letters to the Department of Justice."

"Justice." He rolled the word over his tongue. "How swiftly such a word loses its meaning."

"Look, sir. I know you've spent nearly twenty years trying to get justice for your people. I know you've testified in case after case at the Tribunal. We know about your work with the Mothers of Srebrenica. You've brought lawsuits against the Dutch government. How could you throw that away for one man? Especially a man like Dražen Krstić."

"*Your* government was never going to see justice done. You preached peacekeeping at us while practicing cowardice. We remember your secret pact to evacuate your battalion from Srebrenica by stealth, leaving my people defenseless. It was your representative, Mr. MacKenzie, whose claims about 'ancient ethnic hatreds' satisfied so many. Let the savages fight it out. Except they wouldn't let us fight. They tied our hands and left us to die."

"I'm not sure what you mean, sir."

"The arms embargo," he said wearily. "What else would I mean?" A brief hint of calculation appeared on his face. "Or is it possible you think I meant something else? The day of the fall. The day that dawned without the airstrikes the UN had promised when the Serbs rolled their tanks into 'safe area' Srebrenica. The day the killing began."

Where are the planes? When will they strike?

What further proof did she need?

"You sent the letters to Krstić."

"Did I? Can you prove such a thing?"

"Are you denying it? Everything you've told us comes straight from those letters."

"Does it? Do the letters mention Ahmo and Mesha? Do they tell you that Ahmo was only thirteen years old?"

"Well, no — but everything else."

Hasanović shrugged. "As far as I'm aware, Christopher Drayton fell from the Bluffs, a dangerous place to walk at the best of times. I can't help you with anything else."

"You moved here two years ago, is that correct?" Khattak interjected.

"Yes. As I said, I like this neighborhood."

"Just after Drayton moved here," Khattak noted. "Why did you leave the Bosnian community? You were heavily involved with the mosque in the past."

Hasanović paused. "There's no law I'm aware of that requires Bosnians to live in ethnic ghettos or religious cantons. At least, not in this country."

"Please answer the question."

Hasanović sized him up, his hooded eyes

sharp. "My community has rebuilt. They've found a place for themselves — a way to struggle back to some form of happiness. I have nothing to rebuild."

"Where were you on the night that Drayton fell?"

"At a meeting about the museum. At Ringsong. Anyone will tell you."

"Why did you change your name? Was it to hide your identity from Dražen Krstić until you could find an opportunity for vengeance?"

Hasanović stood up and took the photograph of his family back from Rachel. "Do you think my life's work has been about vengeance? That I feed myself on the same delusions as the fascists?" Misery twisted his mouth. "I changed my name so I could forget who I am. For some, memories are a homeland, a palace. For me they are a prison — a graveyard." He touched his fingers to his youngest brother's face, his dark gaze turned inward. "It's my curse not to forget." His face crumpled. "Will you go? Please just go."

They left him in the shadows, the photograph clutched in his hands.

Rachel's hands shook as she let herself into her car. Khattak paused by her window.

"Was he telling the truth?" She looked up, but Khattak's face was in the shadows. "He never confronted Drayton? He never told him who he was?"

"The man I know Hasanović to be would not stand idly by if he learned a war criminal was living down the street from him. The name change suggests he was biding his time, hiding from Krstić."

"He denies sending the letters."

"I'm not sure that I believe him."

"What about the lilies?"

"He didn't deny that."

"He called the garden a haven. It wasn't his only use of the word."

"He was mocking us. The same way he kept saying 'safe area Srebrenica.' One of six safe havens."

"Christ."

"Indeed. We can't talk here. And we should talk to Nate about what we've learned."

She perked up at once. She wanted to see Nate again, to see if that nebulous connection she'd imagined between them was anything more than wishful thinking on her part. She glanced sideways at Khattak, assuming a neutral expression. He wanted to say something to her, she could tell. And then her hopes were dashed as Khattak took

359

a call, his shoulders tensed against the news. From two blocks away, she heard the sirens.

"Change of plans," he said. "There's been an incident with Melanie Blessant."

28.

Any rape is monstrously unacceptable but what is happening at this very moment in these rape and death camps is even more horrific.

Two cars were parked on the road outside the Blessant house. One belonged to Dennis Blessant. The other was a police cruiser. Khattak went over to talk to their colleagues. Melanie stood just outside the front door that hung askew in its frame, her arms crossed over her overflowing chest.

Dennis Blessant and the girls waited by his car with Marco River. There were scratch marks on the man's face, but he wasn't in handcuffs. Hadley stood in an unconscious imitation of her mother's posture, wrinkling the rose-colored dress she wore. Her hair was pinned up. Cassidy was similarly attired in blue. Both girls looked lovely.

"What's going on?"

"You're cops? Why do we need more cops?" Dennis Blessant asked them.

"We're here on another matter. We're investigating the death of Christopher Drayton." She took note of Hadley's pallor, of Cassidy biting her knuckles. "You're Dennis Blessant?"

"I try not to acknowledge it on days like these."

"Your wife called the cops on you? Did you get physical with her?"

"Good God, no." He hesitated. "Just with the house."

"I called them," Hadley said. "He came to pick us up and give us a ride to our dinner. Mad Mel lost control of herself. She attacked him. I called them so we could get on with our night."

"Hadley," Cassidy whimpered. Tears slid down her face, leaving a trail through the powder she'd applied. "Don't say too much."

Hadley bent down to adjust the strap on a high-heeled shoe. "I'm not letting people think Dad's a wife-abuser. That's exactly what Mad Mel wants."

"Mum, Hadley. Mum."

The gentle correction softened her older sister. She signaled to Riv. He put his arm around Cassidy's shoulder and led her

362

across the street.

"Christ. She does this every time I come to get the girls."

"You share custody, Mr. Blessant?"

His laughter was harsh. "I try to share it. She'd suffocate my girls if she could." He said it loudly enough for his ex-wife to hear. Raging, she flew across the lawn at him. Khattak intercepted her, receiving the full impact of her overblown frontage.

"Inspector," she bleated. "You have to help me — Dennis was threatening me."

"God, Mel. More lies? I've warned you to be careful about Dad. You need to stop the lies."

The woman would have jumped on Hadley if Khattak's grip had let her.

"You have to believe me, Inspector. He hates me and he hated Chrissie. They fought, did you know that? The night that Chrissie fell. Maybe Dennis pushed him just to get at me. Because he knew Chrissie loved me and wanted to take care of me like he couldn't."

Khattak released her. "Is that true, sir?"

Hadley looked between her father and mother, her face ashen.

"Of course it's not true! That man was saving my life. He was taking this witch off my hands. No more alimony. No more child support."

"I knew it!" Melanie shouted. "I knew this whole 'I love my girls' thing was a lie! You wanted Chrissie to take them over. You wanted them off your hands!"

A tearing sob escaped Hadley's throat. She shoved past her mother into the house.

"You useless bitch. You don't know anything. I argued with Drayton because he wouldn't agree to marry you unless I gave you full custody of Hadley and Cass. I told him that would never happen. I begged him to marry you anyway."

"You're lying!" she shrieked. If she could have bulldozed her way past Khattak, Blessant would have been on the ground, shielding himself from the fury of her nails. "The only thing Chrissie *wanted* was to marry me! You wouldn't let him. You wanted to keep me in this rathole forever."

Dennis wiped a hand over his face, agog. "You're a lunatic. Do you hear yourself? I went down on my knees and thanked God the day you met Drayton. You couldn't marry him fast enough for me."

"You followed him." She was howling at him now. "You followed him to the Bluffs and you shoved him over. Maybe you did it because you wanted me to be miserable. Maybe you did it to show you can still control me. Or maybe you did it because you knew Chrissie was a thousand times the father you are. You knew he'd get the girls if I pushed for it."

Just as Rachel stepped forward to intervene, Hadley rocketed out of the front door and threw herself between her parents. She held a large envelope in her hands that she waved at them.

"Your goddamned lies." She swore at her mother. "I warned you, Mel. Don't say I didn't warn you." She upended the contents of the envelope over the lawn. "There's your Chrissie. There's the bastard you wanted to marry. And you're the one who knew about his will. You're the one who followed him. If anyone pushed him, you did."

"No!" Cassidy's wail reverberated across the street.

"I'm sorry, Cass, I'm sorry. But it's true, it's all true."

Rachel stared at the contents of the envelope with horror, Dennis Blessant slackjawed beside her. Hadley had scattered documents and photographs across the lawn between her parents. Rachel slipped on her gloves and knelt on the grass to collect them.

Some of it was pornography. The most depraved and violent pornography she'd come across: terrified women tied up, threatened and debased by knives and guns and other implements of torture. Cross-cutting these were Polaroids. Close-ups of Hadley and Cassidy in their beds at Krstić's house, sleeping. He had drawn their covers aside and photographed their legs, their breasts. There were photographs of Hadley and Cassidy coming out of the shower, their hair wet, their towels slipping.

Bile rose in her stomach.

"Sir," she said to Khattak. Blessant tried to take the photographs from her. She blocked him.

"I'm sorry, sir, these are evidence."

"My girls," he whispered. "My girls. Hadley, did he — ?"

"No," she said quickly. "My God, no, Dad. I never would have let him. I never left him alone with Cassie for a second. But Mel was willing to. She couldn't see what was right in front of her face." Her voice dripped with contempt.

Rachel felt sick. A fifteen-year-old girl was talking about her mother.

"What do you mean?"

"I knew what kind of a man he was when he called my mother a whore every night," Hadley said with disgust. " 'Shut up, you stupid whore. Take it, you filthy whore.' And still she kept pushing him for a wedding date."

"He loved me," Melanie said blankly. "He loved me and I loved him. I don't care what they say he did. He didn't do it."

Hadley grabbed her by the shoulders and screamed into her face. "He was a war criminal, Mother! *Christopher Dražen Krstić!* He killed people. He raped them. Didn't you ever ask yourself why he wanted us at his house? Didn't you ever wonder why he insisted you get sole custody? Didn't you see the pictures?" Her face was soaked with tears. She wiped her nose with the sleeve of her dress.

"No," Melanie whispered. "It's not what you're saying. He was a family man. You're making this all up."

With a swift movement, Rachel blocked Dennis Blessant's sudden lunge.

"Why won't you believe me?" Hadley released her grip on her mother's arms and turned away. "You're my mother. Why would I lie to you?"

Melanie hesitated. "You don't want me to be happy." But her voice lacked conviction. She made a tentative gesture to reach for her daughter, then dropped her hands. "It's just a misunderstanding," she said. "You misunderstood him."

"I didn't, Mum." She hadn't used this name for her mother in years, Rachel was sure. "Honestly, Mum — I didn't." She sank down onto the grass, crying.

Rachel couldn't bear it.

"Sir," she said again.

Khattak motioned the officers from the scout car over. "Take them in," he said of the Blessants. "To separate rooms. We'll meet you there." He looked at Rachel. The color had left his skin, a green tinge beneath its surface. "We'll need someone to stay with the girls."

Rachel swallowed her nausea. This was the last moment in the world to rely upon Mink Norman. She watched him make his call, rose from her knees, and awkwardly gathered Hadley into her arms. Hadley didn't resist. After a moment, she rested her head on Rachel's shoulder.

Riv brought Cassidy back from across the street and all three of them hugged each other.

Hadley gripped Rachel's wrist. She motioned at her sister. "Don't let her see," she mouthed.

Rachel shoved the envelope under her blazer.

Khattak patted Marco River's arm.

"Audrey Clare is coming," he said quietly.

"She'll take you to Winterglass. Stay there, won't you?"

Riv stared at him, man-to-man. "I won't leave until you say it's okay."

He took Rachel aside. "We'll need to get someone from Crisis Response up there, but for now Audrey will be able to handle things. What she does with her NGO is mainly social work."

He could still surprise her.

"And what about us, sir?"

"Was the will among those documents?"

"Yes."

"Then let's begin with Ms. Blessant."

29.

We saw them rape the hadji*'s daughter —*
one after the other, they raped her. The
hadji *had to watch too. When they were*
done, they rammed a knife into his throat.

Khattak didn't want to talk to this woman.
He loathed her. Charles Brining had been
right. There was nothing about Chris Drayton's past that Melanie hadn't known. She
just hadn't cared.

He thought of Hadley and Cassidy, their
luxurious youth and innocence. Their devotion to their father. He rued a system that
left them under the negligent care of a
woman like Melanie. The photographs
sickened him. They weren't something
Drayton had purchased off the Internet and
hoarded like a treasure. They were personal,
intimate. Photographs Drayton had either
taken himself or had his subordinates take
for him. The women were Bosnian. The

photographs were from rape camps.

Khattak had had them copied and dusted for prints. Tomorrow he would send them to Tom Paley with an urgent request that they be forwarded to the tribunal at the Hague. For the twenty thousand rapes that had been reported during the war, much less than the actual number that had taken place, fewer than forty men had been sentenced — less than a handful of these at the international tribunal. Perhaps the photographs would bring other men to justice. After that, he fervently prayed they would be destroyed.

"You knew the code to Drayton's safe?"

He was as far across the room from Melanie as possible. Rachel sat opposite her at the small table in the room. Melanie didn't bother with deception.

"Yes. I watched him open it once."

"You took the envelope from the safe? That's how you knew about the will?"

"I didn't take it. I just happened to see it in there once. I had a look."

"So you knew he was leaving everything to you."

"So what?" She sniffed. "I loved Chrissie. I wanted to marry him. He was no good to me dead."

"I think you'll find that's true, given his

real identity. His policies will be void, his assets frozen until their provenance is determined."

"Come again?" All pretense of kittenish helplessness dropped from her manner at this threat to her windfall.

"His money. It's likely not his to leave. The bequests from his will won't be paid out. Tell me, Ms. Blessant. If you didn't take the envelope from the safe, how did Hadley come to have it?"

Melanie's face reflected her indecision about Hadley's revelations. "She just told you. She was spying on us. That's probably how she figured out the code."

"Her prints weren't on the safe."

This time her answer came quickly. "I like to keep it clean in there."

"Did you see what else was in the envelope?" Rachel asked. "The photographs, the letters to Dražen Krstić?"

Melanie arranged her breasts on the table like two giant lumps of unbaked bread. Rachel backed away. Melanie's façade was beginning to splinter: there were cracks at the line of her jaw, cords that stood out against her neck, white lines in her suntanned cleavage. The faintest blur of mascara discolored the pits beneath her eyes.

"I told you, it was just the one time. I had

a quick look."

Rachel very much doubted that that had been Melanie's only incursion into Drayton's privacy.

"You saw the photographs," she insisted.

"What of it?"

Rachel wanted to smack her self-satisfied face. "What of it? Ms. Blessant, those were photographs of your daughters in various states of undress."

"No," she denied immediately. "He loved them. They're just pictures of the girls asleep."

Khattak jerked forward. "Do you really believe that? After everything your daughter just said to you?"

"Oh honey," the woman said. "You don't think it's possible Hadley was looking for a little attention? Because her father doesn't give her enough?"

And Rachel saw how the woman had already orchestrated an alternate scenario in her mind — one that renewed her vendetta against her husband at the expense of Hadley's need for solace and support. That fleeting moment when Melanie Blessant had truly seen her daughter had already passed.

"You can't honestly believe your daughters weren't at risk."

373

Melanie stared at her, gritty-eyed. "He was a good man. His interest in them was harmless."

Rachel nearly choked. The woman's need to believe in Drayton's single-minded adoration of her had made her blind to everything else.

"Did you find the other photographs harmless as well? Considering their connection to Dražen Krstić?"

She shrugged, the movement rippling through her breasts like an underwater wave. "What man doesn't hold on to a little pornography? Why would I care about that? And who the hell was Dražen whatever to me? No one."

"Not quite," Rachel said. "He was an indicted war criminal, a fugitive from justice. That wasn't pornography you were looking at. It was evidence of his crimes."

"Don't kid yourself, honey. It was women tied up. Or don't you know that most men are into a little kink?"

Rachel wanted to slap her. "You evidently did. Weren't you worried about your daughters in view of the 'kink' your boyfriend was into?"

"Fiancé," she corrected automatically. Her gaze stroked over her sumptuous figure in the mirror behind Khattak's head. "Why

374

would I worry? I could handle anything he wanted."

In a clinical voice, Khattak asked, "You didn't feel a responsibility to protect Hadley and Cassidy from his appetites?"

"I've told you before. The only one Chrissie wanted was me. Hadley's never had that kind of attention from a man — you can't blame her for feeling a little jealous."

It was obvious that she believed this. Rachel didn't know if that increased or lessened her disgust. In her own twisted way, was this how Melanie found common ground with her daughter? Because nothing they were saying about Dražen Krstić was getting through to her.

"Ms. Blessant, did you see your husband follow Mr. Drayton to the Bluffs the night that he fell?"

"I heard the fight. I was with Chrissie that night."

"But not when he went to his walk."

"He asked me to leave. He said his mood was off after Dennis. He wanted to be alone."

"So you didn't see your ex-husband follow him."

"No. But I know he did. He won't rest until he's ruined everything for me."

"You're referring to his desire for custody."

"Yes."

"Then you did know that you and your daughters were a package deal for Drayton."

"You're turning it into something it wasn't. We both knew he'd make a better father for them than Dennis."

Khattak left it. "Did you light candles that night before your ex-husband arrived?"

"Are you crazy? In this heat?"

"It's been raining off and on for the past two weeks."

"Even if it was, it was sweltering."

"You didn't mention any of this to us before."

"You didn't ask. Say," she said, lively with a new thought. "This would be news, wouldn't it? Big news? Who Chrissie really was? The kind of news the papers pay big money for? If they're going to freeze Chrissie's assets, I mean."

She had already forgotten her daughter's anguish.

Revolted, Rachel opened her mouth to speak. Khattak swiftly forestalled her.

He leaned down toward the table, faced Melanie head-on. "Ms. Blessant, I find you appalling."

And when that came up in the inevitable complaint against CPS, Rachel would swear on her life that Khattak had never said it.

"Shall we drive you back to your car, Mr. Blessant?"

"Call me Dennis. You're not keeping me here?"

"We only brought you here to spare your daughters any further unpleasantness."

Dennis barked out a laugh. "That's one word for it, I suppose. My ex doesn't exactly scream maternal devotion from the rafters."

"If you were so poorly matched, why did you marry her?" Rachel asked.

"For the same reason men do most stupid things. She has a great body. I thought that was enough. I had money. She thought that was enough."

He followed them to Khattak's car, settling into the backseat. "I was supposed to take my girls to a dinner tonight. I doubt they're in any shape for it now."

"They're up at Mr. Clare's house. You can ask them, if you like."

He'd been about to leave off his seat belt, then thought better of it. "Cops, right? Look — Mel wasn't always as bad as she is now. She was good to the girls, at first. She treated them like little dolls. When we split up, she took it pretty hard. I would have said that half of what she says and does to the girls is to punish me. It isn't about them. They're her daughters. At some level, she loves them."

Rachel picked on his choice of words. "Would have said?"

"The photographs, Christ, the photographs. What the hell was he? Some kind of pedophile?"

"We don't know. We don't know how deep his perversions ran. He was a sadist, without doubt."

"So Hadley wasn't kidding. He really did call her mother a whore." He sat up straight. "Did he hurt my girls? Did the bastard touch them?"

"We don't know, sir. This is the first we've heard of any of this."

"But you were at our house. Looking into him and Mel. What did Hadley mean when she called him a war criminal?"

Rachel eyed him uneasily. "We're not at liberty to discuss that, sir. It's best if you just focus on your girls for the present."

They pulled up beside his car.

"Mr. Blessant, would you hold up a moment?" Khattak said. "Your ex-wife said that you argued with Drayton on the night of his death. On what subject?"

Dennis fumbled for his car keys. It had been easier to talk to the woman. She looked tough, but her manner was kind. He didn't trust Khattak's courteous detachment.

"Like Mel said. About the girls. He tried to convince me to give Mel full custody." He shuddered. "Thank God I said no. It would always have been no. I'd been counting the days until Drayton took Mel off my hands. I knew the girls would choose to come to me then. Hadley always wanted to, she just wouldn't leave Cassie behind. Thank God," he said again. "Thank God she was watching out for my baby. What the hell was Mel thinking? If she knew about Drayton, how could she have ever let him near the girls?"

Rachel was still wondering the same thing. "I think Ms. Blessant was so focused on getting Drayton to marry her that she didn't pay attention to anything else. What we don't know is why. Was her spousal support insufficient?"

Dennis gave his bark of laughter again. "Mel has expensive tastes. She runs through her monthly allotment in a couple of days. Then she spends the money that's meant for the girls. She always wants more. I gave her money to buy the girls new laptops for school, clothes, other supplies. Mel burned through it all. Since then, I've given Had the money directly. It turned her mother against her, but Hadley's tough." He said the last sentence uncertainly, his voice trailing into silence.

From the shock that made his face sag, she knew he was thinking about the night's revelations. About Hadley and Riv working to shield Cassidy. About Hadley making horrific discoveries and having to contend with them on her own.

"Ms. Blessant knew about Drayton's will. Did you, sir?" Khattak's face gave nothing away. It expressed no more than a mild interest in his answer.

Dennis tried to think. "I didn't. I would never have asked him such a personal question and Mel had no reason to tell me." He flapped large white hands at them. "You have to believe me. I didn't know about any of this. Drayton was worth a hell of a lot more to me alive than dead."

"What about the custody issue?"

"I never thought he was serious. I thought he was trying to make things easier for Mel, trying to show everyone what a nice guy he was. He *was* a nice guy. He was always agreeable. The custody issue was the first sticking point, but I thought we'd both cool off and talk things through sensibly. I wasn't worried. I was relying on Hadley to convince

Cass that her home was with me. That the three of us belonged together."

Both parents had relied on Hadley's common sense and toughness altogether too much, Rachel thought. But one was a man who loved his daughters, the other a woman who balked at seeing reality for what it was.

"Where did you go after the argument with Mr. Drayton?"

"I drove home. I was angry, I had to get out of there." Then he realized what he'd said. "Not like that. I'd been so certain that everything was about to turn around and the news that it wasn't came as a bit of a shock. I needed time to think out a strategy."

"Where was Ms. Blessant while the two of you were arguing?"

Dennis grimaced in disgust. "Upstairs. Preparing her boudoir, as she calls it. Making herself available to Drayton."

"And the girls?"

"At home. Christ! I can't believe I let them stay over there. Anything could have happened to them."

"It didn't, Mr. Blessant. It's likely that Drayton was waiting for the marriage and your wife's permanent move to his house. He wouldn't have wanted to risk jeopardizing his access to the girls."

She had meant it be comforting. She

could see from his face that it wasn't.

Khattak's phone rang. He murmured something into it and waited.

"The girls can stay with the Clares tonight, if you'd like."

"No." Dennis made a visible effort to pull himself together. "They're my daughters, I'm responsible for them. They'll need me. Especially after tonight."

Khattak spoke into the phone again and shut off the call.

"Audrey Clare is a social worker. I'd ask her advice, discreetly, on what tack to take with the girls. I'm sure you'll find her some help to you. We can also arrange for a social worker to come to your house, if you prefer."

Dennis stopped his frantic hunt for his car keys. He could see that they genuinely meant to be helpful. In these few minutes with him, they'd expressed more concern for Hadley and Cassidy's welfare than Mel had done since their divorce. The realization hit him like a sucker punch.

"I appreciate it," he said, quieted.

"We'll need to talk to your daughters at some point, sir."

"Fine. When they're ready. And in my presence, is that clear?"

Rachel liked him a little more. "Of course, sir."

They watched him drive away.

"What now, sir?" she asked. "Nice work with Mad Mel, by the way. Appalling isn't the word I'd have used, though."

A hint of humor appeared on Khattak's face. "I know. That's why I said it. Before you could say something else."

"We could charge her with child endangerment."

"Think of what that would do to the girls," he advised. "All we need is the threat of action. If she persists in denying Blessant custody of their daughters, we can threaten her with criminal charges. She may not have believed that Drayton was a predator, but she should at least have come forward with what she did know."

"That's blackmail, sir."

"I doubt she'll fight us. She has other worries to focus on now. Like how she'll manage without Drayton's money."

"What about the spousal support? Blessant said she's bleeding him dry."

"I'm afraid there's nothing we can do about that. The law will have to run its course."

"Do you still want to talk to Nate?" The

casualness of her inquiry earned her a sharp glance from Khattak.

"Yes. And while I do that, you can go through the photographs."

She couldn't hide her disappointment.

"Bring them with you," he said. "Nate knew Drayton. He might see something we wouldn't."

It was a threadbare excuse, a barely masked attempt to include her, or perhaps he still needed her as a safeguard against Nate's attempts to reconcile the past, but it didn't matter. Rachel was happy to accept any excuse at all.

30.

Mina was crying the most. She said, "We are not girls anymore. Our lives are over."

It was only afterward that she would remember that the women had begun screaming as the soldiers took hold of their arms. They wrested her bruised hand from Mrs. Obranovic's grasp, shoving her neighbor aside. She saw now that though they wore the uniforms of the Dutch, they were Chetniks.

In moments, they had collected her sister Selmira and herself, along with an older girl in her twenties. The older girl was crying, terrible deep sobs where she couldn't catch her breath. Her sister held her hand as though she would never let go, but she could feel her perspiration. Selmira was frightened.

"Let us go," she said. "We're children. Let us go. Show us you are honorable."

She couldn't repeat the word the Chetnik said in response. It was the bad word, the word they called the Muslim women and girls, girls like herself and Selmira.

They were taken to another building where it was dark. Someone had thrown a filthy mattress on the floor. There were people around, but they were trying not to look. She swallowed. One of the Chetniks had left the hall to call another man. The ones who stayed behind grabbed the older girl and threw her onto the mattress.

"Let's start with this one," they said.

Selmira began to scream. She had never heard her sister scream before. It was loud, high-pitched, terrifying. She started to cry.

The Chetniks stopped. They left the third girl on the mattress and came to grab her sister. One of them slapped Selmira across the face. She kept on screaming.

"Should we start with you?"

"Run!" Selmira screamed at her. "Run! Get out of here, go!"

She had promised Nesib she would listen to whatever Selmira told her. She ran for the door, straight into another soldier, this one in the Bosnian Serb uniform. He grabbed her by the arms and dragged her into the room with the mattress.

"Nole," Selmira called, sobbing with relief. "Nole, you have to help us."

She looked up. It was Nole, Nesib's best

friend. The one who stole food for them. The one who had come to tell her brothers to head for the woods.

The Chetniks swore at Nole, who had recognized her and let go of her arms.

"They're not going anywhere," the one who had slapped Selmira said. "They're ours. The general said to enjoy ourselves."

Nole pretended to think about this. She could tell he was pretending because one of his hands pressed softly against her neck.

"The Colonel is calling for volunteers to load the trucks. It's chaos out there."

She held her breath. Maybe the Chetniks would believe him.

"Afterward," the Chetnik said. "They won't miss us for ten minutes."

"We'll get in trouble," Nole said. "Leave them here. They're not going anywhere."

The man who had slapped Selmira yanked her head back by pulling at her scarf.

"You're trying to protect your little slut. The little slut who knows you."

"I'm trying not to get called out by Krstić. I've said they'll still be here. We have all night."

"Liar," said a third man. "They've finished loading the trucks for the night. We're free until the morning."

Nole shuffled his feet, thinking.

The man holding Selmira ripped her blouse

at the neck.

"I've waited a long time for this," he said. "You do what you want."

The Chetniks returned to the girl on the mattress, who had never stopped crying. Nole couldn't stop them.

Selmira began to unbutton her blouse. "Friends," she said. "My sister is a baby. She's only ten years old. You're men, you don't want her. Let the little one go and I won't fight you."

Nole moved decisively. He shoved her away from Selmira and shouldered her to the door. No one moved to stop him. The girl on the mattress was choking, her legs in the air.

Nole hissed in her ear. "Get back to the base and hide. Don't stop for anyone. Hide. Be clever. I'll get your sister."

This time she didn't stop to wave. She looked at her sister surrounded by Chetniks and ran through the door for her life.

31.

It is inconceivable for me all of this that is happening to us. Is life so unpredictable and brutal? I remember how this time last year we were rejoicing over building a house, and now see where we are. I feel as if I'd never been alive. I try to fight it by remembering everything that was beautiful with you and the children and all those I love.

They found Nate in a bright room that led off the kitchen at Winterglass. Its views were of gardens, not the water. In the sinking light, the trees looked like skeletons of themselves, brushed with sweeps of pink and bronze.

Nathan called it his morning room. An embroidered English sofa with matching chairs was set before a raised bronze table. The floor was a blond wood patterned with blue diamonds, a color reflected in a set of

French mirrors on either side of a modest fireplace.

"When will you come with Ruksh?" Nate asked Khattak. "Not that Rachel isn't welcome."

"Not while we're on a case," he answered. "Another time, perhaps."

As Rachel took her seat across from a floor-to-ceiling canvas that featured a frolicking spaniel, she took note of Nathan's pleased reaction. A thaw was setting in.

"You're having difficulties?" Nate asked. "I can tell from your face."

"We're learning difficult things," Khattak said carefully. "We know that Drayton wasn't the only one living under an alias. So was David Newhall."

"Newhall?" Nate tilted his head up to the ceiling, lost in contemplation of its whimsical cornices. "Why on earth would he need an alias?"

"Do you remember a man named Damir Hasanović? The translator for the UN at their base in Potočari?"

"I remember. He testified before the international tribunal."

"He's been living here as your neighbor. You've entertained him in your home."

"Damir Hasanović?"

"David Newhall." Before Nate could

object, Khattak asked, "Is it possible?"

Nate thought about this. Twilight softened the lines at the corners of his hazel eyes. From his pocket, he took a Waterman pen that he tapped against the table.

"It seems ridiculous to have been so blind. First Chris, now David. I thought of these men as my friends."

Rachel wanted to tell him she thought the friendship was sincere, but how would she know? Maybe they had each used Nate for their own ends or as a means of getting to each other.

"Hasanović was one of Dražen Krstić's victims. He lost his family to the Srebrenica massacre. I think he moved here to keep an eye on Drayton. He says he met him at your house and recognized him at once."

"It's true. Mink asked me to invite him as a board member of the museum. That was a little over two years ago. He met Chris that night."

"And moved here when?"

"A week later? Maybe two?"

"He was stalking Drayton," Rachel said. "Once he'd seen him, he had to make sure Drayton didn't disappear."

"And he changed his name so Chris wouldn't know." Nate slapped a hand on the table, making them jump. "The letters.

David wrote the letters?"

"He didn't admit it, but it's the obvious conclusion."

"Are you saying David had something to do with Chris's fall? That he planned for his death?"

"He says not. He also told us he loves to walk along the Bluffs."

"And you think — what? This can't have been coincidence?"

Khattak looked at his friend. His enthusiasm didn't mean that he viewed Drayton's death as an intellectual puzzle dependent on the cleverness of a solution. Nate well understood the human cost, the toll in blood and agony — who better? His warmth and interest expressed his desire to reach out, to offer Khattak his support.

He hadn't been to Winterglass in two years. Nate's openness, his close attention to Rachel, were meant to bridge that distance. Khattak couldn't fault him. He no longer had the appetite to shoot Nate down and watch him suffer.

He knew that Damir Hasanović would have given anything for another moment with his brothers.

He would give anything now to know where Ahmo and Mesha lay buried.

Perhaps he had tried, despite what he'd

392

told them. Tried to wring a last confession from Krstić, a man who knew neither weakness nor remorse. And in that reckless moment of anger, he'd shoved the older man from the cliff, sending him to his death, just as Krstić had condemned so many others.

"It's not coincidence," he said to Nate. "He moved here because he wanted to bring Krstić to justice. He notified the Department of Justice as soon as he recognized him. When his letter-writing campaign proved fruitless, he could have turned to the media. He must have feared that with the first hint of exposure, Krstić would slip away and would never have to account for his crimes. Newhall — Hasanović — would never learn where his brothers lie buried."

"Then you do think he killed him."

"I think he wrote the letters. I think he planted the lilies in Drayton's garden. I don't know if fate intervened and Drayton fell before he could see his plan through, or whether Drayton's fall *was* his plan. We'll check his movements, of course, but that's bound to be inconclusive."

"Like everything else about this case," Rachel said glumly.

"Will CPS be making an announcement about Krstić?"

"With the Department of Justice. Once

393

we've given them an answer about Krstić's death."

"What if there is no answer?"

Khattak's fatigue was evident. "I don't know."

Nate had known him long enough to know what he was really saying. "You don't want David to have done this."

"I wouldn't blame him. Who would? But no. That's not what the people of Bosnia deserve."

Rachel was more prosaic. "Say you do everything by the book and a man like Krstić still walks free. How could we expect Newhall to take that quietly?"

It wasn't an argument for vigilantism. It was Rachel's habit of getting inside the skin of a case, the skin of another's pain.

It was what Khattak most respected about her.

"It's not who Damir Hasanović is. I don't want his life's work to be reduced to Krstić's death."

As he said it, Khattak knew it came down to the same thing it had always been about. Identity. His. Theirs. The victims of genocide.

And what had been different? Only religion.

In Sarajevo, twenty years ago, people had

refused to believe in the war at first.

Different? What do you mean, we are different? We are the same people. We speak the same language, share the same culture. We marry each other, we celebrate Christmas. How are we different?

The greatest general of a Sarajevo under siege had been a Bosnian Serb.

We are one people, the Bosnians.

Until the fascists had killed the enlightenment, burned the countryside, sundered the nation.

Those who hadn't believed in the war had died anyway.

Acts committed with intent to destroy, in whole or in part, a national, ethnical, racial, or religious group, as such: killing members of the group, causing serious bodily or mental harm to members of the group, deliberately inflicting on the group conditions of life calculated to bring about its physical destruction.

Yes, yes, and yes.

He had felt it then, as a student in a besieged city. He felt it now again: the hot flare of rage and futility in his stomach.

Was this what they were? The new Jews of Europe with Bosnia a slaughterhouse whose bloody imprint had faded in memory?

Everywhere the radical right was rising: Sweden, France, Belgium, Denmark, Holland. While a steady stream of vitriol drifted north of the U.S. border.

The war had begun with a program of hate and the steady administration of incendiary propaganda.

You Muslim women, you Bule, *we'll show you.*

You will see, you Muslims. I will draw a cross on your back. You will all be baptized.

We will burn you alive.

And in fourteen days, Srebrenica will be gone.

Damir Hasanović was a man admired and respected the world over, a man whose only mission had been justice. A man who'd sacrificed everything to that end.

For his reputation to be torn down at this last when Dražen Krstić had known nearly two decades of prosperity was something Khattak couldn't bear. It was something he wouldn't do.

One part of him knew that no matter the provocation, Hasanović couldn't have caused Krstić's death. But from a hollow place within himself, the place where identity folded back upon itself to reveal rawer, more vulnerable layers, he acknowledged a more insidious truth — the part that wished he had done it himself.

■ ■ ■ ■

Rachel waited for Khattak to speak, unable to dispel her sense of disquiet. Little things were tugging at the edge of her awareness. Things she had seen or heard yet failed to understand. Maybe it was the night she'd spent reading about Ratko Mladić. Maybe it was the eerie watchfulness of her mother or the newfound sobriety of her father. Maybe it was Zach's continued absence from their lives.

She was missing something — brittle, intangible, and just on the edge of discovery.

She lined up the photographs she had taken from Hadley across the bronze table. She included everything they had collected during their first visit to Drayton's house. Personal papers, the holdings of his filing cabinet. The letters she had read that haunted her like the poetry of the damned. The things the imam had interpreted for them.

Nate came to look over her shoulder.

"You need a cup of coffee," he said. "And then I can help you tackle this."

"I need three."

She was grateful for his support, for his kind eyes and steady hands, or maybe grateful wasn't the word. She chose not to question her strange kinship with Nathan Clare. He was the part of Esa Khattak that opened up to her, sharing himself as an equal. She didn't complain about her relationship with Khattak, she knew they were an excellent team, just as she knew there was something of himself he held back.

Which was fine with her, because there was plenty she was holding back herself.

Khattak stirred from his reverie, shifted the papers on the table. His long fingers pushed a folded sheet of paper toward her.

"What's this? I don't remember seeing it before."

Rachel flattened it out on the table's smooth surface. "Piano music? I found it in Drayton's house. Maybe Nate or Mink gave it to him."

Nate appeared behind her shoulder with a tray of coffee.

"No," he said thoughtfully. "Chris didn't play, as far as I know. And I don't think it is piano music." Rachel studied the minute notations on the five-line staff as Nate set down his tray.

"You're saying this isn't music? It's some kind of code? Something someone sent him?" It reminded her of a spy novel she'd read.

"No, it's music. It's just not arranged for the piano. Look at this. It's written in treble clef. The piano accompaniment below it links two staves: treble and bass."

"What is it then?"

"An arrangement for the violin. I can play the melody for you if you like."

"I don't know that it matters," said Khattak. "Did he play the violin?"

"No. If he were a musician, he'd likely have offered music lessons instead of languages."

Rachel's interest sharpened. "So why did he have it, then?" She'd gotten it from the back of his filing cabinet, crammed in with the first batch of letters she'd found. "It could have been sent to him like the letters. Maybe it means something."

"Shall I play it and see?"

They followed Nate into the great room.

"This will be a bit rough."

It wasn't. He transposed the notes easily, his foot on one of the pedals. It was slow, insignificant. Until it became relentless, urgent. Thick with heartache. A layered anguish inhabiting the room, swelling out from the piano to the upper gallery. Nate's fingers lingered over the keys. The music built to its intolerable climax.

Just imagine this youngest boy I had, those little hands of his . . .

Mummy, I've come. At last I've come.

Where have you been, my son?

I waited for you to come through the woods. Each passing day was an agony. Until there was no hope left that you would come.

I never believed that people could do this.

Her heart was breaking. The music was breaking it.

"Stop," Khattak said.

Nate lifted his hands, placed them in his lap. His face paled at the expression on Khattak's face. "You recognize it."

"Did you give it to Drayton?"

"No. It sounds familiar but I can't place it."

There was a sickness beneath Khattak's skin. "The Adagio attributed to Albinoni. Vedran Smailović played it on his cello in the streets of Sarajevo."

For citizens of a fallen city.

"Do you think Drayton knew what it was?"

"I think a man like Krstić would have made a point of finding out."

"You were right then, sir. It wasn't just about Srebrenica."

"Perhaps there's some symbolism here," said Nate. "Srebrenica was the final movement of the war."

His words hung on the air with the closing notes of the music.

Rachel forced herself to take up the photographs again. It was too much. All of it was too much, the letters, the music, the silenced voices of the missing and dead. Something in the case had to break.

"What are these?" Nate asked, his voice hushed. "A specialized form of pornography?"

"They're from the war. These women may be dead, for all we know."

"I think this one *is* dead. This isn't a photograph, is it? It looks like a color photocopy." He pointed to a grainy image on a faded page. The figure in it was clothed. The body hung from a tree. Dark gold hair framed the face. The pink scarf that spilled down its neck had been used to hang the body.

"These others are prints, this one isn't. Why?"

"It's not from his collection." Khattak's voice was harsh.

Rachel hadn't noticed the photograph before, the disturbing image buried by others even more graphic.

"This is just a girl," she said. Images revolved in her mind. "A girl like Hadley or Cassidy. Look at the way the paper is folded. It was sent to him, like the letters. They murdered women as well?"

"Ten thousand women died in the war. I'd guess the girl in this picture hanged herself."

They looked at each other grimly.

"Someone wanted him to know this. David Newhall?"

"It may have been his cousin or his niece. Perhaps a friend."

Rachel shook her head. This was something else. Something out of place, like the music, the gun, the residue of the candles. A connection she wasn't seeing.

"Drayton had a gun," she said slowly. "He was threatened with exposure. Someone sent him the letters, the picture, the sheet music. The Bosnian lily was planted in his garden. Doesn't it seem like momentum was building against him? He wanted Hadley and Cassidy, but Dennis Blessant stood in his way. He was pressured on all sides: Melanie, Dennis, the letters. He took a walk along the Bluffs at night, the same night he had the argument with Dennis, yet he didn't take the gun. Why not? Why did he leave the gun on the floor surrounded by puddles of wax?"

"Maybe someone took his gun and forced him to go on that walk," Nate suggested.

"His are the only prints on the gun. He left it behind on purpose. I just can't figure out why."

"If Chris really was pushed, someone must have followed him on his walk. Dennis Blessant?"

"Whoever followed him would have had to wait until Melanie returned to her own house. They'd have to wait until Dennis drove away. Neither Melanie or Dennis reported any cars or noise on the street. As far as we know, there were no silent watchers in the undergrowth."

"Melanie's too self-involved to have thought about the presence of others. Dennis was probably distracted by the argument."

"And Drayton's house is secluded from the rest of the street. So there could have been someone there." She balled up her fists in disgust. "Again, that leaves us with nothing conclusive. Just the same old question of the gun. Did Drayton fall, or didn't he? I doubt we'll ever know." She faced her boss squarely. "So where do we go from here, sir?"

"Perhaps we need to widen our net. Find

other suspects."

"No one has a greater motive than David Newhall. His parents, his brothers. Can we really afford to take his testimony at his word?"

"Hasanović worked for fifteen years to identify his parents' bones. What does that say about his patience? This isn't the end he wanted for Dražen Krstić. You won't convince me of it."

Rachel was afraid to dispute it. It was the first time she'd heard Khattak speak with such emotion. He wasn't a man who dealt in ultimate truths; as she did, he traversed the underground cities of doubt and discrepancy where human frailty revealed itself in layer upon layer of incongruity. She owed it to him to try, regardless.

"Maybe he didn't see it as murder. If I were standing in Newhall's shoes, Drayton's fall would look a lot like justice to me."

Khattak's face closed down. If he couldn't convince Rachel, what hope was there? She was only arguing what everyone would think once Newhall's true name was revealed, as it would be. And just like that, the decades of Hasanović's struggle for justice would be washed away, the tragedy of Bosnia swept aside for the cheap titillation of scandal.

Khattak was determined not to let that happen.

"Sir," Rachel said, reading his resistance in the stiffness of his posture, his slightly bent head. "You said we should widen the field. I still think it's possible there's a museum connection here. The average person doesn't walk away from that kind of money."

She flinched from Khattak's look, as cold and remote as if he'd never worked with her, never known her loyalty or perseverance at his side.

"Mink won't take the money — not when she knows where it came from." His tone suggested an implicit faith in the librarian. He turned away. "I need some air. I was planning to walk over to Ringsong. Maybe there's something more Mink can tell us about Drayton or the girls, something she hasn't thought of yet."

This was worse, Rachel realized. Worse than misunderstanding each other over a war in a place that meant little to most people. It was worse that he couldn't separate his work from his desire to return to the museum like a touchstone.

"We're not done here, sir."

"I am. Finish with Nate if you like."

Rachel knew she couldn't change his

405

mind. "Be careful, sir. Let's not give too much of our case away."

Khattak's gaze disquieted her. "I'm not sure what it is you fear from Mink Norman. Whatever it is, you're wrong."

She'd been slapped down but she had to risk saying it. "Then would you ask her about the meeting on the night of Drayton's fall? Because that's where Newhall claimed he was. At least we should know if that much is true."

Khattak didn't argue. His assent was somehow worse than any rebuttal he could have made.

She drove home, avoiding Nate's sympathy, his assiduous offer of help. Slowly through cantering drifts of rain, past the outline of Newhall's house in the gloom and the van parked in its driveway, straight down the highway until an hour later she was home, her thoughts churning, her stomach aboil. It was how her body coped with anxiety. Or with fear and shame. She hadn't done anything to deserve Khattak's rebuff, yet she yearned for his good opinion. Of her work, nothing more, she insisted to herself.

It would have been companionable somehow to review the photographs with Nate, but not after Khattak's cool dismissal. He'd seen into her. Recognized her weakness and exploited it, making her seem feeble and possessive. She shrugged it off. What did her feelings matter when set against Hadley's or David Newhall's? Or the girl who had hanged herself. Perhaps the answer had been here all along.

She spread the photographs she had taken at Drayton's house across her bed.

The gun that lay on the floor. The puddles of wax. The atlas opened to the Drina River. The papers he'd collected: some stored in the safe, some jammed into his filing cabinet, some taken by Hadley Blessant. The yellow-headed lilies. The Adagio in G Minor.

The music made her think of Zach, although not because he'd had the chance to play any more than she had. In her head, she lumped the arts together. Someone who loved music adored art and vice versa. Look at Nathan Clare. A man of letters whose home was filled with exquisite paintings and objets d'art. Who was willing to fund a museum about a long-ago time in a faraway place. The beauties of Andalusia: literature, history, cultural synthesis. A place of learning and libraries, those palaces of memory. The ring songs of Andalusia, the music of a dazzling civilization.

Music, history, art, and lore.

A long ago time in a faraway place — the golden palaces of memory.

Her fingers arranged the photographs she'd taken at Drayton's house in a circle. The music. The photograph. The lilies. The gun. She peered closer.

And now the coagulum that had clouded her perceptions evaporated into discovery.

I feel as though I'm in a pantomime.

Was it the Blessants? she had wondered. From the beginning, the Blessants had been an occlusion.

The music. The photograph. The lilies. The gun.

It had to be. It could be nothing else.

She was playing a hunch, the kind Khattak would discard without a word, but it didn't matter. She had finally grasped the nature of Christopher Drayton's death. She needed to meet the survivors the imam had told them about.

Once she'd taken care of two small matters.

With gut-churning certainty, she found her phone and dialed her brother. When he'd listened to her request and made his promise to help, she made another call, this time to schedule a meeting with Audrey Clare.

The woman who had been at the periphery of Drayton's murder.

The woman who held the key to the truth.

32.

This was the city's still center, the very essence of Islam: in a walled courtyard, water, a tree, and the warm geometry of stone. In the deep blue velvet sky by the minaret hung a sliver of incandescent silver light: the first moon of spring.

There were things he wanted Mink to say, things he wanted her not to say.

Was he there as Esa Khattak, director of Community Policing? He thought not. He thought he was there to listen to the sound of water murmuring through rooms of stone. He was there to cup his hands over the sweet globe of her face. He was there to share the hard things within himself. Things he could not say to Rachel, the language absent between them where words were quietly necessary.

"It's late, Esa," she said, opening the door. He made excuses, lied to them both.

"Something's happened. I must speak with you about Hadley."

The door gave way. The first fresh sails on his personal ship of joy began to unfurl. He followed her, heedless of the tension that narrowed her shoulders, shortening the smooth sweep of her neck.

"Esa," she said, drawing the name out over her lips. "Is it wise of you to come here on your own?"

"I thought we were beyond pretense."

"Aren't you here to ask me questions about your case? About Christopher Drayton?" She sounded angry.

With an effort, he made himself remember Hadley. This was Andalusia, not a garden of bones. Not the darkling meadows of Srebrenica. "May we sit in the courtyard?"

She'd stopped at the forecourt. He stood close, inhaling the scent of oranges from her hair.

"Ask me what you've come to ask."

He thought for a moment of one of the verses Hadley had lettered for the display.

We see / that things too quickly grown / are swiftly overthrown.

"Did Hadley ever speak to you about Drayton? Did she suggest that she may have been frightened of him?"

"Frightened? Why?"

"That's what I'm asking you."

"Yes. I see that you return here time and again to ask me questions."

He studied her face, seeking a clue as to her anger.

"Don't look at me like that. You've come for your work, why else should you come?"

"Mink, I have a duty —"

"I don't care about your duty. Why do you come to Andalusia? What do you want from me?"

He began to feel angry himself. "Isn't it a place of welcome?" He didn't say, as he'd thought so many times, of belonging. "I've come because Hadley is close to you. She was worried about Drayton — I thought you might have known."

"So you've come to taunt me with my imperfect sheltering of my charges. You say Drayton was a fugitive, a *war criminal,* and you accuse me of having left the girls in his path."

"I'm not accusing you of anything. I thought perhaps she may have told you something that would help with our questions about Drayton's death."

"You told me about him, Esa. If I knew something that would have helped you, wouldn't I have said so by now?"

"Not if it was a confidence from a young girl."

"So you expect me to break that confidence."

He stared at her helplessly. Her pale eyes were like moonstones in the delicate light of the forecourt. She wore her hair loose. It fell in soft gold waves that made him want to banish the subject of Hadley altogether. "I thought you'd want to help me. As you did before."

She pursed her lips. The skin around her eyes tightened. "You're pulling me into something ugly. Something that has no place here. Something that defiles this space."

His heart thumped in the silence. Was she right? No matter how virtuous its goal, his work contained within it an unalterable ugliness. Drayton's photographs were visceral proof of that. It was a place Khattak spent his days in, a place his thoughts lived. It would always be so with him. It would always be part of him.

A sense of remoteness closed about his heart. He'd thought more of her than she was, reading into her erudition the same strength and compassion that were second nature to Rachel. Rachel was neither graceful nor poised like this woman. She was

413

blunt, straight as an arrow, and all too human in her personal failings.

Mink was — what was Mink? The illusion of a moment? His heart's long-delayed awakening? He rejected the thought as an unnecessary indulgence.

"I can return in the morning with my sergeant, if you prefer, but I must ask you all the same. Did Hadley Blessant confide in you about Christopher Drayton?"

Her face altered, went soft. "I've made you angry, I'm sorry. I've been so worried about the opening. The girls weren't at the dinner tonight and I didn't know why. They didn't call me so I cut things short, rushed home. And earlier today I received such a distressing call. I'm sorry, Esa," she said again. "These are not your problems. Will you come in?"

She couldn't have said anything more calculated to wipe away his anger. His sense of mistrust faded. He took the hand she held out to him. In moments she was curled up beside him beneath the palm trees' overlapping shade.

"I don't know anything," she went on. "Hadley didn't tell me anything. I wish she had, you've made me worry. What happened tonight?"

Rachel's voice sounded in his head. He

414

discounted it.

"Drayton's interest in the girls was far from fatherly. I thought Hadley might have talked to you about it."

A sharp line formed between her brows. "What do you mean? That he — Was he preying upon the girls? Is that it?"

He held her hand within his own, feeling the rapid beat of her pulse at her wrist. From his touch? He hoped so. "He intended to. The fall interrupted his plan."

"My God. Those poor girls. Why didn't Hadley tell me?"

"She may have feared that her father was involved somehow in Drayton's fall. She may not have wanted to give him a motive."

Mink laced her fingers through his. "That explains why she wouldn't have told you. It doesn't explain why she didn't come to me. You were right. We are close."

"She's a self-contained young woman who's used to managing for herself. With a mother like Melanie Blessant, that's not surprising. Tell me about your call."

"It was nothing. You've more important things to worry about."

She was still caught up in his news about Hadley.

"Tell me."

"A lawyer called me today. He told me

415

about Christopher's will. About the money he left the museum. He also said his assets were frozen."

"Does that pose a problem for Ringsong? Are you in financial difficulty?"

"I would never take his money." Her voice rang with conviction. "Not after what you've told me about him. How would I know where that money came from? It's blood money."

The tightness in Khattak's chest unclenched. He'd expected her to refuse the money, and she had. Why had he expected that this subtle woman whose work celebrated a world both beautiful and fragile would step without a qualm into the dark realm he inhabited?

She went on in a calmer voice, "I doubt there's an art institution in the world that wouldn't benefit from greater patronage, but we've been fortunate in our grants. We planned on a small scale and we're well within reach of our goals."

"I'm glad." He smiled into her hair. The earth was suddenly beautiful; the lush accumulation of blooms hummed with praise through the courtyard. He let the field of silence stretch between them. "Will you send me an invitation to the opening?"

"Are you sure you want to come?"

"I can't think of anything I'd like better."

"Then I will. Esa," she said urgently, "if Chris is all that you say he is, does it matter so much if he fell or was pushed? Isn't the service of his death enough? Can't you leave it alone?"

"What if it was Melanie Blessant, as a shortcut to Drayton's will? Or Dennis Blessant himself, to put an end to any possibility of losing custody of his daughters? Motives wholly unconnected to Drayton's true identity?"

"What if it wasn't?" Her large clear eyes sought out the sliver of moon on the horizon. "What if his crimes came home to his doorstep? Don't his victims deserve some form of redress?"

"I think what we owe his victims is the truth. Whatever it turns out to be."

Mink shook her head. He felt the movement against his chin.

"What is it?"

"I was just thinking how absurd it would be if this man who posed as our friend and benefactor — this dangerous war criminal — buried himself in this corner of the world only to be murdered by the woman he intended to marry."

"It's not the right narrative, is it?"

"So do tyrants meet their end. In these

strange, ignominious ways."

"We've no evidence that he didn't fall. We can't place anyone at the scene, we can't prove or disprove anyone's alibi." Abruptly, he remembered Rachel's caution. "I think I'd better go. I still have some work."

And this wasn't the way a man of his convictions should proceed. Not if he wanted from Mink what he'd once had with Samina. However tempting the night, the walled garden, the woman.

"One night you'll stay longer," she said.

His ship of joy set sail, his silent restraint forgotten.

"Ask me again when this is over."

33.

We saw our sons and husbands off to those woods and never heard anything about them again.

Today no man from our family is older than thirty.

It was their last dawn.

He and Hakija had survived the night on the bus to witness a final dawn. The air in the bus was soft and warm, his brother was still asleep. The killing had stopped for the night.

He thought of observing Fajr prayer in that moment. He thought of words his mother had taught him when he was small.

"Say: I seek refuge in the Lord of Daybreak, from the evil of that which He created. From the evil of the black darkness whenever it descends."

He wouldn't dream of praying now, not with Chetniks all around them. A prayer was as good as a death warrant. He could think of it, though: the Sustainer of the Rising Dawn had seen them through to the morning.

The engines roared into life, as Hakija jerked awake. He put his hand on his brother's neck and cautioned him to silence. Hakija wanted water but there was no water. If he put his head out the window to ask, a Chetnik would shoot him.

The bus moved on, heading north. He recognized the valley town of Zvornik. He knew the fates had been no kinder here. He couldn't afford to think about Zvornik or Srebrenica or the people left behind at Potočari when his mission was survival.

The bus turned off the main road and his stomach fell.

If they weren't going to a camp to be exchanged, where were they going? He tried to measure the time by the sun but quickly lost track. He was thirsty. He admitted to himself that he was also terrified. He wasn't alone. Every face on the bus reflected the same fear back to him. The uncles and older boys who might have comforted them could only think of themselves. It made him think of the Day of Judgment when not a single soul would speak up for another.

Was this their judgment, then?

They pulled up in front of a school in the village of Grbavici. He counted the vehicles in the convoy. Five buses, six trucks. As the men were made to disembark, terror rose like a wave through his body, strangling his throat, expiring through his fingertips. The bus meant life. The school, he knew, was the end of the road.

He whispered into Hakija's ear. "They're letting us rest now, don't worry. Just don't say anything out loud. Pay attention to me. I'll tell you when it's time to go."

Soldiers milled all around them. He was careful not to catch anyone's eye. He pushed Hakija before him through the crowd into the gym, where the men were packed in tight. The heat and fear coming off the other men's bodies seared his skin. Clammy and sick, he clung to his little brother.

Chetniks came into the hall, laughing and talking. They passed water around the gym. A wave of energy pulsed through the men who fought for the water. He and Hakija were close to one of the Chetniks. The soldier saw them and pushed a bottle at them. He grabbed it and pulled Hakija into his chest, where he forced half the bottle down his brother's throat. The men around him caught sight of their prize. They shoved Hakija aside and the bottle fell from his grasp to spill on the floor. Like the others, Avdi dove down and licked it from the floor, his dry tongue taking swift swipes like a cat. They shoved at him and pushed him, each fighting for his turn. He heard his brother's high-pitched call. He clambered out from beneath the crush of bodies and fought his way back to Hakija's side.

"Did you drink?" he asked. Hakija nodded. "Me too."

They grinned at each other, two survivors of the ride to Grbavici. He grabbed his brother's hand and moved him through the crowd as close as he could to the back of the gym. His watchful eyes had realized an opportunity. Like the other boys, they were shorter than everyone else. They couldn't be seen from the front.

Then a rustle went through the crowd. Someone whispered, "The general."

He craned his neck to see. Around the crush of emaciated men, he saw the reason for this new wave of fear. It was Mladić himself, slapping his men on the shoulders, laughing with some, rolling back on his heels.

"We are taking you to a camp," he said.

Avdi didn't believe him. Especially when they picked two men out of the crowd and told them to blindfold the others as they passed through the door.

The crowd in the gym began to narrow into a river, men pressing them from all sides as they were taken to the door, blindfolded and led back to the trucks and the buses. Around them in the gym, men were fainting. The heat of the day was building.

He tried to fight the tide, Hakija's hand slippery in his, but the crush was too great. There were too many Chetniks in the building now, corralling them from the back and the front.

When they arrived at the door, he squeezed himself and Hakija through before the other men could blindfold him. He needed to see. If he didn't see, he wouldn't know the moment for escape.

"Don't worry," he whispered to his brother. "We've had water, next we'll have food. Remember? The general gave out chocolate at the gate."

He said it to reassure Haki. To himself, he thought: it was a taste of sweetness before dying. Some of the children had taken it. He'd known that no matter how hungry, he must not take anything from the hands of the executioner.

There was a terrified murmuring on the bus, but like the men themselves, it was weak and subdued. This time the distance the bus traveled was short. When Avdi peered through the window, he saw that the Chetniks had brought them to a field in the raging heat. It was a pretty meadow, a place where children must have played before death had come to his country.

He knew what was coming. He could see the bodies in the field where the Chetniks had their guns cocked.

"Are we going to die?" Hakija asked him, almost calm.

"No," he whispered back, fiercely. "I didn't bring you all this way just to die. You stay by my side. You move when I move. Don't do anything else."

Rows and rows of men were lined up in the field. He could smell the blood leaching up from the earth. It made him want to vomit. If Hakija hadn't been with him, he would have given himself long-denied permission to faint.

The moment the Chetniks turned their attention to the next load of men to disembark, he grabbed Hakija's hand and squeezed in between two of the rows. They couldn't run, but maybe the first round would miss them.

He waited for the Chetnik commander to give the order.

"Now!" he hissed.

He threw Hakija forward and tugged his body beneath his own. The men behind them fell on top of him just as he landed on the shoes and legs of the man in front of him.

None of the bodies moved. They lay still and

quiet: a perfectly arranged series of corpses.

Pinned beneath warm, bleeding bodies, his hand made a furtive search of his brother's torso. No wetness, no wounds. Lord of Daybreak, Lord of the Angels, his maneuver had worked. Haki's face was turned sideways. He could see his tears. He licked them up quickly. There were Chetnik boots behind them. The soldiers were patrolling for survivors.

Blood from the neck of the man who lay on top of him dripped onto his face. Moving his hand a little at a time, he brushed the blood over his brother's spotless face.

"Don't move," he said directly into Hakija's ear. "Don't breathe."

His brother obeyed him, eyes closed, body frozen. For a second, he thought Hakija was really dead.

He couldn't think of any prayers so he said his mother's name over and over again in his head. Shots fired all around them. Haki flinched but the bodies around them covered the small movement. Boots receded in the distance.

"Is anyone alive?" a soldier called.

"Please," a man answered weakly. "I'm alive. Please help me."

The soldier went over and fired a single shot.

Another group of men was led from the buses to the field. There was another volley of shots, another round of thudding bodies hitting the earth. The scent of the meadow turned sick with decay. And still he listened.

"Please," an old man called, as his turn came to be lined up. "Children, we didn't do anything. Don't do this to us."

He was silenced by a shot.

Someone else begged for his life. Another shot followed.

A man cried and murmured for his daughter.

"Fuck your daughter."

"Better yet, let us fuck her." Another shot.

The other men stayed quiet. They knew it was a game now. Speak and die. Stay silent, die. Move. Die. Lie still. Die. Stay on the bus. Die. Stumble through the field. Die.

Death was the only outcome.

He and Hakija lay facedown in the blood-soaked grass. Underneath their bodies, he held his brother's hand, stroking his palm. The hours passed, the heat of the day building to an excruciating crescendo. They both lost consciousness after a time. When Avdi woke again, it was to feel the ants crawling over his face, his arms, his legs, their tiny incursions unbearable as they delved in the stickiness of blood. He felt them in his mouth. His body itched to scream.

After a time, the sun went down. Now the field was lit by the bulldozers the Chetniks had brought to dig the graves. Newly drunk, they were braying at each other, firing sporadically, shooting at men already dead as a diversion.

He checked his brother's face. Hakija's eyes were closed, there was no sign of life.

He spoke into his ear. "Are you all right?"

Haki's eyelids flickered.

"Good. We have to move soon. Before they come to bury us."

"Everyone is dead," his brother said.

"I know. But we're still alive. Wait for my signal."

It began to rain, a steady, drilling, persistent rain. The soldiers had moved to a distant part of the meadow, firing at random. He turned Hakija's face toward the rain and opened his own mouth. The rain began to wash the ants away. He felt the heaviness of the body that covered his. It was slowly stiffening, turning cold. All this time, he'd been determined not to look. Now he thought maybe he should. Maybe he would be able to tell someone that their brother or father or son hadn't made it. Before their bones disappeared into the earth, he would know what had happened to at least one man among these thousands.

He looked at the corpse's face. It was thin like his own, narrow like his own, hungry like his own. Marked by the madness of terror like his own. He was a boy in his late teens wearing tennis shoes. He would have taken his papers if there were any but none of them had any papers. The Chetniks had stripped every trace of their identity. They would bury their bodies nameless and faceless.

He memorized the face, pondered the young man's shoes.

"You are my brother," he thought of the man whose body he had used as a shield. "I won't ever forget you."

The lights of the bulldozers went dead. The taunting stopped.

Drunk with killing and soaked in brandy, the Chetniks began to withdraw from the field.

He gripped Haki's hand. This was their only chance before they swapped in a new patrol. "Get ready," he said. His legs were numb beneath the weight of bodies, he didn't know if they would work. He didn't know if Haki could walk. But it was walk or die, so they would walk.

He counted to five hundred in his head.

There was no more sound, no more soldiers. Perhaps they'd gone quiet on purpose, waiting to see if any bodies rose from the dead. He'd have to risk it. There'd be no way to crawl free from the bulldozer's pit.

"Now," he said. He freed Hakija from the shelter of his body. He struggled to shove aside the bodies that had toppled over them both. It was hard work. The men were thin but their corpses were fixed in death. At last, he freed them both. Panting, he said to Hakija, "Don't stand up, just crawl. Follow me. If you hear anything, freeze."

Moonlight cut a swath through the field. He traced its path to the woods at the edge. His pace quickened. Every five seconds he looked behind to make sure that Haki was at his heels. Reassured, he moved on, his hands slippery with sweat and blood.

Now he didn't look. He couldn't. He felt bodies give way beneath him with odd concavities, he found tiny patches of grass redolent with blood, he thought at one time that he heard a bone snap from the pressure of his body. He blinked salt from his eyes and kept at his task.

It took them thirty minutes to reach the woods. He climbed into the shadows, pulling Haki up behind him. He grabbed his brother close to his chest and hugged him jubilantly, kissing his rain-washed face over and over.

"See? We made it. I told you we would." He ran his hands over Hakija's arms and legs, an action he hadn't dared undertake before. "Are you hurt? Were you shot?"

Hakija shook his head, a ragged smile on his lips.

"Let's find our mother."

But for a moment he didn't move. For a moment, as he hugged his brother close, he looked out over the field they had left behind. A field so full of bodies that he couldn't see the earth. The shadows of the bulldozers hulked over the ground.

In every direction he looked, there was death.

Until this moment, he hadn't cried. For Hakija's sake, he hadn't cried. Now he could do nothing else. Sobs tore through his body. He stifled them by biting his fists. He said the prayers the Chetniks had ground to dust beneath their boots. He asked God to accept his single Fatiha as an offering for all his people. His tears were the only comfort his brothers would know at the place of their dying.

He didn't let Haki look.

As they slipped into the woods toward sanctuary and life, he glimpsed an unearthly vision in the moonlight that hallowed the ground. He was headed for Tuzla down a death road.

The ghosts in the field rose in rank after rank at his shoulder.

34.

I knew all of them who did it. They were my neighbors.

As Rachel drove to the location of Audrey's clinic downtown, rain began to fall, slowing traffic to a crawl. Audrey was coming from an out-of-town appointment, a longer drive than Rachel's, yet she appeared as calm and lovely as on their first meeting. Even the rain had chosen to spare her: her hair was beautifully styled, her makeup tasteful and fresh. They met in the parking lot in front of Audrey's clinic, a humble space whose windows were decorated with posters of hands reaching out to the hands of women around the world. The clinic's name was lettered in white on a cherry-colored backdrop. Unpretentious and welcoming, much like Audrey herself.

"Shall we go inside?" Audrey asked her.

"This won't take long." Rachel withdrew

431

the envelope that held Drayton's papers from under her jacket. "I wanted to learn about your work here. And your clinic."

She liked the fact that Audrey didn't seem to mind the rain, taking the time to consider her question with her laptop case over one shoulder, the keys to her Jaguar cupped in her hand.

"It's called Woman to Woman. We do advocacy work on behalf of victims of violence."

"What kind of violence?"

"Rape victims. Torture. Girls who've been reclaimed from the sex trade. In some rare cases, domestic violence, although there are other organizations for that."

"What kind of background do you need for that?"

"Mostly you need money, if you're truly passionate about it. But if you're asking about my credentials, I've done a master's degree in psychology and another in social work."

Exactly as she'd thought. There were depths to Nathan's sister that were going to prove invaluable. "Do you have a moment? I'd like to show you something related to this case."

Audrey waited as Rachel produced the

photograph of the girl who had hanged herself.

"Who is that?" Audrey breathed. "Where did you get it?"

"I'm showing you this in confidence. It was among Drayton's papers. You said you've worked with victims of rape and torture, which means you must have an international clientele."

Audrey nodded. "Refugees, mostly, or women with landed status who are just beginning to open up about the violence they've endured."

"Which parts of the world?"

"Congo. The Sudan. Burma. Rwanda." Her eyes narrowed in realization. "Yes," she said. "Bosnia and Croatia, as well."

"Why might a girl from Srebrenica hang herself? Like the one in this photograph."

Audrey set down her laptop case to study the photograph more closely. "It's impossible to say conclusively. The uncertainty of the war may have been too much for her — a kind of existential dilemma. She may have lost loved ones that day or earlier in the war and felt she couldn't go on without them."

"And what if she was raped?"

"Is that what happened here?"

"I don't know. Would suicide be a likely consequence?"

Audrey spread her hands helplessly. "It's possible, Rachel. Rape was a feature of the war."

"Isn't that true of all wars?"

"As a side effect of chaos, lawlessness — the powerful preying upon the helpless. But in Bosnia, mass rape was a policy of the war, systematically carried out, implicating neighbors, paramilitaries, soldiers. Those who wouldn't participate were threatened, they were told it was a bonding ritual. The policy was to terrorize and humiliate their victims so they would never return to the scene of their degradation, thereby ethnically 'cleansing' entire cities and villages. Any building could be transformed into a rape camp. A school gymnasium, a town hall — in Foča, it was the high school and the Partizan Hall." She twisted her keys between her hands and drew a breath. "I can't begin to tell you. We've helped women from Foča at Woman to Woman." She studied the photograph again. "The men there were drunk on rape. Once you've demonized the Other so thoroughly, it doesn't matter what you do to them. They cease to be human. A woman subjected to that type of brutality might well decide to bring her suffering to an end. I wouldn't rule it out."

"This was a kid," Rachel said. "Maybe

fourteen years old."

"That wouldn't matter to the perpetrators. They gang-raped children as a matter of course."

Rachel's stomach heaved. She'd dealt with terrible things in the course of her work but nothing as dark and sinister as this. This man who'd lived among them — a teacher of languages, a lover of gardens, a patron of the arts — he had given these orders, let his men run wild, held none to account. She thought of Hadley and Cassidy. The war had not exhausted his menace.

She considered Audrey with her pixie haircut, her designer jewelry and clothing: a girl raised in wealth and privilege to enjoy a lifetime of the same. Yet she had founded an organization dedicated to helping the vulnerable, when sharing their stories must have been a trauma in itself.

"Why do you do it? This kind of work, I mean. You don't have to, right?"

"Ah, I see." Audrey collected her laptop. "I could live off my brother's wealth or my trust fund, jet-setting about the globe, is that what you mean?" She shrugged. "I'm no saint, Rachel. There are plenty of luxuries I haven't given up." She waved her keys at Rachel. "My Jag, for example. I suppose you think I'm just another dilettante dabbling in celebrity causes."

Rachel swallowed uncomfortably. Until this graphic conversation, she had to admit the thought had crossed her mind. She cleared her throat. "No. I can't see a dabbler sweating it out in graduate school. It's just — I'm a cop, and I still find this stuff hard. You've had to immerse yourself in misery."

"There's hope as well. The women we work with demonstrate incredible bravery. We learn from them every day, it's hardly a one-way street." She fluffed up her rain-dampened hair with one hand. "It's what our parents taught us, both Nate and me. If you're given a gift, you have a responsibility to put it to use. That's why Nate is so invested in immigration policy and multiculturalism: it's a buttress to the work of our NGO." She smiled impishly. "That and the fact that we grew up with Esa and Ruksh."

Rachel had noticed a common factor about people whose work she admired. They made themselves the smallest part of the equation. As if reading her thoughts, Audrey's smile softened into reflection.

"It was my mother, really. Wherever my father traveled on his adventures, she found a way to reach out to the women, to work with them."

"She sounds remarkable," Rachel said. She wondered what it would have been like to have been raised by such a woman. "You mentioned Foča." She pronounced it gingerly. "Would your organization have assisted anyone from Srebrenica? Would you be able to put me in touch with any of the survivors?"

"I'm afraid not, no. If you'd like to speak with one of the families from Foča, I can ask them. We haven't dealt directly with anyone from Srebrenica."

Audrey reached out and grasped her hand.

"I'm glad you came into our lives, Rachel. I'm glad Esa brought you. Let me know if you need my help with anything else."

Rachel pulled into the mosque's parking lot with more speed than care, her tires screeching. It had taken an hour to fight through traffic, her worst suspicions confirmed by Audrey's revelations. She hustled her way inside through a larger crowd than usual to Imam Muharrem's office, where she banged on the door.

He didn't answer so she tried the knob. The charming room was empty. As she pondered her next move, a man appeared at her elbow. Small, slight, with twinkling eyes, he asked if he could help her. She introduced herself as Esa Khattak's sergeant.

"I'm looking for the imam. Imam Muharrem. He said he could introduce us to some of the survivors from Srebrenica."

The small man's face relaxed. "Muharrem is away at a lecture. He will be back tomorrow. My name is Asaf, perhaps I can help you."

She seized on the name at once. He was the mosque's full-time imam, the man Muharrem had been asked to relieve. "Asaf? Imam Asaf? I think you know my boss."

"I know him well. I would be delighted if I could be of service to any friend of Esa's."

"Would you be able to help me locate some of the survivors? Would any of them be at the mosque today?"

The young imam ushered her into the office. As if sensing her agitation, he went directly to the samovar and poured her a cup of tea.

"Please take a seat, Sergeant, and tell me how I can help you. I can make calls and ask if anyone is available to meet you here. I'm sure you understand that I prefer not to give out numbers until I've learned a little more about your interest. Many of these people have struggled to put the past behind them."

"Imam Muharrem didn't tell you about our previous visit?"

"I've been on holiday." His blue eyes twinkled at her. "I'm sure you understand that those are the moments one chooses to get away from the pressures of work. He may have called me, I regret I didn't answer."

"No, it's all right. Look, to be honest with you, I'm trying to understand a little better about what happened in Srebrenica during the war. It's relevant to a case we're working that involves a man named Damir Hasanović."

"Damir?" The imam sat back in surprise. "I haven't seen him in some time."

"Two years," Rachel said.

"Yes, two years. He was an active member of our congregation, on the board of the mosque and so on. He did a great deal of work with the community and he was very much in demand internationally, as well. I hope he is not in any difficulties."

"I hope not as well. Would you be able to tell me a little more about his work? What kinds of things he did?"

Asaf had a quick, intelligent face enhanced by the gentlest of smiles. He would be good at his chosen vocation, she thought, providing spiritual solace to many.

"He acted as a translator and an advocate. He helped many people come to this country as refugees. He advised our students on access to education. He arranged driver's licenses, housing, he explained the immigration settlement services to them. If anyone had difficulty with any level of government, he acted as their representative until their issues were resolved. He wrote letters to the media, he gave tours of the mosque. He lectured at schools. Most of his time was spent on behalf of the memorial."

"The memorial?" Rachel echoed.

"The genocide memorial in Srebrenica. To recognize the dead by name when names were all we had. It was an international project but we had a devoted group here in our city. It's strange," he mused.

"What is?" She found both his tea and his manner soothing.

"It's not only Damir the community has lost — we still don't know why or where he went. He was invaluable to us."

"Who else?" Rachel prodded.

"The others who worked on the memorial. Survivors like those you wish to meet."

"Survivors of Srebrenica?"

"Yes. Of the killing fields, there are only a handful of men who survived. Damir arranged to bring Avdo and Hakija here."

440

Rachel stared at him, dumbstruck.

"What is it, my dear?"

"I'm sorry, Imam. What names did you say?"

"Avdo and Hakija. Osmanović. They were to be executed at Grbavici. By some miracle, the boys escaped when the executions were halted for the night. They made it through the woods to the safety of Tuzla."

"Your gardens are beautiful," she mumbled through lips that felt numb.

The imam quirked an eyebrow at the irrelevance of her remark. "I think you need more tea, dear Sergeant."

She handed him her cup without protest. She wouldn't have objected if he'd added a shot of whiskey.

"Yes, that is Avdo and Haki's work. It's good that they came here — thanks to Damir, they were able to build productive lives, even with Haki's condition."

"What condition is that, sir?"

"The boys were buried under a mountain of bodies. That's how they escaped. Avdi had a plan, it seemed. He knew they would end up at an execution site. From the moment he was loaded on a bus, he plotted their escape." Asaf's voice marveled at it. "I don't know how he did it, how he managed. He's very resourceful. Sadly, by the time he found their mother in Tuzla, Haki was catatonic. After that, it was a simple matter for Damir to arrange their evacuation. And Haki's had wonderful, ongoing treatment in the city. It's helped him a great deal, although it's doubtful he will ever fully recover."

"No," Rachel agreed, thinking of Harry Osmond. "I can't imagine what that would be like."

Asaf made a reassuring noise in his throat. "If you are interested, their testimony is available on the Web site of the tribunal. It has been used in several of the Srebrenica convictions."

"And these were the people who worked with Damir Hasanović on the memorial?"

"Tirelessly. Damir tried to bring the Sinanović family as well. The boys were killed in the woods — some have said by chemical weapons. Their bodies have been identified. Selmira, their sister, died on the base."

Rachel was having trouble assimilating the information.

Everything she had imagined was true.

The music, the photograph, the lilies, the gun.

Her voice husky, she asked, "She was killed?"

Asaf's face clouded over. He lifted a Qur'an from the desk and placed both hands over it as if to calm himself.

"I don't know if I should speak of it, dear Sergeant. I'm not sure I have the right."

Rachel wasn't trying to trick him when she said, "We would like to do her justice." She produced the photograph of the girl hanging from her scarf in the darkling woods of Bosnia. "Is this Selmira?"

Asaf's gentle face crumpled.

"I seek refuge in Allah," he whispered. "Where did you get this?" His fingers gripped the Qur'an.

"Tell me about Selmira," she said. "Did they kill her at Potočari?"

He shook his head from side to side. Like Imam Muharrem, he murmured prayers under his breath.

"She was fourteen years old when she took her own life. She was taken by the Chetniks and raped. It was Damir's dearest wish to place her name on the memorial, but the rape of our daughters is something the community struggles with. The shame is a lasting stigma. It was why Selmira hanged herself."

"Shame and horror," Rachel agreed.

It was what Audrey Clare had taught her, well-versed in the trauma endured by rape victims through her work with her organization, the work she had lightly dismissed. Rachel had remembered Nate's description of his sister as a human rights advocate.

The photograph had been her first clue. When she had paired it with the lines of one of the letters, she'd understood.

Keep the good ones over there. Enjoy yourselves.

"You said Damir Hasanović tried to bring the Sinanović family here. What did you mean?"

He poured more tea for them both, his hands trembling on the samovar.

As she listened to his explanation, she irrevocably understood why Khattak had defended Hasanović from the heart.

The music, the photograph, the lilies, the gun. The clues arranged in a circle on Nathan's table. The words that whispered their damning indictment.

On Tuesday, there will be no bread in Sarajevo.

The besieged city of Jajce has fallen to the aggressor.

They are shelling Bihać.

They are shelling Goražde.

They are shelling Tuzla.

They have shelled Srebrenica.

They have killed Avdo Palić, the defender of Žepa.

They assassinated our prime minister while the French troops watched.

Everything around us is on fire and we ourselves are nearly smoldering.

The National Library is burning, it's burning. Will no one save it, save us?

They will burn us all.

They will burn us all.

Rachel left the sanctuary of the mosque and stood outside, breathing deeply. The thunderheads massed on the horizon echoed her own turmoil. The words meant something. They were chosen for a reason. They directed Drayton to a revelation, an accusation.

A revelation she feared. Especially because Khattak was nowhere to be found.

The rain that had been so mild during her interview with Audrey picked up, muffling the sound of her phone ringing. She hoped it was Nate, the one person who could reach Esa.

The number was unfamiliar. Three rings later, she registered it as Zach's. When she answered the phone, the first thing she said was, "Zach, I love you. Not for a moment have I stopped. Whatever this is with Mum, we'll figure it out together, I promise. You won't have to choose. Just — don't stay missing from my life."

Her brother made the awkward humming noise that substituted for tears with him. He mumbled under his breath.

"What was that?"

He said it again, this time more clearly. Rachel heard him out: his confession of love, his apology in turn, his promise not to disappear again. She told him about the missing and the dead, what it did to your heart and your sanity never to know. The emptiness, the terrible black hole of the pain and dread that consumed you. He whispered and cried and apologized all at the same time.

Then he gave her the information she'd asked him to check and as she listened, her breath blew out in a blasphemous whistle. "Holy saints of Heaven and Hell."

Everything she'd feared had come true.

35.

The dead are not alone.

When Khattak still didn't answer, she called Nate.

"I can't find Esa." His name slipped past her lips of its own accord. "Is he with you?"

"No, I'm sorry, but he isn't. You sound worried."

Instead of using her earpiece, she was cradling her phone against her shoulder while the hard rain drilled her windshield.

"It's not like him not to answer his phone. He doesn't do that."

"Unless he's at Ringsong," Nate concluded. "Shall I find him?"

A rush of gratitude for his offer swelled up in Rachel's heart. It wasn't just the book he'd written; the roots of his friendship, once offered, ran deep.

"Yes. And get him out of there, if you can."

"I think you might be blowing things out

447

of proportion."

"Trust me, I'm not. Please, Nate, go now."

She let the phone fall into her lap and turned on her siren.

Nate found them in the flex room between the portico and forecourt. Mink was wearing a white smock over jeans and a T-shirt, a carpet vacuum beside her on the floor, a duster tucked into the pocket of her smock. A large clear jug filled with water suggested she'd been watering the plants. She'd been chatting with Esa but her smile for Nate was unambiguous.

"How lovely to see you. It's been much too long."

From the look on his face, Esa didn't agree.

"You've had my books to keep you company," Nate said.

Many of the books on Moorish history were from the collection at Winterglass.

"They were a donation, please don't forget." Mink's delight in the words was obvious, just as it was obvious that her reaction brought Esa no pleasure. Nate frowned. He was unsettled by the tension Esa's body language communicated. Surely Esa didn't think that he was interested in Mink when he'd paid such unequivocal attention to Rachel.

"You've made wonderful progress since my last visit," he said to Mink.

She grasped him by the elbow. "This is nothing. Esa knows, he's seen the great room. We've taken a more amateur approach to things, though I doubt anyone would judge Hadley's efforts as less than superb. I like the idea that we've done things with our own hands, like the craftspeople who bound books and built mosques of such immaculate beauty."

"Still living in the past, I see," Nate said.

She smiled, though for a moment her fingers bit into his elbow. "A historian's natural provenance, I'm afraid. Esa, are you coming?"

He followed them to a great room ablaze with light.

"I've just refurbished the lanterns," she said. "I wanted to see what the effect would be on the exhibits."

Her worktable was gone. In its place, she'd added numerous display cases and pedestals, some with modulated lights arranged above them to illuminate well-chosen treasures. Previously, where there had been photographs and manuscript pages, Mink had added woven carpet fragments, an ivory casket and a game box, stone capitals inscribed with Arabic calligraphy, a geometric panel from the Alhambra, glazed earthenware bowls, and swords beside their scabbards: artefacts that ranged from the tenth century to the fifteenth.

The pride of the collection was six folios from a blue and gold Qur'anic manuscript dated to the late fourteenth century. She hovered over the display.

"It's on loan," she said. "Just for the opening. They've installed their own alarm system, so don't get too close."

"It's breathtaking."

On a single manuscript page on vellum, Esa painstakingly identified the Verse of the Throne. The majesty of it made him swallow. Nate read his emotion and tried to distract Mink with his passable recollection of Rachel's questions.

"I can't believe you pulled all this together in two years."

"I had to call in a lot of favors."

"Those regular meetings must have helped as well. Directors, donors. They need constant assuaging."

Mink laughed, arresting Esa's attention. "An excellent description. It will be worth it in the end."

"I hope Chris's death hasn't cast a cloud."

Her eyes widened. "Does he know?" she

asked Esa.

He nodded in response.

"It did at first. Chris was — if not a friend, at least someone I could interest in Ring-song. But now that I've learned who he was, although it sounds callous, I've no reason to miss him."

"It isn't callous," Esa reassured her. Nate watched his friend take Mink's hand in his own. The luminous warmth of her smile encouraged the gesture. No wonder Rachel was worried.

"Was there a meeting on the night that Chris fell? I think David mentioned it to me."

"Yes," she agreed, without looking away from Esa. "We did meet. David and I and some of the other directors. They wanted a progress report. We hadn't gotten this far then, so I missed my chance to impress them. However, we do have another meeting at the end of the week. It should put everyone's fears to rest."

Nate pounced on the word. "Fears?"

"The usual, I'm sure," Esa answered for her. "Deadlines, budget — will the museum open at the time and on the scale promised."

"You've either been reading my mind or my literature," Mink teased.

"How long have you known David?" Nate

could see his questions were unwelcome, at least by Esa, but he kept them up.

"Two years? A little more? Ever since we began work on the project."

He ambled through the room, trying to think of ways to attract Esa's attention, distracted by the exhibits. He enjoyed the great room in Ringsong nearly as much as the same space in his own house. The dark timber, the white stonework, the clerestory windows: they were a concert of loveliness.

Mink had kept personal touches away from the house's main floor. Presumably, she kept her personal effects and furniture in her own rooms. As he drifted from manuscript to manuscript, he realized he knew little of her beyond their shared passion for the finer things in life — music, art, books. She had appeared in his life at the moment he'd lost Esa, filling in the space Esa had occupied with their common history and interests. With Mink, he'd found a link to Esa through Andalusia. He'd known from the first what the museum would mean, the resonances Esa would find within it.

A place where pluralism thrived, where languages and lives intermingled.

He'd known Esa thought of Bosnia as a second Andalusia, with its Ottoman mosques and the library that housed the histories of its peoples. What he hadn't guessed was how largely Mink figured in Esa's thoughts. He'd assumed his friend would find a woman like Samina in time, a woman of his own faith and culture, whose view of the world harmonized with his friend's.

There was nothing to fear from the gentle entanglement of Mink Norman, and yet Nate was uneasy. Community policing was the most unforgiving of mandates: Esa needed his objectivity. If there was a connection between the museum and Drayton's death, he needed to isolate it. He wandered back to them, well aware that his presence was an intrusion. Their heads were bent over the Qur'anic folio, dark and gold together.

"Do you know Albinoni's Adagio?" he asked idly.

Mink didn't look up. Her hand rested on Esa's. "I'm sorry?"

"It's a piece of music. Esa knows it. Perhaps if you don't, Sable might?"

"If it's well known, I'm sure she does. She may even have played it. It's been kind of you to loan her your music."

"I'm looking forward to hearing her play. After I meet her, of course."

"You'll have to throw one of your parties."

He gazed about the room, a thought striking him. "Where do you keep the piano?"

"In our private quarters. The board didn't want responsibility for it."

"The sound would be lovely down here, drifting out to the courtyard, vanishing over the water."

"You have the writer's gift of evoking a mood." Her laughter encompassed both men. "It would be exquisite, I agree, but one can't have everything. I've been fortunate enough to realize a dream — I'm more than content."

"You've a lot to be proud of here. I doubt anyone else could have accomplished as much in just two years."

"As I said, my friends have been good to me." She looked from one man to the other. "Is anything the matter? Is this something other than a friendly visit?"

Nate waited for Esa to say something, anything. When he didn't, Nate sighed heavily and shoved his hands into his trouser pockets. "I should get back. I'm sorry if I intruded." To Esa he said, "Walk me out, would you? I've a message for you."

They had developed their own code of silent signals during their misspent youth. Esa couldn't miss what he was asking.

"I'll just be a moment," he said to Mink.

Uneasy, Nate felt the weight of Mink's stare on the back of his neck

He waited until they had reached the terra-cotta steps to grab Esa's arm. "Come with me," he said. "You shouldn't stay here alone."

"What are you accusing me of?" Esa's eyes were hard green stones.

"Nothing, you fool. Rachel called me. She said to get you out of here. You need to take a step back."

"I need to step back?" He shook off Nate's hand. "You've been involved with the museum for two years —"

"Yes, two years!"

"— and it's taken you until my arrival to realize that Mink's a captivating woman."

"I'm not interested in her!"

"The hell you aren't. You've been hanging all over her."

"I was asking Rachel's questions, questions you were supposed to ask. Did you listen to her answers?" He lowered his voice with an effort. Even now she might be standing by the portico.

"I saw the way she smiled at you."

"She doesn't give a damn about me. It's you she's interested in, and either way it doesn't matter. There's something wrong

455

with the museum, something about the meetings or David Newhall — I don't know what it is, just something. Can't you feel it?"

"I deal in facts, not suppositions."

"Well, what do the facts tell you?" Nate asked desperately. "Chris moved here two years ago. David came two years ago. And the first I heard of the museum was two years ago."

He faced Esa's wrath without flinching.

"What in God's name are you talking about? The museum has nothing to do with Drayton. Newhall told us he was at the museum on the night of Drayton's fall and he was. Along with other members of the board."

"Which members? Ask her to tell you." He could handle Esa's contempt, if he could just get him to look at the truth.

"What's your theory, then?" Esa challenged. "That Mink is covering for David Newhall? Why would she? You asked a question, she answered it. You wanted to know about the music, she told you."

"And you believed her?"

"Are you saying you don't? You used to have more faith in the women you claimed to love."

And there it was. The indictment he had

waited for all this time.

Brutal, bitter, the words hung in the air between them. Then Esa thought better of it. "Nate —"

"No. I'm glad you finally said that. I was a fool over Laine, I admit it. Everything I believed about her was wrong. Everything I did was wrong. But if you're angry, it shouldn't be over this. Mink is a friend, that's all. It's not me who stands in your way, it's Rachel."

Nate blinked rapidly as he descended the steps. "There was a time when you didn't assume the worst about me, Esa. I was your friend. That's all I'm trying to be."

36.

I cannot find words for what happened there.

Rachel found Nate pacing the gardens behind his house. He looked wet and cold and very much alone.

"Where is he?" she demanded. "Wasn't he at Ringsong?"

"He's still there now. He wanted me gone."

"Christ. We need to get over there right away."

They had raised their voices over the wind, a wind so fierce and sudden that it picked apart Rachel's ponytail, sending dark strands whipping about her face.

Nate shrugged. "Not me. I've told you, he doesn't want me around." He shivered as the wind began to howl.

Rachel was too full of urgency to feel the

cold. "Grab your jacket, you're coming with me."

She had the unique ability to override his better judgment, her voice sounding in his ear all the way to the cloakroom and back again to the drive. He shouldered his way into the jacket he reserved for walks along the escarpment. A steely rain slanted against the horizon, the lake beyond arranged in little thrusts of chaos against the shadowy outline of the shore, the white bone of the Bluffs at a treacherous distance.

As her voice carried on, his pace sped up. He came to an abrupt halt at the museum. "That's Aldo's van, the one they use for landscaping. It wasn't here earlier."

"I've seen it before. Last night outside David Newhall's house."

She sprinted up the terra-cotta stairs and jammed her finger on the doorbell. When there was no answer, she moved through the portico and forecourt to the great room. The only person in it was Hadley Blessant. She was taking photographs of the exhibits through the powerful lens of a camera.

"Where's Inspector Khattak?"

"He's not here," said Hadley, a slight frown sketched between her brows. "Is something the matter?"

"Do you know where he is?" Rachel

couldn't conceal the anxiety in her voice. Hadley lowered the lens of her camera.

"They went for a walk on the Bluffs."

"In this weather?"

"I told them. It's not a good idea to walk the Bluffs in the dark. Mink said she needed the air and your inspector wouldn't let her go alone."

"Damn chivalrous fool," Nate muttered under his breath.

"Does this have anything to do with my father?"

Rachel spared a moment from her own worries to address the girl's concern. "No, Hadley, nothing at all. Don't worry about your dad, he'll be fine."

She didn't thank Rachel, but as she shifted her weight from one foot to the other, Hadley offered, "Do you want me to come help you look? There's a flashlight in the flex room."

"I'll find it, thanks." Rachel's gaze searched the room and the courtyard beyond, the windows lashed by rain. "Why is Aldo's van parked out front?"

"They were here. Mink called them a little while ago but she decided not to wait for them, so I told them she took the path along the Bluffs. If the van's still there, they probably went after her."

Rachel's voice climbed an octave. "His brother was with him?"

"And their friend. Mr. Newhall. They meet about the museum every now and again. The Osmonds come to look in on the gardens."

"Thanks." She grabbed Nate by the elbow. "Let's go."

They made their way outside, the rain driving against their faces in little spikes. Rachel began to run, Nate at her heels. Within five minutes, she'd turned her ankle.

"This is crazy," Nate said. "There's nothing to be afraid of. What you've told me simply doesn't make sense."

"You needed to read more as a kid" was her answer. She hobbled along behind him, blinded by rain, the flashlight skipping ahead down the muddy, rain-soaked path. Lightning pulsed against the sky, the Bluffs outlined like the hollows of a skull. The tumbling waves of the lake roared into the silence.

"There!" Nate pointed ahead in the distance, where shadows were grouped against an outcropping of white clay. Three men stood huddled together, shouting against the wind. A man and a woman were balanced in each other's arms at the very edge of the cliff.

Rachel tried to resolve the picture in her mind, dashing water from her eyes. Once she understood what it was, she raced past Nate down the path, her ankle forgotten. Nate tracked her, his feet slipping in the mud.

"Esa," he called. "What in God's name are you doing?"

The group at the edge froze in position. Rachel skidded to a halt in front of Mink Norman.

"Come back," she heard Esa say. "We'll walk here another time."

The three shadows against the rock loomed larger as Nate joined his friends.

Mink turned to Rachel defiantly, her blue eyes blazing, her gold hair a sodden tangle against her face.

"So you've come at last, armed with your weapons."

Khattak glared at her. "What are you doing here, Rachel?"

"It's what you're doing that concerns me, sir. I don't have any weapons," she said to Mink. "Were you expecting that I would? Did you expect me to arrest you?"

Harry Osmond jerked in his brother's hold.

"Rachel, I'm warning you —"

"I'm sorry, sir. You have to know the truth

about her. You have to realize why it matters so much that Drayton was Dražen Krstić, the butcher of Srebrenica." A palpable shudder ran through the men behind her. "You knew this, didn't you? Not just you, Mr. Newhall, but the others as well. Avdo and Hakija Osmanović, the survivors of Srebrenica. You recognized Krstić from the base at Potočari. That's why you moved here."

Harry jerked his head back and forth in a strange repetitive motion. "No," he said. "Oh no."

Rachel spoke to Mink. "I thought it was Mr. Newhall — Damir Hasanović — but I was wrong, wasn't I? You sent the letters. It was you, all along. There is no Sable Norman studying at the Mozarteum University of Salzburg. And there's no Mink Norman either. But there was a Selmira once, wasn't there? That's who the girl in the photograph is, the picture you sent to Krstić. The girl who hanged herself — your sister, Selmira."

Esa turned toward her, shielding Mink from her questions.

"What in God's name are you talking about, Rachel? Do you have any idea what you're doing to your career? I took you on when no one would touch you!"

"I know, sir, and I'm truly sorry."

"Esa," Nate interrupted. "Krstić came here two years ago, the Bosnians came two years ago. And the plan for Ringsong was set in motion two years ago. Andalusia, Esa. What was Bosnia if not a second Andalusia?"

Cradling Mink closer under his arm, Esa pulled her back from the edge. Bright with fury, he turned on Nate. "If our friendship ever meant anything to you, you'll shut up right now. You'll take Rachel and you'll leave this to me."

"It's not just Andalusia, Esa. It's the music, the Adagio. She didn't just send him the photograph and the letters. She sent him the Adagio. Of course she knew what it was. She's literate in music."

"You don't know what you're talking about."

"They know," Rachel said desperately, pointing at the Osmond brothers. "Avdo and Hakija. They're from Srebrenica. I've been searching for my brother, sir, he was missing for seven years — that's when I understood what must have happened here. What happened to Krstić. It's the missing men, the missing boys. That's why they don't have families. That's why it's only Damir, only Avdo and Hakija, only Mink Norman. Nobody else survived, sir, you know this. It's about the dead of Srebrenica, the men Krstić ordered to their deaths. That's why she sent the letters and the photograph of Selmira. Tell him, Mink. Tell him your real name. He fought for your people, he's earned the truth."

"No one fought for us," Mink said tonelessly, drawing away from Esa. "Isn't that so, Damir? Let him tell you."

David Newhall shrugged, the rain on his glasses obscuring his eyes. "What do you want to know? I've told you the story of the base. I begged the Dutch for my brothers' lives, for my mother and father, but Mesha said, 'Don't beg for us, that's not how I want to live. There will be a prisoner exchange, that's what Mladić promised us. You see, he's given candy to the boys?' " David removed his glasses, studied the others through shrouded eyes. "He strode around the base, gave speeches to the refugees, some to us, some to others, dispensing chocolates to the children when all the time he knew there was never going to be a prisoner exchange. We didn't have any prisoners to exchange." He drew a ragged breath.

"Mink," Esa said. "Tell me what this is."

Rachel hated the hollow sound of his voice, the disbelief in it. It presaged an

465

emptiness within her own heart as Mink Norman moved from the shelter of his arms without a qualm. She turned her face up to the rain and reached out a hand to hold Harry Osmond's.

"Selmira *was* my sister, your sergeant is very clever. I don't know how she identified Selmira from that photograph when the tribunal never could. She and I hid with the other girls inside the base on the day that the Serbs overran Srebrenica. Our parents were dead, our brothers had gone to the woods. We wouldn't learn for some time what had happened to them, and then only because of Damir." She nodded at the man whose gaze was fixed on her. "That night, Chetniks came to the factory looking for girls. They were dressed like the Dutch, so I waved at them. That's how they noticed us. Nesib, my brother, told us to hide, to make sure we didn't attract their attention, but I was young, I didn't listen. They took us because I didn't listen. But I was lucky because Nesib had a friend in the Serb army. He warned my brothers to leave Srebrenica at once. And he rescued me from the Chetniks. I know he tried, but he couldn't rescue my sister. The others wouldn't let him."

Harry pressed his face into the back of

her neck. "Don't," he sobbed. "Please don't tell them."

"We've come to it," she said gently. "Don't you see, Haki? We've come to it." She stared straight at Rachel. "What do you know of any of this, Sergeant Getty? All you've thought of is justice for Christopher Drayton." Rachel choked at the unfairness of this. It wasn't for Drayton she had shed her tears, sorted through testimony that would haunt her nightmares forever.

Mink continued her story in a monotone, rain beating against her head. "My sister told the Chetniks if they spared me, she wouldn't fight them. And Nole helped me escape from that room. 'Be clever,' he told me. 'I'll get Selmira.' And he did. When she came back to the base, she was covered in blood. They had torn away her clothes. One of our neighbors tried to clean her. Selmira said we were no longer girls — we would never be girls again. And then she stroked my hair and told me to rest. She said we would find Nesib — isn't that what she told me, Damir?"

"It is, Yasminka. You don't have to do this."

"I do. They need to understand." She drew a deep breath. If she was crying, Rachel couldn't tell her tears from the rain. "In the morning, the Chetniks came to take the boys from the base, all the boys, the young boys. While they were taking them, I lost sight of her. The Dutch were pushing us to the buses, it was a terrible crush. I was looking for Selmira, I was frantic. I forgot to look out for the boys, forgot to ask where they were going. Then our neighbor said, 'She's in the woods outside. Someone found her there. Don't go there.' But I went."

They had arranged themselves in a circle, the circle of survivors: Damir Hasanović, Avdo and Hakija Osmanović — and at its center, Yasminka Sinanović.

"She was hanging there. She had hanged herself with her own scarf, the scarf one of the Chetniks had nearly strangled her with. I couldn't recognize her face but I knew her scarf. I asked our neighbors to cut her down but they said we didn't have time. They said I had to get on the bus before the soldiers came back. It was my only chance or the soldiers would come for me again. Mrs. Obranovic — she rubbed dirt on my face to make me ugly. And I got on the bus. I didn't see my sister again. I don't know where she's buried. Her bones were never identified. All I have is the button from her sleeve and the sight of her body hanging in those trees." She rubbed her own sleeve self-

468

consciously. "Why have you come here?"

Esa wiped the rain from his face with trembling hands. "Your name is Yasminka Sinanović?"

"Yes." She stared back at him with the eyes of a stranger.

"You wrote those letters to Christopher Drayton? It was you who sent them?"

"To Dražen Krstić, yes. There was no Christopher Drayton."

How little he had known her. How little he had understood the motivation behind her warmth, her instant closeness.

"Did you plant the lilies?" Rachel asked. "The Bosnian lilies in Drayton's garden?"

Aldo stepped forward, drawing Mink toward him. "That was my gift to Drayton. A gift from the Bosnian people. A reminder. That what he killed didn't die."

"Then which one of you killed him?"

They had drawn together in a little circle, sheltering each other from the cold gusts of the wind and the rain that slashed at them all.

Esa looked at Mink as if he were waking from a dream, a look composed of horror and betrayal. "You killed him."

Mink ignored him. She nodded at David Newhall.

"No," he answered. "He fell to his death."

469

"But you did something," Rachel said slowly. "For two years, you stalked Dražen Krstić. He must have felt terrorized."

Newhall laughed, a short, sharp bark. Crowded together in the darkness, the Bosnians arranged themselves like a crumbling wall.

"Terrorized?" he spit at her. "You don't know what terror is. Talk to me when you've spent three years strangled and starved by Serb guns, when every member of your family has been taken to an execution site, bulldozed into a grave, and then excavated to a secondary grave, their bones scattered over your homeland to disguise the monstrosities committed against them. Try a month in Banja Luka when your mosques are bombed back into history and your leaders are sent to a death camp to be murdered. Or a week subjected to every form of rape imaginable in Foča, or a day in Brčko where they toss the bodies of the people you love into a furnace. A few letters sent to a man like Krstić do not terrorize. He promised we would be knee-deep in blood. He reveled in it."

A sick feeling rose in Rachel's stomach. "You must have wanted him to feel the things you're describing to me," she said. "These two years of your campaign were leading somewhere, but what was the catalyst that brought about his death?"

Mink stared at Nathan, her gaze unflinching, and suddenly he knew.

"It was the opening of the museum, the opening ceremony for Ringsong. You never planned to take Drayton's money. It was the attempt he made to attach himself to the ideals of Andalusia, its culture of pluralism. It was too much for you to bear."

"I'm sorry, Esa," Mink said to him, abruptly. "You could never understand. Look at your position. You worship at any mosque you choose, and none of your neighbors would dream of saying to you that your minarets are a blight, the symbol of an execrable enemy. Your identity is a gift. It's a badge you wear with honor, and this girl" — she gestured at Rachel, then at Nathan — "and your friend, they respect you for it." She tried not to look at him and failed. "In Bosnia, identity is a curse. In Srebrenica, it was a death sentence. So do not pretend to know us. Please, just do not pretend."

"Did you kill Christopher Drayton?" he asked, his voice tight.

"Dražen Krstić fell to his death." Despite the rain and the cruel roar of the wind, her voice was even.

471

Rachel slicked her wet hair behind her ears. "Why did you mention Foča, Brčko, and Banja Luka?" she asked David Newhall.

"I could name you a hundred other places," Newhall sneered. "Have you heard of Omarska, Trnopolje, Manjača?"

The Bosnians exchanged silent looks, huddled closer. A primal certainty electrified Rachel's nerves. She had guessed. Nearly everything, she had guessed.

"The night Drayton died, you went to see him. All of you. I couldn't understand the wax on the floor until I arranged the letters and photograph in a circle. The wax your candles left behind — they fell in a circle around Drayton's chair. It was a vigil — or maybe you saw it as a circle of justice. You must have planned that moment of confrontation, it was too well-rehearsed. But why was his gun on the floor? I've made sense of everything else — the lilies, the photograph, the letters — but I can't figure out the gun."

They looked at each other but didn't speak until Newhall took the lead.

"He was drunk. He was always drunk on Slivovitz in the evenings. It was easy to get him in the study. We told him the time had come to pay for Srebrenica. It was laughable in a way, how shocked he was when we told him our names, when we spoke in our

472

language. We told him who we were and he sobered up quickly. He demanded we get out of his house. He pretended his chest was hurting."

"Maybe it was," Rachel argued. "Maybe he suffered an attack from the confrontation."

"He suffered nothing except our hatred," Mink said coldly. "We told him he was free to go at any time. We asked him if he wanted us to pronounce the sentence he had evaded for so many years."

"What sentence was that?"

"We knew he kept a gun in his drawer. We asked him to use it on himself. An execution. Like he had executed our families, our friends."

"The gun wasn't loaded," Rachel said cautiously.

"Yes." Her lips sketched the parody of a smile. "We knew a man like Krstić would never choose the honorable course. He told me I was a choice piece and that his men would have enjoyed me in the halls of Srebrenica. He said my sister killed herself because she wasn't good enough for them. He aimed the gun at me and pulled the trigger."

"And when the gun didn't fire?"

"He said his chest was hurting. He

pleaded with us to go."

The smoke from the candles rose in spirals around him.

"Please," he gasped. "Acquit me."

The people gathered before his chair made no move to touch him. The gun fell from his nerveless hand to the floor, his eyes darting frantically about the circle, cowed by the piti-less faces.

They were chanting at him in Arabic, the language of the *balija,* the prayers of the Turk. They were asking God to bring down His retribution. To chain him to the fire forever. His eyes searched out the lovely young girl. With a feeble effort, he reached out his hand to her. The girl with the soft face and kind eyes, surely she would acquit him, show him mercy. He would tell her — he would pretend he knew where the bones of her sister lay buried and what he would say would buy him absolution, a day, an hour, a moment to es-cape.

His skin was clammy. He could feel the color drain from his face, the loss of motor control in his hands. The gun hadn't fired. Why hadn't the gun fired? What had been done to him?

"Please," he said again. "Absolve me. Let me go."

The girl raised her hand yet didn't touch him.

She made the three-fingered Chetnik salute in his face, the salute Serb children gave the survivors of Srebrenica when they came to bury the bones of their loved ones.

"Absolve me," he cried piteously.

"So did our brothers plead before their murderers." Her cold eyes studied him. Had he ever thought her gentle, kindhearted? Had he fantasized about conquering her in bed?

"Beg," she said. "And remember them now."

The last thing he heard before the world went dark was the language of the enemy — Andalusia's golden idiom, the sacred name of Allah.

"He fainted," Mink said simply. "And so we left him there. If he chose to go to the Bluffs, it was God who held his reckoning at the last."

"You threatened him anonymously for years and then confronted an elderly man in a state of extreme agitation with a gun," Rachel contradicted.

David Newhall shook his head. "It was his gun. The only weapon in our hands was the truth. We asked him to admit his name, his nature. Did that endanger the butcher of Srebrenica?"

Rachel didn't argue. She hoped Khattak would say something. As a police officer she knew something needed to be said — this couldn't go unchallenged. He stood by, mute, silenced by the weight of so much deception.

"Come out, come out," Harry sang out. They turned to look at him. "Come out of the woods. Come to your families, your fathers. Come out of the woods."

But every man or boy who had ceded his hiding place in the woods had ultimately found his destiny in a ditch, in some cases after digging it himself.

His brother cradled him in his arms. "We didn't come down again, Haki. Remember? We stayed in the woods. We took the road to Tuzla. We found our mother."

"My brothers were not as fortunate," said Mink. "Neither was my sister. I am the sole survivor of my family. And he thought he could touch Andalusia, honoring not its glory but the calamity of its end. Tainting it with his name and his money. This from the man who destroyed Andalusia." She spit on the ground. "You take something beautiful, you raze it to the ground, and then you claim you didn't know what you had? You try to rebuild it and assure your status as a patron of things that are priceless and holy like the Sarajevo Haggadah, like the National Library of Sarajevo, when you burnt

476

our history to ashes around us? Erasing us, erasing memory."

"You called it a memory palace," Rachel said. "You said the museum was a memory palace like the great cities of Andalusia."

"This is what we have now, the peaceful people of Bosnia. Palaces of memory. Everything else is lost or destroyed. A hundred thousand people are dead — and the women. Will you weep for the women of our country as we do? Will you help us? You couldn't even bring Dražen Krstić to justice." She broke free from the others to back away to the edge of the Bluffs. Rachel froze in place.

"Please," she said. "You can't give up."

Mink laughed, the sound acrid in her throat.

"I am not like these men who pretend to long for the country they destroyed. Momir Nikolić wants to serve his sentence and return to his home in Bratunac to live there in peace and harmony 'such as prevailed before the outbreak of the war.' Why don't they call it a slaughter?" She asked the question of herself, poised on the edge. "While my people are scattered across the globe, denied any semblance of justice."

"Mink, be careful!" She had been down this road before. In Waverley, where Miraj

Siddiqui had died. That final moment when Rachel could have saved a life, could have foreseen the truth and had failed utterly at both. She still dreamt of it. She couldn't face that outcome again.

"Please," she whispered.

"Bratunac," Harry whispered, jerking at his brother's arm. "We stayed on the bus in Bratunac. They didn't take us into the school."

"No," Aldo said patiently. "We stayed on the bus in Bratunac, Haki. It saved our lives."

"The bus is life," Harry repeated, as if he had memorized it. "The school is death."

"Haki." Mink's voice broke. Harry covered his ears. A wild keening rose above the wind.

"They're shooting," he sobbed. "They're killing everybody."

"Don't." His brother covered his mouth. "Don't Haki, it's over. It's over. We found our mother in Tuzla, remember?"

Harry fought his way free. "Everybody is dead, everybody is dead." He chanted the words in a helpless rhythm. "Get them off me, Avdi! Get the dead ones off me! The ants, Avdi! I can't breathe — help me!"

Aldo drew in his breath, sheltered his eyes from the rain, let his brother break away perilously close to the edge of the cliff.

478

There was resolution in his face.

"Lie still," he said to Harry. "Lie still and don't move until I give you the signal. Can you do that, Haki?"

"I can do it. I'm doing it, Avdi."

Harry fell to the muddy ground and lay flat, burying his face in the mat of coarse grass.

"I'm dead, Avdi," he said. His brother's strategy had worked. He'd removed himself from the edge of the cliff.

"You're dead," Aldo agreed. "We're both dead, Haki. That's how we make it." He looked at David Newhall. "Help me," he said.

"Mink," Rachel said again. "You're not safe there, please. Please move away."

Deaf to her words, Mink gathered her hair from around her face and twisted it into a rope. "Hold fast to the rope, Esa," she said. There was mockery in her voice, a mockery that sliced at his heart. "You thought we were the same, and we aren't. For you, Andalusia was an idyll, a golden dream. But it was real to us."

"Mink." Her name was a plea on his lips. Rachel saw the hopelessness on his face, the painful entreaty.

"My name is Yasminka Sinanović, and I am the last of my family. You cannot help me, Esa." She turned her attention to Rachel, stepping away from the edge. "I am a witness to genocide. My work is not done."

She took David Newhall's hand within her own. Together, they reached down to gather Harry Osmond's body from the ground, boosting him to his feet. As a group they shouldered past Rachel and Nate down the path toward Ringsong.

"Wait!" Rachel called. "How can you prove you didn't follow Drayton that night? How do we know you didn't take justice into your own hands?"

Mink answered her by turning up her hands. "We called a meeting for the museum that night. We were all there, well into the night. And so were Hadley and Marco."

David Newhall paused on the path.

"If there was one thing you should have learned from the letters, it is that we did not want what the fascists wanted. The destruction of all that we built together, the country that we shared. Our legacy isn't death." He shook his head at their inability to understand the simplest lesson in the world. Oblivious to Esa's pain, he kissed Mink's hand.

"Believe it or not, it's hope."

37.

Nothing can give me resolution. Nothing can give me consolation.

Nate passed Esa a towel. They were ensconced before the fire in his library, Rachel taking care not to drip onto the velvet sofa, despite Nate's reassurance.

"I'm all right." She warmed herself by the fire. "We're nowhere, sir. We're no further forward."

"Would you leave us for a moment, Rachel?"

He'd been too dignified to pursue Mink when her rejection was so complete. Something had broken between them; Rachel hoped it was irreparable.

"I'll help myself in the kitchen, shall I? How hard could your espresso machine be to work?"

"A fine mind like yours will solve the riddle in no time," said Nate. His face was serious despite the laughter in his voice. He watched her go. He stood by his friend's side before the fire, warming his frozen hands.

"Rachel told you?" Esa asked finally.

"She went back to the Bosnian mosque. She met with your friend Asaf, who told her about David Newhall's work — Hasanović's work, I mean. And he told her about the other survivors. He recognized the photo of Selmira. The rest was Rachel's doing. She kept talking about a circle and somehow — I don't know how — she deduced that a confrontation had taken place the night of Drayton's fall." He was afraid to test his friend, until the thought rose in his mind that if he couldn't say to Esa those things that had been natural and automatic in their friendship before, what point was there in continuing? "Do you believe what the Bosnians told us?"

Esa nodded. "I've no doubt of it. Hasanović isn't a killer."

"And Mink?"

Esa turned to him, rubbing the moisture from his hair with an absentminded gesture. "I want to ask you something," he said.

"Anything."

"I need to ask for your forgiveness. Because I didn't know. Until Mink, I didn't know the power a woman could hold over your thoughts. Over everything you knew of yourself. For me, it was black and white: myself or Laine Stoicheva, I couldn't see how you were torn. I didn't know a person could be torn like that." He laid the wet towel over the fireguard. "You tried to tell me, I know. You wrote *Apologia* and still — I couldn't find it in myself to let it go. I couldn't see how wrong I was until now."

He looked away from the pity in Nate's eyes, the warm compassion.

"Rachel was right when she accused me of having lost my objectivity. The clues were there for me to decipher — the letters, the lilies, the true identity of David Newhall. And yet it didn't occur to me that the others were acting a charade as well. Who better to have planted flowers than a gardener? How was I so blind to the connection between Andalusia and Bosnia? How could I have asked Mink nothing about her family, her history? She didn't need to lie to me. I gave her nothing to lie about. I was lost."

"You were caught," Nate corrected. "Don't blame yourself. I've lived with my neighbors for two years and never suspected that anyone was anything other than he or she pretended to be. As for Drayton, Mink had some sense that Hadley and Cassidy were in danger. I never did."

"Rachel made the connections."

"I can see why you chose her for your team. Her instincts are excellent. Be grateful she's on your side. Because she is. She's loyal to you. And maybe she guessed at all this because she knows what it means to lose a brother. She knows what a powerful driving force it can be. And since she didn't know any of these people, she could sense it was a charade. She knew it wasn't real. She also told me I should have read more as a child."

"Why?" Lightness tempered the grief on Esa's face.

"She said she finally made sense of the candles because of *Murder on the Orient Express*. It wasn't about a single person with a singular motive. It was something the Bosnians enacted together to serve a common end. Mink wrote the letters. David Newhall helped her. The Osmonds planted the lilies. And then they faced Drayton together."

"Because of the museum."

"Not just that." Nate pressed his friend's shoulder, aware that the reason would hurt him.

"Then what?"

"Because the Department of Justice didn't

take them seriously. They must have felt they had no other choice."

Esa mulled this over. "Drayton would have disappeared," he agreed. "Before anyone could do anything."

"And that would have been too much. Much too much for Mink and the others."

The sound of rattling teacups drew their attention to the door. Rachel entered, bearing a tray of miniature espresso cups in their saucers. The room filled with a woodsy aroma.

"Don't ask me where I found these," she said.

"My sister's dollhouse?" Nate guessed.

"Just drink before you catch cold."

She said it lightly, her concern for Esa evident. Her hair plastered to her face by the rain, her soggy clothes bunched about her body, she was still the most interesting woman Nathan had met in years.

"Where does that leave us?" he asked. "Will you do anything further?"

"I'll advise Hasanović to leave the neighborhood. And I'll recommend that Tom release his statement immediately."

"You believe them, then," Rachel said.

"You don't?"

Rachel slurped her espresso, scowling when she scalded her tongue. "So much anger, so much hatred. Such practiced deception — I'm sorry, sir. I know you wanted her to be above this."

"I've no right to expect that of her," he said quietly.

"She had no right to lie to you. I can't figure out what it is that I haven't figured out."

Esa wasn't listening to her. He'd braced himself against the table, his thoughts abstracted. "Rachel," he said, "show me the photographs again."

Surprised, she retrieved the envelope from her bag and shook its contents out on the table. Esa sorted through them until his hand came to rest on the photograph of Drayton's study. The chair surrounded by puddles of wax.

She followed his gaze and his outstretched finger as he made his count.

She saw it too. And now what Damir Hasanović had told them on the Bluffs rocketed into place, fusing the pieces of the puzzle together.

"Great Holy God."

"I can't help but think that's appropriate."

They knocked on the door of his living quarters, sequestered behind the mosque,

486

hidden from view by the overhanging maples.

He answered the door dressed in his customary long robes, his head bare, his beard neatly trimmed.

"Damir said you would come."

Under the wild rain on the Bluffs, David Newhall had told her about terror.

Banja Luka. Foča. Brčko.

"Why did you mention Banja Luka, Foča, and Brčko?" she had asked Newhall, oblivious to the answer.

They were the same cities Imam Muharrem had named. Rachel felt a momentary respite from horror as Nate squeezed her hand. Realization, sickeningly conclusive, tumbled through her thoughts. Why hadn't the imam told them about Damir Hasanović, the highest-profile member of their congregation? Why hadn't he mentioned the circle of Srebrenica survivors that had included Avdo and Hakija Osmanović, Yasminka Sinanović, and Damir? She had viewed photos of the genocide memorial online. She had read the long list of Osmanović dead, a list that seemed to trail down forever into history. So many men from one family dead, she had thought. And just these two boys to survive.

"Today no man from our family is older than

thirty," Mirnesa Ahmić had said in her testimony before the tribunal.

Why had the imam told them the entire grand narrative of the Bosnian war, yet left out everything that made it so personal? The worst part was that she knew the answer to her question. Her previous scenario of the confrontation had been catastrophically incomplete.

Khattak had shown her the proof of it, counting out the number.

"There are five spots on the floor. Five places for the candles. Who else was there that night? Avdo, Hakija, Damir, Yasminka — that only makes four."

She saw their faces again in the rain, the silent exchange as they clutched each other's hands. Wounded as they were, none of the people poised at the edge of the Bluffs had set this plan in motion. And none of them had chosen to name him. The man who knew Srebrenica, knew Brčko, knew Banja Luka, knew Foča.

"You were there that night."

Muharrem led them inward to his rooms. A prayer rug was spread out on the floor, the Qur'an at its head balanced on a small wooden stand. One wall in the room was decorated, the wall in front of a comfortable chesterfield. Facing them was a poster

488

of the sixteenth-century Ferhadija mosque. "Shall I make us tea?"

"We'd rather have the truth."

No one sat. After a moment, the imam gathered up his Qur'an and placed it on the coffee table.

"It was you," Rachel repeated. "You recognized Krstić from the moment you first saw him."

"And if I did?"

"You told the others."

"Was that a crime? Was it not a greater crime that Krstić was here in your country, safe and happy, thriving at every turn? Did you ask how he gained immigration? Can you explain why your Department of Justice did nothing when we reported who he was? Or why you ignored our pleas for assistance?"

There was nothing in his demeanour to recall the patience and forbearance of the man they had interviewed on two previous occasions. His bearing was proud, stiffly unapologetic. No suggestion of his former friendliness lingered about his eyes.

"We are investigating now."

"Now," he mocked them. "Two years later and only because the butcher himself is dead. We were prepared to wait for you to act. You chose to do nothing. And now you worry about your reputation, your government agencies, the black mark on your credibility as peacekeepers."

"Imam Muharrem —"

"You are the worst of all, Inspector Esa. You pretended solidarity, promised me an answer, and yet what did you have your colleague do? Did you tell the world about Dražen Krstić? Did your government admit its mistake? Were you even aware that a man known for sexual sadism had children in his care?"

"If you had told us what you knew, we would have been able to act more quickly."

"Well." The imam shrugged. "I didn't know there was such a person as the righteous Inspector Esa, defender of the Bosnians, did I? I knew of your War Crimes Commission, so we began there." His bleak gaze encompassed Rachel and Nate. "And nothing came of it."

Rachel swallowed noisily. "So what did you do about it, sir?"

"What did I do? What did I do? What did you expect me to do? I talked to you. I told you about Banja Luka, about Prijedor. I told you what happened in the rape camps of Foča. I told you what they did to my family in Brčko. Broken. Thrown into the furnace like refuse. What did *you* do?"

490

"We tried to find the truth. We followed every possible lead to prove that Drayton was Krstić."

"His gun, his tattoo — they were not enough? The tattoo I pointed you to. The JNA-issued military pistol. Not enough?"

"Then you were there that night," she breathed.

"Of course I was. It was my plan from the first. Did you think I would let my children face it alone? My poor Haki? My lonely lost Yasminka? Our beloved Damir, whose quest for justice has been blocked again and again? It is only because of Damir that Haki and Avdo made it to Canada. Why? Because when Avdi made it to Tuzla, he gave Damir his brother's tennis shoes. Mesha's body falling over Avdi was what saved him from the artillery fire. And Avdi — so young, so brave — made himself look at the body that saved him, made himself remember so he could tell one person what had happened to someone he loved. Damir will carry this debt all his life. And he saved Yasminka as well. Because of his efforts, she was able to bury her brothers and place their names upon the memorial. Did you think I would abandon these children to face the devil alone?"

"What happened that night?" Rachel

asked him. "The others said they confronted Krstić and he fainted. They say they left him alive."

"Did they also tell you that he rose from his chair, threatening us with his gun? And that when he fell back drunk, he said our people had died because they were weak — too weak to fight, too worthless to live. He boasted about his accomplishments in Srebrenica. He said he would pull the same trigger again. He fired at Yasminka but his gun was empty. We had checked it beforehand — that seemed to surprise him. We weren't foolish enough to trust in his rehabilitation."

"Then where did you go that night? After the confrontation? Yasminka didn't say you were at the meeting for the museum with the others."

"I wasn't."

"Where were you, then?"

He sat down in a single motion, balancing the Qur'an on his lap.

"Was I here in my rooms, offering prayers of gratitude and perseverance to the Almighty Protector? Or did I walk along the Bluffs in the dark to see what the butcher would do? He didn't have the strength or the humanity to point the gun at his own head, as we had asked him. Perhaps he chose another way."

Rachel bit back a gasp. "Are you saying he jumped? That Krstić committed suicide because you had tormented him for so long?"

"Would he do such a thing?" His smile was bleak. "Perhaps it was the ghosts of Srebrenica who haunted him. Perhaps they followed him wherever he went, the way they followed Avdo and Haki from the killing fields of Grbavici. Isn't that possible?"

Rachel's lips were stiff. "What did you really do, Imam Muharrem? Tell us the truth."

He caressed the Qur'an in his hands. "I did not begin hostilities."

"I'm asking if you finished them."

"Although he was a man who deserved death, I think you will find that my people are not murderers."

"And if you saw the men who murdered your family today? Marrying, having children? What would you do?"

"I would hunt each one of them down if I could."

"Were you on the Bluffs that night? Did you follow Drayton?"

"I'm very tired," he said. "This day has been a long time coming for my people. I would ask you to leave me to finish my prayers."

"We can't just leave it like this. Surely as an imam, you have a duty to the truth."

"No, my dear Sergeant. You had a duty to the truth and you failed it completely. I've fulfilled my responsibilities, one and all."

"With Krstić's death?" Esa asked him.

Imam Muharrem replaced the Qur'an on the table. He took up his stance on his prayer rug.

"How formidable is your desire for simple answers, Inspector Esa. Was I there or not? Did I follow Dražen Krstić? Did I send him to his death?" He raised his hands from his sides to his ears, to fold them over his stomach, oblivious to their urgency. "Allah knows the answer. Shall we leave it with Him?"

"If you're guilty of this, Imam Muharrem —"

"Then you will have to prove it."

They crowded together in the shelter of the mosque, its slender minaret backlit by the moon.

"Was that a confession?" Rachel asked. Her hands were trembling.

"I doubt we'll ever know." Nate said it, and Esa didn't contradict him.

"Then what do we do, sir?"

494

She wanted Khattak to know. She wanted to believe he had the bedrock certainty of right and wrong, truth and falsehood, that she herself lacked. There wasn't a single person who would mourn Dražen Krstić's death, whether murder, suicide, or accident. And yet, and yet — didn't they have a duty to the truth?

Khattak placed one hand on Nate's shoulder. "We call Tom Paley at Justice. The rest is up to them."

"Then come back to Winterglass."

She knew the invitation meant more than it seemed on the surface: it was Esa and Nate clearing away the wreckage of the past, the dross of Laine Stoicheva. It was Nate's warm eyes approving her as a person, a woman without artifice. It was the chance to sit by his fire and make a phone call to her brother without fear, without hopelessness, after he had helped her determine whether a girl named Sable Norman was a student at the Mozarteum.

Yet at this moment, it was the light of the minaret that seemed to hold the truth in the balance.

They had come full circle. Murder, suicide, accident, coincidence. There was no certainty to be had.

But Khattak thought he knew. He thought

he knew what Muharrem had done. The man who had hounded Dražen Krstić and brought him to his knees would not have let him walk away at the last.

There had been a tussle in the dark on the edge of Cathedral Bluffs.

Justice had found the butcher of Srebrenica.

And the shadow of the mosque was no consolation.

AUTHOR'S NOTE

This novel is based upon events that occurred during the 1992–1995 war in Bosnia, formerly a republic of the nation of Yugoslavia.

In 1991, Yugoslavia dissolved into its constituent republics, each of which was to wrestle with the question of independence. In 1990 and 1991, respectively, Slovenia and Croatia staged their referenda on independence from Yugoslavia. When Bosnia followed suit in 1992, it put forward a vision of the future that attested to its uniquely blended heritage. In Bosnia, Serbs, Croats, and Muslims spoke the same language, intermarried without controversy, and embraced each other's traditions in the fullness of history. In this vision of the future, the Bosnia that rose from the ashes of Yugoslavia was a nation of equal citizens, with rights guaranteed under a democratic constitution, in recognition of a centuries-old pluralism.

What came to pass instead was the vision of ultranationalists in the republics of Serbia and Croatia. In their formulation of Bosnia's future, a "Greater Serbia" or "Greater Croatia" could only be achieved by the annexation of a Bosnian territory rid of its non-Serb or non-Croat inhabitants. Thus followed a series of acts that began with the siege of Sarajevo in 1992, and culminated in the Srebrenica massacre of 1995.

For the first time since the Second World War, a genocide campaign of staggering ferocity and ruthlessness was unleashed against a civilian population in Europe, nearly in tandem with the international intervention that eventually became complicit in the suffering of Bosnia's people. In his influential work *Slaughterhouse,* journalist and author David Rieff calls the Bosnia of this period a "slaughterhouse" and describes the conflict within its boundaries as a slaughter, not a war. Through Bosnia's many well-documented agonies, the terms *ethnic cleansing, cultural destruction,* and *rape camps* would also become commonplace.

The term *ethnic cleansing* first entered the parlance as a description of Serbian tactics that "cleansed" the land of its Muslim inhabitants. The substitution of this term for the actual crime of genocide went some distance toward undermining the international legal obligation to prevent the genocide while it was still under way. (See *Prosecutor v. Radislav Krstic* IT-98-33 [2 August 2001].)

Cultural destruction encompassed the deliberate campaign to eradicate mosques, Catholic churches, and countless other representations of religious and cultural identity — foremost among these, the architecture of Bosnia's Ottoman past. Finally, although an endemic part of the overall war strategy, it was for the widespread and systematic use of rape in the southeastern town of Foča that a historic legal precedent was set: rape was recognized as a crime against humanity under international law. (See *Prosecutor v. Dragoljub Kunarac and Radomir Kovac,* IT-96-23-PT [22 February 2001].)

For those who seek to learn how it was possible for the Bosnian enlightenment to be obliterated so swiftly and steadily, there are several key works I recommend. On the nature of the war crimes and cultural destruction that took place, see Roy Gutman's Pulitzer Prize–winning *A Witness to*

Genocide and Michael Sells's *The Bridge Betrayed: Religion and Genocide in Bosnia.*

Rabia Ali and Lawrence Lifschultz's essay "In Plain View," in their edited book *Why Bosnia?*, remains a landmark in the study of the war, alongside *The Death of Yugoslavia* by Laura Silber and Allan Little. For perspective on the role the international community played, there is David Rieff's *Slaughterhouse: Bosnia and the Failure of the West,* Brendan Simms's *Unfinest Hour: Britain and the Destruction of Bosnia,* and Samantha Power's *A Problem from Hell: America in the Age of Genocide.* Human rights reports, war crimes testimony, and UN reports are listed extensively in the notes section.

A comment on names used in this book. Although not based on actual persons, the characters Avdo and Hakija Osmanović were named for two Bosnians who did not survive the war. In 1993, Bosnia's vice president, Dr. Hakija Turajlić, was shot and killed by a Serb fighter while traveling with a United Nations Protection Force convoy. Surrounded by Serb forces on a road ostensibly under UN control, the French commander on the scene opened the armored personnel carrier transporting Dr. Turajlić, resulting in his immediate assassination.

Colonel Avdo Palić of the Army of Bosnia-Herzegovina defended safe area Zepa against Serb siege for more than three years, volunteering himself for negotiations with Serb forces during the fall of Srebrenica, so that the people of Zepa might escape a similar fate. Ordered to investigate and fully account for Colonel Palić's disappearance, the Palić Commission found that Avdo Palić had been held in a military prison until he was disappeared by Serb forces on the night of 4 September 1995. Avdo Palić's remains were subsequently located, exhumed, and returned to his wife, Esma, bringing her fourteen-year search for her husband to an end. He was buried with honors in 2009.

Though not based on any single individual, Dražen Krstić was named for two figures who were instrumental in the carrying out of the Srebrenica massacre. Dražen Erdemović was a soldier in the 10th Sabotage Detachment of the Bosnian Serb Army. He participated in the executions of hundreds of unarmed Bosnian Muslim men from the Srebrenica enclave and was the first person to enter a guilty plea at the International Criminal Tribunal for the former Yugoslavia (ICTY). General Radislav Krstić was the Deputy Commander of the Drina Corps. He took command of the

Drina Corps on 13 July 1995, giving him direct command responsibility for the Srebrenica massacre and the forcible de-population of the Srebrenica enclave. He was the first person to be convicted of genocide by the ICTY.

As to the tireless prosecutors and fearless investigators of the International Criminal Tribunal, who carry out such difficult yet necessary work: nothing has struck me more than the statement of the Chief War Crimes Investigator, Jean-René Ruez, when he said of Srebrenica, "It was a crime committed against every single one of us."

In that spirit, I wish to thank Professor Cherif Bassiouni, President Emeritus of the International Human Rights Law Institute. Professor Bassiouni took time out of his very busy schedule to educate a twenty-three-year-old law student about war crimes in Bosnia, at a time when he was investigating those crimes as Chairman of the United Nations Commission of Experts. His compassion and dedication have stayed with me all these years.

I worked briefly with the Bosnian Canadian Relief Association during the war and had the privilege of meeting many members of Bosnian communities and their imams. I particularly wish to thank Imam Muharrem, who shared his story with such courage and humanity. I have also had the opportunity to learn from the work of many Bosnian witnesses, activists, and scholars over the years, foremost among them Hasan Nuhanovic, whose efforts in the cause of justice have served so many without ever faltering.

I hope what couldn't be articulated at that time has been articulated in this book.

A last word on the people of Bosnia — Serb, Croat, and Muslim — who defended the Bosnian enlightenment in the face of the fascist drive for ethnic and religious uniformity. Their courage, perseverance, and dignity in the face of appalling carnage remind us why Bosnia was a place worth saving.

NOTES

Chapter 1.

I will never worship what you worship. Nor will you worship what I worship. To you, your religion — to me, mine.
Sura Al Kafirun, "The Unbelievers." Qur'an 109: 4–6.

They are going to burn us all.
Paraphrased from the statement of Emil Čakalić, relating what he heard a soldier say to him and other prisoners at the Vukovar military barracks in 1991, after he narrowly escaped execution at Ovčara. He testified on 5 February 1998 in the case against Slavko Dokmanović; on 13 and 14 March 2006 in the case against the Yugoslav People's Army officers Veselin Šljivančanin, Mile Mrkšić, and Miroslav Radić; and on 16 July 2003 in the case against Slobodan Milošević. *Prosecutor v. Slavko Dokmanović,* IT-95-13a-T [5 February 1998], Witness

Chapter 2.

I keep wondering, where have all the good friends gone?

Letter of Muhamed Čehajić, former mayor of the Prijedor municipality, as read by his wife, Dr. Minka Čchajić, before the International Criminal Tribunal for the former Yugoslavia at the trial of Milomir Stakić. In its judgment of 31 July 2003, the Trial Chamber stated that it had no evidence at hand to establish beyond reasonable doubt the reason for Muhamed Čehajić's death. It said, however, that "even if Čehajić was not directly killed, the conditions imposed on a person whose health was fragile, alone would inevitably cause his death. His ultimate fate was clearly foreseeable." The Trial Chamber argued that due to Milomir Stakić's position as president of the Crisis Staff, the National Defense Council, the War Presidency, and the Municipal Assembly in Prijedor, and due to his close ties to both the police and the military, he could not "have been unaware of what was common knowledge around the town, the municipality, and even further afield." The Trial Chamber stated that "[i]t was Dr. Stakić himself [who] triggered the deplorable fate of this honorable man." On 22 March 2006, the Appeals Chamber confirmed the convictions against Milomir Stakić and sentenced him to forty years' imprisonment. *Prosecutor v. Milomir Stakić,* IT-97-24-T [31 July 2003]. Minka Čehajić's complete "Voice of the Victims" statement is available through the International Criminal Tribunal for the former Yugoslavia at http://www.icty.org/sid/186.

Chapter 3.

He was a modest and reasonable man.
Minka Čehajić, a Bosnian pediatrician, speaking about her quest to find out what happened to her husband after she last saw him in May 1992. She testified on 14, 15, and 16 May 2002 in the case against Milomir Stakić. Čehajić's complete "Voice of the Victims" statement is available through the International Criminal Tribunal for the former Yugoslavia at http://www.icty.org/sid/186.

This is part of a cat-and-mouse game.
Letter dated 19 October 1992 from the Permanent Representative of Bosnia and Herzegovina to the United Nations, addressed to the president of the Security Council. S/24685, 19 October 1992.

You can either survive or disappear.
General Ratko Mladić, Commander of the Bosnian Serb Army (the VRS). Available online at *Justice Report:* http://www.justice-report.com/en/articles/interpretation-of-Mladić-s-words.

Because I tell you that the sky is too high and the ground is too hard.
Bosnian proverb.

Lo, with hardship comes ease.
Sura Ash-Sharh, "The Relief." Qur'an 94:5.

Chapter 4.
Father, take care of my children, look after my children.
Mehmed Alić, a Bosnian Muslim victim of the Omarska camp, speaking about how he tried to defend his son Enver from Serb soldiers who were about to beat him. He testified on 23 and 24 July 1996 in the case against Duško Tadić. Mehmed Alić was transferred to the Manjača camp on 6 August and released on 26 August 1992. Alic's complete "Voice of the Victims" statement is available through the International Criminal Tribunal for the former Yugoslavia at http://www.icty.org/sid/195.

Chapter 5.

I took my mother's head into my hands and I kissed her. I never felt anything so cold before . . .

Testimony of Indira Ahmetović, Srebrenica survivor. Her full statement is available through the Cinema for Peace Foundation at http://cinemaforpeace.ba/en/testi mony/indira-ahmetovic/46.

Chapter 6.

Do you still believe that we die only the first death and never receive any requital?

Sura As-Saffat, "Those Ranged in Ranks." Qur'an 37:58–59.

Muslims, you yellow ants, your days are numbered.

Old Chetnik war song.

Bend down, drink the water by the kerb like dogs.

Emir Beganović, a Bosnian Muslim man, was severely beaten and held under horrific conditions at the Serb-run Omarska detention camp, located just outside Prijedor, Bosnia and Herzegovina. He testified on 19 July 1996 in the case against Duško Tadić and on 4 and 5 May 2000 in the case against Kvočka et al. His complete "Voice of the Victims" statement is available through the International Criminal Tribunal for the former Yugoslavia at http://www.icty.org/sid/10120.

Give us some water first, then kill us. I was sorry to die thirsty.

Witness O (he testified with name and identity withheld from the public), a seventeen-year-old survivor of the Srebrenica executions, speaking about their perpetrators. He testified on 13 April 2000 in the case against Radislav Krstić. Witness O's complete "Voice of the Victims" statement is available through the International Criminal Tribunal for the former Yugoslavia at http://www.icty.org/sid/184.

Chapter 7.

Under a big pear tree there was a heap of between ten and twelve bodies. It was difficult to count them because they were covered over with earth, but heads and hands were sticking out of the little mound.

Ivo Atlija, a Bosnian Croat, speaking about killings that occurred in the area around his village in 1992 in the Prijedor municipality of Bosnia and Herzegovina. He testified on 3 and 4 July 2002 in the case against Milomir Stakić. His complete "Voice of the Victims" statement is available through the

International Criminal Tribunal for the former Yugoslavia at http://www.icty.org/sid/190.

There's never any joy.
Saliha Osmanović, Srebrenica survivor, as quoted in "Srebrenica Memorial Day: Our Continuing Horror," *The Independent* (10 July 2013).

On Tuesday, there will be no bread in Sara-jevo.
Letter dated 18 October 1992 from the Permanent Representative of Bosnia and Herzegovina to the United Nations, ad-dressed to the president of the Security Council. S/24677, 19 October 1992.

The tragedy of Srebrenica will haunt our his-tory forever.
UN General Assembly, *Report of the Secretary-General Pursuant to General As-sembly Resolution 53/35: The Fall of Srebren-ica,* 15 November 1999, A/54/549, para-graph 503. Available at http://www.refworld.org/docid/3ae6afb34.html.

It took some persuasion to convince my Serb neighbor with whom I had lived my whole life that I was suddenly his enemy and that I was

511

to be killed.
Dr. Idriz Merdžanić, a Bosnian doctor who treated victims of the Trnopolje Camp, speaking about how he tried to have two injured children evacuated from the north-western Bosnian town of Kozarac. He testi-fied on 10 and 11 September 2002 in the case against Milomir Stakić. His complete "Voice of the Victims" statement is available through the International Criminal Tribunal for the former Yugoslavia at http:// www.icty.org/sid/202.

I am aware that I cannot bring back the dead. Momir Nikolić, "Statement of Guilt" (29 October 2003). Momir Nikolić was an as-sistant commander for Security and Intel-ligence in the Bosnian Serb Army. Nikolić was at the center of the crimes that took place following the fall of Srebrenica in July 1995. He did not raise any objections when informed of the plan to deport Muslim women and children and to separate, detain, and ultimately kill Muslim men. Nikolić did nothing to stop the beatings, humiliation, and killing of thousands of Bosnian Muslim men. He also personally coordinated the exhumation and reburial of victims' bodies. He testified in other proceedings before the Tribunal, including the trial of his two co-accused, Blagojević and Jokić. Nikolić was sentenced to twenty years' imprisonment. His complete statement is available through the International Criminal Tribunal for the former Yugoslavia at http://www.icty.org/sid/ 218.

Chapter 8.
All my life I will have thoughts of that and feel the pain that I felt then and still feel. That will never go away.

Witness 87 (she testified with name and identity withheld from the public), a Bosnian Muslim girl talking in court about the effects of the rape and the abuse she suffered during the nine months she was held captive by Serb soldiers. During this period she was also raped by Dragoljub Kunarac and Radomir Kovač. She testified on 4, 5 April and 23 October 2000 in the case against Dragoljub Kunarac, Zoran Vuković, and Radomir Kovač. Witness 87's complete "Voice of the Victims" statement is available through the International Criminal Tribunal for the former Yugoslavia at http://www.icty .org/sid/10117.

Chapter 9.

I addressed one of the wingborn singers,
who was sad at heart and aquiver.

"For what do you lament so plaintively" I
asked,
And it answered, "For an age that is gone,
forever."

Ruggles, D. F., "Arabic Poetry and Architectural Memory in al-Andalus," *Ars Orientalis, Pre-Modern Islamic Palaces* (1993, Vol. 23), 171–78.

Chapter 10.

Easily predictable events have been proceeding inexorably in the cruelest, most atrocious fashion.
Ambassador Ahmed Snoussi, Representative of Morocco to the Security Council. *Provisional Verbatim Record of the Three Thousand and Eighty-Second Meeting, held at Headquarters, New York Saturday, 30 May 1992: Security Council.* S/PV.3082, 30 May 1992, p. 25.

Today a funeral procession was shelled. The whole city is without water.
Letter dated 28 September 1992 from the

acting president of Bosnia and Herzegovina to the United Nations, addressed to the president of the Security Council. S/24601, 29 September 1992, p. 2.

Charred bodies lie along the street.
Letter dated 9 September 1992 from the Permanent Representative of Bosnia and Herzegovina to the United Nations, addressed to the president of the Security Council. S/24537, 9 September 1992, p. 2.

Chapter 11.
All my joys and my happiness up to then have been replaced by pain and sorrow for my son and my husband.
Srebrenica survivor Sabaheta, as quoted in Selma Leydesdorff, "Stories from No Land: The Women of Srebrenica Speak Out," *Human Rights Review* (April 2007, Vol. 8:3), 191.

Chapter 12.
Whoever was on the list to be killed would be killed.
Quoting Schefik, a thirty-eight-year-old construction worker taken to Manjača. Charles Lane, "Dateline: Croatia," *The Black Book of Bosnia,* ed. Nader Mousavizadeh (New Republic, 1996), 84.

I have just been informed that the besieged city of Jajce has fallen to the aggressor.
Letter dated 29 October 1992 from the Permanent Representative of Bosnia and Herzegovina to the United Nations, addressed to the president of the Security Council. S/24740, 29 October 1992.

Massive air attacks continue in Bosnia today. We cannot defend ourselves yet no one is coming to our aid.
Letter dated 28 September 1992 from the acting president of Bosnia and Herzegovina to the United Nations, addressed to the president of the Security Council. S/24601, 29 September 1992, p. 2.

For having uttered a wrong word, people are taken away or killed.
Letter dated 9 September 1992 from the Permanent Representative of Bosnia and Herzegovina to the United Nations, addressed to the president of the Security Council. S/24537, 9 September 1992, p. 2.

The camps remain open.
Letter dated 4 November 1992 from the Permanent Representative of Bosnia and Herzegovina to the United Nations, addressed to the president of the Security Council. S/24761, 5 November 1992.

The enemy ring around the city is being strengthened with fresh troops.

Letter dated 22 June 1992 from His Excellency Mr. Alija Izetbegović, President of Bosnia and Herzegovina, to the United Nations, addressed to the president of the Security Council. S/24214, 22 June 1992.

For the past three days, Serb forces have been conducting a fierce offensive against the town of Bihac.

Letter dated 9 February 1994 from the Permanent Representative of Bosnia and Herzegovina to the United Nations, addressed to the president of the Security Council. S/1994/142, 9 February 1994, p. 2.

Today Serb forces shelled the city of Tuzla. While writing this letter, the city centre is under heavy mortar attack.

Letter dated 14 January 1994 from the mayor of the City of Tuzla to the United Nations, addressed to the president of the Security Council. S/1994/45, 14 January 1994, p. 2.

The famous National Library has been set on fire and is still burning.

Joint letter dated 26 August 1992 from the acting president of the Presidency and the

Prime Minister of Bosnia to the United Nations, addressed to the Security Council. S/26500, 26 August 1992, p. 2.

Defend us or let us defend ourselves. You have no right to deprive us of both.
Alija Izetbegović, President of Bosnia and Herzegovina, before the Security Council. As quoted in Paul Lewis, "At UN, Bosnian Presses His Plea for More Land," *New York Times* (8 September 1993).

If Allah helps you, none can ever overcome you; but if He should forsake you, who is there after Him that can help you? In Allah, then, let the believers put their trust.
Sura Al Imran. Qur'an 3:160.

Chapter 13.

No one knows what will come tomorrow
and no one knows in what land he will die.

Sura Luqman. Qur'an 31:34.

Chapter 14.
Somewhere life withers, somewhere it begins.
Srebrenica survivor, from *Srebrenica: A Cry from the Grave,* directed by Leslie Woodhead ([distributor Thirteen/WNET PBS], 1999).

Chapter 15.

While the Serb soldier was dragging my son away, I heard his voice for the last time. And he turned around and then he told me, "Mummy please, can you get that bag for me? Could you please get it for me?"

Witness DD, a Bosnian Muslim woman, speaking about how she lost her husband and two sons in the July 1995 Srebrenica genocide. She testified on 26 July 2000 in the case against Radislav Krstić. Witness DD's complete "Voice of the Victims" statement is available through the International Criminal Tribunal for the former Yugoslavia at http://www.icty.org/sid/10124.

Chapter 16.

The National Library of Sarajevo is burning.

Joint letter dated 26 August 1992 from the acting president of the Presidency and the Prime Minister of Bosnia to the United Nations, addressed to the Security Council. S/26500, 26 August 1992, p. 2.

A radio broadcast instructed Muslims to put white ribbons around their arms, go outside, form columns and head towards the main square.

Emir Beganović, a Bosnian Muslim man. He testified on 19 July 1996 in the case against Duško Tadić and on 4 and 5 May 2000 in the case against Kvočka et al. His complete "Voice of the Victims" statement is available through the International Criminal Tribunal for the former Yugoslavia at http://www.icty.org/sid/10120.

Chapter 17.

I don't have a photograph of my child when he was small . . . I want to apologize for crying," Mrs. Čehajić told the court, "because you cannot compare this with what has happened, but this is also something that is important to many people.

Minka Čehajić, a Bosnian pediatrician. She testified on 14, 15, and 16 May 2002 in the case against Milomir Stakić. Čehajić's complete "Voice of the Victims" statement is available through the International Criminal Tribunal for the former Yugoslavia at http://www.icty.org/sid/186.

Chapter 18.

Simply, they left no witnesses behind.

Emir Beganović, a Bosnian Muslim man. He testified on 19 July 1996 in the case against Duško Tadić and on 4 and 5 May 2000 in the case against Kvočka et al. His complete "Voice of the Victims" statement is available through the International Criminal Tribunal for the former Yugoslavia at http://www.icty.org/sid/10120.

I would like to appeal to you to ask, Mr. Krstić, whether there is any hope for at least that little child that they snatched away from me, because I keep dreaming about him. I dream of him bringing flowers and saying, "Mother, I've come." I hug him and say, "Where have you been, my son?" And he says, "I've been in Vlasenica all this time." So I beg you, if Mr. Krstić knows anything about it, about him surviving someplace . . .

Witness DD, a Bosnian Muslim woman, appealing to Judge Rodrigues at the Krstić trial. She testified on 26 July 2000 in the case against Radislav Krstić. Witness DD's complete "Voice of the Victims" statement is available through the International Criminal Tribunal for the former Yugoslavia at http://www.icty.org/sid/10124.

Chapter 19.

How is it possible that a human being could do something like this, could destroy everything, could kill so many people? Just imagine this youngest boy I had, those little hands of his, how could they be dead? I imagine those hands picking strawberries, reading books, going to school, going on excursions. Every morning I cover my eyes not to look at other children going to school and husbands going to work, holding hands.

Witness DD, a Bosnian Muslim woman, speaking about how she lost her husband and two sons in the July 1995 Srebrenica genocide. She testified on 26 July 2000 in the case against Radislav Krstić. Witness DD's complete "Voice of the Victims" statement is available through the International Criminal Tribunal for the former Yugoslavia at http://www.icty.org/sid/10124.

Collect your ammunition and let's go to the meadow to kill the men.

Gojko Simic, Commander of the Anti-Tank Platoon of the Fourth Battalion, 1st Zvornik Brigade, as quoted in *Srebenica: Reconstruction, Background, Consequences and Analyses of the Fall of a "Safe" Area* (Netherlands Institute of War Documentation, 2000): part 4, chapter 2, p. 72. Available online at http://www.srebrenica-project.com/DOWNLOAD/NOD/NIOD%20Part%20IV.pdf.

Chapter 20.

All wounds will be healed but not this one.

Bekir Izetbegović, Bosnian member of the Presidential Council of Bosnia and Herzegovina. As quoted in Markar Esayan, "Srebrenica, Cain's Sign and Poetry," *Today's Zaman* (10 July 2011). Available online at http://www.todayszaman.com/columnists/markar-esayan-250045-srebrenica-cains-sign-and-poetry.html.

Chapter 21.

I apologize to the victims and to their shadows. I will be happy if this contributed to reconciliation in Bosnia, if neighbors can again shake hands, if our children can again play games together, and if they have the right to a chance.

Dragan Obrenović, Statement of Guilt (30 October 2003). Dragan Obrenović was a senior officer and commander within the Bosnian Serb Army in July 1995. He was convicted for persecutions carried out through the murder of hundreds of Bosnian Muslim civilians, committed in and around Srebrenica. Under the plea agreement, he agreed to testify in other proceedings before the Tribunal, including those trials related to Srebrenica. Obrenović was sentenced to seventeen years' imprisonment. His complete statement is available through the International Criminal Tribunal for the former Yugoslavia at http://www.icty.org/sid/219.

Chapter 22.

Mr. Stakić is here. He's a physician just like I am, and he made decisions concerning the camps. He knew that we were there. He knew that his colleague Jusuf Pasic, who was facing retirement, had been taken to Omarska and killed there. He knew about dozens of doctors, physicians being taken to Omarksa and killed. Why? These people were the Muslim intelligentsia and they meant something. Is there an answer to all of this?

Dr. Idriz Merdžanić, a Bosnian doctor who treated victims of the Trnopolje Camp. He testified on 10 and 11 September 2002 in the case against Milomir Stakić. His complete "Voice of the Victims" statement is available through the International Criminal Tribunal for the former Yugoslavia at http://www.icty.org/sid/202.

Chapter 23.

Verily God will not change the condition of a people until they change what is in themselves.

Sura Ar-Ra'd, "The Thunder." Qur'an 13:11.

Chapter 24.

We heard it on the radio. They will send the airplanes now. They will save us now.

Witness DD, a Bosnian Muslim woman, appealing to Judge Rodrigues at the Krstić trial. She testified on 26 July 2000 in the case against Radislav Krstić. Witness DD's complete "Voice of the Victims" statement is available through the International Criminal Tribunal for the former Yugoslavia at http://www.icty.org/sid/10124.

I'm not going to any safe place. The Serbs are going to take me.
Hasan Nuhanović, translator at the UN base at Potočari, discussing the fall of Srebrenica. As cited in Joe Rubin, "Srebrenica: A Survivor's Story," *Frontline/World* (28 March 2006). Available online at http://www.pbs.org/frontlineworld/stories/bosnia502/interviews_hasan.html.

Chapter 25.
30 Dutch = 30,000 Muslims.
Note handed to a Dutch lieutenant by a Muslim officer in Srebrenica. Mark Danner, "What Went Wrong?" (PBS.org, 1999). Published online in conjunction with *Srebenica: A Cry from the Grave,* directed by Leslie Woodhead ([distributor Thirteen/WNET PBS], 1999). Available online at http://www.pbs.org/wnet/cryfromthe grave/aftermath/t2_essay.html.

Chapter 26.

It is a crime committed against every single one of us.

Jean-René Ruez, Chief War Crimes Investigator, Srebrenica. *Srebrenica: A Cry from the Grave,* directed by Leslie Woodhead ([distributor Thirteen/WNET PBS], 1999).

Chapter 27.

When I close my eyes, I don't see the men.

Srebrenica survivor. *Srebrenica: A Cry from the Grave,* directed by Leslie Woodhead ([distributor Thirteen/WNET PBS], 1999).

In fourteen days, Srebrenica will be gone.

A statement made by a VRS (Bosnian Serb Army) soldier to one of the military personnel trying to get through to Srebrenica on 4 July 1995. It is unclear if it was a DutchBat driver or a company medic who was warned. *Srebenica: Reconstruction, Background, Consequences and Analyses of the Fall of a "Safe" Area* (Netherlands Institute of War Documentation, 2000): part 4, chapter 5, p. 260. Available online at http://www.srebren icaproject.com/DOWNLOAD/NOD/ NIOD%20Part%20IV.pdf.

When the Serbs took Srebrenica, they wiped from the earth three generations of men.

Mirsada Malagić, a Bosnian Muslim woman, speaking about the women whose husbands were killed in the Srebrenica massacres in 1995. She testified on 3 and 4 April 2000 in the case against Radislav Krstić and on 16 February 2011 in the case against Zdravko Tolimir. Mirsada Malagić's complete "Voice of the Victims" statement is available through the International Criminal Tribunal for the former Yugoslavia at http://www.icty.org/sid/191.

The young boys were crying out for their parents, the fathers for their sons. But there was no help.
A survivor of the Srebrenica massacre, describing the preparations for executions. *Srebenica: Reconstruction, Background, Consequences and Analyses of the Fall of a "Safe" Area* (Netherlands Institute of War Documentation, 2000): part 4, chapter 2, p. 71. Available online at http://www.srebreni caproject.com/DOWNLOAD/NOD/NI OD%20Part%20IV.pdf.

I realized then that nothing good was in store for us in Potočari.
Mirsada Malagić, a Bosnian Muslim woman. She testified on 3 and 4 April 2000 in the case against Radislav Krstić and on 16 February 2011 in the case against

Zdravko Tolimir. Mirsada Malagić's complete "Voice of the Victims" statement is available through the International Criminal Tribunal for the former Yugoslavia at http://www.icty.org/sid/191.

Chapter 28.
Any rape is monstrously unacceptable but what is happening at this very moment in these rape and death camps is even more horrific.
Semra Turkovic, women's rights advocate in Zagreb, Croatia. Quoted in Angela Robson, "Weapon of War," *New Internationalist* (vol. 244, June 1993). Available online at http://www.newint.org/features/1993/06/05/rape.

Chapter 29.
We saw them rape the hadji's daughter — one after the other, they raped her. The hadji had to watch too. When they were done, they rammed a knife into his throat.
Alexandra Stiglmayer, ed., *Mass Rape: The War Against Women in Bosnia-Herzegovina* (University of Nebraska, 1994), 82.

Chapter 30.
Mina was crying the most. She said, "We are not girls anymore. Our lives are over."
Stephen Kinzer, "Bosnian Refugees' Ac-

counts Appear to Verify Atrocities," *New York Times* (17 July 1995).

Chapter 31.
It is inconceivable for me all of this that is happening to us. Is life so unpredictable and brutal? I remember how this time last year we were rejoicing over building a house, and now see where we are. I feel as if I'd never been alive. I try to fight it by remembering everything that was beautiful with you and the children and all those I love.

Last letter of Muhamed Čehajić to his wife, Minka Čehajić, 9 June 1992. Minka Čehajić is a Bosnian pediatrician who testified on 14, 15, and 16 May 2002 in the case against Milomir Stakić. Her complete "Voice of the Victims" statement, along with the translation of her husband's letter, is available through the International Criminal Tribunal for the former Yugoslavia at http://www .icty.org/sid/186.

Any of the following acts committed with intent to destroy, in whole or in part, a national, ethnical, racial or religious group, as such:
(a) Killing members of the group;
(b) Causing serious bodily or mental harm to members of the group;
(c) Deliberately inflicting on the group condi-

tions of life calculated to bring about its physical destruction in whole or in part;
(d) Imposing measures intended to prevent births within the group;
(e) Forcibly transferring children of the group to another group.

Convention on the Prevention and Punishment of the Crime of Genocide (entered into force 12 January 1951), Article 2 (United Nations, *Treaty Series,* vol. 78, p. 277).

You Muslim women, you Bule, *we'll show you.* Witness 50 (she testified with her name and identity withheld from the public), a teenage rape victim from Foča, speaking about how ICTY convict Zoran Vuković raped her. She testified on 29 and 30 March 2000 in the case against Dragoljub Kunarac, Zoran Vuković, and Radomir Kovač. Witness 50's complete "Voice of the Victims" statement is available online at http://www.icty .org/sid/188.

You will see, you Muslims. I am going to draw a cross on your back. I'm going to baptize all of you.
Witness 50 (she testified with her name and identity withheld from the public), a teen-

age rape victim from Foča, speaking about how ICTY convict Zoran Vuković raped her. She testified on 29 and 30 March 2000 in the case against Dragoljub Kunarac, Zoran Vuković, and Radomir Kovač. Witness 50's complete "Voice of the Victims" statement is available through the International Criminal Tribunal for the former Yugoslavia at http://www.icty.org/sid/188.

Chapter 32.

This was the city's still center, the very essence of Islam: in a walled courtyard, water, a tree, and the warm geometry of stone. In the deep blue velvet sky by the minaret hung a sliver of incandescent silver light: the first moon of spring.
Francis R. Jones, "Return," *Why Bosnia?,* ed. Ali Rabia and Lawrence Lifschultz (Pamphleteer's Press, 1993), 33.

We see that things too quickly grown are swiftly overthrown.
Ibn Hazm, *The Ring of the Dove,* trans. A. J. Arberry (Luzac, 1994, Rpt.). Available at Islamic Philosophy Online, Inc. at http://www.muslimphilosophy.com/hazm/dove/index.html.

Chapter 33.

We saw our sons and husbands off to those woods and never found out anything about them again.

Mirsada Malagić, a Bosnian Muslim woman. She testified on 3 and 4 April 2000 in the case against Radislav Krstić and on 16 February 2011 in the case against Zdravko Tolimir. Mirsada Malagić's complete "Voice of the Victims" statement is available through the International Criminal Tribunal for the former Yugoslavia at http://www.icty.org/sid/191.

Today no man from our family is older than thirty.

Mirnesa Ahmić, Srebrenica survivor. Quoted in "Srebrenica Survivor: Today No Man from Our Family Is Older Than Thirty," *Today's Zaman* (8 July 2011). Available online at http://www.todayszaman.com/news-249880-srebrenica-survivor-today-no-man-from-our-family-is-older-than-30.html.

I seek refuge in the Lord of Daybreak, from the evil of that which He created. From the evil of the black darkness wherever it descends.

Sura Falaq, "The Daybreak." Qur'an 113.

Chapter 34.

I knew all of them who did it. They were my neighbors.

Eighteen-year-old rape survivor Ziba Hasanović, as quoted in Roy Gutman, *A Witness to Genocide* (Macmillan Publishing, 1993), 76.

Keep the good ones over there. Enjoy yourselves.

General Ratko Mladić during the fall of Srebrenica, July 1995, as quoted in Adam LeBor, *Complicity with Evil: the United Nations in the Age of Modern Genocide* (R. R. Donnelley, 2001), 44.

Everything around us is on fire and we ourselves are nearly smoldering.

Paraphrased from Abdulah Ahmić, a Bosnian Muslim man, testifying about the massacre in the central Bosnian village of Ahmići, one of the conflict's most brutal acts of ethnic cleansing. His brother and father were murdered in front of him by Croat soldiers and he survived attempted murder. Abdulah Ahmić testified on 10 and 11 June 1999 in the case against Dario Kordić, member of the Presidency of the Croatian Community of Herceg-Bosnia, and Mario Čerkez, commander of the Vitez

Brigade of the Croatian Defense Council (HVO). They received their final judgment on 17 December 2004. Abdulah Ahmić's complete "Voice of the Victims" statement is available through the International Criminal Tribunal for the former Yugoslavia at http://www.icty.org/sid/10118.

Chapter 35.
The dead are not alone.
Paraphrased from "Remarks by High Representative and EU Special Representative Valentin Inzko at the Memorial Ceremony for Victims of Genocide, Srebrenica, 11 July 2009" (Office of the High Representative, 2009). Available at http://www.ohr.int/ohr-dept/presso/presssp/default.asp?content_id=43702.

Chapter 36.
I cannot find words for what happened there.
Slobodan Milošević speaking to the European Union President Javier Solana about Srebrenica. *Srebenica: Reconstruction, Background, Consequences and Analyses of the Fall of a "Safe" Area* (Netherlands Institute of War Documentation, 2000): part 4, chapter 2, p. 91. Available online at http://www.srebrenica-project.com/DOWNLOAD/NOD/NIOD%20Part%20IV.pdf

Your Honours, I feel that my confession is an important step toward the rebuilding of confidence and co-existence in Bosnia and Herzegovina, and after my guilty plea and sentencing, after I have served my sentence, it is my wish to go back to my native town of Bratunac and to live there with other peoples in peace and harmony, such as prevailed before the outbreak of the war.

Momir Nikolić, "Statement of Guilt" (29 October 2003), available through the International Criminal Tribunal for the former Yugoslavia at http://www.icty.org/sid/218.

Chapter 37.

Nothing can give me resolution. Nothing can give me consolation.

Hasan Nuhanović, translator at the UN base in Potočari. *Srebrenica: A Cry from the Grave,* directed by Leslie Woodhead ([distributor Thirteen/WNET PBS], 1999).

ACKNOWLEDGMENTS

To the many people who deserve my thanks for contributing to a book that has been so personal to me. My deep gratitude to everyone at Minotaur Books and St. Martin's Press for taking a chance on *The Unquiet Dead* and bringing it to life. I am especially indebted to my exemplary editor, Elizabeth Lacks, who believed in this book so wholly, and who championed it with such unwavering commitment. Her many brilliant suggestions improved it in every way.

My thanks to Inspector William Ford (Retired) for his invaluable and very kind advice on policing in Ontario. And to Mir Ali, Director of the Amherst School of Guitar, for generously taking the time to explain how Albinoni's Adagio might be written and orchestrated. And my sincere appreciation to Professor D. Fairchild Ruggles, who graciously permitted me to use her exquisite translation of Ibn Arabi's

Ringsong. And to Stephen Hirtenstein of the Ibn 'Arabi Society for his expert guidance on sources.

My warmest thanks to Faye Kennedy, Steve Bowering, Elena Kovyrzina, and Rob Hunter, who taught me so much about publishing, and whose values embody the Canadian spirit better than anyone I know. Just know — we'll always have Paris.

And I owe an immeasurable debt of gratitude to my family and friends, for their continual love and support. Especially my parents, whose lifelong example taught me the dignity, compassion, and human decency to be found in faith. I owe them more than I can possibly express, but I hope this book will speak for me.

And to my sister, Ayesha Shaikh, my first reader since childhood, my greatest friend in life, and the most ardent believer in all my dreams, including this book. Thank you for bringing my milk money to school, just the first in a lifetime of rescues. And to Omer Shaikh, big brother, for letting me tag along everywhere.

To my brother, Irfan Khan, for everything he contributed to Esa Khattak, and for making me think about Bosnia in much more rigorous ways. I'm more grateful than I can say for his love and generosity — it enriches every aspect of my life, and always has.

To my brother, Kashif Khan, co-founder of the Republic. For taking care of me for so long, and with such love, that I can't imagine anything else. For Pennygrams, phone calls, time-share vacations — and that constant stream of presents in the mail. (Send another one soon.)

To my niece, Summer Shaikh. For bringing so much love, laughter, and adventure into my life. And my nephew, Casim Shaikh, for being my champion from the beginning. Both, the most precious of all precious things. When you get knocked down, remember to get up again.

To Dr. Nozhat Choudry, reader of ragged manuscripts, keeper of writing timetables, and awe-inspiring, undisputed soul sister. For all the ways she encourages and guides me, and for the love of those beautiful girls, Zahra, Hanna, and Maariya.

To Hema Nagar, for taking this manuscript to India and nurturing it in a magical place, just as she's nurtured me. And for being my other, more wholesome and nefarious, half. The love and decency of her friendship mean everything to me.

To Farah Bukhari, for the most genuine love a dearly loved friend and sister can give while suffering heartbreak. She has the courage of the lionhearted, which perhaps she does not know.

To my adopted parents, Uncle Munir and Auntie Aira, for lifelong encouragement and love. And for the unmitigated belief of a feisty little Finn.

And to Mum and Baba and the Hashemi family, for all their love and faith. Especially Fereshteh, with whom I have shared such a deep love of books. And my companion in adventure, Noor Shaikh (allo, matey!).

To my family in Pakistan, Canada, and England, who transmit their pride and encouragement across oceans and continents, particularly my aunt, the distinguished novelist Shakila Khan, my devoted aunt Sameena Tahseen, and my unconquerable grandmother Niaz Fatima Khan.

And to my cousins Saad, Athif, and Akif Khan, and Zohaib Siddiqui, for helping in so many ways.

And to a deeply cherished group of friends, for the moments that have made up the whole. Farah and Saima Malik, Afshan Ahmad, Najia Usman, Haseeba Yusuf, and Seema Nundy: readers of early works, partners in memorable performances, and steadfast companions in various hijinks.

Afshan Javed, for incomparable letters

from Arabia and friendship beyond measure.

Farah Choudhry and Nihan Keser, for those years of fearless joy and discovery in Ottawa. And all the times we skated at midnight.

Yasser Khan for being so much a part of those years.

Asma Amjad, for making me welcome.

Aysha Nusrat, for so much kindness in a strange city.

Wisam Karawan, the most beautiful girl from Gaza. With whom I crossed impassable borders.

Jennifer, for travels through Cairo and Jordan, and the Nuweiba crossing at dawn.

Lena Johansson, for *Samarkand,* dreams of Alamut, and so much else.

Yara Masri, for laughter and solidarity at the Dome of the Rock. And all the girls of Qasr al-Hamra.

Iram Ahmed, for larks. And for the love she gives to what is priceless to me.

Uzma Alam, my much-loved sister, for the conversations that have warmed the years and made us wise. And for reading the stories I write for Layth, Maysa, and Zayna, my light and joy.

Yasmin, Semina, and Kamran Ahmad, who grew up to make me so proud with their courage, grace, and boundless hearts.

And most of all, to my husband, Nader Hashemi, the love of my life. For the matchless faith that has made my dreams possible. For encouragement, advice, and the easing of every hardship. And for being who he is. How sweet this life has been with your love.

ABOUT THE AUTHOR

Ausma Zehanat Khan is a British-born Canadian living in the United States, whose own parents are heirs to a complex story of migration to and from three different continents. A former adjunct professor at American and Canadian universities, she holds a Ph.D. in International Human Rights Law, with the 1995 Srebrenica massacre as the main subject of her dissertation. Previously the Editor in Chief of *Muslim Girl Magazine,* Ausma Zehanat Khan has moved frequently, traveled extensively, and written compulsively. *The Unquiet Dead* is her first mystery novel featuring Inspector Esa Khattak and Sergeant Rachel Getty. A follow-up is in the works.